F   Goldsmith, Olivia.
Goldsmit Young wives.

DATE			

Mynderse Library

Seneca Falls, New York

YOUNG WIVES

Also by Olivia Goldsmith

The First Wives Club
Flavor of the Month
Fashionably Late
Simple Isn't Easy
The Bestseller
Marrying Mom
Switcheroo

YOUNG WIVES

A Novel

Olivia
Goldsmith

HarperCollins*Publishers*

YOUNG WIVES. Copyright © 2000 by Olivia Goldsmith. All rights reserved. Printed in the United States of America. No part of this book may be used or reproduced in any manner whatsoever without written permission except in the case of brief quotations embodied in critical articles and reviews. For information address HarperCollins Publishers Inc., 10 East 53rd Street, New York, NY 10022.

HarperCollins books may be purchased for educational, business, or sales promotional use. For information please write: Special Markets Department, HarperCollins Publishers Inc., 10 East 53rd Street, New York, NY 10022.

FIRST EDITION

Designed by William Ruoto

Printed on acid-free paper.

Library of Congress Cataloging-in-Publication Data has been applied for.

ISBN 0-06-017553-2

00 01 02 03 04 ❖/RRD 10 9 8 7 6 5 4 3 2

In memory of the late Jane O'Connell, a dedicated reader

Acknowledgments

Having written seven novels, I'm beginning to find writing the acknowledgments the most difficult part of the entire process. As you can imagine, there is the chance that I may forget to mention someone important to me. Regretfully, I considered dropping acknowledgments altogether, but it seemed so ungracious. Plus, I've been told over and over that readers actually pore over these pages. Every steady reader of my work apparently expects to find pages of "thank yous" even though most of them don't know any of the people mentioned. Readers, voilà!

Come to find out, Nan Robinson is no longer a Robinson but a Delano and still must be thanked not only for her wonderful help but also the fabulous epigraph. Only note Carl and Rita at Green Tree Nursery make me as happy (keep that sod coming). Like most writers, I am fairly solitary during the day except for my two new loves: Spice Girl and New Baby, brought to me through the careful ministrations of Harold Sokol. Likewise, I need to thank my Line Dogs, Tom and Tony, for giving me my wall and stairway to heaven and Jeff for making the earth move. In addition, I need to correct an error in my last two books. Not since *The Bestseller* have I thanked those unsung heroes of the publishing world—the sales reps at HarperCollins—for getting my work into bookstores all over the country. Special thanks to Marjorie Braman, Joseph Montebello, Jeffery McGraw, Jane Friedman, and Leonida Karpik for all their endless support.

Construction has played a large part in my life this year—not only in my work but in my living space—so a huge thank you to the Chelsea Hotel for making room for me when I didn't have one of my own. Also, thank you to Jay and Lewis Allen for sharing Tody and Villa Allen with me—and for introducing me to Ed Harte, who shares my love of architecture. Nieces and nephews must always be mentioned or they expect bigger gifts on birthdays, so kisses and hugs to Rachel, Ben, Ali, and Michael. There are also some dearest girlfriends who continue to put up with me, even when I disappear into my writing mode: Susan Jedren, Jane Sheridan, Sara Pearson, Linda Gray, Karin Levitas, Lisa Welti, Lynn Phillips, Dale Burg, and Rosie Sisto.

Serious thanks for legal (and philosophical) help from: Paul Mahon, Cliff Gilbert-Lurie, Skip "Bait and Switch" Brittenham, and Bert Fields. Even though agents have always been a difficult area for me, I want to thank Nick Ellison for changing my mind about agents and for straightening out all of my publishing issues and to the lovely Alicka Pistek, Jennifer Edwards, and Whitney Lee from Nicholas Ellison, Inc., for their tremendous responsiveness. Likewise, I would like to praise my foreign rights co-agents: Eliane Benisti of France, Ann-Christine Danielsson of Scandinavia, Roberto Santachiara of Italy, Isabel Monteagudo of Spain, Sabine Ibach of Germany, Marijke Lijnkamp of the Netherlands, and Jovan Milenkovic and Ana Milenkovic of Eastern Europe. Literary Guild president Roger Cooper was one of the first to believe in me and I'm grateful for his response to this book as well as the care and enthusiasm shown by Marcus Wilhelm, Susan Musman, John Bloom, and the other delightful staff.

Finally, there are the legendary people in the movie industry who are working hard to turn this novel into a great film. Ivan Reitman, Tom Pollack, Dan Goldberg, Joe Medjik, and especially Michael Chinich of Montecito Pictures are brilliant, funny, and understand my purpose with this book. Candy and flowers should also go to Laurie Sheldon for her female input. Totally male as Montecito is, I think you Lost Boys are going to do something great. ICM and particularly Jeff Berg, Barbara Dreyfus, Nancy Josephson, and my cutie Bob Levinson are my Hollywood supporters and all have my gratitude. Oh, and I never leave out Sherry Lansing, my touchstone and friend along with other Paramount people including Alan Ladd, Jr., Jon Goldwyn and Deedee Myers, David Madden, and Robert Cort. Nunzio Nappi, the Bitch of Perkinsville, Carol Sylvia, Robinette Bell, Lenny Bigelow, Debbie, Katie, and Nina LaPoint, Ann Foley, Jerry Offsay, Jacki Judd, Barbara Howard, David Gurenvich, Louise, both Margarets, Michael Kohlmann, Dwight Currie, Charlie Crowley, Lenny Gartner, Pat Rhule, Judy Aqui-Rahim, Barbara Turner, Lexie, Max, and Freeway.

RING ONE

For a woman, marriage is like a circus. There are three rings:
the engagement ring, the wedding ring, and the suffering.

Nan Delano

I

In which we meet the improbably named Angela Rachel Goldfarb Romazzano Wakefield, on the occasion of her paper anniversary, and the strange outcome of that celebration

Angela Wakefield had arrived early, partly because she was a compulsively prompt person—law school had taught her the wisdom of that—but equally because she wanted to savor these moments before their little party began. So she sat, her legs neatly crossed at the ankle, her purse on the third chair, and stared out the window at the water. Marblehead, Massachusetts, was so beautiful that it was not a place she'd ever imagined making her home—her, a dago Jew mongrel from Queens, New York. Even now, though it was well into autumn, sailboats were tacking their way across the harbor, fishing boats were pulling into dock as the sunset turned to twilight. Distant lights had begun to twinkle in homes along the water.

Reid had picked the restaurant and, just like Reid, the club was perfectly groomed. The white cloths on the table glowed in the waning light; the glass and silverware gleamed. The starched napkins had been folded into complicated shapes, kind of like the newspaper soldier hats she used to make to play army, though these napkins were much prettier.

Angie looked around self-consciously. She was never so neat, so well-pressed as the napkins. Her hair was wild, black and curly, long and not really styled; her clothes were always wrinkled or losing a button. She was told often by Reid that it was part of her charm. Why else would Reid have married her?

Angie looked around the club dining room. She knew not to expect much from the food in places like this: go to a Brookline deli or Boston's North End for good food. Here the martinis would be dry, the service impeccable. Angie never felt very comfortable alone in the club. She shifted in her chair. In just a little while—since he was usually late—Reid Wakefield III, her husband of one year today, would be sitting opposite her. Reid was comfortable anywhere. He belonged not only to this club but the birthright club welcomed by all.

When the waiter approached Angela inwardly groaned. He asked for her drink order, but she didn't want to start without Reid, so she apologized and said she'd wait, if it was okay. "He should be here any minute," she added, checking her watch. Reid was already twenty minutes late, but he was chronic that way, always overscheduling, always so involved with whatever he was doing that he forgot about whatever he was committed to do next. Well, not forget about, exactly. He just juggled a little and—because of his charm—everyone forgave him.

Angie used the time now to pull out her makeup kit and surreptitiously check her face. It was a pretty face—roundish, with round dark eyes, and a generous mouth. Okay, let's face it—a big mouth in both senses of the word. Now her mouth needed more lipstick—why did it wear off her lips but not off her teeth? She ought to comb her hair, though she knew she shouldn't do that at the table.

Angie sighed. She was what she was, and Reid had picked her, not one of these real blond, anemic poster girls for Miss Porter's School. They all had names like Elizabeth and Emily and Sloane, but they—in their understated, unwrinkled clothes and untreated hair—hadn't attracted the prince that she had. *Take that, you Waspettes!*

Reid represented sunshine, vitality, and the kind of life that did not have to acknowledge defeat. Cushioned by money and contacts, his family boated and played tennis and celebrated birthdays and weddings and even funerals in a dignified way that boasted of order and control.

Not that Angela was proud of her heritage. Anyway, all of them were new immigrants compared to Reid's family. The Wakefields had come over after the *Mayflower*, but only just. Reid's mother, on the other hand, was a Daughter of the American Revolution—and looked it. She didn't color her hair or worry about fashion. She was a Barbara Bush type, but prouder. She'd never said that she was disappointed in Reid's mate, but when Angie thought about it, she didn't know what they had to be so proud of—they'd stolen their land from the Native Americans. Angela figured they got some credit for stealing it early. And they still owned plenty of it in and around Marblehead.

Angie put her lipstick away and pulled out the wrapped gift she had for her husband. It was their paper anniversary and she had racked her brain to come up with the right present. Here it was: an autographed first edition of Clarence Darrow's autobiography. Reid—a newly minted lawyer working for Andover Putnam, the most old-line of Boston's old-line law firms— worshipped Darrow. He'd *plotz*. Angie patted the package and grinned.

She didn't allow herself to get too excited by the prospect of his gift to her, though. Men weren't that good with gifts or romance. Especially WASP men from old money. She'd learned that already: for their first married Christmas, Reid had given her a pair of ski gloves—even though she didn't ski. When she'd suggested they spend their first romantic weekend away, he'd opted for Springfield, to visit the Basketball Hall of Fame. As if. Worst, for her birthday he'd given her a coffee grinder. She shook her head now, remembering the scene when she'd opened the elaborately wrapped box. "But don't you *like* fresh ground?" Reid had asked, shocked when in answer she'd thrown the thing at him. They'd had a huge fight. Later she'd called her mother. "A coffee grinder?" she'd asked. "Is it a Braun? Hey, he's trainable. Your father once gave me an ironing board."

Angela had neglected to point out to her mother that she and Angela's father had divorced, and that she didn't want that to happen to her and Reid. Instead, "What did *you* do," Angie had wept, "when you got the ironing board?"

"I made him swallow it," her mom admitted. Angie had begun laughing. "Look. Mixed marriages never work," Natalie Goldfarb-Romazzano said in a comforting voice.

"Don't tell me that now, *after* I married a Protestant," Angela had replied.

"I don't mean mixed religions. I mean mixed genders. Men and women. Mars and Venus. We're not from other planets. We're from other solar systems."

Now Angie shook her head again at the memory. Her mother was, as her father put it, a real piece of work.

"What's that about?" a voice asked. "We allow no 'nos' here. 'Yeses' exclusively. This is a *very* exclusive club."

Angie looked up at Reid—her tall golden boy, a water skier, a rock climber, a Princeton grad. In the last reflected light of the sunset, she could swear he glowed. Reid, who had already taken his seat across from her, got up, came over to her chair and bent down and kissed her—a long, lingering one. A public display of affection! She could hardly believe it. And at the club, where no one ever *had* any feelings, much less *showed* them! His lips pressed hers. God! He'd been so sweet lately. Angie found his tongue with her own. She felt herself blushing. He took her breath away. Big deal about the coffee grinder. She was so lucky!

Eventually Reid moved back to his chair, untousled, unflushed. The waiter stood behind him. "So, what will you have, Angie?" Reid asked. Then he hesitated, moved her purse, and took the chair beside her. "Too far away from my girl," he explained, his voice low. Then unexpectedly he put his right hand—the one closest to her under the tablecloth—high on the inside of her thigh. A wave of longing washed over her, so intense that she had to look away, out at the lapping tide. "I want you," Reid whispered. Then he raised his voice to give their drink order to the hovering waiter. But that interruption didn't stop him from stroking her thigh. She blushed again while the waiter nodded and left to fetch for the scion of the Wakefield family. Angie always apologized to "the help," while Reid made them wait, yet they served him better.

"So, what's this?" Reid asked, placing his other hand on the little package. "Who could it be for?" His voice was full of assurance and teasing.

"Oh, nothing," Angie said innocently. "For no one. A little anniversary present, maybe, if anyone you know is having an anniversary."

"Oddly enough, *I* am. And so is my wife. Could it be for her? Or for me?" He didn't reach for his gift, though. Instead, to her delight, he pulled a little box from his inside jacket pocket. "Does this look like a Braun?" he asked.

Angela's heart began to beat even faster. Jewelry? Real jewelry? Aside from her engagement ring and wedding band, he'd never given her jewelry. She tried to be calm as she reached out for the box. It was navy blue leather, unwrapped, and had SHREVE, CRUMP & LOWE stamped in silver letters across the top. Only the best jewelry store in Boston! And the most overpriced, but hey, this was a present. Angela still couldn't get over the fact that Reid paid retail for things. But on this occasion she was glad. Maybe her mom was right. He was trainable.

Angie stared at the enchanting box and told herself to be calm. It was probably only a sterling key chain or thimble or something, but she'd treasure it forever. "Animal, vegetable, or mineral?" she asked, vamping for time.

"Well, I'm the animal, you're the vegetable, and the gift is certainly from the mineral world," he told her.

Yes! She took the little case in her hand. Mineral world. As in gems? Ready to faint, she flipped open the lid; a small but exquisite sapphire surrounded by seed pearls winked at her from the satin interior.

A ring! "Oh, God. It's beautiful." She stared at it. "Oh, God," she repeated.

"It's a funny thing," Reid said dryly. "Is this a religious difference? I can't tell if it's a Jewish or a Catholic one. But only sex and jewelry get you to mention the Lord's name." He squeezed her thigh again and laughed. Angie vowed she'd get to the gym tomorrow after work for sure. She was so grateful to him that she'd keep those thighs thin and toned forever. She reminded herself that her father had started cheating on her mother after her mom had gotten a little—well, *zaftig. I'll eat nothing but fruit salad tomorrow*, she thought. *The kind packed in water. And I'll drink four bottles of Evian—the big bottles—even though it means I'll pee like a horse all day.*

"You know what I'd like?" Reid asked her. "I'd like you to promise to do something for me."

As if she wasn't already starving and flooding herself for him! As if she wouldn't give up breathing if he asked her to. "Anything except prostitution or getting my nose fixed," Angela told him.

He laughed. That was one of the reasons she loved him: he was an easy laugh. Then his face took on a sort of choirboy earnestness that she rarely saw. "Let's renew our vows," Reid proposed as he took her hand. "I want to marry you all over again."

Angela was so touched she felt herself flush. Reid had been unusually romantic lately—flowers, little gifts—but this was so . . . so very, very *sweet*. She felt she could either laugh or cry, so she went with the first option. After all, it was a Goldfarb-Romazzano family tradition, especially on her mother's side. "Might as well laugh," her mother always advised in crisis. "Then you don't have to fix your mascara later."

Angela put her hand out, covering Reid's beautiful long fingers. "Oh, honey. It's a wonderful thought. A lovely thought, but . . ." She paused. He watched her face, as attentive as a puppy, but a lot less mature. She didn't, now or ever, want to hurt him. So how could she explain? "We only married a year ago, sweetie. It's . . . it's inappropriate to do it again so soon. If you want to say our vows privately I will, tonight or tomorrow or—"

"No!" Reid interrupted. "I want to say them publicly. I mean, with people there. People from work. My family. Yours. You know. A ceremony."

"A renewal ceremony?" Angela tightened her hand around his. "I just got over the wedding! It took me this long to write and thank your family for all those cheese boards. Anyway, sweetie, people just don't do it." His family was usually the one that talked about what was "done." She thought of the pain she'd caused her mother-in-law already with her social gaffes. They'd nearly fainted when she'd had both a rabbi and a lapsed—and married—former Catholic priest at their ceremony. "It's . . . not done," she repeated. "Not for at least ten years, anyway. Or twenty-five."

"Why? I love you more now than I did when I married you," Reid protested. "I want everyone to know that."

Angie felt tears of total happiness rising. The hell with the mascara. "And I love you more, too," she agreed. "It's just that people might think that it's . . . well, you know, greedy. Like we expect presents or something."

"Angie, will you do this for me?" Reid asked earnestly. "Your eyes are so beautiful now, so warm and wet." He lowered his voice. "I want you this minute. I want to kiss you on your eyelids and make love to you, right here on the floor. But instead, just say yes to the ceremony."

She couldn't, not ever, say no to that level of desire in him. She was ready to nod her assent when he continued. "Look. You know my parents didn't want us to marry. And you didn't like most of my friends. Plus, let's face it, they didn't like you. People said you wouldn't fit in. Hey, even I had some doubts."

Angie nodded, still smiling though he'd never mentioned his doubts before and the news surprised her. Of course, she'd had plenty of doubts—about him. His fear of commitment, his family's coldness, his lack of . . . well, depth. She'd thought he might back out of the wedding right up until the moment when he turned to the rabbi and said, "I do."

"Anyway," Reid continued, "It wasn't an easy year. I admit we've had to take some time to adjust. And then, five months ago, I started this affair. I thought things between you and me weren't . . . well, I thought maybe my parents had been right."

Back up! Angela wasn't certain she'd heard him. "What! I mean, who . . . ?"

Reid made a gesture with his hand, a sort of flutter that matched the one her heart was making in her chest. "An older woman. From work. But she meant nothing. The affair . . . I don't know. It just showed me— after the first gloss of lust wore off—it showed me just how much I really love *you*." He leaned forward. The setting sun gleamed behind him. "I want to show that I'd choose you over any woman in the world, Angela. It was a mistake, but my affair taught me something. And I just want to make that knowledge public. I want to—"

His affair? Angela couldn't really hear anymore. She saw Reid's lips moving, but she couldn't hear him. Deafness wasn't the issue. She was afraid she might die right there at the table. But her pride wouldn't let her. Her heart was beating so loud that Reid must have heard the noise. She certainly couldn't hear anything else. She sat, frozen in shock, and watched her husband's lips move. Lips she'd just kissed. Lips that had lied to her and kissed another woman's mouth, another woman's. . . .

"I have to go to the toilet," Angie said. Then she stood up abruptly and almost ran across the dining room.

2

In which we meet Michelle Russo, Pookie the dog is walked

Michelle got Frankie into bed, which wasn't easy now that he was six. She shrugged into her jacket and told Jenna she was going out to walk Pookie, their cocker spaniel. In the driveway she looked around guiltily. Frank always yelled at her when he caught her walking the dog. "It's the kids' job. You spoil 'em," he said. It was just that it was easier for Michelle to do it herself than nagging at Jenna. And she could use the air.

As Michelle walked the dog through drifts of leaves she took a moment to look up at the stars. It was chilly and Michelle took her hair out of the scrunchie that bound it up. It fell down below her shoulders in an unman-ageable cascade of blond curls that would keep her warm and make Frank hot. She shivered. Elm Street was dark, and despite the cold, this was a time Michelle really enjoyed. It was perhaps the only moment of the day that she spent alone—if you didn't count Pookie as a companion. The dog pulled on the lead a little bit and Michelle stepped along the sidewalkless curb.

Pookie paused. Uh-oh. Her neighbors, the Shribers and the Joyces, went ballistic if Pookie even lifted a leg anywhere near their property, so she discreetly tried to tug him in the opposite direction. But then she noticed the Joyces' windows were dark. Maybe they were traveling. Since Mr. Joyce had retired, they had been doing a lot of that. They had lived on this block longer than anybody else. They were pleasant, but never really warm.

Still, Michelle loved them, just the way she loved the entire street and every house on it. This was where she and Frank had chosen to live. The place she had brought both of her children home from the hospital. Frank had taught Jenna to ride without training wheels right here, and one winter afternoon Frankie Junior had gotten his tongue frozen stuck to the lamppost that Pookie was now sniffing. This street was filled with, if not friends exactly, then friendly acquaintances; it was the place they all called home, where their children and their cats and their dogs ran in the grass and fought and played.

Michelle hadn't had a home growing up. Her mother usually worked as a waitress and came home with some take-out and a six-pack of beer. Her father was always involved in some scheme or other, none of which ever made any money, but did require hours spent in bars.

For a moment Michelle shivered, as if someone had walked on her grave. There was no reason for her to wind up so lucky, unless it was a payback for a really rocky start. Michelle had been born in the Bronx, which was only twenty or thirty miles south of here, but a whole other world. Her mother was Irish, straight from County Cork. Her father was Irish-American, the son of a fireman and a fireman himself—until he reported to work one night so drunk that he walked into a burning building and, feeling invincible, fell six stories when it collapsed.

Michelle hadn't missed her loud, frightening father. But Michelle was that rare Irish entity, an only child, and she'd been left with her depressed, unreliable mother. And when her mom's mom got sick "back home," Sheila returned to Ireland to help. Michelle, only a little older than her own daughter was right now, had waited and waited for her mother's return. A month seemed a long time to a child; half a year seemed a lifetime. The two years it took before Sheila came back had been enough to do a job on Michelle, dumped as she was with her paternal grandparents, lonely and suspecting that her mother stayed away because she couldn't face coming back. Michelle had decided then that nothing was as important as loving your husband and your children. She would *never* be a Sheila.

If Michelle could do it all over again, every bit of her hard, sad early life, she would live through it all as long as she could be assured that she would wind up with Frank Russo, her two kids, and her dog in the safety of this clean suburban harbor in Westchester County; no crime, no grime, no horrors. Healthy food on the table. Clean sheets on the bed. Clothes folded in neat piles in dresser drawers. A yard full of flowers, and two nice cars which never broke down. In the first couple of years of their marriage, Michelle had watched every glass of dago red that her husband drank, expecting him to get drunk and for the picture to fall apart. But he never had. Not once.

Michelle walked the dog up and down the street and, as she did nearly every night, couldn't help feeling grateful for the fact that her family, her marriage, and her friendships were going so well. She knew that just five houses down the street, Jada was having to deal with her unemployed husband sitting on his butt while Jada worked hers off all day at the bank. Michelle also couldn't get over the fact that Clinton, Jada's husband, was "acting up" again. How did Jada put up with it? Michelle was only a little sorry the partnership that Frank had tried to put together with Clinton had never worked out.

Michelle knew she was a survivor, the lucky one, satisfied with her life, stable in a time of instability. Up and down the block marriages had failed, families had split, and houses had gone up for sale. Not hers. The two things she knew for sure were that her friendship with Jada had survived during all of the upheaval, and that her own marriage was secure.

It hadn't always been so perfect here. When she'd first moved in, she'd been a little lonely. Then she met Jada. Every morning for the last four years, since Jada moved in, the two of them had been walking what people in the neighborhood called "the circuit," following the curving route of the old suburban streets at the fastest pace they possibly could with a dog in tow. They'd been religious about it, forty minutes of walking, no matter what, and Michelle believed that Jada found the habit as comforting a way to start the day—and lose some weight—as she did. It was the only time they gave to themselves, and it bolstered both of them. At first they'd only talked about the kids, their school, that sort of stuff. But then when Michelle's mother died, they talked about that. And Jada had told stories about growing up. Finally, Michelle had opened up about her own lousy childhood. They'd been best friends since then. They gossiped about the neighborhood. And recipes. And clothes. And all the other girl stuff. Now, since this problem with Clinton had surfaced, they talked about that.

It was a luxury Michelle hadn't had since her school days. Since her marriage she'd been so busy with Frank and the kids that she'd lost touch with the gang back in the Bronx. She stretched her long legs and walked down toward the Jackson house. She could see Clinton, but not Jada, moving around the kitchen. Michelle took a deep breath, enjoying the crisp air, and started back toward her house. She got to the edge of her property and waited while Pookie sniffed the leaves, admiring her house.

Michelle took pride in her home. She kept her house, her body, her children, and her life neat and clean and regular. She looked down at Pookie. The dog was a purebred cocker spaniel, not like one of the mutts that were always getting run over down home. "Right, Pookie?" she asked out loud. The dog looked up and cocked his silky head. "Let's go in," Michelle said, and the dog turned toward the front door light.

Jenna was out of her bath by the time Michelle got back inside and she went in to clean up the kids' bathroom. "Hey. What's this?" she asked Jenna, and pointed to the full bathtub, which was just starting to drain.

"Come on, Mom!" Jenna said. "I'm not going to drown. It's too cold to wash in two inches of water."

"You know the rule," Michelle told her. "No baths higher than the tape." She pointed to the red line she had affixed years ago to the inside of the tub, along with the nonskid rubber stick-ons she'd glued down to the ceramic bottom. It was hard to get the dirt out from their edges but it was worth it. Most fatal accidents occurred in the home.

"Mo-o-o-om." Jenna stretched the single syllable out until it was an aria almost as long as Tony singing out Maria's name in *West Side Story*.

"Most accidents happen in the home," Michelle told her eleven-year-old daughter for what, conservatively, had to be the three-thousandth time. She followed her daughter into Jenna's perfect bedroom—a room Michelle would have killed for when she was eleven. "I'll give you ten minutes for VH1—no MTV—before you have to shut off the light," she told Jenna.

"Won't I get to see Daddy before I go to bed?" Jenna asked, ready to pout. Trying to be more like a teenager every second.

"No, sweetskin. He's working," Michelle told her, and watched the glower of disappointment bloom on Jenna's perfect pink face. Michelle knew just how she felt. The Russo women—Jenna, Michelle, and Frank's mother Camille—all adored their Frank.

"Daddy might be taking us all out to dinner on Friday. And then it's the weekend." Frank never worked on the weekend. He was a really attentive father, and both Frankie and Jenna worshipped him. "Look, Daddy's been working very hard for us lately. Let's bake him a cake for tomorrow. Okay?"

"Yes!" In a second, Jenna turned from sulky preteen to delighted child. "Can I frost it all myself? And can I lick the bowl?"

A sugar promise did wonders in attitude adjustment, Michelle knew, but she wasn't a total pushover. "You can frost it alone, but you have to share the bowl with Frankie," Michelle told Jenna for what also must have been the three-thousandth time. She looked at her watch. "Now just *five* minutes of VH1. Then lights out." Jenna smiled, snuggled under her quilt, and sighed. Michelle knew she'd be sleeping in less than three minutes and made a mental note to come back in after straightening out the bathroom to shut off the TV.

She wiped up the splashes, put two washcloths up to soak, then picked up and refolded three bath towels (Two children and three towels? It didn't add up.) She Soft-Scrubbed the sink and Windexed and wiped the mirror. Frankie, she noticed, had remembered to put his dirty clothes in the hamper (good) but he'd also thrown in one of his little Nike Airmax sneakers (bad—there would have been chaos before breakfast). Michelle left the bathroom, its towels hung, its tile gleaming, and looked in on Frankie, who had already tossed off his quilt. She put his sneakers beside the bed, covered him, and kissed his sweet, high forehead—just like his father's. Then she shut off the TV in Jenna's room. Jenna murmured something in mild protest from her bed, but the lure of sleep was too strong. Jenna held Pinkie, the toy rabbit she'd had since she was a baby, in a stranglehold that was her precursor to sleep. When she turned toward the wall, Michelle smiled.

Then she went into her bedroom. She got out her best silk night-gown, took the Joy perfume bottle from the bureau, and went into the bathroom she shared with Frank. She began to run a bath but first, care-fully, hung the shimmering gown over the shower door so the folds would fall out. Then she looked into the mirror.

Michelle smiled. She was taller than average: she liked to say she was five-foot-eleven, though she was really only five-ten-and-a-half. Frank was her height, but he liked her tall. Way tall. So she *always* wore heels, except on her walks with Jada. Height helped her—it made her look much more attractive. But she admitted she was good-looking. She'd been lucky—she'd gotten the pert nose and strong jawline of her Scotch heritage without the really narrow mouth. In fact, her mouth was so full that it made her self-conscious. In school girls had made fun of her—call-ing her "fish mouth" and "trout"—but the boys had flocked to her.

She shook her head and her hair gleamed, but the roots. . . . She'd have to make an appointment to touch up her blond color. Her com-plexion could carry off the lightness. The only disadvantage she had was her skin; it was so delicate it showed every change in her mood by flush-ing or paling, but also—if she wasn't careful—wrinkling like the poppy petals she swept off the patio all summer. Michelle perpetually slathered on creams and potions. Even with them she knew she had less than a decade left before the lines, a tiny network of wrinkles, kicked in. Oh, well. She still looked good.

With the steam from the bath filling the room she could look into the reflective glass and see herself as she'd been at twenty-one, a decade ago, and it didn't seem as if there had been a lot of change for the worse. Maybe her highlights were helped along just a little bit, but *that* wasn't a bad thing. Okay, her waist had expanded from her pregnancies, but only by an inch or two. She peered at herself, her green eyes moving along her mirrored form. Her breasts. . . well, they had also expanded from the pregnancies, which was good—at least it made her waist look smaller. She pulled her sweater off and admired herself. Not bad. She allowed herself a smile. In an hour Frank would be home and admire her even more. She reached over her head to do up her hair—but just for now. Frank liked her hair down in bed. And she liked Frank to get what he wanted, as long as he wanted *her*.

3

*In which Angela rings her father, rings the airport,
and rings up a tab*

"Five months. I don't know. Uh-uh. Because he *told* me."

Angela was crying, getting mucus and tears on the receiver of the phone in the vestibule of the Marblehead Yacht Club. Some man, leaving the restroom, gave her a look, then averted his eyes as if from an accident. Well, it was a wreck, or she was. She looked down at the Shreve box, still clutched in her right hand. She doubted she could open either of her fists again.

"He *told* you?" her father was asking. "The cold Wasp son-of-a-bitch rat-bastid *told* you he'd been sleeping with someone else? And on your anniversary?"

Angie couldn't speak. She nodded—not that her father, four hundred miles south in Westchester County, could see her. But he heard her gurgle. "Brutal," he said. "Where are you right this minute?" he snapped.

"At a pay phone. At the club." Now a woman walked past Angie, glanced at her, then actually turned back to stare. Her cold eyes seemed to say, "Don't behave that way *here*." She was about Reid's mother's age. She probably knew both Reid's parents. Fuck her! Angela defiantly wiped at her eyes, then her nose, with her hand. The woman shook her head in disgust. Angie looked down. Her fingers were a mess, covered with eye makeup, but she managed to flip the bird at the old bat, who stalked off.

"Angie, baby, didn't I tell you never to trust a man with Roman numerals after his name?" her father asked. Oh God. Was she going to get a speech? Angie had tried to call her mother first, then her best friend Lisa, but had only gotten their machines.

"Please, Daddy. No lectures. Not from you." She wiped her eyes with the back of her hand. "I can't believe it. I want to kill him. What should I do?"

"It's okay, baby. It's okay," her father soothed.

He was using the voice she trusted, the one she always obeyed. He'd used that voice when he had told her not to worry, she'd ace her SATs, the one that promised her she'd get into law school. Her daddy, despite his flaws, did love her.

"Listen to me," he said. "Here's what you do. You hang up the phone. You walk out of that hellhole and get into a taxi. The last Delta shuttle to New York leaves from Logan in forty-five minutes. You can make it, easy. And I'll be at the Marine Air Terminal to pick you up. Not one of my drivers. Me."

"I don't know if I can make the plane. When I tell Reid I—"

"You don't have to tell that bastid a single fucking thing," her father spat. "Don't you go back to that table."

"You mean just . . . leave? But . . . I don't even have my purse with me," Angie said. She felt naked, helpless. But the thought of crossing that room, looking at Reid—impossible! While just leaving at least had . . . dignity. "I have no money, no I.D. . . . ."

"I'll have a prepaid ticket waiting at the counter," her father told her. "They'll ask you to tell them your mother's maiden name and give your social security number." Angie nodded.

"But security. I.D. I . . . I don't have *anything*." That wasn't technically true. She still clutched the Shreve box in her hand.

"I'll tell them how your grandma is dying and how close you were," he said.

"Nana? Okay." She began to cry again. "Thank you, Daddy," she said. "God, I'm so ashamed."

"Ashamed? What have *you* got to be ashamed of?"

"Being so fucking stupid," Angie told him. "You never trusted him."

"Well, there is that," he admitted. "Forget it. Women are all blind or else there'd be no human race. Just leave the bum. Let him sit there and wonder if you fell into the shitter and drowned." Anthony Romazzano waited for a laugh but didn't get one. "Okay," her father said. "You promise me you'll hang up and walk right out the door?"

"Yes," Angela agreed. She hung up the phone and turned herself around. She took a deep breath and pulled down on the cuffs of her sleeves as if the gesture built up enough courage for her to take the first step. She ought to go into the ladies room and clean up, but what difference would it make? She'd only cry some more. When she walked toward the exit door, she felt as if everyone was watching her and that they knew what had happened. She couldn't believe she'd never see Reid again. But the fact was that she caught a last glimpse of her husband as she walked past the dining room door. He was calmly leaning back in his chair, looking out at the water. Why was it he always looked as if nothing bothered him? So pulled together?

With all her built-up rage, Angie pushed hard on the club door and was blasted in the face with cold salt air. She waved to the first taxi in line. "Logan Airport, please. Delta shuttle." Then she again burst into noisy tears.

It wasn't until they got to the Callahan Tunnel and its inevitable traffic that Angie realized she might miss the flight. But since she didn't have a penny on her, she couldn't even pay the driver. "Please hurry," she said. He'd already looked at her once or twice in the rearview mirror.

"Did you say Delta or USAir?" he asked. He had a lilt in his voice. Irish. Just off the boat. Driving a cab the way her father had, back in New York; but her father had gotten into the limo business, gotten rich, and married a nice Jewish girl.

"Delta," she told the driver, and then explained about Nana. What would he do when she tried to stiff him? Call the cops?

Well, if he did, she'd telephone her father. She thought of Tony, waiting at the other end of the trip. She was grateful to him for his help, but at the same time she couldn't avoid remembering that he had done the same thing to her mother that Reid was doing to her now. The only difference was, her father did it *after* he and her mom had been married for twenty-something years, and he hadn't told her mom until he'd been caught. He still swore that it shouldn't have broken up the marriage.

"Oops. Sorry. I missed the Delta turn. I'll have to go around again," the cabbie said. Perfect, she thought. Now she'd probably miss the shuttle and wind up sleeping in the airport. As if she could sleep. Sleep! She wasn't even sure she could go on breathing. She felt as if there were jagged pieces of bone or steel or glass in her chest. Every time she attempted a deep breath, or when a sob shook her, the pieces would meet and rub and tear. How had this happened to her? She'd been so careful.

She'd waited until she was finished with college and almost done with law school before she had allowed herself to become serious about a man. She'd always been smart, and independent. She'd wanted to do something with the law to help people. She'd dated, but had been wary of men, and she'd worked hard during her internships and summers, giving her time to Legal Aid instead of dinner dates. She still gave money to "Save the Children," participated in AIDS walks, and worked for Meals-On-Wheels once a month. She was a good person, a strong person. She had judgment, intelligence, and persistence.

She'd listened to her mother's advice, and absorbed the lessons—all bad—of her mother's friends' marriages. She'd avoided alcoholics, neurotics, and the generally misogynistic. And she'd finally picked the man who pursued her, not a man she'd pursued. He'd come from a family in which there seemed to be no history of womanizing: Reid's father was cold, not hot. She'd worried that Reid might not marry her, that her family wasn't up to his social standards, but never that he'd cheat on her. *How had this happened to her?*

The taxi was pulling up to the Delta terminal. Angie looked down at her hands. One held the crumpled mass of yellow pages, now all sodden, that she'd torn from the phone booth at the club. In the other she still clutched the Shreve box that contained the perfect sapphire ring.

The driver pulled up to the curb and braked. Then, in an act of courtesy usually unknown to North Shore cabbies, he actually got out of the cab and opened the door for her. "Sorry for your pain," he said, his Irish accent thick. "I really loved my granny, rest her soul." He looked at her, and Angie knew her hair must be wild, her face a swollen, streaked mess. "That'll be forty-one dollars," the driver added, almost reluctantly.

There was only one thing to do. She opened the Shreve, Crump & Lowe box and took out the ring. "Here," she said, handing it to him. "I forgot my purse. But you can have this. It's worth a lot. I know my Nana would want you to have it." Then, the empty box still clutched in her hand, she walked through the airport's electronic eye doors, away from her marriage, and up to the Delta ticket desk.

4

Wherein we meet Jada R. Jackson,
and we discover the cost of living in Republican Westchester,
as well as the state of her union

Jada looked at her watch, realized it was too dark in the car to see the dial, and checked the clock on the dash. Damn! It was half past eight already. The kids would have eaten and—if she was lucky—be settled down to bed and homework. Her eyes flicked away from the dash but not before she noticed, with a start, that the gas gauge was almost on empty. Damn it! Now, when she was so late, she'd have to take the time to stop and fill up. Why was it that Clinton, who was unemployed and had the whole day to get errands done, had used her car yesterday but not bothered to fill it up?

She burned with indignation. She knew why. Clinton's mind was on things other than her convenience.

Jada pulled into the island at the Shell station, turned off the ignition, and waited for full—or, for that matter, even partial—service. She'd had to learn from experience that her time was more valuable than money, but if they kept her waiting here for this long at the pump, what was the point of paying more? She beeped and reluctantly an older man came out of the glass enclosure to help her. "Fill it up" was all she told him and, to speed the process along, she flipped him her Shell card at the same time before she rolled up the window to keep out the October chill. The card slipped from the geezer's fingers and she watched as it skittered across the oily macadam; he had to squat to pick it up. She sighed and turned up the heat setting, not that it would do any good with the motor off.

Jada shivered, and the movement was reflected in the rearview mirror. Her eyes looked very bright in the darkness. Her lips were chapped and there were already patches of dry skin under her eyes—a sign of winter. Jada sighed. Only in her early thirties, she was still a striking woman, but as she glanced into the rearview to check again on the attendant she wondered how much longer her looks would last in the harshness of these winters.

The old coot had finally picked up her card and gotten to the nozzle, but now seemed to be fumbling with the Volvo's gas cap. Jesus H. Christ! It was what she called the RTSYD syndrome: Rush and They Slow You Down. She'd experienced it at the bank. Why was it that, when you were in a hurry, morons were invariably at their slowest?

Jada jerked opened the door, got out of the car, and moved to the back fender. In a single motion she threw back the gas cap, took the nozzle from the old man's filthy hand, and inserted it into the gas tank opening herself.

He probably wasn't grateful for her help, but she was paying three cents a gallon more for full service and she'd had to do it herself. Jada felt that was the story of her life—she had to do everything herself—and she was ready to burst into tears.

Sometimes she doubted her faith. Her parents, island people, still had a deep faith. But somehow it seemed easier to believe when you lived in a warm climate. Right now, shivering in the chill of a New York State wind, she wondered if her God loved her. God had created marriage, she figured, to see just how much two people could irritate one another. If her theory was right, she and Clinton had certainly done God's work. The two of them were barely speaking at this point, and she was pained to realize that not speaking was an improvement in their relationship right now. Of course, they'd have to speak tonight. She'd have to force this issue that had come up between them.

Jada climbed back into the Volvo. The old man, after too long a pause, came back with her card and receipt. Shivering, she rolled down the window to take the little tray he held out in his greasy hand so she could sign. She grabbed it, scribbled her name, and tore off her copy, thrusting the tray back at him.

But instead of taking it and pulling back, the old man merely leaned forward. "Pretty car," he said in a conversational voice. As if she needed to talk to him! Get a grip. It was almost eight-thirty! But he continued. "And a real pretty woman in it," he said. She was about to say thank you and roll up the window when he added, "Pretty damn uppity." She hit the window button, closing him off as best she could. Then, as if she couldn't predict, didn't know the next word that would come out of his mouth, the "N" word did, followed by his spit on the side of the car.

The stupid bigoted cracker! Jada gunned the motor and pulled out of the station and onto the Post Road without even checking the left lane. She cut off a tanker truck and was rewarded with a deafening hoot from the diesel's whistle. Tears of rage rose in her eyes, and she almost missed the left turn she had to make on Weston.

In the darkness and comparative quiet of that winding road, she tried to calm herself. To be fair, the incident with the disgusting, ignorant old man was her fault: she knew that constant vigilance and never-failing politeness were the price she and Clinton paid—along with high property and school taxes—for living in this part of Westchester County. Being black in wealthy white suburbia wasn't as hard as it had once been, but it still wasn't easy. They were not the Huxtables. Despite everything she did, they were barely keeping their heads above the financial water line. But they were giving the children the kind of life that all Americans dreamed of. Still, there was a very real cost involved.

They lived under constant financial pressure. And they were cut off from their church, back in Yonkers. There were no black families in their neighborhood, and few kids of color at the school. Shavonne's friends were white, and Kevon spent all his free time with Frankie next door. Sometimes Jada worried that they weren't just fair-skinned, but also fair-weather friends. Even she had become best friends with her (white) neighbor Michelle and sometimes, though she loved Mich, she felt . . . well, alone. Worst of all, though, was Clinton's alienation.

Sometimes Jada wasn't sure if all the struggle was worth it. When Clinton had first begun as a carpenter, he and Jada had lived in Yonkers and rented a two-room apartment. Then he'd gotten a job that changed everything. A wealthy executive in Armonk noticed Clinton's work on a commercial project in White Plains and hired him to convert a three-car garage into a guest house. Clinton had learned the ins and outs of contracting right on the job. He didn't make a dime of profit on that first one, but he had used it as a springboard to other jobs. The boom times, and perhaps a little white liberal guilt, had gotten Clinton work at least as often as it had stood in his way.

But he was equipment crazy. He spent all the profits on a backhoe, a bucket loader, and a bulldozer. He had T-shirts made up that said, JACKSON CONSTRUCTION AND EXCAVATION. IF WE AIN'T BUILDIN' WE'RE DOZIN'. Well, he was probably dozing right now—on the sofa. Because he had mismanaged everything.

At first they'd both thought Clinton's touch had been golden. Both she and Clinton had been sure he would create their fortune. In the darkness, Jada shook her head. Maybe he'd gotten a little cocky, a little arrogant even. He felt like he was different than most of the other men back at their church. "They're employ*ees*," he used to say. "I'm an employ*er*." He didn't go as far as turning Republican, but he did buy a set of golf clubs. And she had had total faith in him.

It was funny. When she'd seen Clinton working on a building site or directing his men, she'd gotten off on it. He was DDG—drop-dead gorgeous. He seemed so "take charge," so full of authority. Now he was just full of it.

Blind faith, as it turned out. They didn't know they were merely riding the fiscal tide of the times. When corporate downsizing began, all of Clinton's business dried up and blew away, just the way so many white executives' jobs and minds had. He couldn't make payments on the equipment, couldn't make salaries, had to let people go. The trickle-down effect took a little longer, but Clinton's mind and pride were eventually blown, too. For almost four years he tried to hang on, giving detailed estimate after detailed estimate on houses that were never built, extensions that were never added.

Finally, all his pride, her faith, and their money were gone, but their mortgage payments still had to be paid. Jada begged Clinton to get a job, and when he couldn't, or wouldn't, she—who hadn't worked since their first child was born—got the only job she could—as a teller for minimum wage. Even for that she had needed the help of her friend Michelle to get the position. There were a lot of job-hungry wives in Westchester. The money Jada had earned just barely covered groceries, but at least from that day on they were paying cash for their Cap'n Crunch instead of Mastercarding it.

Clinton, though, hadn't been relieved. In fact, he'd been made even more miserable by her working. He moped and loafed and slept and ate and griped. He said he didn't like her out of the home, that the job paid too little and was beneath her. She agreed, but knew they were in no position to negotiate. Somehow, Clinton just never accepted that. He lived a bitter, private life, waiting for "the climate to turn." He'd gained at least forty pounds. He yelled at the kids and seemed to blame her for everything.

If it had been impossible to cope at home, Jada had found it surprisingly easy to persevere at work. The bank was a relief: what they expected of her was so much more doable than her task at home. To her own surprise, she'd been promoted almost immediately to head teller— a black woman with three other black women *and* a white girl reporting to her! She'd never supervised anyone but her children. Then, when she'd been made a loan officer, and later head of the whole loan department, she'd been as astonished as any of them. Mr. Feeney, the branch manager, had liked her—they got on real well and up to his retirement, she'd been his assistant branch manager. When he'd retired, well, she'd hadn't been surprised at anything except her reluctance to tell Clinton the good news.

Only one woman, Mr. Feeney's old secretary, Anne, seemed to resent her. Now she was branch manager, with two dozen people, including Anne and Michelle, reporting to her! She coped with Anne and depended on Michelle. Thank God it hadn't changed their friendship: Michelle wasn't the least bit jealous. Michelle liked being a loan officer and didn't want to put in any hours after three o'clock. Not, of course, that Jada *wanted* to—she just *had* to. The bank was paying her about half what they had paid Mr. Feeney, but they still wanted blood. Two months ago they'd sent some management consultants through to see if there was some way they could "reduce overhead through more efficient paperwork flow-through and staff utilization." What it really meant was finding a way to fire a couple more people, though Jada's branch had larger deposits and transactions than any other branch of its size in the county.

Of course, everyone had been shaken up. They all needed their paychecks—except for maybe Michelle—as bad as Jada did. Sometimes Jada had to shake her head at the way men managed things. They gave lip service to the idea that human resources (never "people") would perform better if their morale was high, but then the sons-of-bitches were always doing things that *lowered* morale.

The report had come back two weeks ago and—thank the Lord—the branch had been given what television movie critics might have called a big thumbs up. But Jada had been left with frightened, resentful employees. To combat that she instituted a weekly meeting to get and implement the staff's suggestions for improvements. The problem was, there were very few real ways to improve, while everybody wanted to use the meeting to showboat. Well, at least the men did. They all had to repeat old ideas over and over as if they were new and their own. The women had to talk every single damn thing to death.

This evening's meeting had been so stupid, a waste of time. Why was it that a person alone could make a decision in ten minutes, but an organization of ten people could take two hours to come to no decisions at all?

Jada sighed as she turned the Volvo into the driveway. She could see the unweeded dahlia bed by the streetlight. Her mother, a great gardener, would be ashamed. At the very last minute she saw Kevon's bike lying on the blacktop near the garage door. She swerved and braked. God-double-damn it! Goddamn, Goddamn, Goddamn! So much for not taking the Lord's name in vain. Jada stormed out of the car into the cold, jerked the bike up, and leaned it against the side of the garage. She opened the door (*Why hadn't Clinton fixed the automatic door opener? The man was useless as handles on a glove!*) and then put the bike away, pulled the car into the garage, got out, closed the garage door, and stamped across the lawn.

It was bedlam inside. Clinton was lying on the great room sofa. He gave her a look that said "I *do* help around the house," when all he'd managed to do in the last week was put a towel in the hamper once. Now he was talking on the phone while Shavonne was eating cookies *and* watching TV. Both were forbidden to her preteen daughter before homework and a chapter of reading. Meanwhile Kevon, Jada realized with a shock, wasn't anywhere to be found. At least the baby was sleeping, unless Clinton had left her lying in the driveway, too.

"Where's your brother?" she asked Shavonne.

"I don't know," Shavonne murmured, without taking her eyes off the screen. "Are we going to eat soon?"

"You haven't had dinner yet?" Jada shot a murderous look at Clinton and went to the refrigerator. She took out the milk, grabbed a box of Kraft Macaroni and Cheese, took out the last can of tuna, and decided to add the leftover string beans. There were plenty of 'em—why did she bother with green vegetables at all?

In nineteen minutes the table was cleared and set, the television off, Shavonne washed, Kevon was found in his room, and the casserole was being dished out to the four of them. Life took on order and she could see even Clinton was marginally grateful. That sense of order, and the children, were the only reasons he hung around. But his lapses were getting worse and worse. She would have to talk to him.

Jada looked across the table at her husband. He averted his eyes. His skin gleamed and his hair, in a new cut, was in a handsome fade. For a month this new crisis had been hanging over her head. She should talk to him tonight. Confront him. But she was so tired. *I'm the real casualty in this family,* Jada thought. She knew that, despite her incredible fatigue tonight, she still had to put Shavonne and Kevon to bed, check in on Sherrilee, as well as confront her husband and demand his decision, a decision he didn't want to make and she didn't want to hear.

Jada began to spoon what was left of the casserole into a plastic refrigerator bowl. The limp, twice-cooked green beans—certainly a misnomer, because they were no longer anything even close to green—lay there before her. They looked worse than dead—used up and wasted.

Somehow the sight of them made her inexpressibly sad.

5

*In which two people achieve orgasm
and boots are made for walking*

When Frank Russo walked into the master bedroom a little before eleven that night, Michelle, her hair down, lay across their bed in her satin nightgown, her breasts bursting out of the white foam of lace at the straps, reading. She looked up from the page as Frank caught sight of her. He grinned, then tried to play nonchalant. As if. She smiled to herself, then waited. She knew the scent of her perfume, the one she wore on nights like this and that he still bought her every Christmas, was wafting toward him. She didn't say a word—she only smiled and glanced at the fabric of his trousers, right below his belt buckle. She wondered, not for the first time, if she'd trained him like one of those Russian dogs that salivated when a bell rang. Would her perfume give him an erection anytime he smelled it?

Frank sat down on the bed beside her, his eyes taking her in. "What you been up to?" he asked, his voice husky and intimate. "Painting the garage?"

For a moment Michelle opened her mouth to protest. Then she closed it again. She wouldn't laugh. Instead she shook her head slowly, letting her hair cascade over her shoulders, lowering her eyes demurely back to her book. "Uh-uh," she said, her voice slow. "But I *did* change the oil in the Lexus," she drawled.

"Good girl," he said, and casually began to unbuckle his belt. "While you're at it, my truck could use a tune-up." It was only then that she allowed herself to laugh and put the book down. Then she took Frank's hand and held it to her soft, wide-open mouth. She licked his palm.

Frank couldn't play cool any longer and groaned, then stripped off his shirt and undershirt, and lastly pulled off his jeans and boxers in a single movement. Michelle tried to keep his hand against her mouth the whole time, promising him everything with her eyes, but once in bed he pulled up the blanket as soon as he could and turned his back to her, curving his body into his sleep position. "God, I'm bushed," he said, and lay there quietly, ready for sleep.

"Frank!" Michelle wailed, and then he had to laugh and turn to her, his arms open, his flesh hard.

Making love with Frank, after all this time together, was still great. Maybe, Michelle thought, it was because they knew each other so well but could still surprise each other. Their lovemaking ranged from very sweet to wildly athletic humping. From tiny, subtle movements, just the right word, the right tone of voice, to something wild that felt like sex with a stranger. Yet what Michelle loved was that it was always, in the end, safe with Frank.

There was the night he had come home with a Gap box. He wouldn't let her touch it until the children were asleep. "Later," he said raising his dark brows. From his leer she'd been afraid it might be a sex toy or a porno tape, but when she opened the box it was just a blue dress. She'd looked at him blankly. "Now," he'd said, "go get me a tie."

"Why?" she'd asked.

"Because we're going to play Oval Office," he told her. "I'm Mr. President and you're Monica." She'd laughed and laughed, until he convinced her to become his Secretary of the Interior.

Tonight, though, Frank was playing no more games. He was his most tender self. Without preliminaries, he rolled over and onto her, holding his weight off of her by placing his elbows on either side of her chest. Then he lifted her two hands with his and, holding her wrists, placed their hands on her hair. "Do you have any idea how beautiful you are?" he asked in a whisper.

She shook her head, though their hands held her hair so she couldn't move it very much. "Tell me," she whispered.

"Only if I can be inside you while I do," he whispered back.

"You drive a hard bargain," she told him, and shifted her weight to one hip. He still held her hands, but now with only one of his own. With the other he pulled up her nightgown, the satin bunching deliciously around their thighs. She was already wet as he pressed his flesh into her.

"You're like silk," he whispered. "All over. All over," he repeated. "I look at you sometimes and I'm amazed. You're so beautiful. And every place I touch you is so soft." He was inside her—still and hard—but he moved his hips just once so she would remember where she ended and he began. He looked into her eyes. "Is that enough?" he asked.

She shook her head no.

"You want more?" he whispered. "More?"

She nodded.

"You're greedy," he told her, moving his eyes from hers. She watched him look at her. "Your mouth," he murmured. "Men would kill just to touch your mouth, just once, with the tip of their finger."

She smiled. A little shiver ran through her. "What do you want to touch it with?" she whispered.

"With my palm," he said, covering her mouth, but only for a moment. "With my tongue," he added, and he licked the very corner of her lips. "With my teeth," he whispered, and pulled her bottom lip into his own mouth, biting her gently but firmly. He knew the line just between ultimate pleasure and the slightest bit of pain and judged it perfectly. Frank changed the balance of his hips then and pushed deeper inside her. He kissed her at the same time, his tongue aping the intrusive, wet slide of his penis.

"Your mouth is so beautiful," he said, and it was almost a groan, "but it's not the most beautiful part of you. Not even close." And then he let go of her hands so she could pull him tightly to her. And she did.

Later, when Michelle lay in the dark, her nightgown a ruin, her body loved and relinquished, she savored her happiness. She reached her hand out to Frank's back, so dark, so broad. He wasn't big, but he was beauti-fully, compactly built. She rested her hand on his shoulder. He was already gone, spent, but she didn't feel alone. Their union was a lasting one, and the thousand times that he'd entered her, the thousand times she'd given herself to her husband, had built up a kind of bank balance, a kind of bonus of connection between them, even when they weren't joined as one flesh. Lying beside his sleeping form, she didn't feel alone.

It was cold, and Frank shivered for a moment in his sleep. Michelle got up to close the window he insisted on leaving open. As she silently lowered it, she looked out at their quiet street. Then a limo, moving slowly, drove by. From her perch above, Michelle could see a face, white and drawn behind the glass. She could swear it looked up at her, that their eyes con-nected. She shivered and locked the window. Reflexively, for the first time in years, she crossed herself. Then she turned back to look at Frank, and almost ran to be beside him again in the haven of their bed.

Frank had spent himself on her and their children, Michelle thought. He had built this house with his own hands and skill and strength for them. He fed them and clothed them. He taught his son how to throw, his daughter to dance. He taught all of them how to feel loved, how to be safe.

I'm so very, very lucky, Michelle thought before she fell into another deep, deep dream.

The next morning when Michelle woke up she found the ground outside covered in a deep frost. For a moment she considered climbing right back into the warm bed beside Frank, but Jada, like some dark, heat-seeking missile, would just come up the stairs and drag her out. Michelle dressed with an extra layer, pulled her long tangle of hair into a ponytail, and tugged on her boots instead of her sneakers. She was down the stairs and almost out of the house in just minutes. Pookie was already waiting there at the door, his brown eyes almost as pleading as Frank's had been.

"Okay," she said, though she knew Pookie would slow them down. And Jada wouldn't like that. Michelle loved Jada, but it had been odd at first to become friends with a black woman. There weren't many in their neighborhood. And though Michelle prided herself on *not* being prejudiced, Frank and his family were . . . well, they certainly had special words and phrases that they used when they spoke about African-Americans. But they weren't allowed to do it in front of Michelle, or her children.

It was a luxury to have a close friend. She and Jada got along really well, but sometimes small things stood out strongly and marked the boundaries between them. There was something about the way Jada both excused and blamed her husband that was weird to Michelle. And there were the foods Jada served her kids, unhealthy prepackaged American things. Plus, the different television programs she watched, the different reactions to movies that she had. There were a few things like that that they'd both learned to stay away from. Now Michelle clipped the leash to Pookie's collar and was out the door. She'd learned that if she didn't make it a quick getaway at 5:40 every morning, she wouldn't get away at all.

The frost crunched under her boots and sent that little chill down her spine that everybody got when they heard certain noises. It wasn't really cold, but the frost was a promise of things to come. Michelle loved cleanliness and she liked the freshness of the air in winter. It smelled clean. The dusting of snow, especially when it first fell, was also so clean-looking. Michelle walked down the street, almost reluctant to ruin its perfection with her boot prints and Pookie's little paw spots. The tar of the street surface showed through starkly, black blots on the white sheet of road, as white and soft as confectioners' sugar. Theirs were the only steps marring the perfection. That was the good thing about this time of the morning.

Michelle looked up from the frost and saw Jada coming out of her house. She'd be in a grim mood. Jada hated winter. Well, Michelle was prepared to hear her complain and also ready to hear what was going on in the Jackson marriage.

Jada pulled her hood tighter around her face. Gray flaky patches were already forming on the skin under her eyes. She wasn't made to live in this climate, she thought, though she'd lived in the Northeast all her life. When she'd visit her parents in Barbados, her skin stayed moist. There her hair went into perfect jet ringlets and had bounce. She had what

Clinton's grandma called "good hair"—that meant it wasn't nappy and didn't need a perm to straighten it. Jada knew what it really meant was that it was closer to white people's hair than it was to black people's. She hated that kind of stuff, so she was disgusted with herself to find she was pleased that Shavonne had inherited her hair. It wasn't as important that Kevon get it, and when he didn't—his tight curls were a lot more like Clinton's—Jada had accepted that. That made her a racist and a sexist, she figured. She'd decided she'd let God worry about Sherrilee's hair.

Jada reached for her Blistex stick. In the Caribbean, her full lips never cracked and chapped. She stuck her hand into the pocket of her parka, pulled out a tube of Vaseline and smeared it on her face and hands before putting her gloves on. It was the only way to keep her face from peeling off in little dry flakes all winter. She'd look shiny, but what the hell, nobody saw her but Michelle and Pookie, and the one or two nutjobs who ran past them in shorts, tearing their middle-aged tendons and ruining their knees.

She was exhausted and probably looked it. She glanced at Michelle, who was approaching; she seemed wide awake, her face already glowing in the cold. Her long but perfect nose was merely a little pink at the tip. Otherwise, she looked gorgeous.

Jada liked to walk with Michelle because, among other things, Michelle had legs even longer than hers. They paced each other well. But that little dog slowed her down and Jada *hated* standing still in the cold. There, in the early morning darkness, Jada couldn't help but get agitated at waiting for the dog. Start and stop, start and stop. Michelle needed that dog about as much as Jada needed more stretch marks.

"Make that dog move or I'll have to strangle him and use him as a muff," Jada threatened. Sometimes, though she felt very close to Michelle, in a lot of ways Jada believed there was an unbridgeable distance between them. Maybe it was because of the black/white thing, maybe because of Mich's marriage, which was so happy. Jada knew how Michelle loved Frank, and Jada believed he loved Michelle in return. Most important, he loved his kids *and* brought home money each and every week.

So Jada kept her mouth shut and hoped that Michelle and Frank Russo would be the only damn couple in Westchester County to manage to stay together happily in this decade or the next. Jada loved

Michelle and she wanted her happy. After all, if they *both* bitched all the time, what would happen to their friendship? Not only that, but she needed Michelle as a walking partner. Let's face it, she thought. A black woman walking alone in the dark mornings in this light neighborhood would be a daily invitation for the cruiser to stop by.

"Come on, Pookie, honey," Michelle said.

Jada just didn't get the way white people treated their pets, as if they were children. And, in Jada's opinion, Michelle certainly treated her kids as if they were pets. She let her kids get away with murder—they didn't tidy up after themselves or remember to say "please" or "thank you." Then there was that physical, personal boundary issue. In Michelle's house, Jada would never even *think* to take down a glass from the cabinet or open the refrigerator. But Michelle would do it in her house without permission. Jada had never criticized Michelle for any of it. It was small stuff compared to the warmth of their friendship. And maybe there were just as many things that Michelle held back from Jada.

Now, though, Jada allowed herself to eye the undisciplined dog. Then she looked at Mich's face. "Here," she said, holding out her Blistex. "I swear you are the only white girl with lips fuller than mine. Sure we aren't distantly related? Because I'd hate to kill my own cousin's dog."

Michelle laughed, took the Blistex and the hint, and called out to the dog. "Don't be so down on him," Michelle said, for what had to be the thousandth time.

"Well, he does have two advantages over men," Jada sniffed. "He doesn't brag about who he slept with and he never calls her 'bitch.'"

Michelle laughed. Pookie stopped sniffing and started walking. Jada set a fast pace. Michelle smeared Blistex all over her wide mouth and handed it back to Jada. "Between the two of us this stick won't last out the winter," Michelle said.

"Hell, it won't last out the walk if you use that much," Jada retorted.

They walked for a moment in silence. "Do you think I'm getting fat?" Michelle asked, as she did almost every morning.

"Yeah. And I'm getting white," Jada retorted. Michelle giggled. Then her face took on her serious look, the look that meant that soon the quiz would start, and Jada just wanted to put it off as long as possible.

It was early enough that the streetlights were still on, but as the two women passed under one it blinked off. "So where do things stand, Jada?" Michelle asked, predictable as an actuarial table.

"I don't know. We never had time to talk." Nevertheless, Jada raged about the condition of her kids and home the previous night as she and Michelle speed-walked past the quiet houses.

"You have to draw a line in the sand," Michelle said. "You have to . . ." But Michelle caught herself.

Sometimes Jada thought her friend was afraid to give advice. "I don't think I can stand it. I'm going to have to take an ax to his head, even though he is the father of my children."

"Hey. When did that stop you before?" Michelle asked, and Jada had to grin.

Michelle definitely had a giving NUP—a term Jada had invented to categorize a person's Natural Unit Preferences. Michelle was a generous friend, and generous to her husband and children. But somehow Jada just didn't feel like taking pity from Michelle right at that moment.

"He's gone crazy on you, Jada," Michelle said, "If Frank ever . . ."

Jada tuned out because she loved Michelle—she was her best friend, even if she was from the south, white, had a stupid dog, and was sometimes thick as a plank.

It had been weird when Jada realized that she really didn't have any close black friends anymore. She couldn't hang with the African-American tellers at the bank and she didn't relate to the few neighborhood strivers whose daddies and granddaddies were professionals and who went to college—real sleep-away colleges. She certainly couldn't relate to Clinton's homies, who thought that double negatives were standard and career planning was marriage to a man with a job at the post office.

She and Michelle had a lot in common, but Michelle actually thought Frank was perfect and closed her eyes to all the funny stuff that went on in Frank's business, not that any of it was funny. Jada knew there were county contracts, inside deals. Frank Russo thrived, even when the economy was at its darkest. There was no way that Frank hadn't paid off officials, wasn't connected to . . . Well, Jada didn't like to think about it. It was none of her business. But a few years ago, when Frank had asked Clinton to join him in business, Jada had actually been relieved when, for once, Clinton had made the right decision. It wasn't jealousy that made Jada believe that the Russos had a little too much cash. If Mich wanted to close her eyes to it, that was her business.

The Jacksons had bought Jada's Volvo station wagon from the Russos. It had been Mich's car. But Michelle got a new model every eighteen months or so. Since Jada had gotten the station wagon, Michelle had been through two—no, three—luxury cars, and she'd told Jada Frank paid cash for every one. Jada had to admit Frank Russo was a good man—for a man. Most importantly, he really adored Mich. But that didn't fool Jada: when it came to his NUP, old Frank was a taker, too. In a way he was *worse* than Clinton. He had Michelle completely fooled. Jada doubted if Frank knew where the washer or dryer was in his house, much less the stove. If Michelle were to ever leave Frank home alone with the children for two days and Frank couldn't call his mother over, the Russos would die of starvation, despite a refrigerator full of food. Frank, who could work with his shining dark hair to get just the right lift, was incapable of slapping a slice of Velveeta between two slices of bread, or sorting laundry, or making the bed. He made Clinton look like the black male Betty Crocker. And Michelle never complained.

Hey, girl, she told herself. *Stop the comparisons. Try for a gratitude attitude. Drop the criticism.* This daily walk, Jada thought, this friendship, and this safe and pretty neighborhood, were two of the good things in her life. She said a silent prayer, remembering to be grateful for her strong legs and lungs, her friendship and her home. She looked around at the houses, the gray trees glistening with the last of the frost. Pretty. "Look," she said, pointing to new construction. "They're putting a sunroom on." She and Michelle checked every house improvement project and gave their approval—or not. Michelle looked at the hole knocked into the side of the brick colonial.

"Oh, I'd love that. It looks like it'll be a real greenhouse. I wonder if Frank could build one for me?"

He should build a doghouse first, Jada thought, tripping over the leash as Pookie cut her off yet again. They turned to the right, Pookie pulling Michelle, who was almost slipping as the dog pulled her on the snowy street. As Jada looked away in annoyance, she saw the oddest thing—a face appeared in the window of a Tudor across the street for a moment. It was a face so pale that a trick of the light made it seem almost luminous, although the eyes were so shadowed that they seemed to recede into the darkness of the house. In the back of Jada's mind something about the face seemed familiar, or . . . had she had a dream? She shivered and shook off the feeling. "I'd swear I just saw a ghost," Jada told Michelle. "Otherwise there's a scary-looking woman being held prison in there. Who lives in that house now?"

"Oh, that's the new guy. You know. The middle-aged one who lives there alone. He's Italian or something. Anthony. He has that—"

"The one with the nice cars?" Jada interrupted.

Michelle nodded. "The one with a limo service. And a very small mortgage." Jada reflected that being a loan officer gave you insights others might not have. Michelle continued. "I don't think he's married."

"Well, then he has a very unhappy girlfriend."

"Maybe it's an arranged marriage," Michelle said. "You know, like they write away to Russia and order some young wife."

"That's not *ar*-ranged, it's *de*-ranged," Jada said. They walked on in silence for a while.

"So what are you going to do about Clinton? Will you force him to make a commitment?"

"Clinton? Commitment? The only thing those two words have in common is they both start with a 'c.' I mean, Clinton is the only guy in his 'hood who never got a tattoo. De Beers lies when it says it's a diamond. A *tattoo* is forever."

"I can't imagine *why* he'd do something like this," Michelle said. "You're perfect."

"Why he wouldn't get a tattoo?" Jada asked, deflecting the discussion. Sometimes Mich just didn't get it, Jada thought. Was it her kiss-me-I'm-Irish heritage? "That's just it, Mich. I'm perfect, and that makes Clinton sick. I'm twice as strong as he is. He knows it and he hates it!"

"No! Jada, don't say that! You're going through a hard time—a really hard time—but that isn't true. Clinton admires you. He doesn't hate you."

"I didn't say he hates *me*. I said he hates my strength." Jada sighed. "He could make it ten years ago when it was easy, but he can't make it now when it's hard. I could. I *can*. Shit, girl, I have to. And he resents me for it." They came to the gate, where they turned around. Michelle, as always, patted the corner post. Jada, despite her mood, almost smiled. If Michelle couldn't touch the post, she wouldn't feel as if they had accomplished this bone-chilling, breathtaking three-quarters-of-an-hour of torture. She looked at her friend's long legs, her skinny mane of perfect blond hair pulled back into a ponytail. She looked like a young colt—all legs and eyes and tail. Meanwhile Pookie sniffed and snuffed at the post as if the damn dog had never seen it before.

"But I thought they *wanted* us perfect," Michelle said as they got moving again. "Frank notices if I put on a pound or don't shave my legs. I mean he loves me anyway, but—"

"Hey, it isn't about whether your legs are shaved. And it isn't even that your legs are twenty inches longer than mine. We've got the same thing between them. Men want that without a lot of trouble."

"Jada! That's awful. I work hard to keep myself looking good. It's not just about looks, but it's not just about sex, either. I mean, I know it's impossible, but I used to try to be perfect for Frank."

"They don't want us perfect," Jada snapped. "They want us dependent. Unless we're *too* damn dependent. *Then* they feel smothered. And they want us to take care of them. Unless we do it *too* much. *Then* they feel controlled. And they want us sexy, unless it means we want to make love *too* much. *Then* we're demanding. Because *then* they feel castrated."

Michelle sighed. "That's harsh. You just have to talk to him. He's your kids' father. Talk to him when you get home now. There's no time like the present."

Jada had to admit she was pumped up. Her adrenaline was flowing. "You're right. Cover for me at the bank. I'll probably only be an hour late. I'm serving Clinton a little extra something with his scrambled eggs this morning."

"Just don't be bitter, Jada," Michelle begged. "In spite of this, don't get bitter."

"Too late," Jada told her friend. "I already am."

6

In which Angie compares her father's taste in decor with her own in clothing, and in which she's briefly—very briefly—reprieved

Angela opened her eyes as she did—pointlessly—every morning at a quarter to six. The first thing she saw was the smoked glass mirror of the wall opposite the black leather sofa she was sleeping on. She closed her eyes. She was already so depressed she knew she couldn't get up, and the day wasn't ten seconds old. Her eyes still closed, she collapsed from her side to her back. Well, that could count as her exercise for the day. She pulled the shamrock green afghan over her head. Good. More exercise. Now perhaps the day would go away.

Actually, she wasn't sure what day this was: her anniversary had been on Tuesday, and it felt like she'd slept for days. Hopefully it was Sunday. If so, her mother would be home from her trip to some seminar or other. She'd once again watched TV till dawn and hadn't the strength to leave the den to go upstairs. She was camped at her dad's house, which was decorated in Middle-Aged Suburban Despair. But Angie had no place else to go. Her mother had recently moved into a new apartment and Angela hadn't ever been there. She couldn't even sit in her mother's space and take comfort from her surroundings. So Angela had been holding on, waiting for Natalie Goldfarb, giver of comfort, speaker of wisecracks, to get back so she could pour all of this pain and disappointment into her mother's ear.

But what good would *that* do? Angela asked herself now. Under the blanket—in the bra and panties she'd have to wear for two, or possibly three, days—Angela tried to avoid that thought. But she wasn't a kid with a boo-boo. What good could her mother actually do? Sure, she'd hold Angela while she cried her lungs out, but that was about it. Somehow, till this minute, Angela had felt that her mother could fix things. Not just that she'd comfort her and sympathize, but that she'd actually give Angie the key, the way to stop the relentless pain she was in. No—more than that. She would make the pain disappear, fix the problem, and make it go away. "Oh. The first anniversary I-cheated-on-you announcement. Sure. Daddy did it, too. You just . . . "

But there was no *just*. Lying there, feeling as dead and lank as her own hair felt now, Angie realized that what she wanted, more than anything, was to be back with Reid. Back with him, lying in their bed in the bright clean bedroom they had furnished together. She wanted *his* muscled arm around her, not her mom's. She wanted to open her eyes and see the Massachusetts light of early morning shining, but softened by the white net of the curtains, falling onto the bare bedroom floor. She felt such a tug of homesickness and longing for all she'd left up north that she actually opened her eyes and groaned. Now there was only the empty Shreve, Crump & Lowe box. She reached out for it and nestled it against her chest. Instead of her white bedroom pillows, she had a lumpy leather throw cushion under her head. Instead of her fluffy quilt, she had this old afghan. Instead of a skylight over her bed she had a ceiling repulsively spackled in figure eights, topped off by a light fixture from hell. Angie sat up, sick and dizzy. Who *had* done her father's decorating? That chandelier had to have been bought from a bad Italian restaurant's second-best dining room.

Angela had never lived her life with a man at the center of it. Since before high school she'd had a good group of girlfriends. In college they'd dispersed, but she'd made new friends and kept them, adding more in law school. She had always made time to see movies, and to Rollerblade, and to consistently volunteer for Meals-On-Wheels. She'd been delivering to some of the same people for years. It wasn't as if she'd read *The Rules* and built her life around catching some man. She'd gone to Thailand with her girlfriend Samantha and walked part of the Appalachian Trail with pals from school. So she wasn't just going to fall apart like some pathetic tool. Reid was not her entire life. At least that's what she told herself. So how come she felt so bad?

Something moving past the window caught her eye. It was still fairly dark, but two women were trudging by together, both wrapped up against the cold. One had a knitted cap almost covering her blond hair, but the other turned toward her companion—and in the direction of Angie's window—and Angela was surprised to see the woman was black. Now that was a sight you wouldn't see in Marblehead. The two women were already past the window and making the turn following the curve of the street. As they disappeared from view, Angie felt a pang of loss. What had happened to all her friends? Scattered across the country, working, married. Out of touch. It was ridiculous, but she wished she could bring them all together, like in a movie. *Reality Bites*. Well, she'd call her friend Lisa. But it was so early. She'd give Lisa a break.

Of course, she *had* called Lisa already. Several times last night, for an hour at a time. Wait till her dad got the bill! Angie missed her cellie, but the phone was in her purse, along with everything else. Maybe Lisa could get her wallet for her.

Lisa was an attorney who worked with her up in Needham. When Angela had first met her she'd been repelled by Lisa's tall, blond perfection and her Harvard Law background. Lisa was two years older, but acted as if it was two decades. Then, after working together, Angela had gotten over her prejudice because Lisa had been so friendly.

After a while, they had lunched together almost every day and Lisa regaled her with every horrible date she'd suffered through in the last eight months. Now it was payback time, and Lisa had been counseling her to keep away from the phone and to stick with her resolve not to speak to Reid. Angie had arranged for a leave of absence and Lisa was handling some of her work. She was a good friend.

She thought about taking a shower. Another day or two and her hair would go Rastafarian, but she didn't care. God, she hadn't just lost a husband, she'd lost her hairdresser! Who could do her unmanageable hair like Todd?

She was too tired to stand, and her body felt too limp to be safe in a bathtub. Then again, the idea of rolling under a tub full of water and dying was not an altogether unattractive one. Except for the part about breathing the water in. That would hurt like a bastard. She hated to get water up her nose. If only her father had sleeping pills—lots of them and the good kind, the kind that killed you. None of that over-the-counter Sominex stuff that gave you diarrhea. The only useful thing she'd found in Tony's medicine cabinet was a half-empty bottle of Nyquil. Hey, Angie told herself, she should stop being so negative—the bottle was half full. Or had been till she got a hold of it.

Angela bent over and reached for her sweatpants—well, they were her father's sweatpants—and slipped into them. As she pulled the waistband up over her legs and past her thighs she realized those were the thighs that Reid had just stroked the night before. A hot tear, and then another, escaped from under her right eyelid and immediately coursed down her cheek and into the crease beside her nose. She hated Reid. She hated him touching *her* thighs, and then she wondered who else's thigh he had been touching. What had he said? An older woman? Someone at work. Could it be Jan Mullins, the only woman partner at Andover Putnam? No. She was a fifty-two-year-old wrinkle bunny. One of the drab paralegals? Unthinkable. Maybe a secretary? Oh, who had he touched, who had he kissed? Had he told her he loved her?

The thought made her so angry that she had enough energy to stand and pick up the Rangers sweatshirt from the floor beside the sofa and slip into it. Her dad, unlike most Italian-Americans, didn't care about baseball but adored hockey. He'd taken her to dozens of games. This sweatshirt might be from one of those father-daughter trips.

Well, she'd make him important in her life again. She and Tony. And she'd get a pro bono job, something with kids or old people, not just the usually guilty scum at Legal Aid. She'd bust her butt, and she'd . . . Angela gave up. She'd pull herself together and join Mother Teresa's order tomorrow.

She started to weave her way through the house to the bathroom. As she passed the living room she couldn't help but wonder what frame of mind her father had been in when he furnished his house. The chairs were overstuffed and covered in blue velvet. The sofa was leather and one of those modern Italian shapes that looked like a surreal mountain range. Angie got a chill at the thought of having to continually sit on the leather furniture and touch it with her bare skin.

After his divorce from his second wife—a marriage that had been shorter than a normal menstrual cycle—her father had given up on the Park Avenue life he'd briefly attempted and moved to the suburbs. He'd dated a bunch of suburban women but complained that they bored him. So he worked compulsively, and watched a lot of sports on TV. It must be a work day, Angie realized, because if it was Saturday he'd be here, probably sitting on that cheesy sofa. What a life.

It was frightening to realize that it could become her life, too. She hadn't been here long, but already she was feeling Middle-Aged Suburban Despair. And not just because of the horrible decor. Why was it, she wondered, that after a divorce men decorated so badly while women let their wardrobes go to hell? It was as if each gender blew off an area of good taste in a single legal instant. How long would it be before she was dressing in earth-tone stretch-waist pants and a leatherette jacket, coordinating perfectly with this room? Fuck joining Mother Teresa's. Her life had ended.

Angela shivered, though the sweatshirt was warm. Yes, her life had ended. There had been the childhood phase, the pre-teen years, the high school and college coed period, law school, and the brief marriage. Now she would begin the Miss Haversham of Westchester segment, a segment that might—if she was as healthy as her Nana—last for fifty years. She looked down at the Ranger sweatshirt and wondered if it would also last that long. Not as dramatic as a wedding gown, but more practical, she thought. Now all she needed was a rosary.

She fell onto the couch and back asleep, woke long enough to catch the end of the *Today* show, and then fell asleep yet again. It was almost eleven when she next opened her eyes. It was odd: she had a morbid need to check the time. No place to go, nothing to do. Still, the idea that almost five hours had drifted by since she first woke up frightened her. When the phone rang, she jumped. Should she answer? It could be her dad, who checked in. She picked up and was relieved when Lisa's voice greeted her.

"Hey, Angie," she said. "How are you faring?"

Only Lisa would use the word *faring*. You had to be born in Back Bay Boston to get away with that. "Well, I'll put it to you this way," Angie told her friend. "If I were back in first grade right now, Mrs. Rickman would give me an 'unsatisfactory' for attitude." Angie paused. "I really hurt. I miss Reid."

"Let me tell you what your attitude should be," Lisa said. "You should be furious and hurt and unforgiving. What Reid did means he doesn't love you. He probably never did. You were his pet ethnic. Believe me, I know all about it. A little rebellion for the family. You don't need that. You don't need to do anything except move on."

"I know, I know," Angie agreed. "I'm such a tool. Of course I know it, but I have the weirdest feeling. I have the feeling I just want to hear his voice to ask him one more time whether he really meant to do it."

"He meant it," Lisa said, her voice full of certainty and controlled anger. "Look, it was unbelievable the way he did it, and unforgivable in the way he told you."

Angie was about to agree when the doorbell rang. She started. "Hey, Lisa. Someone's at the door. I gotta go."

She hung up and glanced nervously at the front of the house. What was this? Nobody came to a suburban Westchester door—not in this section of Westchester—uninvited in the middle of a weekday morning. Who the hell could it be? Avon ladies? Jehovah's Witnesses? Door-to-door electrologists? Whoever it was, Angie decided she wasn't going to respond, until she peeked out the hall window and saw the florist's truck. Then she flew to the door, threw it open, and had grabbed the two dozen white roses and snatched the note from the cellophane in less than thirty seconds.

It was from Reid! Obviously, it wasn't in his handwriting, but he had dictated the words. *I love you. Don't punish me for telling the truth. Forgive me, Reid.* The fragrance of the roses was faint but sweet. Oh God! He loved her. He'd fucked up—big time—but he loved her. One act of generosity on her part could free her and Reid from this pain. With one stroke, her conversations with her father and Lisa were stripped from her mind.

Yes. Yes! She *would* forgive Reid. What he had done was horrible, unforgivable, but she would forgive him. She was hot-tempered, like her father and mother. But she'd be big enough to do it. He had learned his lesson. Angie would look at this horror, this incident, as a last fling. Oh, she'd grant that most last flings came *before* the wedding, but Reid had always been a little slow emotionally. You couldn't completely blame him. Look at his parents. He would promise to never do it again, he would shower her with more Shreve, Crump & Lowe boxes and they'd go back to their big white bed. She couldn't restrain a shudder. Well, maybe they wouldn't go *right* back to it, Angie realized. Maybe there would be some healing time necessary.

Then, in a single instant, the image of Reid alone, miserable, lying curled in a fetal position on their big white bed came to her. Guilty. Despairing. It had taken him this long to track her down. He had been frightened, then remorseful. She knew that without her he was lost. He needed her energy, her drive, her warmth.

Clutching his card to her Ranger sweatshirt, Angie ran to the phone and punched in their number. She heard the first ring and knew the stretch, the exact arc of his beautiful back as he reached for the phone. She could perfectly imagine that four hundred miles away in Marblehead, his hand was reaching across the sheets to the receiver. He was there, she knew it, too desolate, too sick, to go to work. He had been lying there in a painful pool of guilt and regret worse than her own misery. Because he *did* love her. Despite his cold parents, despite their disapproval, despite his own limitations, he loved her. The card in her hand said so, and Angie knew it deep in her gut.

When the phone was lifted from the receiver on the second ring Angie smiled in vindication and waited to hear his voice, a voice as deep and clear as the sea off the Marblehead coast.

"Hello," a high-pitched woman's voice said in a breathy exhalation. Angie nearly dropped the phone. "Hello?" the voice said again, this time in a questioning tone.

Angie pulled her hand from the receiver as if it were on fire. She dropped it into its cradle. "Oh my God," she said aloud. "Oh my God."

She'd called her house. Who had answered? Not a relative or an in-law. She didn't have any sisters and neither did Reid. The voice certainly wasn't his mother's. *What is going on?* Angie looked down at the phone. She must have misdialed. She'd misdialed or, worse, Reid had already had the phone disconnected. Somebody new had their phone number. It must be one or the other. Angela snatched the receiver up and punched in their old number, but much more carefully this time. Had she remembered to dial the area code? Maybe she hadn't and it had been a Westchester call.

The phone rang and Angie held her breath. She pictured Reid again, but this time the picture was a little . . . well, mistier. This time, again on the second ring, the phone was lifted and again the soprano voice said, "Hello."

It wasn't a wrong number. Reid had obviously changed numbers. But did they reassign phones so quickly? She should inquire. But her voice box was paralyzed. Maybe it was a cleaning lady. Yes. That was it. Or a stranger making a delivery or reading the meter. It could happen, she told herself. She looked down at the florist's card she was still clutching to her chest.

"Hello?" the soprano said again. "Hello. Reid? Is that you?"

Since it wasn't, Angela hung up the phone.

7

Wherein Clinton and Jada have their talk, we learn about the nature of man, and the difference between milk, water, and blood

"Clinton, we have to talk."

"*Again?*"

"I'm afraid so," Jada said. Once the kids were on the bus, she closed the kitchen door and turned away and started wiping down the stove top. She could still see his face in the reflection of the stainless steel. She wondered when he had last cleaned the stove. "I'm afraid so," she repeated, but she wasn't really afraid. She was outraged. He had finally gone too damn far bringing dirt into the house.

Jada had suspected for years during their marriage that Clinton may have occasionally strayed. It was something she preferred not to think about, though awareness had sometimes been thrust upon her. That rich, bored woman in Armonk who had installed the two-hundred-thousand-dollar pool had called a little too often. And so had that black record producer's wife, the Pound Ridge one who wanted to sing. Jada had decided to ignore them. They had never interfered in her marriage, never stopped Clinton from bringing home his paycheck, playing with his children, or loving her. Since then she'd learned that, in sales parlance, overly attentive client handling was called "petting the goldfish," and if Clinton's work had sometimes gotten a little up close and personal, Jada had turned a blind eye. He was a man, after all. And a good-looking, virile one. When men were offered what she thought of as POP—pussy on a plate—it was hard for them to walk away. Especially in Pound Ridge.

Jada sighed. That was back then, when her marriage was good and the children were small and she stayed home with them. Now her life was made up of working all day and cleaning all evening. Of getting meals on the table, laundry folded, and then waking up to do it all again. Clinton's life, as far as she could see, was made up of lying around watching television, having it off with this new girlfriend of his, and in his free moments making sure the kids didn't burn down the house. Jada wasn't complaining about her life; she was doing this for her family and she could keep on doing it as long as she had to. It was just that when she looked at Clinton's life, if he would only make a few changes, everything could be so much easier for both of them. Easier and worthwhile. And she knew a part of him wanted a worthwhile existence. But a part of him was also willing to risk what they had by being lazy, taking her for granted, and tickling the fancy of some woman in Pound Ridge. "Well, I'm not in Pound Ridge," Jada said aloud and strode into the dining room, snatching up a tray and a rag as she passed her husband.

"Say what?" he said and followed her into the messy dining room.

Jada began throwing empty cups, cereal bowls, and a couple of crumpled paper napkins onto the tray. *I'm losing it*, Jada thought. It wasn't just the glassware that rattled; she was, too. She was speaking her thoughts out loud. It was a family trait—her mother did it when she was disturbed. "I was saying we have to talk," Jada snapped.

"Don't you have to go to work?" he asked nervously.

"No. Why? Are you expecting someone over here? Let me straighten up for your guest." She wiped down the table. It amazed her, even after all these years, that Clinton could stand there watching her do for him without lifting even a fork. That's what came of marrying a man who was DDG. Well, that was the least of it. Jada felt she had risen above the small stuff; long ago she and Clinton had promised each other that if they had children—and they obviously had—that unlike the two generations of Jacksons before Clinton, their kids would grow up *with* a father.

That was the big stuff. Until now, despite whatever brief flirtations might or might not have arisen from his work, Jada had never doubted that Clinton's NUP was taking. Like most men. But there was a limit.

Jada, even now, with Clinton standing hang-dog and useless behind her while she picked up the placemats, tried not to make a moral judgment about it. People just had their NUP, like the color of their hair. Jada had to admit that Shavonne's NUP was taking, too. Kevon, at least at this age, was more like Jada; his natural preference was to give. When she and Clinton had first met, the truth was Jada had *liked* to give. It had made her feel important and useful. Clinton needed to be taken care of and Jada guessed she needed to be needed. She'd cut his hair, she'd bought his clothes, she'd cooked for him. All Clinton had to do to make her happy was to say, "Nobody makes cornbread like Jada's. Can't eat no one else's cornbread," and Jada excused the double negative, feeling happy and content and ready to bake another fifty pans of cornbread. Now Jada knew Clinton-speak. "Can I help with dinner" meant "Why isn't it on the table yet?"

From the time Clinton's business had begun to fail, it had been one long slide on his side. Bit by bit. First he stopped bringing home money, then he stopped looking for work, stopped coaching Little League, stopped doing carpentry around the house. He'd even stopped what, in her opinion, was a married man's most primal task—taking out the garbage.

Her parents' marriage hadn't prepared her for this. Her mother and her father loved and respected each other. They'd been bitterly disappointed when Jada married an American black man. Though she'd been born in New York, Jada's parents were Bajans and they still thought of Barbados as home. "Americans. Forget them. They have no drive," her father had said. "They have no morals," her mother had warned her. Jada felt they were old-fashioned and definitely prejudiced, even more so against blacks than whites. Most of all they were prejudiced against other Islanders: they despised Jamaicans, were competitive with Antiguans, and were suspicious and contemptuous of the French islanders. American blacks were beneath them all.

It was ridiculous. Jada had laughed at them. But now occasionally Jada wondered if her parents hadn't been right, at least about Clinton. She hoped her marriage calmed down again, because she didn't look forward to giving them bad news. She wasn't certain about all American black men, but hers was undependable and lazy.

Maybe it wasn't true, but it felt true now. Maybe there had once been some kind of equilibrium between her and Clinton, when her giving had been balanced by Clinton's money-earning and the wonderful loving, but both had ended long ago. He hadn't earned even a dime in almost five years and they hadn't made love in almost three (except for the New Year's Eve when both of them had been drunker than they should have been and Sherrilee was accidentally conceived). They hadn't had sex in so long that her diaphragm must have been torn. She wasn't sure how it happened, but she'd gotten pregnant and—after what had happened once before—she couldn't bear the thought of not bringing the baby into the world. She'd prayed over it, and God, or her heart, had spoken. Sherrilee was an adorable baby, good as gold, and though it had been difficult to work through her pregnancy and was difficult now to leave the baby behind when she went to work, Jada didn't regret her decision. She had thought the baby might bring them closer, and Clinton had acted delighted and involved. But, as with most things, Clinton didn't follow through and now she wondered if she had done the right thing.

"Jada. Please have patience. I need you," Clinton said.

Need? Jada had been so damn needed that she'd run out—not out of giving, but out of feeling happy about doing it. The children had shown her that it was as natural as breathing to give to a nine-year-old, but definitely unnatural to have to give in the same way to a thirty-four-year-old man. Natural or not, Jada was damn tired of it.

"Yeah. You need me. But you say you *love* her." Jada couldn't believe he'd told her about this latest affair. She hadn't wanted to hear a word, but he'd insisted. "Go need her," she told Clinton, and turned her back.

Jada stuck her head into Shavonne's room looking for dirty laundry, Clinton behind her. She picked up the pile and moved down the hall. Tonya Green, the woman Clinton was seeing, claimed to love children, though Jada had heard that her two were living with her mother. What did *she* do all day? Jada wondered. She didn't work. She had a reputation in their church for being very pious. She taught Bible school. Did she go to prayer meetings? Hang out in bars, hoping to meet a buff married man? Maybe she alternated. Monday, Wednesday, Friday, prayers. Tuesday, Thursday, Saturday, her prayers were answered.

Jada snorted. The oddest part of all this to Jada was that when it came to the sex—Clinton and Tonya together—she just didn't care. Ten years ago she would have been filled with jealousy. She had thought that making love to Clinton was central to her life. Now she didn't even miss it. Sleeping beside him was bad enough. Sex would be . . . well, she was too angry, too tired, and too disappointed in him to want it.

Jada didn't think Clinton loved her. He just needed her, wanted her to love him. And she couldn't. Clinton sometimes still wanted to make love to her. Clinton had wanted their baby. Clinton took good care of the baby now. But Jada didn't feel like making love to him, and she didn't feel like taking care of him. She wanted *him* to take care of *her*. She'd lost respect for Clinton and perhaps she had some responsibility for this pathetic affair with Tonya.

Jada had only been surprised that Clinton had bothered to tell her at all. He'd never bothered before. Surprisingly, she had merely thought, "One fewer thing I have to do. Let Tonya listen to his bullshit rap about the next useless, unrealistic scheme he's going to fail at." Jada realized then that she hadn't really listened to him in years, after dozens of plans she had listened to, had critiqued and prayed for, had ended in nothing. Yet men had to be listened to by someone.

What *she* had to have, what she was working herself to the bone for, was a stable family. She wanted to live in their house, the house Clinton had begun but still hadn't ever finished, and she wanted to see the kids do well in the community and really well in school. She wanted to see Shavonne win the local ice skating finals and go to the prom. She wanted Kevon to get his math scores straightened out and wind up with a scholarship to a really good college. She wanted the children to grow up with a father, as they'd both pledged before God. They all needed him there. He had to watch the baby while she worked. He'd promised to help raise the children. She didn't think about the quality of her marriage—what was the point? But they had to have this Talk. Too bad she was so damn tired. She was always tired. Jada got to the door of their bedroom, and Clinton was right behind her. "I'm getting ready for work," she said.

"I thought we were going to talk," Clinton said.

Of course, he was right. She had begun this, but somehow between the kitchen clean-up, the dining room, the laundry check, and the assorted other things she had tried to get done, she had very little energy left. "You're right," she admitted. "I did say that."

"I'm going to make up my mind," Clinton said. "I promise you. I'll get my life in order."

He was making her crazy. "Déjà vu all over again," Jada said without attempting irony or humor. She turned around and faced Clinton for the first time since they were in the kitchen and realized she still wanted to slap his face. "Do you realize that you said the exact same thing, in this exact spot, in the exact same tone of voice, one month ago?"

"What are you talking about?" Clinton asked, already defensive. The man was DAS—dumb and stupid—if he didn't see what was coming.

"Let me refresh your memory." Jada started straightening up the bed. She hated to lie down in a rat's nest of messy bed clothes. It amazed her that Clinton couldn't even pull up the sheets and blanket when he got out of their bed—hours later than she did—each morning.

"You explained about Tonya back then," Jada said, keeping her voice neutral. "When you started drinking truth serum along with your Bud Lite in the afternoon." It was unproductive to use sarcasm, she reminded herself. She stood on her side of the bed. But Clinton didn't react. This man was oblivious to everything. "Clinton," she said to him, "to tell you the truth, I don't care what you do with your johnson. But I *do* care about this family. And I'm not letting your selfish-ass ways destroy it. I've given my blood for this family. I've given up my personal life, I've given up my outside interests. I get up in the dark and leave my babies sleeping in their beds to put food on the table. I don't like my job. Never have. I never wanted a career. I never wanted to be successful, to be a boss. I only did it out of necessity—"

"Okay. Enough," Clinton interrupted. "I remember. Don't try to make me feel worse than you usually do." Clinton looked down. "I try hard."

For a moment Jada was filled with enough anger to really smack him up-side the head. As if she was saying any of this to make him feel bad!

With Clinton, everything was always about Clinton. Try hard? The man didn't make the damn bed! "Shut up, Clinton. Give your excuses, run your mouth to Tonya. What I'm saying is that you can move in with her and I can go on with the kids, or you can give her up and try to keep us together, as a family. What's it going to be, Clinton?"

Jada thought of a proverb her mother had told her. It might have been from the Bible or it might have been an old Bajan expression. "A drink that is given when it isn't asked for is like milk. The same drink given only when it's asked for is like water. But a drink you have to beg for, that's given resentfully, is like blood." Jada had to ask and ask Clinton for even the smallest thing, and then half the time it remained undone. Her house still needed flooring in the kitchen and a dozen other finishing touches. Jada knew that Michelle didn't have to ask for anything. A moment before she even knew she was thirsty, Frank would offer that girl milk. Jada tried not to resent her friend, but sometimes it was hard.

"Jada, I know you're hurt. I know you're frightened." He climbed back into bed, under the blankets, as if he needed to be shielded from her. That enraged her. She needed protection from him, not vice versa.

Jada opened her eyes wide. "Clinton, I'm not hurt over this. I'm hurt that you won't work to keep this family together."

Clinton lifted his head from the pillow and started to say something, but Jada raised her hand and opened her mouth in time to stop him. "And I *was* afraid when I thought I couldn't earn a living. But I'm not hurt and I'm not afraid now, Clinton. I'm just telling you again, straight and plain, that you have a choice to make." She began to strip off her walking clothes but then, suddenly, felt that she didn't want to be bare in front of him. He was still a good-looking man. His chest was flat and wide. His stomach was tight even with his weight gain. His skin never chapped or grayed, while she had stretch marks and wrinkles. It was a strange feeling—modesty in front of her husband of so many years. "It's you that's breaking a commandment, not me. I'm trying to live righteous." Jada opened the closet door and stood behind it as she struggled into her work clothes.

"Jada, you don't understand . . . this thing with Tonya and I isn't just about the flesh. We have a spiritual connection."

Jada put her head around the closet door and stared at him. Mercy! Sometimes she couldn't believe the bullshit that came out of this man's mouth. *Sweet Jesus, you made this man,* she thought. *Now make him see the light. Or, alternatively, pluck out his eyes.* She thought of her parents. On Barbados, a small island where everyone knew everything, people learned compromise as an art form. Not Clinton, though.

"I can forgive you," she said. "I can live with you. And I can try, even harder than I have, to keep this family together. But not if you talk to me about that woman's spiritual qualities. Everyone has to draw a line, Clinton. I don't want to hear one damn thing about her. Don't insult me with a comparison."

"I wasn't comparing," Clinton began, his version of an apology, then saw her murderous expression and stopped. "My family means everything to me," he added quickly. "You know that. Maybe we haven't been getting on so good, but there have been times when it was smooth and times when it was rough." He rubbed his long fingers through his hair, then held the back of his neck as if it ached. Too bad he was DDG, Jada thought. "It can be smooth again," he said. "I know that. I hope for that. That is where my commitment comes from. But with Tonya . . . well, I feel like what happens there is for *me*. Not for my children, not for the family, not to keep the mortgage paid down. Just for me." He paused. "And I feel like I deserve something." He shook his head. "This is making me unhappy. And it's making you unhappy. And Tonya, she's a good woman. It's making her—"

"Don't tell me how *she* feels, Clinton. That is not a way to open my heart," Jada snapped.

"It isn't easy to be a black man in a white man's world," Clinton said.

"Oh, spare me. It isn't easy to be a black woman. And I'm starting to think it isn't easy to be a white woman, either. It isn't easy to be *anything* in this world, Clinton. That's why we have churches."

"Jada, I have prayed over this. Tonya and I have prayed over this together." Jada rolled her eyes, but Clinton ignored that. "All I want to do is try to explain how hard it—"

"Stop explaining, start deciding," she said. "Look on the bright side, Clinton. You have the choice—your family or your mistress. That's a lot more choices than most people get. But I'm telling you, you can't have both. So if you don't make a decision, I'm making it for you. And this time, Clinton, there is *no* flexibility. Next week I move all your stuff out of here and into the garage. I'll tell the children and I'll tell Reverend Grant. I'll go to a lawyer. So by next Wednesday, your decision is made, either by you or by me." She turned her back on him and tucked in her blouse. She did it so hard she broke a nail and caught it on the waistband of her pantyhose. Well, first her marriage, now her nail was broken. And it wasn't even ten o'clock yet. She glanced at the clock on the bedside table. Beside it was a photo of Shavonne holding Kevon when he was an infant.

Her babies. Her family. Jada knew the last few years had made her hard, and she didn't like it, but there was nothing she could do about it now. Meanwhile, if she could only save her babies, give Shavonne and Kevon and Sherrilee something more to start their lives off with. She couldn't let this decision be made for her as Clinton dithered and the clock ticked.

She found the strength to turn around and look at her husband. "Clinton, just think a moment. Your daddy ran out on you. *His* daddy ran out on *him*. You're free to run out on your children, too. But that's not what we promised them. They're *your* babies, too. I think you want something better for them. I know I do, but I'll take what you give me, Clinton. It's just that I won't put up with you and Tonya together, and have all of them at church talking. Plus allowing you here, takin' up space in my house and my bed."

"It's *my* house, too," Clinton protested. "For Christ sake's woman, I *built* this bed."

"Then take the damn bed over to Tonya's," Jada snapped. "And don't take the Lord's name in vain in this house. Point is, you can live here with me and the children if you want to try again to be a family. Or you can live with Tonya. She's got kids, don't she? Two? Three? Four? By how many men? Well, you can have them or yours. You just can't have both."

"I don't want both," Clinton whined. "I just don't know what I want."

As if she cared, Jada thought. "Well, you have a week to figure it out," she told him. Dressed now, she clicked across the floor in her high heels. She was in the hallway before she remembered, turned back, and put her head back into the bedroom. "Oh, and Clinton," Jada told him. "You better begin to find your own gas money." She slammed the door and went to say good-bye to Sherrilee before she left for work.

8

Economically containing both Michelle's bustier and bust

Michelle squatted to the floor to pick up yet another Disney action figure, pushing the bones of the bustier she was wearing up into her ribs. *Don't do housework dressed like Nasty Spice,* Michelle told herself. *This is what you get.*

Ah, the pull between passion and prudence. Of course, she could just leave the stuff lying around, but though she sometimes wanted to dress like a high-class hooker for Frank, Michelle knew beneath her uplifted cleavage beat the heart of a very tidy housewife. In fact, she was probably a little neurotic about it. Having grown up with filth around her, as an adult she was constantly cleaning. Maybe she should get a French maid's costume. She smiled at the thought as she picked up the red plastic toy. Frankie had so many of the things Michelle couldn't tell who they were anymore. Was it because he was a boy or the second child? Back in Jenna's day, Michelle had known the difference between a Little Mermaid and a Belle, but now the Hercules/Aladdin/Moses continuum was too confusing. She sighed, and guiltily wished Frankie had stuck with the Lion King. Somehow he had more toys but less attention than Jenna had gotten.

Once down at carpet level, Michelle noticed half a dozen Legos under the ottoman—good thing she hadn't vacuumed. She'd hoovered up more Micro Machine pieces than any Electrolux could be expected to eat. Pookie was chewing on his plastic bone and growled at her. Michelle shook her head at the dog, throwing back her hair, left down for Frank. Then she reached past Pookie for the Legos and gathered them in her right palm, balancing them with the action figure—she thought it was Jafar—in her left hand. She managed to straighten up in a single movement without using her hands from her squat on the floor. Not bad for a thirty-one-year-old woman.

She turned her head. Over the back of the sofa she could see Frank's dark hair, and the very top of Jenna's head, leaning on his shoulder. Jenna was clutching Pinkie with her right arm. Frankie must be lying across his dad's lap by now, lulled to sleep long ago by the bleeps and yeeps of whatever Nintendo game his dad and sister were playing. Michelle smiled. They had all had a good night; Fridays were always good nights. She and Frank had split a porterhouse and pasta while the kids had had hamburgers, their favorite. Frank had played wiffleball with Frankie for almost half an hour, then he'd suffered through a *Rug Rats* video, followed up by a Nintendo marathon. Jenna had let her brother play with Daddy while she helped Michelle clean up the dinner things. Her reward was getting Frank all to herself for the last hour while Michelle policed the area. Mich's reward would be her time alone with Frank in bed. Her smile, which created a parenthesis on either side of her wide mouth, deepened.

She moved to Frank and, very gently, touched his shoulder. She'd learned a long time ago not to come up behind him and touch him too hard—it really startled him. Now Frank bent his head back against the sofa cushions and looked up at her, though neither Jenna nor Frankie made a move. Nothing moved except the dancing Zelda image on the TV screen. The kids were both sleeping and Frank was playing the idiotic game alone!

"Time for bed," Michelle said in a throaty whisper and Frank's smile echoed her own. "You carry Frankie. I'll walk Jenna up," she told her husband. Frank nodded, then reached out and took a Lego from her right hand.

"Did you bake these just for me?" he asked, his voice low.

"You don't bake plastic," Michelle said. "You extrude it."

"I thought we'd do that later, upstairs." He waggled his eyebrows. Michelle shook her head and moved her hand to Jenna's shoulder.

"Come on, big girl," she murmured to Jenna who, very reluctantly, came out of her doze and, propelled by Michelle, got on her feet.

"Bed time for Bonzo," Frank added as he placed his sleeping son across his shoulder, cupping the boy's head gently in one hand.

"Be careful with him. Most accidents happen in the home," Michelle reminded him.

Upstairs, Michelle got Frankie out of his clothes and into his pajama top while Jenna got herself into bed. Michelle took pity on her firstborn and didn't insist that Jenna wash her face and brush her teeth. Just for one night it would do. She knew just how tired Jenna felt. She looked forward to lying down herself.

When she entered their bedroom, Frank was already stripped and under the sheets. As usual, he hadn't folded down the bedspread, so Michelle did it for the three-thousandth time. He was a good man and a good father. They had had a lovely night, but she still couldn't train him to take the bedspread off before he lay down. Oh well. There were a lot worse traits.

"Come here, gorgeous," Frank said, his voice already thick with sleep. Michelle sat down on her side of the bed, pulled off her shoes, and wriggled out of her skirt, but left on her panties and bustier. She wanted Frank to notice how nice she looked in it. Frank took a curled tendril of her hair in his hand and gently pulled her face down to his. "Hey, hot stuff. How much for the whole night?" he asked.

"A lot," she informed him before he kissed her.

"Worth every penny," he said. He reached for her upthrust breast. "Take that thing off," he said. Michelle followed his order in less than sixty seconds. "That's more like it," Frank murmured, wrapping his arm loosely around her, resting his hand on her hip and pulling her against him.

"Better than Nintendo?" Michelle teased.

"Well, not as exciting but . . ." he mumbled. She poked him between two ribs. "Okay, okay. Better than Nintendo," he admitted and kissed her on the neck. She sighed deeply and she heard her sigh echoed by him.

Fridays were always long, exhausting evenings, but good ones. She was happy and tired and so was Frank. "Baby, you know I want you, but . . ."

Michelle kissed him on his sexy, stubbled cheek. Later perhaps, some time in the middle of the night, he would wake her up with his arm tight around her and the rest of him insistent.

But it wasn't Frank who woke Michelle. It was a horrible, rending sound and the noise—lots of noise—of feet on the stairs. From somewhere downstairs the usually quiet Pookie was barking ferociously. Michelle barely had time to sit up before she was aware of the red light flickering round the room. *My God,* she thought, *the house must be on fire.*

"Frank!" she screamed, but his eyes had already flown open, just as the bedroom door did. And then their bed was surrounded by men, some in uniform, some not, all with guns drawn.

"Police!"

"Police!"

"Police! Don't move! Put your hands up over your heads!" The voices were shouts, harsh as punches. Michelle turned to look at Frank, but one of the voices brayed "Don't move!" in her ear. "Hands up! Don't move!"

Michelle wondered, for a brief instant, if this could be a dream—a very, very bad dream. But before she could find out, one of the uniformed cops leaned over and slapped handcuffs on her. She knew, from the cold reality of the metal on her wrists, that this nightmare was real. Pookie was now in the room barking; suddenly he was interrupted mid-bark and went silent. What had they done?

"Frank," she cried out again.

"Don't fuckin' touch her!" Frank yelled, and the two men holding him at the shoulders began struggling with him. The struggle pulled the top sheet and blanket down, and Michelle, paralyzed with horror, felt her left breast exposed to the cool bedroom air in front of a dozen men.

"This must be a mistake. You have the wrong house!" Michelle cried. "We're the Russos. The Frank Russos."

"No fuckin' shit," one of the men said.

"Mommy?" Michelle heard Frankie's bleat from down the hall and, despite her nakedness, sat up. "Mommy?" The bleat now sounded more certain of being terrified and Michelle called out to her son.

"It's okay," she shouted, though it wasn't. "Leave my children alone," she cried out hoarsely. "This is some kind of mistake. Leave my children alone."

"Tell her what kind of mistake this is, Russo," one of the cops holding Frank down said. Frank went into a diatribe of swear words, some of which Michelle had never heard come out of his mouth. "Get your hands off her, you cocksuckers!" he screamed. "Leave my kids alone, you stupid fuckin' bastards."

Two of the officers had gotten her up, standing between them. She hoped her hair covered most of her. She had to get to her children. That was all she knew.

When Frank swung to hit the guy on the left with his shackled wrists and called them cocksuckers for the second time, Michelle saw the cop throw a mean knee into Frank's groin. Frank screamed as Pookie had, then crumpled at the side of the bed.

"Mommy? Mommy?" Frankie's now ever-more-urgent voice was joined by his sister's, and by the terrifying noise of crashing from below. Michelle began to shake. Pookie ran past her, past all the watching men, maybe to protect her children.

"For chrissakes, collar the dog and give this woman something to put on," a plainclothesman said, entering the bedroom, and threw a blanket at her.

"Fuck the coke whore," another one retorted, and then Frank was on his feet, naked and screaming, fighting first one, then three of the cops.

"Frank!" Michelle yelled out to her husband as the two officers beside her began to pull her out of the room.

"Get her outta here," the man who had given her a blanket told the police. "Call McCourt in. Make sure she's gotta woman officer with her all the time."

"McCourt's taking the kids."

They were already in the upstairs hall. Behind her, Frank was bellowing. "*Where* are you taking my kids?" Michelle asked, frantic. "Stop! Please! Where are my children?"

They paid no attention to her. It was as if her voice was unhearable. "Get McCourt, goddamn it!" the plainclothes policeman yelled. "We should have two women officers. And what the hell are the state guys doing here? This is our jurisdiction."

"It's RICO, baby. Everyone wants in. Even the county's here."

"Frankie? Jenna?" Michelle called. "Where are you?"

Someone grabbed Michelle roughly by the shoulder and propelled her down the hallway. *No!* She wouldn't. Where were her children? What was happening? She heard another howl from Frank. Trying to hold the blanket around her despite the handcuffs, she also clutched at the banister outside Frankie's room. There were two cops in there and, as Michelle looked, they began to throw action figures, blocks, and Legos off the counter to the floor, pulling the mattress off the bed, throwing open cabinets. Frankie was being ushered out of the room by a woman police officer.

"Mommy!" he yelled, the tears and snot already mingling on his face. "The bad man let Pookie out."

"Let's go," the officer behind Michelle said, and gave her shoulder a push. "McCourt, stick with her. Johnson can take the kid."

"No!" Michelle said. She held on to the banister but bent forward to her son. "*I* take care of the kid," she said, her voice harsh.

"Not now you won't," the voice behind her answered and gave her another, harsher push. Her long hair fell into her face. She lost her hold on the railing and fell to her knees. Her son began to wail. "Frankie, it's all right," Michelle said, though it had never been less all right, not ever.

"Johnson!" The woman officer—McCourt, or whoever she was— yelled out in a tough voice down the hall stairs. The sound of glass smashing obscured the response. "Johnson!" McCourt yelled again. Behind McCourt, Jenna was being pushed out of her bedroom, still almost sleepwalking.

"They have Pinkie," she said. The whole group at Michelle's back was blocked from moving forward because of her. She couldn't hold the blanket on, conceal the handcuffs from her children, and grab them all at the same time. She didn't know what to do. She was still on her knees. She had no idea what was going on. It took all of her willpower not to break into sobs louder than Frankie's.

"They have Pinkie!" Jenna cried again and as Michelle was pushed past Jenna's door, she saw a policeman tearing off the back of the stuffed animal, pulling out the kapok, and scattering it. "No! No!" Jenna shrieked, lunging for her rabbit. Someone behind him was beginning the destruction of Jenna's room.

"Get up," someone behind Michelle commanded, and she felt herself lifted by her hair. Just then another uniformed woman ran up the stairs, took Michelle's daughter by the shoulder, and moved her around the banister and onto the stairwell.

"Let's go," she said. The policewoman looked up at the screaming Frankie, struggling against McCourt. "I'll take him, too," she said, and flashed a look at Michelle. It was a look of compassionate concern, the only human thing about this nightmare. "It'll be all right," she said. "It'll be all right. Tell them to go downstairs," she told Michelle. "We'll all come downstairs."

Michelle, on her feet now but still panicked, nodded automatically. "It's okay," she said, though she wasn't sure if Frankie could hear her—or anything. "It's okay," she said to Jenna. "Let's all go downstairs."

But it wasn't okay. Not downstairs or outside, not now or anytime soon. The Russo living room had been transformed in moments from a showplace to a scene from hell. There were more than a dozen men tearing books from the bookshelves, pulling the sofa cushions apart, tearing up the carpet. The desecration was so shocking that Michelle herself shrieked.

Somebody put her into a coat, taking the handcuffs off her to do so, but recuffing her afterward. "Frank!" she yelled. "Frank!" Her Lalique vase was smashed, Frank's flowers tracked across the floor. "Watch out for the glass," she called out. "Be careful of the children. They're barefoot."

"Get some shoes on them," someone yelled.

"Pookie! Here Pookie!" Frankie was calling out.

"Frank! *Frank!*" Michelle screamed again. There was a lot of noise going on overhead and then, faster than she could believe possible, Frank's bloody face moved past her down the stairs and out the door, surrounded by a coven of police.

"It'll be okay, Michelle. It's okay," Frank called. Behind him the cop who had given her the blanket was again issuing orders.

"Get the kids into a car," he barked to Johnson. "Get them some warm clothes. We'll take them over to Child Welfare."

Michelle's eyes opened wider. "No! Please!" she said. "Please. I don't know what this is. But please, can't I leave the children with my neighbor?"

"Sorry. No." He turned away. "Get her clothes. Put her in my car. Keep her away from Russo."

"What is going on?" she managed to scream to him as her children were hustled out the door. "This is against the law. *What is going on?*" A line from some television show came to her. "I demand my rights!" she screamed.

"Oh Christ." In a tired voice someone began a drone. "You have the right to remain silent. You have the right . . . "

This was like a bad television show, Michelle thought, as if she were at the movies, or in some kind of daze, watching the news. It couldn't be real. But Michelle was read her rights, forced into shoes, and walked out into the cold night air. The children were already gone, but other people, neighbors, were standing staring at her. Her neighbors! The Joyces. The Shribers. And strangers! What was happening?

Flashes went off. Who the hell could be taking pictures? She turned her head toward the garage only to see the lawn furniture strewn around. The driveway was filled with unmarked vans and men dressed in black wearing headsets. Six, maybe more, cruisers and troopers cars were pulled up around the house, their lights flashing. Lights were being turned on in houses farther down the street, and more people were gathering. Michelle even thought she saw Jada. She put her hand up to block the lights and get a better view. But before she could call out to her friend, she felt a hand press on the top of her head and force her into the police car waiting at the side of the curb.

9

Wherein Jada increases her already heavy workload

Jada sat at her desk, the office door closed. That was unusual: when she had to work Saturday mornings, Jada liked to keep an eye on what was happening on the bank floor. But today her own state of mind was unusual. Last night—well, at 2:10 this morning, to be precise—she had opened her eyes and gone to the window to see her friend's life being destroyed: police two-tones, unmarked cars, ominous gray vans, all with lights flashing and gun racks, had surrounded Michelle's house. Jada, shocked, had roughly shook Clinton awake and flung on her coat. She was at the Russos' gate in time to see both Jenna and Frankie being dragged off by a uniformed woman. When she had shouted out to them, Jenna had managed to look up, but Frankie was way beyond noticing a friendly face.

Jada had turned back to the crowd when the car drove the children away. The other faces around her were anything but friendly. Neighbors from the block and even one street over had assembled. If the night was colder, Jada wondered whether they would have rushed out into it so quickly to share Michelle's tragedy. Such alacrity, when with advance notice you couldn't get them out for recycling.

But what the hell was going on? Jada overheard a few nasty murmurs and then some even more unpleasant rumors. "A kiddie porn ring," Mr.

Shriber said, and his wife, a pleasant plump woman whom Jada had always liked before, nodded her head knowingly. "There were always a lot of kids around," she intoned.

"That was because their children were popular," Jada snapped. "And because Michelle let the whole neighborhood play in her yard." The Shribers were notorious for the perfection of their lawn and flowerbeds. No one was allowed on their property, ever. They had once put in a formal complaint about the mailman when he stepped off the walk. "You better watch out you don't get sued for slander and lose your landscaping."

Jada had then struggled through the rest of the crowd, wondering what the hell could be so wrong. What really had worried her was that there wasn't an ambulance in sight. The irony that seeing an ambulance would be good news was not lost on Jada. At least there wasn't a van from the morgue. She had stood there helpless a few more minutes. Finally, after she—and all the damned locals—had seen a handcuffed Michelle put into a police car and driven away, she had asked one of the black cops, one of only two she'd seen among the dozens there, what the hell was going on.

"Drug bust," he had said. "Big dealer. We'll get a couple of new cruisers out of this." Jada's mouth had fallen open.

It was still open. She sat at her desk, the memo that needed correction unmarked in front of her. She could barely take it in. A drug bust—a big one—on her safe street, and happening to her friends. Not that she believed Michelle was involved or guilty. Just that it could happen, that wealthy, working white people who owned their home could have their lives—and their furniture—wrecked and left on public display.

This morning, as she drove past the house, roped off with yellow crime scene tape, she'd seen two of Michelle's dining chairs, the upholstery torn, the filling ripped out of them, sitting forlornly on the drifts of leaves in front of her house. All sorts of other household goods were strewn over and among the leaves: throw pillows, Frank's footstool, the lamp filled with shells that Michelle loved and Jada had always thought was a little tacky.

Seeing Michelle's things strewn like garbage in an abandoned lot had given her such a pang, such a sense of doom and the inevitability of death, that it was almost as bad as seeing corpses out there. Jada knew just how often Michelle polished the wood of those dining room chairs. She'd even been with her when she picked out the rose and ivy fabric they'd been reupholstered in, fabric that was now slashed and flapping like torn eyelids in half a dozen places.

Her elbow on the desk, Jada put her forehead against her hand and rested it there, closing her eyes for a moment. She could feel her long fingers pressed against her skull through the thin skin at the top of her head.

When she'd come home last night, Clinton had been standing in the front doorway holding the baby. He hadn't asked her a single question. He'd only admonished her.

"You shouldn't be out there," he'd said as she walked up the steps.

"Why the hell not?" Jada had asked, thinking he was criticizing her for rubbernecking like the others. "I was trying to see if I could help. She's my best friend."

"You shouldn't be out there because we don't want to be attached to this thing." She had walked inside and Clinton had closed the door behind her. "Frank Russo has always dealt from the bottom of the deck. How do you think he got those county contracts?" For years Clinton had been anti-Frank. Jada had never been able to figure out if it was because Frank was so successful and Clinton was jealous, or if there really was something to Clinton's concerns.

Last night, Jada had snapped at him. "It's not about a damn contracting dispute," she told him bitterly. "It's about drugs."

"That motherfucker's been dealing drugs?" Clinton had exploded. "Unbelievable." The baby started, woke, and began to cry. Clinton began to pace and handed Sherrilee off to Jada. "I told you not to mess with them. Cops will be all over us, questioning us tomorrow. They see drugs, they see niggers. Jesus! How dare he? That greasy little fuck puts our whole family in jeopardy."

"Not quite as much as he jeopardized his own family," Jada had said coldly and had begun to stomp upstairs, soothing the baby but not knowing how to soothe herself. "If it was a black man, you wouldn't think he was dealing. You would think he was framed," she flung at Clinton from the stairs. "We don't know what the story is."

Of course, Michelle hadn't come in to work and Jada had said nothing about last night to anyone. She'd made more than a dozen calls to police stations and to the courthouse. She'd also checked her answering machine twice to see if Michelle had, by any chance, called. But there was no message.

When Anne, Jada's secretary, gave her little double knock on the door, Jada quickly lifted her head from her hands and picked up a pen. "Yes?" she asked and Anne came in, her eyes so big they seemed to precede her.

She carried a newspaper, not the *New York Times* or the *Wall Street Journal*, which Jada had learned to look through for business news every day, but the local county rag. "Look," Anne said and flapped the newspaper onto Jada's obsessively neat desk. Jada didn't want to, but Anne was going to make her look at the scene of the crime. Trust jealous Anne to gloat at someone's misery. Jada sighed. This woman needed a lot of churching.

She looked at the paper. There, spread out in two pages of tabloid pictures, was Michelle's house, a close-up of Frank's bloody, obviously beaten face, and—oh dear Lord—Michelle herself in her blue winter coat and handcuffs. Jada put her hand up to her mouth. SUSPECTED DRUG KINGPIN BUSTED, the headline read. She could hardly believe it.

"Isn't that something?" Anne asked. There was something in the sound of her voice that gave Jada the feeling Anne was enjoying the excitement of this.

Jada grabbed the newspaper and crumpled it. "That headline is outrageous. Why don't they just write 'guilty'? This man has only been accused, not convicted," she reminded Anne. "The press has already gone too far." She looked up at Anne as she flung the newspaper into the garbage. "When Michelle comes back to work, I hope you will all remember that she hasn't even been accused of anything. Now, don't you have something better to do?"

After Anne left, Jada walked out onto the floor, spoke to a few of her staff as naturally as possible, and greeted an important customer. She returned to her office, trying to look casual, closed the door, and retrieved the newspaper from the trash. Smoothing it out as best she could, she gobbled up the dearth of information. Despite the bad underwriting, it didn't seem as if any drugs had been discovered, thank God, and it did seem as if the police had been incredibly harsh both to Frank's face and to the house. Jada knew that since the RICO Act had been passed, police had been gung-ho about busting for profit. She also knew that success bred resentment, and Frank, cocky as he was, probably had a lot of envious enemies in the county.

The intercom rang. "It's Michelle," Anne announced in a breathless voice, as if Al Capone were back from the dead and calling bankers. Jada picked up the phone, watching to make sure that Anne hung up.

"Have you heard?" Michelle's voice asked.

Jada wondered if Anne, not visible now, was still listening on some other extension. "Honey, *everybody's* heard," Jada said. "Where are you?"

"I'm at home," Michelle managed and then she gasped, making an awful sound that Jada didn't like to hear and hoped that Anne wasn't hearing. She lifted the phone base off her desk and pulled it as far as she could. Then, setting it on the floor next to the credenza, she stretched the handset as far as she could and just managed to get to the door and look out. Anne and several of the other women had their heads turned toward her but immediately telescoped around, avoiding her. None of them was on the phone.

"Oh God, Jada this is terrible. This place . . . it's . . ." Michelle began to cry. "I have to go. I have to go pick up the kids. They were fostered out last night. Can you imagine?" She started to choke up; Jada could barely understand what she was saying. Something about Frank and making a list and the mirror and something else.

"Be cool, Michelle," Jada said. "All the shit you're looking at, all the broken stuff, isn't important. The babies are important and they're all right. You can come to my house tonight. We can clean up your place tomorrow." The poor girl. Kneeling there in the wreckage, she probably *did* look like Cinderella but it wasn't the time for Jada to make a "Cindy" joke.

"Oh, Jada." Michelle made another horrible noise and then said something else about Frank.

"Is he home?" Jada said. She didn't want to be too inquisitive. She'd known a lot of people who'd been in trouble and now wasn't the time for twenty questions. "Is he there with you?" she asked.

"No," Michelle answered, sobbing. "They wouldn't let me talk to him, but a lawyer came and said he would be home tonight or tomorrow. Jada," Michelle whispered, "it's a nightmare. Frank didn't do anything. How could the police do this to us?" She lost it then, and tears rose in Jada's own eyes.

"Michelle? Michelle? You cry, but then wash your face and fix your hair and pull yourself together for Jenna and Frankie. You want me to come with you to pick them up? I know how Child Welfare can be."

"I can do it," Michelle whispered, pulling herself together. "I can do it," she repeated, as if she were giving herself a pep talk, which Jada figured she was doing.

Jada used an old joke they'd run through together during the trials of raising suburban kids. "Are you calm?" she asked.

"Yes."

"If you're calm, I'm the Dalai Lama," Jada said.

"If you're the Dalai Lama, I'm Richard Gere," Michelle answered weakly.

"If you're Richard Gere, I'm outta here," Jada finished. "I'll leave work real soon, pick up some pizzas, and we'll have a pizza party at my house. If you want to sleep over with the kids, that's just fine."

"Sleep?" Michelle asked. "Oh God, Jada. I'm never going to be able to sleep again."

"Just as well," Jada said. "It's overrated. A big time-waster, generally. And you got a lot of cleaning to do. You okay?" she asked, just to be sure.

"Under the circumstances, yeah," Michelle said. "Under the circumstances. And Jada?"

"Yes," Jada said.

"Thank you. I won't forget this."

"I hope you do. I hope you forget the whole thing once it all gets straightened out. Meanwhile, tell me what's really important. I forget if the kids eat sausage on their pizza or not."

10

During which Angela sleeps through a riot and is subsequently read the riot act twice

"You're going to have to do *something*, Angela," Tony, her father, was saying from the doorway of the study. "It's not healthy to just lie here. You don't even look healthy." He craned his neck forward. "You're not taking an interest in anything. You didn't even get up last night during that riot."

"What riot?" Angie asked dully.

"You didn't even hear the cop cars and the commotion down at the end of the street?" Angela just shook her head. She'd found the number of a pharmacy that delivered, and a combination of Nyquil and Tylenol PM had put her in something close to a coma. "Well, you saw the police tape around the house today, didn't you?" her father was asking. "The bastids wrecked the joint."

Angie shook her head again. She didn't have a clue about what he was talking about, and she didn't care.

"Angie, there was a huge drug bust round the corner, about ten houses down." He looked at her appraisingly. "Hey, when's the last time you went out?" he asked, suspicion in his deep voice.

"I'm going out later," Angie told him, avoiding the question. It had been a few days. She was still in the Ranger's sweatshirt, still on the sofa.

"Great! You gotta date?" He approached her and sat on the arm of the couch.

"Yeah. With my mother," Angie said grimly. He better not get too close. She hadn't washed, brushed her teeth, or been out of her father's house since she arrived, and even she was willing to admit she was getting a little strange.

"Oh, she's back?" her father asked. Angie couldn't help but notice how he pretended to be totally casual, but she could sense his very real curiosity behind it. Desperation knew desperation. Angela was almost certain that her dad regretted the divorce. As far as she knew, her parents didn't speak. Her father had simply disappeared from her mother's conversation. But somehow Anthony Romazzano always knew Natalie Goldfarb's whereabouts.

"You're not going to get involved working for those *schnorers*?" he asked. "I didn't pay for law school so that you could help out a bunch of freeloaders."

"You didn't pay for my law school," Angie reminded him. Her father was very odd about money; he'd been poor and then he'd been very rich. He tried never to let the women in his family know where he'd stood. But they'd ignored him, and he'd always been disturbed that neither Natalie nor Angie seemed influenced by his money. Though he'd suffered a few business reverses recently, he was still well off.

"Please, Angie. You could get a job with a Park Avenue firm in a minute. I could help you."

"I'm not interested in Park Avenue. And you're helping me right now," Angie said. "You've been great." She kissed him on the cheek.

Tony awkwardly shifted his weight, reached into his back pocket, and took out his wallet. He pulled a wad of bills from it and handed them to her, without getting too close. "Look, you're a beautiful girl. Go out. Get your hair done. Get a manicure."

She sat up, kissed him again, and let him hand her the money. She didn't want it, but she knew it was his way of being kind. "Next you'll be telling me to buy a hat."

"You want a hat?" Tony asked, pulling open the wallet again. "I'll buy you as many hats as you want."

Angie couldn't even smile at his cluelessness. "No, Dad. It was a figure of speech. Men used to think that when women were unhappy, they
could just buy a hat to cheer themselves up."

"When?"

"Back in the fifties, I think."

"No, they didn't. I was alive then. Your grandfather never told Nana
to buy a hat. I never told your mother to buy a hat."

"Just as well," Angie said darkly. "It saved your life, no doubt." She
flopped back down on her back, already used to the warm but unpleas-
antly sticky leather waiting for her. Probably that dead cow hide was the
only skin that would ever touch hers again, she thought morosely and
stared overhead at the hideous figure eights in the ceiling.

Her mother was arriving home tonight and Angela knew she should
be showering. Since she hadn't brought any clothes with her, and since
she'd rather die than get into that stupid dress she'd worn to the club, it
wouldn't hurt if she stopped off at the Cross County Mall and bought a
pair of jeans and a couple of shirts. But the idea of doing either of those
things tired her to the point of exhaustion. The thought of getting vertical, getting into the car, getting to Poughkeepsie, parking, and finding
her mother's apartment was daunting enough. Angie felt as if all energy
had been drained from her. She had no "gets" left in her. But she had to
go: her mother was her only hope. Natalie Goldfarb would tell her what
to do. Her mother had to because otherwise, Angie figured, she was
doomed.

Her friend Lisa was still telling her to just stay away, to try not to
think about Reid, to remember how unforgivable his action had been. It
was good advice, and Angie was almost embarrassed when she thought
of how often she'd cried talking to Lisa.

She couldn't cry with her dad. It would upset him too much. He
would either cry, too, or threaten to kill Reid. Angie looked over at
Anthony. His fingers were pulling uselessly at the corduroy of his
trousers. He got up and moved to the end of the couch and motioned
with his head for her to retract her feet. She did so, curling up into a
semi-fetal position, her back now pressed against the stupid leather sofa.
The hide was cool on her back, since it hadn't been leaned on. Angie

shivered. Yes, that was what she should get used to. She would spend her life untouched by real skin. She would spend her life pushing herself against coldness, hoping for a tiny bit of warmth.

Angie looked over at the flowers her son-of-a-bitch husband had sent. She hadn't put them in water and the heads were already drooping, the edges of the petals already brown. The bouquet was a metaphor for her life—she would wither long before her time because of a tragic lack of caring. She hadn't taken all those comparative lit courses for nothing. When her father put his hand on her ankle, she turned away from her dead flowers to look at him.

He'd done this to her mother, she thought as he began to speak. "Angie, listen to me. You can't just lie here. Reid was a spoiled bastid. He always was. You can get over this. What he did was wrong, but the fact that he *told* you was unforgivable. You—"

"What do you mean?" Angie asked, but she knew about her father's double standard. It was an Italian thing. "You mean it would have been okay if he was screwing some other woman as long as I didn't know about it?" She pulled her knees the rest of the way into her chest, away from her dad, and shook her head. "Thank God he was guilty—or idiotic—enough to tell me. Otherwise I might still be there, a marble-head in Marblehead, living a lie."

At that moment, Angie hated her father and all men. Clueless, rotten, selfish, insensitive bastards. But Reid was the worst. As she lay on her back all these days—what, five? a week?—Angie had played scene after scene from her courtship, wedding, and marriage in her mind. The week she and Reid went to Vail and never got onto the slopes. The fight they had once in a Boston supermarket over mayonnaise. The way he had looked at her the first time she wore that taffeta dress. All gone. All useless, stupid memories of a stupid girl.

But a part of Angie couldn't believe that the good times were over forever. If Reid had died, she thought, she would be able to cope because she would have known that he wanted the good times to continue as much as she did. Knowing that their lives could continue, *were* continuing, but with Reid having the good times with someone else, just tore her apart. The idea that she alone had experienced some of their most touching moments together, while he was merely waiting to go meet the Soprano, was unbearable to her. Her stupidity, her lack of insight, her bad choices . . . all of it was unbearable. Angie knew that many, maybe even most, people had to compromise and adjust their view of marriage once they were actually married. But she hadn't *had* a marriage, though she'd thought she had. He'd been cheating on her, not married to her, except perhaps for the month or so after their wedding. She had had a one-sided fantasy.

Her father, at the foot of the sofa, began moving one of his meaty hands up and down the sole of her foot. Hot tears rushed to her eyes. Being touched was excruciating. She wanted to kick him away and then crawl into a ball of shame and fear and rage, but instead she smiled and accepted the massage. He meant to be comforting. He loved her. But Angie stared at him and could only think that he, too, had betrayed a woman—her own mother. Well, at least Anthony hadn't snuck around behind Natalie's back. He had just gotten tired of Natalie, dumped her for another woman, and at the same time tried to hold on to every nickel he had ever made. He was her father, but he was also a man. She pulled her feet away from him.

The only one now who could help her was her mother. Suddenly all Angie wanted was to be away from Anthony, to be next to Natalie and listen to Natalie tell her how she could fix her life. Her revulsion was the only thing that gave her enough energy to pull herself up from the sofa. "I'm going to go and see Mom," Angie told him.

"Angie, enough with the poor personal hygiene and the self-pity," Natalie Goldfarb said to her daughter as she leaned across the table. "You lie down with dogs, you get up with low self-esteem." Natalie reached out and stroked her daughter's hair, but then pulled her hand away. "Wow," she said wiping her hand with the napkin. "I need some of that in my Buick's crankcase." She opened her purse and took out a lip balm, handing it silently to Angie, who had been furiously chewing on her lower lip all week.

As Angie applied the lip balm, her mother watched, then heaved a sigh. "I love you, honey, but a part of you always knew what a spoiled little bastard Reid was. Maybe you're shocked, but you can't tell me you're really surprised."

Mother and daughter were sitting at the tiny table in the minuscule kitchenette of the small studio that Natalie sublet. It didn't seem like a home—it was more of a big storage room, with cartons, books, and papers everywhere. Two chairs sat one on top of the other, rolled-up rugs leaned against the wall, and no paintings or pictures or photographs were displayed anywhere. Angie thought of the cozy home Natalie had made for her family, as well as the domestic way Natalie used to live with her law partner, Laura. She looked around with fear and distaste at this. Had her mother given up? Could she only make a home for other people? This was not a comfortable place to live and certainly not one that would give *her* shelter.

"You should work in a shelter," Natalie said. "You should see how bad some of our sisters have it. I was just in India, and let me tell you, when a husband is tired of a wife over there, he and his mother douse her with kerosene and set her on fire. They have a name for it. 'Stove accidents.'"

Angie shuddered. "Very nice. So am I supposed to be grateful that Reid didn't use me as a luau torch?" she asked. Natalie got up, took the untouched sprout and sunflower seed salad away from Angie, and bustled over to the sink.

"Do you want something else?" she asked Angie. "I think I have sardines, but I'm not sure about crackers."

Angie shook her head. She hadn't eaten anything real in days, but if she did it wouldn't be something as disgusting as that. All at once she felt very sorry for herself. Didn't her mother even remember that she hated sardines? She'd always hated them, since she was little. Her mother and father had been such an odd mix: her mother was so domestic but not a physical person, while her father craved being taken care of. They'd battled over who should take care of whom for almost twenty years. Meanwhile, who'd taken care of her?

Suddenly Angie felt as if she were very, very young. Five years old, or maybe four. And lost, like the time she'd been lost at the zoo and had wandered into the park only to realize she couldn't find her way home.

At the time, she'd decided she'd just sit down on a rock and wait until she grew up, because she knew she couldn't make a home for herself until she was older. When her mother had found her, she hadn't cried. She'd just felt very, very lucky.

Her luck, though, had changed. If she *had* sat on the rock all those years until she was grown up, the way she was today, she still wouldn't be able to make a home for herself. She thought of all the care and attention she'd poured into the apartment in Marblehead. Picking out the sheer curtains, buying the sofa, and carefully stacking their wedding china—it had all been exciting but exhausting. She couldn't do it again.

She looked around her. Was this what she was doomed to, then? A room like a warehouse with nothing but a few cans in the larder? Her mother had once run a household and served warm nourishing dinners and put starched linen pillow cases on all the beds. Angie remembered the comfort of that. What had happened? Was her mother falling apart, Angie wondered? She seemed cheerful, though distracted, and now concerned for Angie. Was this the way every woman lived when they weren't living for somebody else? Or was her mother in more pain than she was showing? The break-up with Laura could not have been easy for her.

Whatever it was, however her mother felt, it was clear to Angie that there was no place for her here. Angie might as well go out and find a rock to sit on.

With that knowledge, all of her loss seemed to tumble in on her. She began to cry and then not to cry, but to sob. Her shoulders began to heave in spasmodic jerks and the noise she was making was almost obscene.

Natalie's arms were around her in a moment. "Oh, baby. Oh, sweetheart," Natalie said, stroking Angie's greasy hair lovingly. "Oh, my little baby. You loved him that much? You loved that idiot so much? Mourn as long as you have to. But I think it couldn't hurt you to start doing something for yourself. You definitely need your hair touched up. You want me to ask my guy to do it?"

"Mom, my problems won't be solved by highlights."

"No, but it's a start." Natalie took a deep breath. "You never really liked that job up in Needham. You just took it to be close to Reid."

Angie couldn't remember now why she had taken the job, but she knew she was lucky to get it. It hadn't been easy to get the month's leave of absence, either. But Angie wasn't ready to go back or to quit. She put her head down and hunched her shoulders, knowing what was coming.

"Why don't you give up those rich people's wills and trust funds?" her mother asked her. "Why don't you join our practice?"

Angie looked up from the Formica tabletop and stared at her mother. Natalie ran a women's legal services clinic where the clientele was primarily women so down and out, so pathetic, that they didn't have a few thousand to ante up to an attorney.

"I can't work there," Angie said, frightened of both the idea and her snobby repulsion. Her mother's practice served mostly poor or embattled women coping with everything from a disastrous divorce to immigration problems to harassment. Angie wasn't ready to spend her time helping other depressed women. She was too depressed herself. "I'm not registered with the bar here."

"That doesn't mean you can't drink. I can swear you in until you get the bar," Natalie said, and with a flourish brought a bottle of burgundy over to the table. She poured herself a glass—a jelly glass with blue dinosaurs on it—and then one for Angie. "Listen to me," Natalie said, leaning forward and holding her glass of wine. "What the hell is the point of going back to the scene of the crime? What's the point in going back to a selfish life where you're thinking of nothing but your own pleasure—or your own pain? Believe me, one is worse than the other. Join us. We'll get you through the bar in no time and we have a hundred women with problems so pressing, they'll make your adventure with Reid look like a day at the circus. Did I tell you about the eighty-two-year-old woman evicted from—"

"Mom, I don't want to hear about her pain," Angie interrupted, and took a swig of her wine. "I have my own." This wasn't what she had craved, what she had expected and needed. She wanted her mother to fix her old life for her, not offer her a new one . . . a boring, awful new one with a house like a garage and a job worse than social work.

"You think I don't understand?" Natalie asked, raising her brows. "Of course I understand. All you can do is think of him. How maybe it didn't happen, how you are looking for excuses, or, if there is no excuse, how maybe it was your fault and then you can forgive him anyway. How just because it happened once before, doesn't mean it'll happen again. Yup, I know what you're thinking. But those are all the desperate configurations of a rat trapped in a maze, looking for the little bar to press to get the cocaine that the scientist administers at the end of every test. You're obsessed with your future former husband because you're still hoping somehow you can get that hit of affection. That hit of sex."

Angie turned her head away. Her mother might be accurate, but accuracy didn't feel like what she needed right now. Natalie leaned across the table, trying to get closer, but Angie kept her face averted. Natalie's voice softened. "You feel like without it you can't go on, that you're trapped. But I'm here to tell you that being 'in love' is only an addiction. It keeps delusions going. It separates you from your real life, from real love, which you can feel for a friend, God, an animal, even a man. 'In love' sets you up to worship Prince Reid, some false idol you've erected within your temple. You were only with him for a year, Angie. You're young—only twenty-eight. Oh, there can be a man, later, if you want one. A good man, one who could be there for you." Natalie's voice toughened up then. "One who doesn't look like Brad Pitt in any way."

Angie stood up and reached for her purse. Somehow she felt more depressed but less hysterical then she'd been. Her mother hugged her. "You look beat," Natalie said, patting her on the shoulder. She hugged her again and Angie, too weak to hug back, let herself melt against her mother. That was what she wanted: to melt, to disappear, to lose herself forever.

"Do you want to sleep over?" Natalie asked. "I can unfold a cot I use when we get full at the crisis center."

Angie restrained herself from shivering. The idea of sleeping on a bed of misery here in this warehouse made her father's sofa and the plaster infinity signs overhead seem almost heavenly. "No," Angie said. "I'm just fine."

"Yeah," her mother said. "You're fine and I'm skinny."

Angie managed to give her mother a watery smile before she shrugged into her coat and left.

II

In which dinner and an ultimatum are both served

Jada and Michelle had planned to rendezvous at Post Road Pizza, but Michelle had called back to say she had to go down and pick up Frank. Jada pulled the car into the driveway, got out, and opened the rear door for Jenna. Jenna got out, moving slowly, as if overnight her eleven-year-old body had been transformed into an old woman's. But at least *she* was moving. Frankie seemed to have become paralyzed, turned into a block of stone, or maybe ice, by the trauma of the last twenty-four hours. When Jada lifted him from the backseat, she was surprised by his heaviness. The kid couldn't weigh more than forty pounds, but as dead weight he felt like the huge bags of Sacrete that Clinton used to throw so easily across his shoulder in the old days. Jada hugged the little boy to her, freed up a hand, and put it on Jenna's shoulder as she led them into the house.

When Clinton looked up from the kitchen table, Jada knew immediately that there would be trouble. She decided to ignore him for as long as she could. Normalization was the goal here, and since she normally ignored Clinton anyway, that was the route to take.

"Hey, Kevon! Hey, Shavonne! Guess who's here?" she called out. Shavonne wasn't crazy about Jenna lately—sometimes they got along and sometimes they fought—but Kevon adored Frankie. Kevon ran into the kitchen, but skidded to a stop when she put Frankie down on the linoleum. Kevon stood almost as still as his friend, then his eyes flicked from Frankie's face to his mom's.

"What's wrong with him?" he asked her in a hoarse kid's whisper, as if he could already tell that Frankie wasn't talking and maybe couldn't hear.

Jada felt Clinton's disapproval from all the way across the room. He was such a hypocrite! He'd hung with some neighborhood brothers who'd gotten in plenty of trouble, and once or twice had even brought the kids along until she'd put her foot down.

"He had a bad sleepover," she said. "Remember when you had that sleepover at Billy's?" Kevon nodded. It wasn't easy for her son to be the only African-American in his grade. "Well, it was scarier than *that*. But he's okay now. He's with us." She tightened her arm around Frankie, really talking to him. Kevon, bless his heart, reached his hand out to Frankie, who still stood immobile.

"Come on, Frankie," Kevon said. "We hate Billy." Jada realized that Kevon thought Frankie had spent the night with Kevon's little enemy. But she wasn't going to bother to correct the picture because, thank the Lord, Frankie allowed Kevon to pull him out of the room. She turned to Jenna, who was chewing the end of her hair.

"Is my mother coming back now?" Jenna asked.

"She's having dinner with your dad. He wanted pizza. We'll be eating in a little while," Jada said. Then she raised her voice and called her daughter again. Shavonne came into the kitchen clutching the baby.

"Oh, hi," she said, overly casual. She looked at Jenna. "I can't really play with you now," she told her self-importantly, "I'm baby-sitting my little sister."

"Jenna's going to help you baby-sit," Jada said. She felt like strangling her daughter, and the girl wasn't even a teen yet. "If you both do a good job, I'm going to pay you both." She could actually feel Clinton's stare, though he was behind her. "Don't go up the stairs with the baby," she admonished more gently than she felt disposed to be. "Play with her in the living room," she told them. Reluctantly, it seemed, Jenna moved with Shavonne through the living room, Jada right behind them. *Be nice to her, Shavonne*, Jada thought. *Now's not the time to stand off.* The baby gurgled and then spit up on Shavonne's shoulder.

"Oh, yuck! Gross," Jenna said. She'd inherited her mother's clean gene.

"That's nothing," Shavonne told her. "When she had a cold, you should have seen her snots."

Normality—such as it was—had been achieved. Jada felt relieved and left them. Graphic descriptions of bodily functions would bind them. She closed the dining room door, then entered the kitchen, but avoided even looking at Clinton. Jenna had refused pizza, so Jada pulled out two bags of frozen french fries and a cookie sheet, sprayed the pan with vegetable oil, opened the oven door, and threw the tray in. She filled a pot with water to boil hotdogs. At least they were turkey dogs, not the other junk. Guiltily she looked for something green to serve with them. Nothing but very old strawberry yogurt (which ought not be green). She hadn't had time and Clinton hadn't had the ambition to clean out the refrigerator in the last two or three weeks. Well, she told herself, she'd just give them green Jell-O and pretend it was a balanced meal. They deserved better and so did she, but she was working under a lot of adversity here.

Even more adversity than she thought, however. Clinton rose from the kitchen chair he'd been sprawled in and came up beside her. It wasn't to help with the damn dinner, but to take the refrigerator door out of her hands and close it behind her. He leaned on it. "What do you think you're doing?" he asked.

"Making the dinner that you should have made?" she responded. He was worse than DAS. The man was *dead* and stupid.

"Don't try to get smart. You've already been dumb," he told her. "What are those kids doing over here?"

She narrowed her eyes. "*Those* kids?" she asked. "You mean Frankie and Jenna? *Those* kids are always over here, or our kids are always at their house."

"Not anymore," Clinton said.

"Oh, Clinton, don't start with me." She did not have the patience for this kind of bullshit. Not today. Not now. Not from this bastard, who was spending his days with his dick in some other woman and his nights taking his kids for granted.

"Those children shouldn't be over here."

"*Shouldn't?* Why *shouldn't* they?"

"Because I don't want them influencing my children."

"Oh, today they're *your* children?" she glared at him. "When did they become *your* children? They weren't yours the other night, when Shavonne had her book report to write or the day before, when Kevon had diarrhea. You think Jenna is a danger to Shavonne, who bullies that girl shamelessly? And do you think that Frankie could influence anything right now?" She crossed the kitchen, her steps fast and angry, not that they made much noise against the plywood of the unfinished floor. She started to set the table.

"Are you through running your mouth?" Clinton asked. "Because you're just missing the point. Number one, they're the children of a drug dealer. Number two, if you don't think the police are watching them and everything they do right now—"

"The police are watching everything that Frankie does? Well, that's an easy job. Even you could do it. 'Cause Frankie isn't doing dick."

"Don't show a smart mouth to me," Clinton said, narrowing his eyes. "I'm telling you that a black man in Westchester don't need a connection with a drug lord."

"Drug lord? Goddamn it, Clinton. I know you don't like Frank and I know you're envious of him. But maybe, just maybe, he's not guilty." She threw the napkins on the table. "Every time one of your damn useless White Plains home boys gets busted, you're telling me about police conspiracies and frame-ups all night long. Now they're just? Clinton, they didn't find any drugs next door. I don't think the man's involved with drugs. Maybe some bribes, maybe some crooked contracts, but not drugs."

Jada walked closer to him, but not within arm's reach. She had let her voice rise. She didn't want the children to hear this, and she didn't even want to be having this conversation with Clinton. But she wondered if she should be jeopardizing her marriage and her family for her friendship with a white woman. It occurred to her that Mich probably wouldn't do it for her.

"You know Michelle," Jada continued anyway. "You know these children. And you know how much Frank loves them, so just stop it, Clinton. Have some compassion. Would you want to have to bring your children home to this house after uniformed vandals tore it apart? Michelle is over there crying her heart out and cleaning up, and after dinner I'm going over to help her."

"You are *not* going over there," Clinton said, and came around the table and took her hand. He held it hard.

She snapped it out of his grip and held it up in front of her face. "Talk to the palm, Clinton. Because the ears aren't hearing." She turned away. "Didn't you ever hear of due process? Let's try to be Christians about this, Clinton. Don't be so holier than thou. *You* only go to church to meet your lover."

"Come on, Jada. Frank Russo is the kind of white man who—"

"This has nothing to do with race, Clinton," Jada snapped. "I don't know what Frank Russo did or didn't do. But I know *he's* not sleeping around, tearing his family apart. I know *he's* not using his church as a singles bar." All at once her rage rose within her and she felt it pushing words out of her mouth. "You've had plenty of time to make your damned decision and I'm tired of waiting for you to make it. I have waited and I hoped that you would make a decision—any decision. But you haven't. So I have to. If you go down to Tonya's again, don't come back, Clinton. I mean it. The deadline has long expired."

"Don't you threaten me," Clinton warned her. "You can't take my children away. You didn't even want the baby."

Jada snapped her head back as if she'd been slapped. "Don't go there," she said. "I'm not making you give up anything. You're choosing to leave it, to leave us."

Clinton moved very close to her, and for a moment his size and the anger she could feel in him frightened her. She didn't—*wouldn't*—let herself take a step backward, away from him, but she was scared, though she hoped it didn't show. "Don't you dare go over there tonight," Clinton said to her.

"Don't you dare give me orders," Jada spat right back at him. "Why don't you give the children their dinner instead? Something useful, instead of stupid threats." She leaned toward him, just to show him he didn't scare her. "I listen to God and my conscience before I listen to you. Michelle's my friend. She would do it for me." And with that Jada spun around, away from him and out the kitchen door into the relief of the cool darkness.

12

Wherein Angela stops playing hooky and instead gets hooked

Angela was dressed, for the first time in almost a week, in real clothes. She was wearing what she thought of as "a cheap legal suit"—one of those rayon-and-wool blend, navy blue jacket and skirt jobs that was a knock-off of what all the women at her ex-law firm used to wear. This one, though, was a *real* cheap one. And big. She'd gone up to double digits. You didn't want your size or your IQ to be there.

Yesterday she had forced herself up and out of the house, and had dragged herself over to Hit or Miss. Now she looked down at herself, sitting behind the wheel of her father's Dodge Dart, the one he referred to as "the spare." This outfit certainly couldn't be called a hit, so it must be a miss. She was a miss now, too. Or on her way to becoming one. An unmarried miss.

She needed the suit, because today she was showing up at the White Plains Women's Legal Crisis Center. Her mother, definitely for Angela's own good, had insisted that Angie show up today. She didn't feel like it, but she didn't feel like doing anything. She was even tired of lying on her back and staring up at the ceiling. She hadn't seen anything good on television, not even on A&E, in the last four or five days. There also wasn't anything good to eat left at her father's—she was down to no-fat

Snackwell cookies and she'd just as soon eat cardboard, or nothing. She
was still miserably unhappy but, she had to admit, she was also bored.

"You have to *do* something," her mother had insisted. "Just visit us."
So Angie agreed. It might as well be the Women's Center, though now,
squeezed into the cheesy size ten (she'd been an easy six when she'd
boarded the Boston shuttle), and driving this car in this disembodied
place she'd never lived in, she longed for the black sofa again.

Angie pulled up to the building off the Post Road, where the WLCC was
located. She pulled into the lot. Parking here, she noticed, was a lot different than at her suburban Boston firm, where every car that wasn't a Lexus
was a Volvo. Or a Jaguar or a Mercedes or a BMW, when you talked about
the partners. Here the cars looked like automobiles from another culture
altogether—people who had to make payments on used cars they couldn't
quite afford. The Dart fit right in. Angie got out of the car and walked past
the dented Chevys, the late-model Buicks, the rusted Ford Escorts.

When she got to the lobby, there was no sign, so she had to ask for
legal services offices, then walked the stairs to the second floor instead of
taking the elevator. What the hell. It would be the first exercise of her
new life. She was breathless by the time she got to the top, even though
it was only one flight. She, who used to do the Stairmaster for forty-five
minutes! Well, she reminded herself, she had just spent several days horizontal.

Now to face Natalie. Angie waited for her breathing to even out.
She'd need it to face Natalie. After her divorce, her mother had become
all fired up about a whole bunch of things. Angie guessed it was a good
thing. Her mom had gone to law school, gotten her degree, and since
then had only practiced law for women who were in need. Angie had
been inspired, and she was sure one of the reasons she'd gone on to law
school was because of her mother. On the other hand, it wasn't always
convenient to have a mother whose priorities were so political.

Hesitantly, suddenly feeling shy, Angie walked into the WLCC office.
A black receptionist looked up, but behind her Laura Hampton was
looking over some papers.

Laura saw her and smiled. "Oh. Hi, Angela. Good to see you." Laura
walked around the side of the reception counter and kissed her cheek.

Angie liked Laura, the woman who had handled her mom's divorce and then who had . . . well, handled her mother. The two women had lived together for almost five years, but had split last Christmas. Angie had never asked why.

Now Laura took Angie's left hand in both of hers and held it. "I heard from your mother about Reid," she said, her voice low. "I'm *so* sorry."

Angie nodded, then took a quick glance around the waiting room they were standing in. There were two heavy middle-aged women sitting at either end of a battered sofa like a pair of bookends, and a painfully thin Indian woman in a sari sitting at attention in one of the straight-backed chairs on the other side of the room, jingling her bracelets nervously along her arm. Angie's heart sank. It was as bad as she had pictured it, maybe worse. All three looked drowned in their own misery, but Angie figured at least she didn't have to share her own. She merely nodded at Laura, who took the hint.

"Where's my mother?" Angie asked, and felt panic rising.

"Your mother had to show up at court, but just for a little while. She'll be back in the next hour." Angie tried to smile, but only managed to nod.

She hung up her coat and followed Laura down a short hallway to a tiny room with only one window high up in the wall. The rest of the room was jammed with metal file cabinets, a battered desk, and two chairs. Papers and files were stacked on every surface. "Karen Levin-Thomas is the attorney who usually works here," Laura told her. "But she's in the hospital right now and she'll be out for a few months. Why don't you sit here?"

"Take a look at these while you're waiting for your mom," Laura had suggested, pleasant and cool and oblivious to Angie's total emotional collapse. Angie did, and once she'd begun to read through the first fat file she forgot about her surroundings.

Angie wiped the tears out of her eyes with the back of her hand. But, for the first time in days, they weren't tears of self-pity. They were tears of pity for others, as well as something else . . . something frightening that she couldn't exactly define. It seemed as if the hour or so she'd been in this messy room had stretched into days—or as if she'd been in the room long enough to experience other people's lifetimes. Angie had looked at file after file. Every one had shocked her; the stories were horrible. They weren't all betrayals by husbands, though there was a lot of that. There were other betrayals, but almost all of them were betrayals of women by men—men who held power because the women loved them, or men who held power because they were a woman's boss, or because the court had given them power.

The files raised a lot of questions that Angie couldn't answer. Except perhaps for one—why she was there. So many of the cases had shocked her with the disservice the legal system had done and the horrors that the women clients were going through: a woman with restraining orders but being stalked by her violent ex-husband nonetheless, another who had lost her house and was living with her children in a shelter while her husband had taken all of their assets and was living in Canada. Deadbeat dads. Several older women bilked by "investment advisors." Oh, the lists went on and on. Every one of these women couldn't have had a shoddy lawyer—although there were certainly enough of them to go around.

The women who came here needed help, and Angie realized she could help them. But she'd been avoiding the knowledge for a long, long time. In law school, after graduation, while she looked for a job, when she got engaged to Reid. She'd always known about her mother's grim work. She just hadn't wanted to cope with this kind of unfairness. She wanted to have her perfect selfish life, preferably with Reid.

So, now that she wasn't going to have Needham and Reid, why didn't she want this? She did feel the injustice, and feel it deeply. But there was something in the way. Difficult as it was, Angie sat with the feeling. And then she recognized that under her pity and compassion, it was a kind of nausea, and she knew it for fear. These grim files, these grim lives, could have been her own. She could wind up as alone and unloved as these women seemed to be. The fear that had been building in her stomach almost rose to her throat. For days and days she had been fighting off the impulse to call Reid again.

She'd tried to think of a million reasons why the Soprano would answer the phone: he could have hired a maid, he could be staying at his parents and a neighbor could be checking on the plants, he could have found a sister who had been missing for thirty years, he could have taken a eunuch as a roommate. More realistically, Angie admitted to herself she could be in denial. Because however far-fetched the reasons, she actually wanted to believe one of them. So far she had resisted the phone and refused the two other deliveries that Reid had sent—another bouquet and something from a bookstore. So far she'd held out.

But now, here, surrounded by lives encased in manila folders, lives that seemed as empty and loveless as hers did, Angie reached for the phone. She dialed her husband's office number. As the phone rang at the other end she knew she should hang up. She should call Lisa and get talked down, like from a bad acid trip. But the feeling, the compulsion, was so strong she couldn't control herself.

"Andover Putnam," the switchboard operator said.

"Reid Wakefield," Angie requested, and just saying his name aloud sent a shiver all the way down the back of her neck.

Just then the door to the overcrowded little office swung open and her mother walked in. Angie put the phone down quickly, as if she'd been caught with a vibrator instead of a receiver in her hand. She felt her face flush and hoped her mother didn't notice.

"Having fun?" Natalie asked.

"Fun? I'm so upset I can't see straight," Angie admitted. She didn't have to admit *all* the reasons she was upset. She took a breath or two and looked down at a couple of the folders. "I mean this Carolyn Stoyers custody case, and the things immigration did to that Vietnamese woman . . ."

"That's nothin'," Natalie said and threw a fat file down on the desk in front of Angie. "Take a look at this one. You want injustice, see what they tried to do to JoAnn Bloom. Too bad Karen got sick," Natalie said. "But she's a tough bird. She'll be back. At least until she's through chemotherapy." Angie sat and looked at the folder.

"What happens in the meantime?" Angie asked, finally looking at her mother's blank face. She knew that her mother was holding out the hook and hoping that it stuck, and she was afraid that maybe it might.

"You know," Angie said, before her mother could answer, "ever since you and Daddy divorced, I thought you were, well, a little adamant. I know he tried to give you a raw deal, but I just didn't believe that all women were being given raw deals. I thought that maybe you were . . . paranoid."

"You know what Willam Burroughs used to say, don't you?" Angie shook her head. "'Paranoia is having all the facts.'" Natalie's gaze swept the room. "Nice office space, huh?" she asked.

Angie looked up at her. "What are you asking?"

"Whether you want to give a few hours of your time to help out."

"A few hours?" Angie laughed. "It would take my whole life time to fix this."

"Oh, a lot more than that," Natalie said. "But you could take a small bite. Just something to chew on while you find your feet."

Angie knew her mother, knew her strategy, but nodded anyway. She wouldn't get sucked in forever. Still, she could do this now. She couldn't go back to Needham.

"Okay," she said. "But it's just temporary. It's just for right now."

13

In which Michelle cleans up the debris
with a little help from her friend

Michelle was on her hands and knees trying to pick the bigger pieces of broken glass out of the carpet. She'd stopped crying a long time ago—sometime after she'd quit looking for Pookie out in the dark, and before she'd tried to put some order into the wreckage of her children's rooms upstairs. She'd had to settle for eliminating, filling six big garbage bags with all of the torn pillows, smashed toys, broken knickknacks, shredded posters, and other mangled bits and pieces of her two children's material lives. Frank had helped her put their son's bunk beds upright but, battered himself and with at least one rib broken, he had at last gone to lay down. Neither she nor Frank wanted the children to see their father's face tonight, and maybe not tomorrow. It even frightened Michelle. She had put ice on it, but it was really too late for that. He would look frightening for the next week at least.

Michelle knelt there. She thought of the joke Jada always made. She was like Cinderella now, but there was no fairy godmother. She was about to get up from her knees when she saw yet more glass, these shards glinting from under the ottoman. As she reached to extract them she realized she'd used the exact same motion only twenty-four hours ago, though her house had been perfect then and she was only reaching for innocent Legos. Tears began to roll down her cheeks, and with both hands now full of broken glass, she couldn't wipe them away. What was the use, anyhow? she asked herself hopelessly. She'd probably be crying for years. She felt like a car crash victim. How right she'd been. Most accidents did happen in the home.

After the horror of last night, Frank had called a lawyer. The lawyer had gotten her and—after a considerable delay—Frank himself out of jail. The guy, named Rick Bruzeman, was a small very well-dressed man who seemed effective but far from sympathetic. Michelle wanted to tell him how outrageous, how awful the police had been, how she and Frank were innocent, and how this outrage, this unjust invasion should be on the front page of the newspaper. "Don't worry. It will," he said, "but not with that spin." He didn't seem to want to listen to her. Perhaps he'd heard it all before, and from people who weren't innocent. What he'd done had been effective and efficient—he'd picked her up, he'd gotten the children released into her care, and he'd gotten Frank's bail reduced and had him sprung—if that was the word you used for a legal exit from the Westchester Detention Center— but he seemed worse than cold. He seemed professional. He made Michelle feel more like a criminal than the police had.

Now Michelle stood up, the glass still in her hands, the tears still on her cheeks, and looked around again at the destruction. It was incredible, unbelievable. If the police had to search for drugs or whatever they suspected was hidden, did they also have to break, tear, and rip apart *everything* in their search? She started walking to the garbage bin she had placed in the center of the room and, as she did, her foot crunched against something spread in the carpet.

She looked down. What the hell was this? She crouched and looked more closely. At first she thought that it was potting soil from her corn plant, but then she recognized it was coffee. Coffee? Someone had opened—well, it looked like two or three of her sealed fresh cans of ground coffee, and had not only pawed through the stuff, but then thrown it onto the floor here. It had already sunk down into the weft of the carpet, but in some places it was thick enough to form little hills. Ironically she wondered if maybe Frankie would like to use the setting for his action figures—it would make a realistic battleground diorama.

She rose again, threw the glass into the garbage, and looked around. Framed pictures had been pulled off the walls, the canvases torn, the frames broken. The big mirror beside the credenza had been cracked. The contents of every drawer and cabinet had been pulled out and were lying now in mounds on the floor. There wasn't an upholstered piece of furniture that hadn't had its guts pulled apart, its cushions torn. Empty, the cushion covers now lay on the floor like giant crumpled condoms.

It was a nasty image, but there was something almost brutally sexual about all this, Michelle thought as she went for the Dustbuster. Her home had been rent apart. She felt almost as if she'd been invaded or raped. And look what it had done to Frank and her children. She'd pull it together as best she could, but the cracks and tears and dirt couldn't be erased.

She looked past the dining room table into the hallway. She knew she should go outside and bring in her chairs, the chairs that were sitting in her front yard like drunken relatives advertising her family's tragedy. She should also go out again and look for Pookie. But the fact was, she didn't have the courage to do it. She had felt the neighbors' eyes on her when she was outside. Anyway, she had to get this place decently cleaned up before the children could come in, but the task was so overwhelming that she didn't know exactly what to do next.

So, instead of pulling out a new box of trash bags, she turned around and walked back up the stairs, passed the children's emptied and scarred rooms, and into the master bedroom. Frank, one eye blackened, both cheeks bruised, was lying on the bed, perhaps lightly dozing. She should let him try to recuperate, but she couldn't. As she got onto the bed, he opened his eyes. That was all she needed—to see his dark, pained eyes staring into hers—to start her crying again. "Oh, Frank, it's so horrible. They've destroyed us, Frank."

"No, they haven't," he told her and put his right arm out and around her. He winced with the pain of moving, but his arm felt so good on her shoulder and back. He soothed her while she wept against his side. "Michelle, babe, they attacked us. But they didn't destroy us," he said in his deepest, most serious voice. "I don't know why, and I don't know who decided to pull this horrible bullshit on us, but I'll find out and I'll take care of it, babe. I swear I will. We got the best lawyer. They busted us and there was nothing here. Nothing." She nodded, her head now against his chest. "Thank God they didn't plant something here." Michelle shuddered at the thought. "We'll sue the town, we'll sue the county, we'll sue the state. Keep a list of everything torn or broken. They'll pay." He looked at her. "They didn't hurt you? They didn't touch you?"

"No. No," she answered him.

"They'll pay. A few people will pay in other ways, too. I swear it, Michelle."

"But why, Frank? How could they—"

"I don't know, babe. But I'll find out. Bruzeman is connected. He's expensive but he's worth it." Michelle didn't want to tell him how she felt about Bruzeman. "Maybe it was because of that shopping center deal," Frank mused. "I don't know. But they didn't destroy us. They didn't touch you, did they? Nobody at the police station touched you?"

She shook her head. "But look at what they did to you, Frank. And the children. They—"

Frank's hand tightened on her back. "Fuck those corrupt bastards."

"They've ruined the furniture, Frank. My chairs. The sofa. They wrecked the carpet and . . . Pookie's gone. He doesn't come when I call him. And the neighbors . . . "

"He'll come back, don't you worry. And tomorrow you go out and buy new furniture," Frank told her. "You hear me? Get what you want, what they can deliver immediately. Furniture doesn't make a family. And keep that list, Mich. Write down everything that's been spoiled. We'll get it all back. We all stick together, nothing can hurt us." He moved his hand to her cheek and cupped it gently. "You know I would never do anything like drug dealing, Michelle. You know that, don't you?"

Michelle looked at his bruised face and nodded. "We stick together and nobody can hurt us," Frank repeated. He leaned forward and kissed her. Then he put her head against his shoulder and gingerly leaned his cheek against her hair, as if its cool glow could comfort his throbbing cheek.

Michelle rested there, against his strength, until his breaths deepened and evened out. Then, much comforted, she went back downstairs to again deal with the wreckage.

"Oh my God!" Jada felt like bursting into tears, but looking at Mich's face she knew she had to keep it light. "Have you been decorating again?" She asked and shook her head. "Um, um, um. Martha Stewart doesn't live here, Cindy. How could they have done this to a white girl's house?" Jada looked around the room. "Sweet Jesus, help us."

Michelle was tugging out yet another bag of garbage. "If Jesus decides to help, tell him to bring more trash bags," she said.

Jada shook her head at the irreverence and put down one of the dining room chairs she had carried in. "I'll go get the others," she said.

"Have you seen Pookie around your house?" Michelle asked, though she didn't have much hope.

"He's gone? I saw him running up the street the night the police were here." Jada touched Michelle's arm. "God, I'm sorry. The kids must be . . ." She shook her head. "Man, this does look like an accident scene."

"Well, you know what I always say . . ." Michelle began to make a joke, but she couldn't finish. She was moved that her girlfriend had crossed that horrible line of tattered yellow police tape and was here beside her, that she understood her. Michelle wasn't stupid, even if she didn't have a college education. She knew that on their quiet, deserted-looking block, there were eyes from every house surveying hers. Everyone was constantly assessing and reassessing property values. Would the pocket park refurbishment upgrade the value of their lot? Would the rise in school tax lower the selling price of their house? What, she wondered, did a drug bust next door do? Probably it depressed house values almost as much as it depressed her.

Michelle didn't know if she'd ever be able to stand in her yard again, waving at Mr. Shriber when he slowly jogged by or saluting passing neighbors' cars. And for Jada, a woman who had worked so hard to find acceptance for her family here, to ignore all those invisible but watching eyes and step over the line, well . . . Michelle felt herself choke up. It was more than what she should expect, but she didn't want to collapse and show Jada just how bad she felt, how bad it was. She supposed she didn't have to. Jada's eyes, open wide, showed that she knew.

"I'm so sorry to drag you into this," Michelle began. "I know you have your own problems."

"There's sure enough to go around," Jada agreed, beginning to pick up debris.

Michelle felt suddenly guilty. She hadn't even asked Jada what was going on with Clinton. God. There *were* enough troubles to go around.

"Did you finally talk to Clinton?"

Jada nodded as she began to pick up torn paper. "I told him he had to make his mind up by the end of the week or I was going to get an attorney."

"Oh, Jada. I can't get over it. How could he?" Michelle tied a twist wire around her trash and shook her head. "He's gone crazy on you."

"Crazy? Forget Clinton! You should see *Tonya*. She thinks Clinton's a catch! Is she going to support him? The ridiculous way she likes to dress up, she can't support herself. She's a fool from Martinique, who gets herself confused with the Empress Josephine." Jada opened the last trash bag and began to throw stuff into it, including the box it had come in. Garbage made garbage. Kind of like Tonya having children.

"You mean she's the one I met at your church pageant?" Michelle asked in disbelief. "The one with the hat, and the awful hennaed hair? *No!*"

"Uh *huh*." Jada snorted again, bent over, and threw some sofa stuffing into her trash bag. "I want you to believe me when I tell you I'm not jealous. I don't want to sleep with him. But he's my husband and he is committed to the family or he's out the door. I just can't get over his bad taste. You'd think fifteen years with a man would improve that. I weaned him off Colt 45 and got him drinking Budweiser. I threw out that Peach Glow hair dressing and taught him Paul Mitchell gels. But the man's heading right back to funky Yonkers."

"Forget him. How did the kids seem to you?" Michelle asked.

"A little shaken up," Jada admitted. "But who wouldn't be? This wasn't a search, it was a vendetta." She surveyed the visible damage as she swiveled her head around.

"It was worse," Michelle said. "You should have seen it before I picked up the first eleven bags of garbage."

Jada shook her head. "These men were out to find something," she said. "And you mean to tell me they didn't? Hell, you tear my house apart like this, you're gonna find a marijuana seed left over from the sixties." She shook her head again and bit her lips. "Um-um," she said. "I didn't know police ever did a job like this on white people."

"Frank says they were out to get him."

"Looks like they did get him, from the picture," Jada said.

"What picture?" Michelle asked.

Jada shook her head and held up both her hands. "Don't ask, don't tell," she said. She got real close to Michelle and took her by the shoulders. "I know you're not a church-goer, Michelle, but this is a time when everybody needs to fall back on God, because it's gonna get worse before it gets better."

"I fell back on Frank," Michelle said. "And it can't get worse than this," she added, looking at the ransacked rooms.

Jada sighed. "Please God, I hope so. But people can be really, really cruel. And the courts can be worse than the cops. Believe me, I know plenty of people in White Plains who've been through it. Innocent people. And some guilty ones who still didn't deserve to be treated like dog shit." She let go of Michelle's shoulders but patted her gently on the back for a moment. "Okay, honey, that was my version of a pep talk. Now let's clean this place up the best we can before the kids have to get in here."

Michelle looked at her friend. "Should I keep them home from school tomorrow?" she asked. "Let them recover for a day, or would it be worse to do that?"

Jada thought of Anne at the bank and her morbid curiosity, even pleasure, at Michelle's bad luck. "Kids can be cruel," Jada said. "Real mean. But you figure, if they have to face it, they might as well face it on Monday."

14

In which Jada clears up and goes home to find Clinton's cleared out

When Jada got back to her own house it was well past three A.M. She was dead meat. She and Michelle had filled more than twenty bags of trash, vacuumed the entire downstairs, put away the still-operational appliances, pots, and pans, thrown out all the broken china and other smashed bits from the kitchen, then swept and washed its floor. The house hadn't looked really good, but it had lost some of its nightmare quality.

Jada, home at last, took her shoes off and put them on the mat by the door. The little area there was supposed to be a mud room, but Clinton had not finished the job. The floor was plywood and the slate for it lay where the bench and cabinet to hold boots and shoes should be. Jada, way too exhausted to be annoyed, took her coat off and put it across the back of a kitchen chair. Although she yelled at Clinton and the kids for doing the same thing, she was too tired to hang it up now. All she wanted was some sleep.

Cleaning up the wreckage next door had not only been physically exhausting but also emotionally draining. And it had frightened Jada. Somehow, despite her own massive problems, it had seemed that most other people's lives were more secure. Ha! She knew that everything was in God's hands, but to see Michelle's home destroyed, her husband beaten, and her children paralyzed with fear frightened Jada, too.

She thought of Anne and the other girls at the bank. Two of them were single mothers and she knew that, like her, they lived from paycheck to paycheck. She looked around her unfinished mud room and plywood kitchen floor. At one time she'd been proud of Clinton. She'd seen him as a builder, as a man who took action and made people and things come together. But now he was tearing them down and apart. Well, she had to try and be grateful. She said a short thanksgiving prayer. Things could always be so much worse.

She walked up the stairs as quietly as she could and passed the door of the baby's room. That was one job Clinton had finished. He'd painted the room and built a changing table for Sherrilee. He'd even put her name on the door. Now Jada pushed it open and poked her head into the room for just a minute, only to check. But Sherrilee wasn't there. She hoped that Clinton hadn't let Jenna and Shavonne sleep with her. Walking more quickly to Shavonne's door, she looked in. Jenna lay curled on one side of Shavonne's double bed, but neither Shavonne nor Sherrilee was there.

That was strange, Jada thought, but perhaps they'd both crawled into bed with their daddy, though Shavonne didn't do that much anymore. Of course, Shavonne could have had one of her frequent fights with Jenna and wanted to get away. Jada walked down the hall. Somehow this didn't feel right. Not at all. But, she told herself, she was probably just spooked by the problems next door. Still, she couldn't stop herself using unusual force.

She got to the door of their bedroom and threw it open. *Nothing's wrong,* she told herself, but something was. No baby, no Shavonne, no Clinton. Only a note, lying in the middle of the unmade bed. Frightened, Jada strode over to it and snatched it up.

Jada,

I have made my decision. I have taken the children and I am leaving you. Your work schedule, your attitudes, and now your friendship with undesirables has led me to believe

that you are not only a bad wife but also a bad mother. You
will hear from my attorney, George Creskin and Associates.
My children told me they didn't want to stay with those drug
kids.

Clinton

Jada's eyes ran over the page a second time. Then a third. Clinton didn't
write like this. What *was* this? Was he insane? Her heart began to beat so
fast that it felt like a thumping on the outside of her chest. She didn't care.
She didn't matter. She ran to Kevon's room and pulled the door ajar, but
only Frankie was sleeping on the bottom bunk. She turned and ran back
out into the hallway. She threw open the door of the linen closet where
they kept their suitcases and backpacks. All the bags were gone. Like some
kind of mad thing, she ran back into Shavonne's room and slid open the
closet door. Many empty hangers greeted her. She turned and pulled open
the drawers of Shavonne's bureau: underwear, socks, and T-shirts were
gone. Gone. And her children gone, too.

Now, crazy with fear, she ran back down the hall to her own room.
All of Clinton's shoes were missing, along with his two good suits and
his leather jacket. He was a madman! A madman! He had taken her children. Did he think that she would stand for this? Did he think that she
had scrambled and worked the way she had so that he could take their
family and walk out of the house? And what the hell would he do with
them, with her children, now that he had them? He didn't even take care
of them *here*. Clinton had nowhere to go. How would he pay for a hotel,
a baby-sitter? He had no job, no money, no help. He wasn't even on
good terms with his mother—hadn't been since they married.

She began to run down the bedroom hall, but at the top of the stairs it
all hit her. She stopped and stood statue-still. A fear deeper than any she
had ever known hit Jada in the chest so hard that she had to sit down on
the top step, one long leg tucked under her. Who should she call? What
should she do? She put a hand up to her mouth so that she wouldn't
scream out loud. There were two children still sleeping in the house,
though they weren't hers.

She couldn't call the police—this wasn't a police matter, was it? She couldn't call a lawyer at this time of night. Anyway, she didn't know a lawyer. Her mother and father were in Barbados, and neither was young anymore. She couldn't, *wouldn't*, shock them with this.

Jada's right hand clutched the railing of the banister as she sat at the top of the stairs, frozen. Clinton couldn't do this to her. Surely he didn't hate her *this* much. And the children: would they willingly leave her? Had he forced the kids to go? Had he lied to them? Jada shook her head back and forth as if trying to shake the reality out. But it wouldn't go.

Her marriage was over. That was clear. Her family was broken, but Jada knew she would find her babies, bring them home, and save them. This house and those children were what she had sacrificed her life to and no one was going to take them away. She was still strong enough to make sure of that.

But now, in the darkness at the top of the staircase, Jada lowered her head to her knees and quietly began to sob.

15

Containing a visit to Marblehead by a marble-head

"You want, I'll come with you," Tony offered again as he dropped Angela at the shuttle. "You don't have to do this. And you sure don't have to do it alone. I can postpone my business trip, and I'd love to come."

"I need to go alone, Daddy," Angela told him, and patted his arm. "Mom offered to come with me, and I could have made a big deal out of it, but I'd rather just get in and get out. For my stuff. Reid can keep the stereo and the blender. I'm just getting some of my clothes, my pictures . . . you know."

"He going to be there?" Tony growled. "Because that son-of-a—"

"He doesn't even know I'm coming," Angela assured her father. "I'm not going up there to see him. Don't worry. He's a sick puppy and he's out of my life. I just want my own clothes." She looked down at her cheap lawyer's suit.

"Okay. So you got the movers all set up like I told you?"

"Yeah," she said, and gathered up her purse and her scarf. "Just two guys with some boxes and a van. They go back and forth between Boston and New York all the time and they'll bring the stuff down to your house next week."

Anthony Romazzano nodded and bent awkwardly across the bucket seat to hug her. "Okay, baby," he said. As Angie started to get out of the car, he added, "You sure you don't want a limo to take you?" She shook her head. "Do you need any cash?"

Angela nodded. She hated accepting his offer, but she was really pretty strapped. Tony handed her a few hundred dollar bills and a credit card with her name on it.

"Just in case," he said. Her eyes teared up. She bent her head to look into the front seat of the car. "Thanks a lot," she said.

"No problem," he answered. "And you'll be home tonight?"

"Absolutely," she told him. "I might see Lisa for a drink before I leave, but I'll call your machine if I do."

Angela was early, so when the plane started to board she got one of the bulkhead seats near the window. At eleven A.M., the shuttle wasn't packed, though the flights at seven, eight, and nine must have been jammed. When the doors closed the seat beside her was still empty. She crossed her legs.

She wasn't one hundred percent sure why she was going to do this thing—a sort of cat burglary cum/slash-and-burn operation. She hadn't told Lisa, nor Reid. She didn't have to tell him. She was determined not to touch his stuff. Anything that was his or theirs was repugnant to her, but she wanted to remove any trace of her that had existed there, to be sure he knew she was gone forever.

Angie had always felt that a space took on the attributes of the person or people who lived there—even if they didn't want it to. Her father's new house seemed as desolate and lost as he did. It was the house of a family man who'd lost his family. Her mother's place seemed worse in a way. But Angela remembered the apartment they had all lived in back when they'd been a family. It had been crowded with warmth—well-used pots in the kitchen, throw pillows on all the stuffed furniture, family pictures and drawings and report cards and mementos everywhere. It had been a comfortable place. She'd begun to make a place like that for Reid. But now she'd never finish the job.

This was going to be harder than she'd realized. The more Angie thought about it, the more she was convinced she needed help. The only person she knew of who could help her was Lisa. Angie lifted up the handset in the seat and slid through her credit card, then punched in the number. She hoped Lisa wasn't out of the office. Lisa's voice mail picked up. Shit. Well, she'd just leave a message and hope that Lisa wasn't spending the day at a deposition or something.

Angie guessed it was better than having a secretary answer the phone, though if one had, she could go looking for Lisa. But the secretaries were all gossips. God knows what they were saying about her disappearance. They had always eyed Reid when he picked her up at work, and she'd bet that they were talking about this now, if they knew. Did they take Lisa's voice mail messages or did Lisa do it herself? Angie decided to be very discreet.

"Lisa," Angie said to the machine. "I don't know when you'll get this, but I have a favor to ask of you for today. I'll call you in about an hour." She hung up, pressed END to finish the call, then wondered if Lisa would recognize her voice because she hadn't mentioned her name. She slid the phone back into its casing and slumped against the wall of the plane, staring out the window at the clouds.

All at once her energy had deserted her. This was going to be harder than she'd expected. Going back there, seeing their home, their hopes, their bed. Well, she'd have two strong Irish lads to help her, she'd do it as quickly as she could, and maybe, *maybe* Lisa would be able to show up. But it occurred to her that if she could just see Reid one more time, she might have closure. If she could speak to him and tell him how he'd ruined a part of her forever, she might feel better. She might get the weight of this shock off her back, even if it wasn't dignified.

Somehow the idea of seeing Reid gave her a nervous energy despite her exhaustion. She pulled the phone out of the handset again, fumbled for her credit card, and called him. God, she hoped it wouldn't list this number when her dad got the bill. He'd wig out. Definitely.

Reid's secretary, an older woman named Shirley, answered. When Angie asked for him, Shirley asked who was calling, please. Angie noticed, for the first time, how high-pitched her voice was. For a moment she wondered if Shirley was the Soprano. But she'd seen Shirley. Shirley was really old. Angie had to mouth the words 'his wife' as coldly as she could just to get through it.

"Oh," Shirley said, obviously startled, but she was wise enough not to say anything else.

Angie heard the tiny click as she was put on hold, but she was only on hold for a moment. Then Reid's voice was in her ear.

"Angie? Is it really you?"

"Yes," she said.

"Oh God, Angela. I thought I'd never get to speak to you again. I thought that—where are you calling from?"

"I'm on a plane," Angela said and, oddly, that made her feel a lot more confident. It sounded so glamorous, calling him from a plane in her busy life. For a moment she wished she could say she was on a plane on her way to Rio, or some place even more exotic.

"Angie," he said. "Thank you for calling me." He paused and she could actually hear him swallow. "I know what I did was inexcusable . . ."

What he did? How about what he was still doing? When Angie heard the past tense, she wondered about her calls to the Soprano. Was it possible that it *was* past tense? *Angie, get a grip,* she told herself. God, what was she thinking about? What did it matter? She looked across the aisle of the plane to see if anyone could overhear her. It was crazy to have this conversation in such a public place.

"Yes, it was," she said. "It was inexcusable because it hurt me in a way nothing ever will again. I let myself be open to that and you never, ever should have taken advantage of my trust."

"Angie," he said again.

He said it in a way that nobody else did. His voice had the sound of his desire in it. He was the only one, the only man who had ever made her feel beautiful and loved. The idea that she would never feel that way again was unbearable, and Angela closed her eyes against it.

"Angie, listen. This may be the most important talk we'll ever have. I see now how stupid I was, telling you what I did. How I did. But Angie, Ange . . ." He paused. "I did it to clean the slate. I did it to tell the truth and make things right between us for the rest of our lives. I promise, Angie."

She was silent; her eyes were closed but a hot tear escaped from the corner of one of them.

"Are you still there?" he asked.

"Yes," she managed to say.

"Thank God. Listen, I love you. I'll always love you. And nothing like this will ever happen again. I give you my word." He paused. "Don't punish me for telling the truth."

She told herself she should ask him about the Soprano. That she should curse him and hang up. That she should . . .

"Ange, don't move out. Move back in. Please," he said.

"The flight is landing now," she told him. "I have to hang up."

"Landing where?" he asked and she heard the desperation in his voice. She had hurt him by walking out, by not speaking to him until now, and she was glad. "Where are you?"

"I'll be in Boston," she admitted. "But just for a few hours. I am going to stop by and pick up a few of my things."

"Boston! Angie, I—"

"I hope you have no objection," she said with as much dignity as she could muster. Then she hung up.

In the taxi on the way to Marblehead, Angela put on her makeup. Her face looked good. Her round blue eyes, with just a little mascara, perked right up. The sleeping she'd done had actually improved her face and her excitement had given her color—she didn't need any blusher. She took out a dark lipstick, then decided on a pinker color.

Her hair was a total loss. She should have made an appointment with Shear Madness before she'd left New York. She fluffed her hair as best she could, hoping it would do.

She had called the movers from Logan, confirmed they were on their way, and had left another message on Lisa's voice mail telling her that she was going to the apartment. In a way, she hoped that Lisa didn't show, because she was hoping that Reid would.

Angie nervously palmed the key to their condo. It had become hot in her damp hand. She looked out at the grim November landscape. What was she doing? This was insanity.

Was there still a chance, the smallest chance that Reid might somehow make it all right? She knew it was possible to live without him, hurt and empty, but going on. Was it still possible that there might yet be a way for her to live *with* him?

She wasn't thinking anymore. She had her plan. Just get her stuff. If Reid appeared, she'd simply see what happened next.

"Wait a minute," Angie said as she pushed at the door. "I think I accidentally double-locked it." The key was slick with her sweat. She turned to Sean and Thomas, the two handsome, young Irish immigrants who were helping with the move.

"Want some help?" Sean asked, his eyes open wide with the question, his lilt delightful.

Angie's fingers slipped again on the key. It had occurred to her that Reid might have changed the locks, but she didn't like to think about that. And he hadn't said anything over the phone. She tried the door again.

Her heart pounded. She was an attorney, she reminded herself. What she was doing was not illegal. Until the divorce action was filed and a settlement was drawn up, this place and its contents were as much hers as Reid's. She told herself that, but her hands and now her armpits were sweating. Her stomach flip-flopped. Suddenly she felt so sick that she thought she might vomit. She tried to take some deep breaths but the nausea didn't go away.

Why wasn't the door opening? At last she remembered that the door was a little warped and had to be pulled in as the lock was disengaged. She did it, and the welcome sound of the spring opening allowed her to push the door in. "Here we are," she said and hoped that the panic she'd felt wasn't showing on her face.

She stepped into her own living room as a stranger, but very little had changed. Well, she'd only been gone a week. She looked at the denim sofa they'd bought at Pottery Barn, the long table near the window that she'd ordered through a Crate & Barrel catalog sale. She'd leave all of that, even if she'd paid for part of it. *Don't think about Reid,* she told herself. All she was interested in were her really personal possessions.

"Open some of the book boxes," she told the movers. She went over to the shelves, pointing. "All of these and all of these," she told them. "I'll come back and look at that shelf later. And if one of you could make a couple of wardrobe boxes up, I'll need them in the bedroom."

Sean nodded and passed a glance to Thomas. Were they realizing now what kind of an operation this was? Did they have a lot of divorced-women break-up scenes as a part of their ongoing business? Without wondering anymore, Angie left them and went into her bedroom.

It surprised her that the bed was unmade. Of course, she had always been the one to make it, but she thought that Reid needed things neat. The whole room, in fact, looked disheveled. Not dirty, but messy, with clothes on the floor, newspapers and piles of magazines strewn randomly.

Then something about the room hit Angie almost like a force field. For a moment she felt as if she were trying to move underwater, or as if the air had solidified and was heavy on her shoulders, her arms, her chest. Her stomach tightened and she felt her nausea return. This room, where she had been so happy, felt very, very threatening. It made her somehow feel deeply sorrowful—sorry in a way that sapped her anger. She knew that both of them had been happy here. How wasteful that that happiness had been destroyed.

Angie did a quick visual inventory; she would only take the things around the room that were hers. She began to collect them, cradling them in her arms like groceries off the shelf in a convenience store. Her perfume, the two stone turtles Reid had bought her in Mexico, the Rosenthal bud vase she kept by the side of the bed. She didn't like to actually touch the bedclothes, but as she snatched up the throw pillow she'd had since college—the one with the beaded flowers—she nearly dropped everything else.

She called for Sean to bring in a box. He did, and she filled it with the knickknacks. Then she went into the bathroom and filled another box with her deodorant, makeup, hair dryer, brushes, and her other non-sense. She didn't want any of the stuff, but she certainly wasn't going to leave her tampons or spray gel for the Soprano—or any other strange woman Reid might march through here.

She stopped for a moment and looked at herself in the mirror. Her mascara had smudged on one side of her lashes, and she stopped to fix it and brush her hair. While she was at it, she might as well put on fresh lipstick. She studied herself in the mirror. "You're hoping he'll come," she said, and the face there nodded at her. "You're disgusting," she said aloud, just as Sean came back into the bedroom. He heard her.

"Excuse me?" he said.

Embarrassed, she told him it was nothing. He smiled, and gave her an appreciative once-over. She must look better than she thought. "I need that wardrobe box over here," she added, and slid open the closet. She began stuffing dresses, suits, and jackets into the wardrobe box, pushing them against each other to pack them tightly. But it seemed that there were more clothes than she remembered. She noticed a blue silk dress because it stood out from the usual brown and beige and red that she wore. She took it out and held it away from her, her other arm weighted down with a load of clothes on hangers. Angie looked it over and dropped her own clothes on the floor.

"Here, let me help," Sean said, thinking her action had been accidental and picking up the dumped outfits.

Angie, as if from a long distance away, murmured her thanks. Then, with the blue dress over her arm, she walked back into the bathroom. She closed the door behind her, locked it, and hung the dress on the hook beside the tub. She sat down on the closed toilet seat and stared at the dress. It wasn't hers. It had never been hers. And even if Reid was a transvestite, the dress wasn't his, either. It must have been a size four. Angie stared at the evil little dress.

It must be the Soprano's. Had Reid already invited her to live with him? Angie and Reid had been separated for less than a month. Could it be that?

Angie left the dress there and walked back into the bedroom. Sure enough, there in the closet was a jacket, a couple of pairs of unfamiliar jeans, two blouses—one white, one blue—and a gray business suit. Below them there were four pairs of shoes, neatly lined up: two pairs of pumps, one black, one navy; a pair of Reeboks, and another pair of flats. Angie crouched down. They were size seven-and-a-half. She picked up one of the black pumps and caressed the suede. Suddenly, squatting there on the floor, Angie felt as if her heart might break.

"I'll take this one out to the hall," Sean said, holding the full wardrobe box. "Shall I bring in the other?"

Angie turned her face to him and nodded.

"You know, I'd wondered if . . . well, before we start up the truck, you'd like to have a beer with me?" Sean asked. "That is, if you drink with the help."

Angie smiled. He was cute, with Irish dimples. But she had other things to think about right now, though she appreciated the compliment.

"I'm married," she said. Sean raised his eyebrows, but said nothing. He left her alone and she got up, still holding the pump, and sat on the little chair in the corner, the one she had taken from her old room. She gripped it with both hands, as if she might be thrown out of it. The shoe lay like a dead thing on her lap. She was taking this chair, she thought. It and everything and getting out.

She couldn't understand what Reid was. She could, perhaps, understand how he might have cheated on her, and even changed his mind and wanted her back. Maybe giving her the ring had been a sincere gesture. But what she couldn't understand was how he could have told her he wanted her, that he wanted to renew their vows, and go on immediately to start living with another woman in just a few weeks' time. Had he *ever* loved her? Would any partner do? Had she merely been a Reid Wakefield accessory, like his golf clubs, his squash rackets, his navy blazers?

The realization that she had called him, opening a door, horrified her. How embarrassing, how weak. Her face flushed deeply. He might yet show up. It was the last thing she wanted. God, she had better get out of here fast.

Angie stood up and called out to Sean. "I'm taking this," she said, meaning the chair, when Reid walked into the bedroom.

"I can't believe it," he said. "Thank God you're home."

"I'm not home," Angie said. "I'm packing to go back there."

She couldn't help but be stunned by how tall, how really beautiful he was. The too-long bones and the too-broad shoulders should have made him hulking, but there was some innate grace, some trick of movement he'd been given, that made him seem graceful. She pulled her thoughts away from his looks, or her attraction to them, although it was difficult to do. Her stomach tightened yet again. She thought she might actually be sick.

Reid took only one step into the room. "Please, Angie," he said. "Tell me you want to stay here."

"Like hell I will," Angie said and pointed into the closet. "Why would I? So she and I could both share the bathroom with you? Just tell me if she's the one you've been sleeping with all year, or if she's some new one."

Angie hated how she sounded—shrewish and, underneath it, so obviously hurt. But what else could she do except try to be a true Wakefield and keep her mouth shut? Forget about that. Reid moved toward her and she took a step backward, stumbling against the chair. Just then Sean stuck his head in.

"We finished with the books," he said. "What's next?"

"The coffee table and the two blue lamps," she told him, her eyes never leaving her husband's face. Sean quickly looked from her to Reid and didn't say a word. Once he had disappeared, Reid took another step toward her.

"Angie, please. Pay absolutely no attention to that. I know it was wrong, and stupid. It's just that I was so lonely without you." He sat down at the edge of their bed.

The thing about Reid, she realized, was there was a certain attractive childishness about him. Perhaps if he wasn't so good-looking, he wouldn't seem as sweet and vulnerable. But to see a sexy, handsome, tall man admit to his weaknesses, to fess up to his fears as Reid had always done, was, in a way, deeply moving to Angie. Like a child, Reid was controlled by his feelings. Maybe that had made her feel powerful. Or maybe it had given her the false feeling that she alone had pierced the shell of his perfection.

"You don't know what it's been like. Just when I realized how empty, how shallow I was, and that your love was the only thing that mattered, you left me." He had his head in his hands, but then cocked it toward the closet. "I've only been trying to hold it together," he said. "I can't concentrate. I can't eat. I'm drinking half a bottle of Scotch each night. I feel like shit. I mean, I know I am a shit, but I also feel like shit all the time." He looked at her and his lashes were wet. "Nothing works for me, except you. And you took yourself away."

Yes. His naiveté was attractive. The thing was, Reid probably meant what he said. But he had probably meant what he had said to whomever the Soprano was. Somehow his simplicity was duplicity. He was so vulnerable.

"So you asked your girlfriend to move in—even though you don't want her," Angie said, and took the suede pump in her hand and chucked it at him as hard as she could. It hit his chest, but he'd got his hands up fast enough to ward off most of the impact. That was Reid—never really without some protection. Angie couldn't help shaking her head. What a stupid, ineffectual woman weapon—throwing a size seven-and-a-half black suede pump at your soon-to-be-ex's heart. Why not a .38-caliber bullet, one of the kind that was scored on top so it would explode once it hit its target?

Reid rose from the bed, dropped the shoe, and moved across the room to her. All at once, it felt to Angie as if everything went in slow motion—as Reid walked closer, he seemed to get farther away. She didn't know if she wanted him beside her or out of the room, out of the building, out of her life. She couldn't move. She felt as if minutes, maybe hours, were going by as he took one step, then another, toward her. At last he was in front of her, so close that she could smell the laundry scent coming from his shirt. He stood silently before her, but even if they didn't speak in words, she felt every cell in her body drawn to him. Was this, she wondered irrelevantly, what they called animal magnetism?

Finally he spoke. "I love you, Ange. I swear I do. If you forgive me, you'll never regret it."

Angie leaned her head against his shoulder, and his arm gently, so gently, tightened around her. "I gave away the ring you gave me," Angie said.

"I'll get you another one," Reid assured her.

"I told my parents what you did," Angie told him.

"I'll spend the rest of my life living with the shame." Gently, tenderly, he stroked her hair. She couldn't help but shiver. Her face was fine, her hair was fine, all of her was fine. Her mind went blank and that was a relief. Any guilt, any doubt she had, she ignored.

It felt so good to be sheltered in his arms. Angie wanted to rub first one cheek and then the other against his chest, the way cats did to mark their territory.

The Soprano meant nothing to him. Maybe this whole bizarre time could be written off, forgotten. Maybe it was just a lapse and Reid had learned a lesson. But at the moment Angie couldn't think. This wasn't about thinking.

There was some noise out in the living room, the sound of something toppling over, but thudding, not crashing. One of the men yelled something, and then a woman's voice answered him. Angie froze. It couldn't be. It was. The voice. The Soprano.

The door swung open and Lisa stood there. Angie, feeling caught out and guilty, took a step back from her husband. Reid took a step back from her as well. "What the hell is going on?" Lisa asked, clearly furious as she looked from Angie to Reid.

Angie felt ashamed. After all, she'd burned up hours of Lisa's time talking about how she hated this man. She stared at Lisa, who looked very, very good; her hair was blonder, and she seemed taller and thinner than ever. "You got my message," Angie began, but at the same time Reid said, "How did you—"

"What the hell are you doing here?" Lisa said to Reid.

"It's my house," he answered, defensive as a child.

"Lisa, it's okay," Angie said. "We've started to talk things over."

"The hell you are," Lisa said, still looking at Reid. "I ought to report you to the department of narcissism. They'd come right in here and shut you two down."

"What are you talking about?" Angie asked.

"Oh, shut up," Lisa said, violently. "Do you know how sick I am of listening to you whine?" She looked at Reid. "What do you think you're doing to me?" she asked.

It took that long for Angie to get it. But then she did—big time. She looked from Reid, who averted his eyes, to Lisa, who stared insolently at her. The blue dress, the shoes, the advice to stay away—now it all made sense. Size four. The Soprano. Why, in all those hours of talking, of complaining and bitching, had she never noticed Lisa's voice? Angie shook her head, pushed past Lisa, and walked out into the living room. "That's it," she told Sean and Thomas. "Wrap it up. I'm out of here."

16

In which Michelle, Brownie Queen, has to let them eat cake

Michelle hadn't been able to sleep since the bust. She was exhausted, but every time she started to drift off, she'd start awake, a cold sweat covering her. She couldn't stop her mind from racing. She didn't want to wake up Frank, so she shuffled down to the kitchen and decided to straighten up the cubicles that held mail, magazines, and Frankie's school papers. There she found a neon green paper with the reminder of the bake sale that was being held today during all lunch periods. Bake sales were always the best fund-raiser, she decided she'd bake. Making brownies at three-thirty in the morning wasn't exactly a normal thing to do, but she needed to do something.

Michelle had to admit to herself as she measured out the dry ingredients—flour, sugar, walnuts—and the eight eggs for the four pans she would make, that baking had a soothing affect on her. As the aroma of chocolate filled the kitchen, she was grateful for the roteness and optimism of the task.

Now Michelle walked up to the front door of the Eleanor S. Windham Middle School with one hand tightly clutching Frankie's and the other hand holding a huge box of her homemade brownies. Frankie was beside her, but Jenna had run ahead to make it less clear that she'd been driven here by her mom; she was already old enough to be humiliated by being seen at any time with her mother at school, and this was a much more abnormal situation.

Michelle was doing her best to recover and help her kids recover from the horror of the arrest, but she wasn't even sure that driving Jenna over was the thing to do; she and Frank were part of the problem for Jenna, so perhaps she shouldn't expect that she could be part of the solution. Normally she thought kids should learn to stand up for themselves. But this wasn't a normal situation. She couldn't let her daughter be picked on by the bus bullies because of her parents' legal problem. It was too much.

Michelle knew how cruel kids could be from her own experience— once or twice her mother had shown up to pick her up at school and Michelle, horrified by the sight of her, drunk and slovenly, had prayed that she would live it down. Afterward there had been taunts and Michelle had simply braved it out, pretending that she didn't hear them. But she was altogether tougher than Jenna—she'd had to be. Michelle didn't ever want her daughter to have to be as tough as she had been. It wasn't good for a child. Now, as she watched Jenna duck into the crowd and join the bunch of little backs that were presented to Michelle as she entered the slate-floored school foyer, Michelle made herself loosen the hold she had on Frankie. She didn't want him to feel just how frightened and desolate she was. She wasn't sure how she could face Mrs. Spencer, the principal, or even Mrs. Spencer's nosy, daunting secretary.

The bust had been bad enough, but Michelle hadn't known the worst— that her private agony had been spread all over the pages of the newspaper. For two days, as bad as it was, Michelle had been an ostrich, silly enough to think that her humiliation had been a private one—or as private as a police raid with twenty cop cars in the middle of the night could be. She didn't realize the whole humiliation had been spread out on breakfast tables all over Westchester County until Rick Bruzeman had mentioned over the phone that the press coverage wouldn't help the grand jury.

"What press coverage?" she'd asked, and he'd thought she was joking. Michelle had driven to his office to see what he was talking about; she had been so shocked that she hadn't cried or behaved badly there, despite the growing distaste she felt for the man. She'd waited until she got home to her wreck of a house, and then had locked herself in the bathroom for two whole hours. She'd set the alarm clock for two-thirty so she would have enough time to soak her face in ice and wouldn't scare the children when they came home from school.

But they'd come home with new horrors. Jenna was crying because two older girls on the bus had pulled off her backpack in front of the whole gleeful group of kids and pretended to go through it looking for drugs. Jenna had run to her room and locked the door. Frankie had come home silent but holding up a note. He went to the window, looking for the lost Pookie while Michelle read it.

It was from Frankie's teacher, reporting that he had wet his pants in class and that she shouldn't be expected to clean up after him. She'd punished him. Michelle had taken off Frankie's urine-soaked Osh-Koshes, bathed him, and sat him in front of the television before she went up to comfort Jenna. Then she let Frank take over that job when he came home. It had all been, it still was, hellish. But she and Frank had decided that facing it down was the way to go.

Now, at the school door, Michelle lifted Frankie up. He was so small, so light. As she walked down the school hallway, surrounded by noisy children, she focused on how all she'd ever wanted was to love her husband and her kids. Why was it the nature of the world to take the one thing you wanted and twist it into so much pain?

Walking into the principal's office this morning was as difficult to do as it had been for her back in the days when she was only eleven. But Michelle wouldn't let them hurt her son or her daughter without fighting back. She didn't expect that the school would be responsible for fixing things, but they shouldn't be allowed to make everything worse.

Michelle walked in, nodded to the random teachers at their mailboxes, and moved directly up to Hillary Gross, the secretary. "I'm here to see Mrs. Spencer," she announced and was proud her voice didn't quaver. "May I leave these here while I go in to meet with her?" she asked, lifting a heavy box onto the counter.

"What is it?" Hillary Gross asked, her voice suspicious.

Michelle was ready to snap something at her—like "Heroin tarts"— but maintained her dignity and instead smiled at Frankie. "Just something for the bake sale," she said in what she thought of as her Professional Mom's Voice. She moved smoothly and directly toward Mrs. Spencer's office door. Someone was just leaving, and before anything else could happen, Michelle put her head in, held Frankie a little higher, and entered Mrs. Spencer's den, shutting the door behind her on all those curious, hostile eyes.

Mrs. Spencer was at her desk, her back to the light. She was one of the older women bureaucrats, a little more modern than the battle-axes that Michelle had been taught by, but certainly not what you could call dedicated or progressive in her thinking. She had over-permed gray hair and her burgundy lipstick was darker, but not by much, than the age spots around her eyes, nose, and mouth. "Don't rock the boat" could have been the motto they ran under her photo in the middle school yearbook. Michelle tried once again to paste on a pleasant smile and sat down in the chair opposite Mrs. Spencer, still holding Frankie against her shoulder.

"Thank you for seeing me," she said, her voice cheerful and soft. "I have to be at the bake sale in just ten minutes so I don't have much time, and I know how busy you are." Mrs. Spencer nodded. She wasn't looking for gossip or trouble. "You know Frankie, don't you?" Michelle asked.

"Yes. Of course," Mrs. Spencer said but Michelle doubted that the woman did. She was strictly a desk model, leaving her office as rarely as possible.

"I'm going to ask Frankie to sit in the chair outside," Michelle said, her voice still pleasant. She turned to her son. "I brought you a book and I won't be long," she promised.

She stood up again, went to the door, settled him on the bench there and gave him not only his *Pat the Bunny* book but a box of juice and a tiny box of raisins. Frankie just stared down at his feet. Michelle's heart broke as she looked at him, but she left him there and went back to sit opposite Mrs. Spencer, again closing the door.

"I'm not sure if you're aware of it," she said, her voice now brisk, "but my family has been upset by a false accusation. Anyway, it's important for you to know that though police were involved, there hasn't been an indictment and there probably won't be. We're considering suing the town and the county for false arrest." Michelle felt Mrs. Spencer straighten up at that. She searched in her bag, as if she weren't acutely aware of the location of the insulting note from Frankie's kindergarten teacher, folded carefully in the side pocket.

Mrs. Spencer leaned forward across her desk as if she was willing to help with the search. "I had heard about the arrest and I—"

"As I just said, there've been no indictments," Michelle interrupted. "My husband and I were held for a few hours, badly frightened, and released. He and I have been the victims of some kind of smear campaign. Anyway, whether you believe me or not, our children are certainly innocent, wouldn't you agree?"

"Well, in these cases the children always are exposed to—"

"In our home my children have been exposed to love, respect, and moral behavior," Michelle said as she pulled the letter out and thrust it forward at the principal. "This, on the other hand, I consider *un*loving, *dis*respectful, and *im*moral behavior."

Mrs. Spencer picked up the letter and looked it over briefly. "I didn't know about this," she said. "I don't know anything about it, but I'll look into it."

"No, *I* am looking into it," Michelle said. "What's needed here is a reassessment. Surely Miss Murchison was aware that my son had been exposed to some stress. And that children can be unkind to one another. Frankie has never had an accident at school before." Michelle's voice began to rise and her hands to shake. "How dare she let him sit in his urine all morning? In front of the other children. In the corner like a bad boy. How dare she humiliate him and betray him that way?"

"You know the administration policy here is that children have to be toilet-trained to attend kindergarten. But I do think that Miss—"

"I know for a fact that these accidents have happened to other children and that when they do, the standard practice is to dry the kid off as quickly and discreetly as possible and move on. Why was Miss Murchison doing otherwise? Why was she punishing my son?" Without waiting for an answer from the useless woman, Michelle stood up. "It had better not happen again, Mrs. Spencer," she told her. "In fact, what better happen is that my son is given some extra kindness and special treatment to make up for this or else this school is going to be slapped with a law suit so gruesome that it will take the pension of every principal in the county to *begin* to pay it off." Michelle turned and walked to the door. "I'm taking Frankie down to Miss Murchison's room," she said. "Then I'm going to the bake sale. I count on you to speak to that woman and make sure that my son gets to be monitor tomorrow and that today he gets to sit beside her at story time. Because he could use a little help right now."

Michelle felt like she had to keep moving. She swooped up her son and her brownies, nodded at Hillary Gross and the rest of the audience that had gathered in the room. Her head was up, her ponytail high, and attitude was expressed in every line of her long, stiffened body. Now, brownies and her son in tow, she turned her back on all of them and strode down the hall.

She dropped Frankie off with Miss Murchison, had a whispered but fierce conversation with her, and then went on to the cafeteria. There two women had already set up the traditional "we're having a bake sale" paper tablecloths and were spreading out the incoming sweets.

Going into the big, echoing cafeteria was hard for her. She really needed Frank. She needed his strength. But the funny thing was that his strength was sometimes a terrible problem. He would have wrecked Mrs. Spencer's office. He would have made things worse. He would have screamed and Hillary Gross and all the others in that office really would have had something to gawk at. That was why, despite his strength, Michelle had learned to do some things on her own. She wasn't really good at them, but in the long run, it was the best thing. Now, however, she missed him desperately.

Keep moving, she told herself, *and keep your head up.* Another mother, an older woman with dyed black hair, was unwrapping an angel food cake while a redhead Michelle had met at PTA—Minna or Mona, Michelle couldn't remember which—sat with a money box, counting out paper and silver change. Michelle swung the heavy box up beside Mona (or Minna) and smiled brightly again. "Hi," she said, putting out her hand. "We've met before. I'm Michelle Russo."

Minna-or-Mona nodded but then looked away, her eyes wandering somewhere over to the closed cafeteria windows. She didn't offer her hand or her name. Michelle knew she should be cold and just shut up, but she had to try to push through this. "I brought brownies," she sang out. "Mrs. Russo's famous double chocolate specials." She turned to the other woman who was watching her, silent. "I know a lot of women bring brownies," she said, "but mine are baked from scratch. I know other people say that, but mine really are. Mine always do well."

The silence was a little frightening. She looked down at the table. Crumbs. She began to put them together into a tiny pile. One was stuck to the Formica and she scratched at it with her fingernail. "I baked four pans," she continued, horrified at her own desperation. "That's forty-eight brownies. And I ground the nuts for them. Don't you find that store-bought shelled walnuts never taste really fresh?"

There was nothing. No response at all. It was as if they hadn't heard her. These two human beings stared at her as if she were a guppy from another planet, floating before them in the air, her mouth opening and closing to no effect.

Michelle didn't have time to reflect. She was there in front of them and had to make contact. She swept the crumbs into her hand, but then she didn't know what to do with them. She couldn't just drop them on the floor, so she stuck them in her pocket. Disgusting. "You know, one of the funniest things that happened when my daughter started school here was when the second grade had a big bake-off to pay for, oh, I don't know, I think more laptops . . ." She stopped for a minute to think and heard a little laugh escape her. The two women simply stared as another woman joined them, a platter in hand.

Just shut up, Michelle, she told herself, but she couldn't. Somehow it had become really, really important to her that she break through the glass to these women's humanity. If she could do it now, everything would be okay. If she couldn't . . .

"Anyway, one of the kids brought in a big banner and they pinned it all across the front of the tables. It wasn't until late in the day that someone noticed the typo. The sign said 'Cake Stale.' Even my brownies didn't sell very well that day." She gave a little self-deprecating laugh.

The woman with the platter put it down on the table adjacent to Michelle's. Unlike the other two, her face, thank God, wasn't frozen. Her eyebrows knitted together. She stared at Michelle, but in an open, assessing way.

"Your face is very familiar," she said. "How do I know you?"

"From the newspapers," the redheaded bitch answered before Michelle could say anything.

She left the brownies.

She went back to Frankie's classroom, looked in and saw him sitting in his little chair beside Miss Murchison. Then, as slowly as she could manage so that it didn't look as if she were fleeing in defeat, she walked out to the car. It wasn't really cold yet. Just brisk. Yet she felt frozen in a weird way, or cracked like a piece of ice.

She got into her car, threw a Celine Dion tape into the cassette player, and turned the ignition key. She made sure she didn't allow herself to peel out of the parking lot. She kept one hand on the wheel but put the other lightly over her heart. She didn't cry. She patted herself instead and said aloud, "That was hard. That was hard, but you did good. They don't matter. You did real good."

She hoped she heard herself.

"Oh, Frank, they were horrible," Michelle told her husband. He was holding her around her waist as she leaned against him in the sanctuary and warmth of their kitchen. "Horrible. I mean, no wonder the kids are so shook up. I'm a grown-up and . . ." She stopped. What was she? Angry, hurt, outraged. Even—she hated to admit it—ashamed.

Frank let go of her and stepped away from the table, pushing the chair loudly behind him. "I'll go over there," he said. "I'll go over there and I'll talk to those bitches."

Oh God! Just what she needed! Michelle could see the headline now: DRUG LORD PUNCHES OUT OLD LADY PRINCIPAL AND BAKE SALE MOTHERS. She grabbed his wrist and pulled him back to the table. Why hadn't she remembered to save some brownies for the family? God, she was a complete idiot! She'd been so hyper and over-compensating that she'd given

all four dozen to the school. She wished she could put one in front of
Frank right now, pour him a calming glass of milk, and draw his attention away.

Sometimes Frank, as strong and good as he was, was way too direct.
Certain things couldn't be fixed with higher volume, or even the truth.
She noticed a smear on the chrome of the refrigerator handle. She
thought she'd wiped down everything after she'd finished baking. She
picked up the sponge and started for the fridge.

"What are you doing, Mich?" he asked.

She stopped, but the smear of batter stared at her. She had to wipe it
off. She did, then put down the sponge and looked at him. "Nothing,"
she said.

In the last two days he'd been out screaming at attorneys or home, on
the phone, screaming at other attorneys. Michelle wanted to tell him
that listening more and yelling less might help, but he was a straightfor-
ward person. Michelle could see that he was already unbearably frus-
trated by the loops and curves of the law. What would it be like for him
if this stuff dragged on? A chill ran down her back. Frank, thank God,
stopped and put his hand around her wrist, too. He pulled her down to
the other dining room chair. She looked at him.

She always told him everything. It wasn't always the right thing to
do—he was so protective that he always wanted to involve himself—but
Michelle had already explained this morning before she left that yelling
at the teachers and other kids wouldn't make them behave better
toward their children. He understood that. Now he looked at her and
tightened his grip around her wrist. She tightened hers in response.

"Mich, I can't believe I put you through this kind of pain," he said. "I
can't fuckin' believe it."

"It's not your fault," Michelle said. She felt cut off from the actual
problem itself. She was only dealing with the aftermath. She put her
hands on the dining room table. She'd try to look calmly at the bigger
picture.

"Frank, what's going on? How can they do this to you?"

"It would take too long to explain." Michelle couldn't help but think
he said that because he himself had no idea how it worked.

"Why don't you try to explain. You know, it's my life, too."

"Look, they're out for someone's blood. But they won't get mine. The DA has some secret informer, but if there was gonna be an indictment, it would have been handed down by now."

"So you won't be charged?"

"No. There's nothing to charge me with."

"And there won't be any trial."

"Of course not. All of this will go away. Keep a list, though, Mich. Keep a list."

"I am."

"Look, after I get out from under this thing, after they apologize to me, I'll have everyone from the governor on down come in here and kiss your feet," he said, his eyes intense. She loved his deep brown eyes. She'd married him for them.

"Shoes on or off?" Michelle asked. For him, she had to show a strong side, to help him through this.

"Shoes on," he said without laughing or losing his intensity. "I don't want them to enjoy it. Only I can kiss your naked feet." He moved his hand to the end of her fingers and pulled them up to his cheek; then he kissed each one. "You've been very brave, Mich. You aren't the same little girl I married."

Michelle didn't know why this terrible thing had been visited upon them. It was unfair, it was frightening, it was horrible. Maybe a tiny, very tiny part of her had wondered if there was the smallest possibility that somehow, she didn't know how, but somehow Frank might be—not guilty, she knew he wasn't guilty—but . . . involved, or . . . aware of something. It had only been a tiny question, but now, looking into Frank's eyes, Michelle was ashamed she had even considered it.

Michelle kept it together the rest of the morning and when Frank left that afternoon to check on a job and asked her if she was okay, she was almost answering honestly when she said yes. She'd kept cleaning and putting things in order. Making lists of broken things they needed replaced had a calming influence. Broken things could be fixed or replaced. Could her life be? She decided to go into work the next morning. She took some deep breaths. So, at three fifteen, when Jenna walked in the door Michelle turned and greeted her with a sincere smile—until she saw Jenna's blank face.

"What is it?" Michelle asked and ran to her daughter. She knelt beside her. "What?"

Jenna pulled the big rumpled bag from behind her. "What is it?" Michelle repeated, this time referring to the bag. But kneeling there, she knew.

"It's the brownies," Jenna said in a toneless voice. "The lady told me to tell you that nobody wanted them."

17

Containing a fruitless search

Jada got out of her Volvo and went to the pay phone just three cars away from where she was parked. She called into the office again, made sure that everything was under control, and gave Anne the briefest directions about what to do. Then she walked into the convenience store, used the toilet, and bought yet another cup of coffee, though caffeine was already singing in the arteries of her head.

Nervously, she looked out the window. She'd been watching for hours now. She knew she ought to eat something, but her stomach rebelled at the sight of the nasty snack cakes and cheap breads and rolls arrayed along the dirty counter. Funky Yonkers. She just took her coffee and went back to the car.

She'd spent three hours in front of Mrs. Jackson's house, but she hadn't seen any activity. Of course, it had been from four A.M. until seven, but now, on this gray November morning, there was not a sign of light or movement in the second-floor apartment of the run-down three-family building that Mrs. Jackson called home.

But Clinton had to be somewhere with her children. He wouldn't have taken them to a motel. First of all, he couldn't afford it. Secondly, even Clinton wouldn't upset the children in such a strange way. And would any decent hotel accept a man with three babies arriving in the middle of the night? She hoped not.

She got into the car and gunned the engine to crank up the heat. Thank God Volvos were built for Scandinavia. She pressed the seat heat button so that she might stop shivering, but she wasn't sure it was from the cold. It was more likely from rage and fear.

The thought had crossed her mind that some deranged fathers had been known to run off with their kids and set them on fire or shoot them or . . . But she told herself firmly as she pushed her back into the warming seat that Clinton was not deranged. Angry, vengeful, vain, spiteful, and self-deluded, yes. But deranged, no. She had to keep her mind off unrealistic insanity and keep it on the insanity of her present reality.

Although Jada had never really gotten along with her mother-in-law, and hadn't spoken to her in the last year except for visits with the children, she told herself that this was no time for false pride. It was past nine o'clock and there was no sign of life up there. Odd as it might seem to Mrs. Jackson, she would have to go to the door to find out if her mother-in-law knew anything. She just hoped she did. And maybe she'd be lucky; when the door swung open she might see Kevon tucked on one end of the sofa with Sherrilee at the other. Then she'd swoop in and take her babies and nobody would be able to stop her. Nobody.

Jada took another slug of the coffee, put it back into the cupholder, turned the ignition off, took the keys, got out of the car, locked the door, and crossed the street. Every single one of those acts drained her, but as she climbed the wooden stairs up to the second floor, she told herself she had a war to fight and she had to be ready for anything—even physical violence. Clinton had never raised a hand to her, but if he even touched her, if he tried to prevent her from taking back her children, she would rip into him with everything she had. It was funny—all the small activities like calling Anne, getting the coffee, even turning off the engine, seemed daunting and beyond her energy, but flying at Clinton with flailing arms and kicking feet seemed like something she could do for hours at a time without tiring.

When she got to the door, she didn't give herself a minute to think. She banged on it and waited for an answer. When there was none, she banged again. She peered through the door's dirty window, but the kitchen was bathed in an even gloom and completely deserted. She rattled the door to no effect.

Jada had never broken the law. As a kid she'd never shoplifted candy, she'd never gotten a speeding ticket. She didn't even jaywalk. A black woman in a white town couldn't. But now she had to get into this house. Maybe Clinton had her children hiding. She wasn't a housebreaker, but without hesitating for a moment she took off her shoe, smashed it against the corner of the glass, and smashed it again to enlarge the hole. She slipped her shoe back on as she reached in, threw the lock, and opened the door.

Once she was inside, she knew that there was nobody there. The air had the still quality of emptiness, not the moist living scent of people sleeping. Still, to be sure, she walked through the apartment, in its usual disarray. Mrs. Jackson was a lazy housekeeper just like her damn son. Jada shook her head at the plastic bags stuffed with dirty laundry, and worse, that were lying around the perimeter of the room.

After checking Mrs. Jackson's empty bedroom, she was about to leave—until it occurred to her to go to the telephone. There, on a bit of cardboard torn off a cereal box, were a few phone numbers. One she immediately recognized as the Yonkers phone number that had appeared so often on her bills.

Tonya Green's. He wouldn't. He wouldn't pack up her babies and take them over to that slut's house. It wasn't possible. She could hardly believe it, but she knew it must be true. They must have plotted it out together. She could see it now. Tonya was "a good Christian woman" who would try to cover up her guilt for her adultery by caring for her new man's children.

"They weren't there either," Jada said. Michelle reached out and patted her knee. "They weren't there, Clinton wasn't there, but Tonya wasn't there either. I think they all have gone some place together. I spent most of the night parked out there in the dark and cold for nothing."

"I spent all night baking brownies so I could have my daughter insulted. Things aren't good." Michelle got up, shaking her head, her long hair swinging in its clip, and went to the coffeemaker to bring the pot over to the table. She poured them each another mug, though Jada figured if she drank one more cup of coffee she would have to be hospitalized.

"Where could they have gone?" Michelle asked. "Oh, Jada, it's so horrible. I thought the worst thing that could happen, happened to me. I know how bad it feels knowing Pookie is out there somewhere and not being able to find him. It's got to be so much worse for you. It's a nightmare. It's a horror movie. How could all of this have happened?"

"Did you ever think it might be because we live on Elm Street? You know, bad luck like in the movie and everything?" Jada asked to lighten the burden.

"Maybe," Michelle acknowledged, her blond hair falling like a shade over her face. "But Lucy Perkins on Maple Drive has a kid with leukemia. That's a lot worse."

Jada nodded, saying a silent prayer for the Perkins child, and one of gratitude that her own kids were healthy, if missing. But she didn't feel better. What she wanted, God forgive her, was for Clinton to have leukemia right now. That, and she wanted her kids back.

And she was burdening her friend with all of this. "I know how much you're going through right now, but I didn't have anywhere else to go," Jada began. "I'm . . . I'm really sorry I—"

"Oh, come on. Listen, you have to see a lawyer and you have to see him right now. And about the only good thing that's come out of this is that I have a high-powered attorney now, and if he doesn't know what to do, he'll know the person who does. You wash your face and I'll call him and we can be over there in fifteen minutes. The guy is the worst sleazeball you've ever met, but he's connected to everyone in the county through favors or business." Michelle pushed her hair behind her ears. "You're going to need a good lawyer, Jada. Rick Bruzeman isn't a good man, but Frank says he's a really good lawyer."

Jada, still trying to maintain some kind of emotional control, got up. "All right," she said. "I do that first. Then I go to my reverend."

"Okay. We have a plan," Michelle said.

• • •

They were in the car in less than fifteen minutes, which, considering the time Michelle usually needed to get ready, was a huge sacrifice on her part. They drove together in Mich's car—Jada had had more than enough of the Volvo for a while. On the way over, as Michelle scanned the neighborhood for Pookie, she gave Jada the background on Bruzeman. As Jada understood it all, the main point seemed to be that time was of the essence.

That didn't mean that his receptionist didn't make them wait for almost twenty-five minutes. Jada picked up a *Fortune* magazine—the kind of magazine white lawyers had in their very white waiting rooms— and leafed through it. She stopped at an article about the reclusive Moyer clan—a bunch of brothers so old and rich from inherited wealth that they spent most of their life fighting about how many billions belonged to each of them. She showed the article to Michelle. "Do you think Charles Henderson Moyer would lend me a few bucks to pay for a divorce?"

"I doubt it," Michelle told her. "If any of them have a NUP, it's taking not giving. That's how they got rich in the first place."

By now Jada could barely speak, she was so hyped, so scared, so angry. There were some other news and financial magazines spread out on the table in the reception area, but she couldn't look at them. She hadn't slept, but she still wasn't tired. She had to do something with this energy. She'd just decided to call in to the bank again when Bruzeman's secretary showed up and ushered them down the hall.

"Hello, Michelle," Rick Bruzeman said as the two of them walked into the huge room. When he looked up at her, Jada saw his eyes register that slight surprise that she was black. He was a little guy with a tan that looked like he'd gotten it in some tropical place—maybe that resort in Barbados less than a mile from her parents' place that they'd never eaten at.

Bruzeman's gray hair was thinning and Jada was tall enough to see down to the monk's spot in the middle of it. His mustache was surprisingly small and seemed to move a lot when he talked. He hugged Michelle enthusiastically, in a way that managed to be cold at the same time. Then he smiled, his mustache twitching, and asked them to sit down on the sofa so they could be comfortable—as if Jada could be comfortable at all. Michelle patted Jada's hand when she sat beside her friend on the sofa. Bruzeman asked if they wanted coffee and they both shook their heads.

"I'd just like to begin," Jada said.

Michelle launched into the whole sorry business. She told Bruzeman a little bit of background and then went right into how Jada had helped her clean up, only to be rewarded by the desertion of her husband and the kidnapping of her kids.

"Well, wait a minute here," Bruzeman said when she had finished. "This isn't kidnapping. This isn't a police matter. He's the children's father, but it is serious."

Jada restrained herself and merely said she knew that.

"It's serious, but it's not uncommon, though usually it's the woman who leaves with the children. What we need is an immediate determination of temporary custody. That means I have to get to the courthouse today and have this heard immediately. We have to go aggressive, as well as fast. What I'm going to suggest is that you also go for a *pendente lite*." He paused and waited for one of them to ask what that was.

Jada and Michelle both said "What?" at the same time.

"A *pendente lite* is a request for immediate support payments for the children until the trial. If we move fast enough we can have first strike advantage. The *pendente lite* will hold until the custody and support issues are heard officially in county court." He leaned forward and smiled for the first time. "The fact is, that that can take months. In the meantime, your husband has to pay support."

"He has no money," Jada said.

"Then he'll have to get some. Because if he doesn't pay, he goes to jail. For contempt. Now, of course, eventually the court may decide to lower the amount or change it, but in the meantime, he pays or he's looking at the sky through bars." He picked up a legal pad and pulled out a gold pen from his pocket. "Three children?" he asked. "Is that what you said?"

Jada nodded, silent. She wouldn't mind beating Clinton almost to death, but the idea of the father of her children in prison wasn't a good one to her. And if he went to prison, it ought to be for kidnapping, not contempt of court, but apparently things didn't work like that.

Bruzeman asked a lot of questions then about her job, her income, their home, its equity, Clinton's business, and the like. She listened and answered as best she could, though now her only thought was to get him moving as quickly as possible over to the courtroom where her future would be determined.

"Hmm," Bruzeman said at last. "I think I see the full picture. You're the breadwinner. That could be a problem, if someone didn't know how to spin it right."

"Never mind spinning. How do we find him?" she asked. Forget his questions about whether or not Clinton had a pension fund or any other significant retirement monies. "How do we find him, get my kids, and serve him with these papers?"

"Oh, I have professionals we retain who will do that. Process service. It's not really that difficult. Not usually."

"She wants her children back," Michelle said. "She just wants her children back as soon as possible."

"Well, this is the fastest way," Bruzeman unctuously told Michelle. "Thank you for bringing in Mrs. Jackson," he added. "I think she and I might have a few things to say to one another alone, if you don't mind." He reached out, patted Michelle's shoulder in his oily way and said, "How is Frank doing? Calming down a little?"

"He won't calm down until we sue all of those sewer rats," Michelle said, and stood up. She turned to Jada. "I'll wait out in the lobby."

Bruzeman put his arm around Michelle's shoulder and walked her out the door. For a moment Jada was alone. She tried to offer up a prayer of thanksgiving; this man seemed to know what he was doing and how it had to be done. Certainly she didn't like him, but she didn't like to think what she would have had to go through on her own. And it was good of him to take her without an appointment. He hadn't even asked about a fee.

Bruzeman walked back in and closed the door behind him. When he sat down across from Jada, something about his manner had changed. In a way he seemed more relaxed, though she couldn't exactly define why. He reminded her of people who have gone backstage after a performance at the community theater; they still had their costumes on, but they were suddenly themselves instead of their roles.

Bruzeman looked across at her. "A black man won't get custody over you unless you've been doing crack or whoring."

Jada blinked. Was he asking her a question? Was he insulting her? "I work at the County Wide Bank," she said. "I'm the branch manager. I just do it for the money. It's a form of prostitution, but it's legal."

"Well, that does lead us to the money." Bruzeman continued to look at her without any discernible human feeling. "Divorce is expensive," he said. "And right now there's going to be a lot of legal tap dancing. I'm going to have to ask for a ten-thousand-dollar retainer and I'm afraid it won't go far—not unless we stabilize the situation quickly. I've never heard of your husband's lawyer, which means I don't expect much trouble there, but I can't move forward until you retain me."

Jada sat there absolutely stunned. Ten thousand dollars? She didn't have *ten* dollars to spare, certainly not a hundred, and definitely not a thousand. Where had she gotten the idea that this guy was going to give her a break?

He kept looking steadily at her. "You have to move fast, Mrs. Jackson. You have to move fast if you want your children back."

"But I don't have the money," Jada was forced to admit.

Bruzeman stood up as easily as if he were on springs. "Then I don't have the time," he said.

Jada still sat there. Looking at him, she knew that words would get her nowhere.

"Speed is essential here, Mrs. Jackson."

Jada figured she might have a little over seven hundred dollars in her checking account. And the mortgage was due, as well as the phone bill, which already made her two hundred dollars short. Nonetheless, she reached into her purse, pulled out her checkbook, and wrote him a check larger than any she'd ever written before. Her hand shook only a little.

She put the check down on the coffee table; when she stood up, she could look down on him. "You had better make this happen right," she said, and walked out of the room.

18

In which the lost is found and home truths are revealed

"Let's go for our walk," Jada said as she stood out in the cold beside Michelle's kitchen door.

Michelle hesitated. "You know, I think I just can't today. I . . ." She paused, feeling a strange reluctance to go out, a pull to the house. If she could just wash the hallway. "I really should do something about the linen closet. And I have laundry . . ." Michelle had been up until two-thirty cleaning, yet she felt there was so much yet to be done. Cleaning was the thing that calmed her; putting order into a disorderly universe was a comfort.

Jada was looking at her, her eyes wide. "Have you gone completely crazy, Cindy?" she asked and pulled Michelle's ski jacket off the hook. Jada began stuffing Michelle's limp right arm into the sleeve. "You have all afternoon to do the laundry. And all evening. I mean, you're not competing in the Miss America pageant tonight or anything, are you? Besides, we can look for Pookie."

Michelle smiled and shrugged into her jacket, though the thought of the towels piled askew in the closet and not yet color-stacked still bothered her. Well, maybe she'd have a few minutes for it after breakfast.

Once outside, Jada critically surveyed Michelle up and down. Michelle realized she hadn't washed her hair in two days, she had

Frank's sweats on, an old shirt of Jenna's, and Jenna's funky, dirty sneakers. "Love the look," Jada said. "Early leper colony. *So* you."

Michelle stopped and looked down at herself. Suddenly she felt better, almost able to laugh. "Okay. So I'm a *Glamour* Don't. What did Bruzeman say?" she asked Jada as they trudged down her driveway. She thrust her hands into her pockets. Damn! She'd forgotten her gloves again. Now her hands would freeze if she used her arms, so she'd have to keep them fisted in her pockets. Less aerobic exercise. Oh well.

Jada still hadn't answered her question, and Michelle, for a moment, thought her friend hadn't heard her. Then they turned off of Elm Street and she saw that Jada was biting her already chapped lower lip. "That bad?" Michelle asked.

"You have no idea," Jada said shaking her head. "He can get me immediate visitation, but he can't get me custody back. He also can't seem to return my calls. I mean, it got me crazy waiting to hear from him."

Michelle nodded. "Frank is going crazy, too," she said. "He's on the phone with Bruzeman's office all the time. I swear, I'm the only thing that's holding him together. Last night—for the first time ever—he almost smacked Frankie Junior when he spilled his milk all over the dining room table."

Jada shook her head. "Men are weak. Unless they're out to getcha."

"So you will see the kids?" Michelle asked. She turned her head, checking the yards of the houses nearby. Something was rustling in the bushes of a yard. But it wasn't Pookie, it was only a bird. Michelle continued walking, her eyes scanning lawns for the dog.

"Yeah. But I can't get custody back. Not until we have a hearing."

"And when will that be?" Michelle asked. "With Bruzeman's connections he should be able to get you right on the family court calendar."

"It's not as easy as that, it seems," Jada said. She turned to look at her friend as they rounded the corner to Oak Street and started down the long hill. "The truth is, I don't think he really gives a shit about this case. He said he was going to move fast, but this isn't fast."

But they were walking fast. Jada took bigger steps than Michelle, and Michelle had to match her stride, which was almost impossible. "I'm also so hungry," Jada said. "I'm sure it's all anxiety, because when I'm not hungry, I'm nauseous."

"Well, I could have brought you four dozen brownies," Michelle said. "I'm stuck with them." When Jada turned a questioning eye on her, Michelle poured out the whole story of the women at the bake sale.

"Those bitches!" Jada spat. "You stayed up all night baking. It's not as if you've even been accused of anything. Damn them!" She shook her head. "I know I should turn the other cheek and pray for their small, pathetic souls, but that was really mean, Mich. And to use Jenna. Who were they? I'd like to go and whap them."

Michelle, despite the cold, felt warmed by her friend's indignation. "Oh, they're Christians, too, I'm sure. They probably turn the other cheek."

"Good," Jada said. "Then I'd whap that side." She looked over at Michelle. "There are Christians and there are Christians," she said.

"Actually, the worst was Miss Murchinson." She told the whole story while Jada nodded her head sympathetically.

"Kevon had her last year. The woman was a witch. And a bigot. Kevon never got to show-and-tell until I went over there and told her a few things myself."

"Hey, can I stop here long enough to check the thickets? Pookie used to run off and come here to chase squirrels."

"Michelle. It's November. There are no squirrels."

Michelle shot her a look and Jada raised her hand as if to ward off the laser beam. "Go for it," she said.

Michelle crouched down, calling for the dog. After a few moments she gave up and they continued to walk down the hill and around the next corner of the circuit in silence.

Michelle was breathing deeply, trying to keep up with her friend. It was really good to get this exercise. She was crazy to want to stay in the house. She hadn't been able to breathe well in there; she'd woken up last night with her heart fluttering, gasping for air. "Hey, Jada, did you ever feel like you couldn't breathe?"

"Yeah. Right now," Jada said as they started up the longest hill of the walk.

"No. I mean like when you're just lying down, or sleeping." Jada turned her head and aimed a long look at Michelle.

"You mean like a panic attack?" she asked. "Or do you mean like asthma? Or heart trouble?"

Michelle felt suddenly embarrassed and looked down. She was always so stupid. "I don't know," she said. "I just woke up last night, and, well . . . I've been waking up a lot of nights and I can't breathe. So I sit up, but I still can't breathe. I don't want to bother Frank, but walking through the house doesn't fix it, and even a hot bath didn't help. I spent the last three mornings from two to five cleaning. That seems to be the only thing that takes my mind off it."

"Oh Lord, Cindy, no wonder you look so lousy."

"Thanks," Michelle managed to laugh.

"Why didn't you say something before? 'Hey, you *look* like shit but I *feel* like shit.' Until I see my babies I just . . ." She stopped talking. Despite their friendship, Michelle knew that Jada was a very private person.

"You'll see them," she assured her. "Bruzeman is going to get them back for you. He couldn't be successful and so repulsive if he wasn't good. It's not a problem." Jada just nodded her head. "You know," Michelle said to fill the silence, "I think I'm going to go to Dr. Brown. I'll tell him about my breathing."

"He'll probably give you a sleeping pill, or a Valium or something," Jada shrugged. "I guess right now it could only help."

"I'm not sure about that," Michelle said as they walked past her favorite house in the development. "You know about my parents. I don't like to drink, or take the chance of getting addicted to anything."

"Hey, come on. Doctors are there to help. Unless they work at an HMO," Jada added. "The bank will pay for it. You've got to keep yourself from falling apart."

"I hope I can do it," Michelle said. She thought about Frank and how erratic his behavior was becoming. She knew the pressure was worse on him than it was on her, but she wasn't taking it out on the children or on Frank—at least not yet.

"I think Frank needs a tranquilizer or something, too," she admitted to Jada. "He's really edgy. But he wouldn't take one."

Jada shook her head. "They can't take care of themselves," she said.

"It's not fair," Michelle said. "None of it's fair." She was beginning to breathe hard from walking up the incline and her breath, just like Jada's, was coming out in white puffs of frosty air. "It isn't fair."

"Tell me about it," Jada said, and promised herself she wasn't going to cry. "We are expected to take care of everything. I've got to take care of my kids. I got to take care of the house. Then I got to take care that I don't get fired and do what I gotta do to keep my job. That isn't enough. I also had to take care of my man, and of how I looked for him. Because if I don't take care of how I look, I'd lose my man, and then I'd be on my own and I'd have to take care of myself and everyone else. But I *been* taking care of myself the whole damn time." Jada looked fierce, her brows almost meeting. "'Cause he never took care of me. He didn't want to know too much about what I was feeling. And he sure didn't want to take care of the kids."

Jada shook her head. "I don't know where he is with them right now, but I do know that one hour of Shavonne's attitude plus one hour of the baby's fussing and he'd put them up for adoption." She bit her lip; Michelle wanted to reach out and take Jada's hand, but she was afraid to. "Clinton has only done this to scare and punish me. He doesn't want, and he can't handle, the responsibility of the children. He won't hear about the troubles that Kevon is havin' at school. Most of the time he doesn't even wanna be told about the broken damn garage door."

"I know," Michelle sympathized. "I really know."

"Of course, you know. Of course, you know. Every damn woman in America knows. But that isn't the worst of it. Nuh-uh. Ask the First Lady. The worst of it is that after a while we get real damn good at taking care of ourselves. We make sure we take care of ourselves because we *have* to. That's the only way we or our children will survive. And then look what Clinton does . . . He sticks in the damn knife. Then they tell us that we're hard. That we've lost our vulnerability. That we ain't the little girl they married."

"That's just what Frank said to me," Michelle said. "But I think he meant it was a good thing."

"Oh really?" Jada asked, her voice edged with sarcasm. "Well, this is only the beginning, honey. If you survive this and take care of yourself and Jenna and Frankie Junior, he's gonna be tellin' you that you're a goddamned castrating bitch before this is over." She increased her pace. "First they promise to take care of *you*, then they need *you* to take care of *them*, then they force you to take care of yourself and your kids. Then they blame you for it."

"Oh my God!" Michelle said. "Those are like the Buddha's Four Noble Truths. Jada, that's it. That's it in a nutshell."

Jada nodded her head emphatically. "The hell with the Buddha. I'm a Christian. But they're the Four Home Truths, baby," she said, and stepped up the pace again.

"Jada, you should start a twelve-step program, like Al-Anon. Except for *all* wives, and instead of twelve steps, there are those four."

"Mich, you're a little too late to the party. *All* married women *all* over have already gone through those steps. And they're damn sick and tired of it, especially the last one." Jada clenched her fists and walked even faster. Michelle was forced to almost run to keep up.

"Wait," Michelle begged. She'd lost some ground looking for Pookie and Jada must have gotten twenty feet ahead of her. Michelle held her hand to her rib cage. "I got a stitch in my side," she called.

"Get used to the pain," Jada said. "It ain't goin' away anytime soon." Suddenly Jada stopped, nearly at the crest of the hill. Michelle, who knew Jada hated to break her pace, took advantage of the opportunity, inhaled deeply, and ran up the hill to reach her friend.

"Thanks for waiting," she said, breathless.

"I wasn't waiting. I was thinking," Jada told her. "Michelle, what the hell are we doin' this for?"

"Doing what for?" Michelle asked. "You mean staying married? You mean taking care of our families?"

"No. I'm talking about this damn walking. In the cold. In the dark. We're doing this walkin' so that we can still look like we're twenty-five when we're thirty-five-year-old grown-up women." Jada looked at Michelle. "Think about it. You're worse than I am, but I spend hours every week trying to stay the same weight I was in junior college. It's ridiculous." Jada turned her back on the rest of the hill. For the first time ever since she and Michelle had started walking, Jada was going to quit. Michelle watched her as she started to walk down the hill.

"Meanwhile," Jada said, "my husband has stolen my kids and is probably lying in a warm bed with a woman who's got a fat black ass. I'm not doing this anymore, Michelle. I am not gettin' up at the crack of dawn, walking out into the New York cold, and dragging myself up and down Westchester hills to make sure that the cellulite on my thighs isn't forming. I got better things to do." Jada kept walking, if anything, even faster than she had before. Michelle had to almost skip to keep up with her. A thrill of fear, not just the chill of November, went through her.

"Jada, listen. I know how bad you feel. Well, *almost* how bad. This thing Clinton did to you is terrible. But we're not doing this just to look good or for health. At least I'm not. Honestly." She reached out and took her friend's hand. "I'm walking with you because I want to be with you. Because I want to talk to you. You're my only real friend, Jada. And you're so good for me. Our walks are the only time I have during the day when I get to be . . ." Michelle searched for the words. "When I get to just be myself. To be honest. And not think I'm stupid or crazy when I am."

Jada looked down at her. "Well, you *are* stupid *and* crazy if you think spending time with the likes of me is good for you," she said, but she leaned over and hugged Michelle hard. Michelle hugged her back. She was amazed at how grateful she felt for Jada's small act of friendship.

"You're right, Mich," Jada said. "I think that's why I pushed you into your jacket this morning. We both need these walks."

"Thanks," Michelle said. They had come to the end of Laurel Street, the place where they turned around. Jada looked over at Michelle.

"Go ahead," she said. "Touch the post. I know you want to."

"The hell with the post. I used to touch it for good luck, but it hasn't worked, has it? Absolutely nothing is going right for either of us," Michelle said. Then despite herself she gave in and tapped it.

"Forget about luck. Think about God," Jada said, and then a big smile broke out on Jada's face. "Just when you think that, God sends a miracle."

Michelle turned to look in the direction Jada was pointing. There, padding out from behind a garage, came Pookie, looking as if he were doing nothing more than following them on their usual walk. Michelle dropped to her knees and clapped her hands and he trotted over. She put her face down against the dog's soft head.

"We found him! Or he found us! It is a miracle," she said.

"No," Jada answered. "I knew we'd find him. The miracle is that I'm happy to see him. The spoiled little spaniel." She looked over at Michelle. "It'll make things better for the kids, won't it?" Michelle hugged the dog and nodded her head. "Let's try to cheer up," Jada said.

And Michelle did. As they walked home, Jada spoke about how much she wanted to see her children, alternating with how much she wanted to murder Clinton. Michelle agreed with her the whole way back.

19

In which realizations are rather thick on the ground

When she got back from Marblehead, Angie had a hard time keeping her head clear. She was glad her father was away—she couldn't face explaining her stupidity to him. The only thing she longed for was sleep. Any thoughts that came into her mind in the mornings when she woke up or at night, back at her father's, were full of such hurt, such rage, and such humiliation that she couldn't tolerate her own consciousness. She'd had a hard enough time believing that Reid, the low-life slime ball, had betrayed her. But it was far more difficult to accept that he had betrayed her with Lisa. What an idiot she'd been! There had to be a name for the kind of jerk, the kind of stupid, trusting, moronic idiot she was, but she couldn't think of one except for "Angie."

On Tuesday, when she didn't call, her mother had telephoned and threatened to come over, get her out of bed, and chase her down. Angie had managed to get dressed and show up at the office, looking more like a desperate client who needed help than a lawyer prepared to give any. But the staff had been so kind: Michael Rice had patted her hand. Bill, the paralegal, had taken her to lunch and confided to her about all the men who'd broken *his* heart, while Susan, the receptionist, had brought her a whole box of Yodels. "And you don't have to share them," Susan told her.

After everybody's kindness, Angie made her decision. She couldn't just spend the rest of her life lying on her father's sofa—although she felt as if that was all she really wanted to do. Instead she could at least help other women. Her mother was right—that was a worthwhile way to spend your life. She would take this job—even if it wasn't permanent—and she'd do her best. She'd make a difference for others, even if it was too late for herself. And if they couldn't use her when Karen Levin-Thomas returned (if she ever returned) then Angie would find another job with Legal Aid or the NOW Legal Defense Fund or something like it, and do the kind of work that she always should have been doing.

She stared at the files in front of her, dozens and dozens of them, but the words in the documents floated in front of her eyes. So much pain, so much betrayal, so much disappointment. She knew she wasn't the only Angie, the only stupid trusting woman in the world who had let her life be ruined through her own poor judgment, but case after case after case of Angies seemed overwhelming.

She stayed late that first night, trying to focus. It wasn't easy, but she could either do that or sleep some more, and she couldn't face the thought of her dad's empty house, her rumpled bed, and her empty future.

Her coworkers said goodnight on their way out. Angie had to turn the desk light on as the darkness outside matched her internal darkness. She kept going through the cases, taking notes, putting down court dates on the big tracking calendar. One thing law school had taught her was how to stick with something, how to work through distraction and fatigue simply because you had to.

She didn't take a dinner break. At about seven o'clock she broke into the Yodel box, and by nine-thirty she'd eaten every one of them. And then something happened. She wasn't sure if it was her mind clearing, or if the sleep had done the trick, or if it was only a sugar high, but as she sat reading her notes she began to get angry. Very, very angry.

None of this was fair. And it wasn't the fault of Mrs. Huang, whose husband had falsely translated and then made her sign documents that gotten her embroiled in all of his malfeasance, and in trouble with the IRS as well as Immigration. And it wasn't the fault of Terry Saunders's that her husband of twenty-seven years had taken all their money, including her inheritance from her family, forged her name, and deposited it in off-shore accounts, where he was now living with her children's baby-sitter.

It was all unfair, rotten behavior. It was better to live life as a trusting soul than to be a J'in Huang or a Henry Saunders, willing to lie and cheat a partner. Better to be an Angie Romazzano than a Reid Wakefield or a Lisa Randall, she thought, and for the first time since her anniversary, the shame that had bound her fell off. She actually stretched her back, as if, like some bug that drops its carapace, something stiff and dark that had enclosed her had dropped off. For God's sake, she thought, what did she have to be ashamed of? What did any of these women have? They had followed the rules, behaved honorably. For most of them, their only sin had been to be too trusting.

She stretched her shoulders back again and made fists with her hands. Anger moved like blood through her whole body. The trouble with most of the women that she'd seen at the clinic was that they weren't mad. They were ashamed or frightened or both.

Angie would focus on the work at the clinic. Oddly, it would comfort her to feel the rage that many of the women clients she spoke to were afraid to express. Her rage was big enough for all of them.

The clinic, she decided, wasn't just her temporary job. It was her mission. With Natalie's help in getting licensed, she would take on these cases and she would win them. She knew she was smart, and more important, she knew how to work hard. This was not how she would have chosen to spend her life or her energy, but it had chosen her. There was nothing for it but to push ahead.

She might have had a life in a pleasant house in Marblehead, working at a respectable private law firm, and raising one and three-quarters children while her husband, a delightful, handsome, popular guy, discreetly cheated on her and she turned a blind eye. But that wasn't the life she was going to live and there was nothing she could do about it now. And she had picked this new focus. She wasn't stuck in it—she was selecting it. She might not have fun, but she was going to make a difference.

She had one more appointment, with a woman who worked two jobs and couldn't come in until after nine. Sometime around half-past, Angie looked up to see the door open and her new client come into the office, shoulders hunched, head down, a woman used to being bested by everyone, an immigrant who didn't know her rights and was afraid of all male authority. Poor Mrs. Huang.

The next morning Angie was ushering a client out the door, patting her shoulder in a pathetic attempt to comfort her, when her mother bounced down the corridor from behind her and tapped Angie on her tush. Mrs. Gottfried left and Angie turned to her mom. "You busy for lunch?" Natalie asked.

Angie raised her eyebrows. "Well," she said, "I do have a date with Brad Pitt, but I hear he's cheating on me with a Soprano, so I could blow him off."

Natalie heaved a big sigh. "Honey, I didn't want to tell you. It isn't just a Soprano, it's the entire Mormon Tabernacle Choir."

"Why am I not surprised?"

The two of them put on their coats. "Maybe you want to comb your hair. Are you letting those streaks grow out or what? And take your car," Natalie said. "I might want to linger."

"Car?" Angie asked. "To go to the deli? I wasn't even going to bring my purse. You're buying, right?"

"Not exactly," Natalie said. "Bring your bag and your car keys." Angie nodded agreement, though she didn't feel up to much more than a quick sandwich. She put on some lipstick, brushed her hair, and added some mascara. She still looked like shit, but now she looked like shit that tried.

They were out the lobby, almost to the parking lot, when she jerked her head and pointed across to the Blue Bird Coffee Shop. "We're not flipping into the Bird?" she asked.

"No," said Natalie. "This is a fancy-shmancy lunch. Just follow me."

So Angie tried to, despite Natalie's driving, which had to be the worst she'd ever seen—and she'd lived in Massachusetts. Since Angie still didn't know the neighborhood, she followed blindly while her mother weaved across the busy streets until they were driving one right behind the other in a mostly residential area on a narrow lane. Natalie drove on the right shoulder, except for when she drove over the white line. As Angela watched, her mother make a left across the other lane without signaling first.

Now her mother put on her left blinker, but she didn't make the next left-hand turn. Angie shook her head. Only a woman who had spent most of her life living in New York City without a car could drive this badly. But Angie lost the smile quickly. It suddenly hit her that she had no life, and living with her dad and driving this old clunker he'd lent her was no way to get a life.

She ought to think about some kind of a living arrangement—not that she was making a living. The clinic had been paying her only a tiny per diem that didn't do much more than pay for her lunches and gas money. She wasn't sure if they could or would pay more, and where would she live if she didn't live with her father? The idea of a place of her own frightened her. Somehow it had been fun and easy to pick out sheets and a vacuum and a coffeemaker when it was for her home with Reid. But doing it for herself? It all seemed expensive, difficult, and maybe pointless. But it was pointless to do it for a man who was sleeping with your best girlfriend, too, she reminded herself. Maybe making a home was important. She sighed. She had too much to think about.

She looked around at azalea, mountain laurel, and privet that dominated the landscaping in the neighborhood they were driving through. This part of Westchester was beautiful and expensive. Like the plantings, it was mature as well. Somehow, Angie couldn't see herself living there. Nor could she see herself in White Plains or the other larger towns in Westchester. She could only see herself in New York City, but she couldn't afford an apartment there and had avoided the city because she knew how difficult it was to get a good legal job. The competition was fierce.

And now, against her will, she was kind of hooked on this do-gooding stuff. The stakes seemed so much higher than in the wills and estates she had done before. And she had so much autonomy—maybe too much. The clinic was so overwhelmed with potential clients that there wasn't a lot of time for supervision from the senior people. And the senior people didn't act particularly senior; everything was friendly. At her law firm there had been a strict hierarchy—like Victorian children, associates were regarded best if they didn't speak to a partner unless they were spoken to.

Just as Angie began to wonder where in the world her mother was taking her, a restaurant on beautiful grounds appeared on the left. It was a huge old house that had been turned into an inn and Angie pulled up and parked just a car away from her mother's. "Who are we meeting here?" she asked. "I think this is more than just a little lunch."

Natalie laughed. "Oh, you'll see. It'll be fun."

JoAnn Metzger looked great. She was a famous writer now, but Angie remembered her from years ago, when she had worked at JoAnn's husband's office for the summer.

"How are you?" JoAnn asked. "What a nice, nice surprise."

JoAnn had been invited to Angie's wedding, but had been away in Japan and couldn't come. Instead she'd sent the most beautiful wedding gift of all that Angie had received: an antique kimono, incredibly embroidered and framed beautifully in a Lucite box. Angela had retrieved it from the condo, and now it was in storage. The thought of the kimono, its beautiful colors enclosed in cardboard and sitting in a warehouse, made her sad. Perhaps she did want her own wall, just so she could hang the kimono.

"I'm fine," Angie said.

Her mother laughed. "Oh yeah. She's just great," Natalie said and leaned toward JoAnn on her right while she took Angie's hand. Natalie told Angie's story to JoAnn while Angie sat there. Oddly, instead of pain, she felt outraged as she heard it. She thought that might be a good thing—a sign of growth or healing. Either that, or it was the beginning of a complete mental breakdown.

JoAnn reached across the table and took Angie's other hand. "I can't tell you how sorry I am."

"Been there. Had that done to her," Natalie told Angie.

When the waiter arrived, the three of them looked as if they were about to perform a seance. All three of them ordered Cobb salad.

"But with the dressing on the side," Natalie commanded. Angie had to smile. She knew her mother would use up all her dressing and probably finish off skinny JoAnn's, too. When their drinks arrived, they stopped talking about Angie and Reid and Natalie began talking about the clinic. Angie knew that JoAnn was on the board, but as Natalie spoke Angie realized that her mother had already told JoAnn quite a bit about Angie's help.

"Here's the thing," she said. "The caseload is increasing, we're paying Karen while she's out, but we've got to have another attorney and we're going to have to pay them. So I'm proposing Angie. Do you think that's nepotism?"

JoAnn laughed. "Of course it is," she said, "but that doesn't make it wrong. I got my son his job in publishing." Their salads arrived. JoAnn looked across the table at Angie. "But are you up to it?" she asked. "I don't mean intellectually. I'm sure you're a good lawyer. What I mean is, are you up to it emotionally right now? After Gerome left me I was, well . . ." She turned to Natalie. "How would you describe it?"

"Deluded," Natalie said. She looked at Angie. "She kept thinking they'd get back together. Which Alaska and Siberia will do again someday, maybe if you wait long enough."

JoAnn looked at Angie. "Are you waiting for him to call you? Are you obsessed? Do you think you will go back to him?"

Angie shook her head. "Never," she said.

"I'm proud of her. She went up there, got her stuff, and came right back down."

Angie took a deep breath. She hadn't told about Lisa. She wasn't sure she wanted to, but looking at the two older women, suspecting they had heard it all, she decided to become another statistic, another dumb woman. "I found out who he was sleeping with," Angie said. "It was my best friend from work."

JoAnn closed her eyes and shook her head. Natalie turned to her daughter. "Oh God," she said. "The little witch. Don't let it make you feel like a jerk, Angie. *She's* the jerk, not you."

JoAnn opened her eyes. "I know it doesn't help to hear this, but it really could be worse," she said. "He could be sleeping with your sex therapist."

Though Angie's mouth was full of Cobb salad, she laughed, or something close to it. It was a relief to tell them about Lisa, and it was a relief to hear these sane reactions. "Yeah, but that doesn't happen in real life."

"Oh yes it does," Natalie said as she raised her eyebrows and inclined her head toward JoAnn. "She was paying that broad two hundred dollars an hour to talk about her sex life with her husband while the therapist was boffing him."

"Is that true?" Angie asked JoAnn.

"Well, I might not of put it exactly in those words," JoAnn admitted. "It was a hundred and seventy-five an hour and I don't think that 'boffing' is what they were doing while I was seeing her. They were moving up to the actual boff." JoAnn smiled. "I cared so much then. Now . . . I don't consider myself a victim anymore," she said. "I've moved on. It's not that that wasn't a bad part of my life, but I'm over it." She smiled, and her smile was gorgeous. "I guess I'd consider myself a recovering first wife."

There was a pause while they finished their lunch. Then Natalie began talking about the clinic and she and JoAnn discussed the budget for a little while until the waiter brought cappuccinos.

"I wonder if we could go back to Adrianne," Natalie was saying when Angie paid attention again. She knew they were talking about Adrianne Lender, the famous actress and producer.

"Does she fund the clinic?"

"Does an ex-husband send his child support late?" Natalie asked archly. "Honey, she is the clinic."

"How much additional funding do you think we need?" JoAnn asked. "Because my new book contract . . ."

Angie decided it was a good time to excuse herself. That was for two reasons: first, she didn't want to hear them talk about her financial possibilities. Second, she suddenly felt dizzy and a little bit nauseated. Maybe she was the one who had had too much of the rich dressing on her salad.

By the time she had negotiated her way across the room and to the small hallway that led to the ladies', there was desperation in her step. She walked into the bathroom, threw open a door to a stall, and threw up. The force of it was shocking—three spasms and her belly was empty,

but she heaved a few more times. She leaned against the wall, her forehead and upper lip beaded with sweat.

She guessed that her confession to her mother and JoAnn had cost her
more emotionally than she had thought. She averted her eyes from the
toilet and flushed it. If it was Lisa and Reid that she was flushing away,
she was glad to see them go.

Nothing like a good projectile vomit to set you up for the afternoon.

20

In which Michelle floats alone and Jada floats away

Michelle pulled the pink sweater over her head, then struggled into the gray flannel skirt. Well, actually, she didn't have to struggle anymore. The terror of the last week had killed her appetite and probably jumped up her metabolism. Anyway, she'd obviously lost some weight, because she didn't even have to pinch the zipper together to get the skirt to close. She looked in the mirror.

Her body, always long and vertical, looked as if it had stretched taller than its normal five feet ten inches. She supposed that she should consider the weight loss becoming, but when she looked at her face her reflection shattered that idea. Her face was bones and hollows, her nose more prominent. Somehow it looked as if her skull had gotten smaller, but the skin hadn't. Her hair was so blond against her face that it drained it of all color. Michelle had always been fairly effortlessly pretty. But this face was going to take a lot of makeup before she could show it at the bank.

Michelle had talked with Jada and both agreed it was best to try to return to their work lives. "If you sit at home all day or keep grooming Pookie for hours you'll wind up in County," Jada had said, and Michelle knew she was speaking for herself, as well.

So last night Michelle had told Frank that today she would be going back
to her job at the bank. Frank, as always, had told Michelle it wasn't necessary, but Michelle wanted—no, she needed—the regularity of her old work
routine. She wanted to be out of this house that had been sullied in a way
she couldn't Windex or Pledge off the walls, windows, and furniture. And
at the bank she had some coworkers who knew her. Not real friends like
Jada, but a few other women that she'd worked with now pleasantly for
years. They had birthday lunches together, and she liked them.

Besides housework, she had her list to keep herself busy. She'd gotten
a notebook, found all her old receipts for her furniture and linens and
stapled them to the new ones. But at the bank, Michelle had her loan
work; that would keep her mind active in a more productive way than
her growing fears over the legal swamp she and Frank had fallen into.
Plus, defending themselves was going to be so costly that they might
actually need the money, though she didn't say that to Frank. Frank was
worried, but he wouldn't talk about the trouble with her.

"Look, they haven't indicted me. They got nothing," was all he'd
repeat to her, but she knew he was spending hours on the phone and in
conferences with Bruzeman. How could Frank afford to spend less time
on work, yet spend more than ever on costs—cleaning up the house and
replacing everything, as well as paying attorney's fees?

Michelle left the bedroom and walked down the hall to get her hot
rollers, which, typically, Jenna had borrowed and never returned. She
heard a noise and stopped, poised to listen. Scratching. Was it the dog?
She immediately ran downstairs, taking two steps at once.

"Pookie! Pookie!" God, it had made all the difference to Frankie now
that the dog was back. He was sleeping through the night again.

The dog was scratching at the door. Was there someone—a cop or
worse—hanging around out there? Frank had been paranoid about even
using the phones, afraid they might be tapped. But Michelle would not
be intimidated in her own house. She flung open the door only to find
the local "freebie" newspaper, one she'd requested they *not* deliver, at
her feet. Michelle couldn't even gather the energy to bend over to pick it
up. She simply shut the door and bent over to scratch Pookie's ears.
"Good dog," she said.

She got the hot rollers, went into the bathroom, opened the little cabinet on the wall where she kept close to forty plastic jars, tubes, and compacts, and selected a handful to begin painting onto her face. She plugged in the rollers, then shook the foundation bottle hard, because otherwise she wound up smearing some oily water with occasional cementlike chunks of color on her face. No wonder they called it foundation! Looking at her pale skin, the sootlike marks under her eyes, and her colorless lips, Michelle shook her head. Then she got busy.

As she rolled up her hair and began painting her face, she thought of the song that began, "Gray skies are going to clear up, put on a happy face." She couldn't remember the rest of it, but she forced herself to hum it. She *had* to stop feeling sorry for herself.

After she finished with the blusher, she started working on her eyeliner. However bad she felt, she reminded herself that Jada was ten times worse off. What was it like right now for Jada, with her children missing and no news since Clinton had taken them, except for a quick call on her answering machine that said "I have the kids and they're all right" in Clinton's voice? It was cold. Jada had made her come over and listen to it.

Yes, Jada had it so much worse. Michelle still had her husband and children. She still had her family intact. She couldn't imagine what it felt like to Jada, adrift, alone, isolated from everyone she loved and cared for. Her horror wasn't public, but in a way that was worse, far worse than Michelle's. Putting another layer of mascara on her lower eyelashes, Michelle had to stop because her eyes had gotten so wet. Well, she was finished anyway.

She looked in the mirror at her renovations. Her skin was now evenly ivory, with no freckles but with pleasantly pink cheeks and a matching mouth. The creases above her eyes had just the right amount of pale brown eye shadow, while the darkness under her eyes had disappeared. *Funny how we're supposed to have shade over our eyes but not under,* she thought. She looked fine. In fact, she'd taken pains, so she looked better than usual. She was ready for the day. Now she just had to be brave and achieve re-entry. As she walked out of the bathroom, as a little encouragement to herself she began to sing about how gray skies were going to clear up.

• • •

Michelle and Jada had talked it over and decided Michelle could come in a little bit late this morning. Jada was going in, too. She couldn't afford to take another day off from work, not with the legal bill she was going to have to pay. And though both women would have preferred driving in together, Jada hadn't thought it was a good idea. For a moment, Michelle had been hurt and thought that Jada might not like to be seen with her in public. Then she got her head straight. They almost never drove to work together before. Why should they do it now?

Michelle pulled up to a parking space just before nine o'clock, got out of the car, and took a deep breath. This was normality, and it felt better than the ups and downs of the last week. *Just be brave and friendly now,* she told herself. *You're guilty of nothing.* She walked to the employees' entrance and rang. Bobby, the part-time security guard, opened it for her. He was a nice kid. "Say, hey," he said casually and she smiled. Maybe this would be easy as pie.

"Good morning," Michelle said in passing, then opened the closet to hang her coat, put her gloves and hat in the place on the shelf where she always kept them, and walked directly to the coffee machine. She'd only been away for a few working days, but she was touched to see that her mug was still in its place. She poured herself an almost-full cup. She took it to her desk, but before she could put her coffee down, she realized it wasn't her desk. Her pictures of Frank, the kids, Pookie, the little ivy plant she'd gotten last Mother's Day—nothing was there that was hers. Her stomach tightened, and shyly, almost fearfully, she looked around at the others.

Was this some awful, mean joke? Were they all watching her to see how she'd react? Several officers were talking with customers. Ben and Anne were on the phone and everyone else seemed to be avoiding her eyes. She sat down anyway, unsure of what to do. Her hand began to shake. She'd spill the coffee if she didn't set it down soon. Then Anne hung up the phone and walked over to her.

"Hi, Michelle," Anne said in a brittle voice. "So, while you were gone the consultants rearranged the desks. Yours is over there now, in the bin." She pointed to the spot where the internal wall took a jog, creating a small alcove near the vault. It was a spot coveted by some, because it gave you privacy from the eyes of the bank customers. Of course, that was why it was inappropriate for an office to be located there.

"But Betsy sits there," Michelle protested. Betsy serviced the lock-boxes and needed easy access to the vault, which was what had made the wall jog there.

"Betsy will be servicing them from the front, over there, so that we don't get interrupted by being asked for the safety deposit person. Something about efficiency." Then, without another word, Anne turned her back on Michelle and moved over to her own desk, where she sat and managed to keep her head down, busily looking through a file drawer.

Michelle, her face reddening under the ivory foundation makeup, stood up slowly and walked over to her new desk. She slid between the wall and the desk and then sank into her own chair. Seated in the alcove, her back almost hitting the wall, the desk became a bulwark in front of her. Michelle could almost have been in a closet; her range of vision was cut off.

She thought of the nuns who had taught her in grammar school. They wore wimples that had acted as blinders, just as this desk's position did. Michelle couldn't see any of the customers as they came in, nor could she see the first two rows of officers' desks. All she could view was Anne's desk and Jada's glass-windowed office behind it. She was all alone, isolated, and out of view. Was it just a coincidence? She didn't think so. Michelle lowered her head and pretended to look at the loan requests on her desk, but she was actually trying to remember how to put on a happy face.

Michelle had worked through the morning, catching up on paperwork and making a few calls to customers who had neglected to complete parts of the loan application properly. She also had had a few approvals, but she was saving those calls to make at lunchtime, when some people might be home. She'd like to give somebody some good news. There didn't seem to be much good news here for her, though.

It was almost eleven-thirty and aside from two loan applicants, no one had spoken to her. She'd been too frightened to get up and walk over to Ben's desk or to one of the tellers and try some small talk. What if they rebuffed her as harshly as the woman at the bake sale had done? Michelle couldn't have taken it.

She wondered again whether her desk had been moved to keep her out of the sight of "decent people." She didn't want to be paranoid, and she didn't think Jada would let the consultants or the bank staff do such a thing, but she wasn't completely sure. After all, Jada was not only her friend but also a working mother who had to take care of her children financially. The job meant everything to Jada.

Now that it felt jeopardized, Michelle realized that emotionally her job meant a great deal to her as well. She liked to help people. She enjoyed teaching them ways to reorganize their financial needs, to fill in the forms, and it was very gratifying to feel that she'd done them some good. It gave her other adults to talk to, even if it was just about a funny *Seinfeld* episode or the new luncheonette that had opened next to the bank.

It gave her something to talk about in the evening, too. When Frank told her about his day, she could tell him about hers. Although some-times the job was complicated, and sometimes she had the heartbreak-ing situation of turning down money to people who were desperate for it, she found most of the work fairly easy and had time to joke and enjoy herself during the day.

But this was no fun; sitting in a lock box away from everyone and being cold-shouldered by her coworkers felt really awful. She thought of the times she'd locked poor Pookie in his crate when he'd been bad. Maybe it was just a combination, Michelle thought, of her first day back, her new location, and her coworkers' awkwardness. If she made the first move, perhaps everything would slide into place and she'd come to see this desk as an advantage. The phone rang and she lifted the receiver.

"Michelle? It's me, Jada."

"Oh, hi," Michelle said. "How ya holding up?"

"I'm sorry I didn't call you when you came in, but first I had to face Mr. Marcus and then I just had an hour-long meeting with Data Processing and I swear I don't know one thing that was said in it."

"Doesn't sound good," Michelle told her. What a relief! Jada wasn't cutting her off. "You want me to come in? Have you got a lunch break? We could go out to lunch."

"Not a good idea. Look, I wouldn't be honest if I didn't tell you there's some pressure I'm getting about your job here. No problem. Just a little pressure. But I think we better . . . well . . ."

"No problem," Michelle said, though her throat seemed to close up as she took the news in.

"Also, I really need your help."

"Sure," Michelle promised. "So, what's up?"

"Open your bottom righthand drawer," Jada said. "And don't look up."

"Is it a present?" Michelle asked. "A present for me?" Slowly she pulled the drawer open.

"Hey, it ain't even a present for *me*." Jada's voice almost crackled over the phone. "Though I need it." Michelle pulled out a piece of paper and recognized it in a second. It was a loan application made out by Jada. An unsecured loan for ten thousand dollars. Uh-oh.

"I got it," Michelle said. "What now?"

"Michelle, I don't know what to do. I already gave Rick Bruzeman a check for ten thousand dollars to pay his retainer."

"Ten thousand dollars?" Michelle whispered. "He asked for that much?"

"That was just a start," Jada admitted. "But he's going to be aggressive and get me my kids back."

"It's difficult," Michelle agreed. "And it's a ransom. I never imagined . . ."

"It's worse than that. I haven't been able to get him on the phone since, just messages from his assistant. He's always in court or in transit or in something."

"Well, he is a busy guy. Because he's good."

"So good he said we have to move real fast and then he took my money and is gone."

God! Michelle wondered what Bruzeman was charging Frank. It must have been lots more, lots and lots more than this. She thought of a bitter joke Frank had told her. What can a goose do, a duck can't, and a lawyer should? Stick his bill up his ass. She was afraid to tell it to Jada, not only because this wasn't the time, but because Jada didn't like vulgarity. "How are you going to do it?" Michelle asked Jada.

"You got the answer right in front of you."

Michelle looked up from the piece of paper in her hand and over to Jada's office. Jada was standing, the phone held to her ear with one hand, the other hand massaging the back of her neck. She shook her head when she saw Michelle's eyes on her and turned away. "Don't be looking over here," Jada almost snapped. They were both silent for what seemed like a long, long minute.

"Listen, Michelle," Jada said. "This isn't any kind of Whitewater scam. I'm not asking you to do something you wouldn't do. I think I can guarantee the loan. I can't touch the equity on the house because I need Clinton's signature to do that. But I can pay this back as soon as I can tap the equity. What I need you to do is look at that application the way you would any other, but make it happen a lot quicker. Because if I don't get cash in my account by tomorrow, I am definitely going to bounce Mr. Bruzeman high and wide. Okay?"

"Okay," Michelle said. "Listen, while I have you on the phone, can you tell me why I've been stuck in this corner?"

"B-O," Jada said.

"Are you saying I stink?" Michelle asked—Michelle, who showered at least twice a day and almost never left the house without freshly washed hair.

"Not body odor. Boss's orders," Jada told her. "Marcus was worried. A few jerks said something. But I think once everyone settles down, you're not going to have any problems except for one or two assholes. But for now they're *all* assholes. I'm looking out this window at a sea of assholes."

"Not a pretty picture," Michelle told her.

"I don't know. I think it's better than their faces," Jada said, and Michelle had to laugh. The laugh freed her up; as awful as all this was, Jada was her friend and they both would live through this.

Michelle had done her best for most of the afternoon filling in the legion of forms it would take to approve Jada's loan. She'd also called around and got verbal approvals segment by segment. The trickiest thing she'd done was to back-date it all so that it appeared as if Jada had been on the queue waiting, and Michelle's absence or lack of follow-through was at fault.

It wasn't hard to call people and say, "You're not going to believe how I screwed up. I'm a week behind in processing my boss's loan." People were surprisingly cooperative when she told them her job might be on the line.

And Michelle didn't mind doing it. The numbers Jada had given her weren't so bad that they made the transaction unlikely or totally out of line.

The problem was, at least as Michelle saw it, that though Jada could pay this loan back eventually (and probably with some big difficulties) she couldn't afford any further legal bills and the divorce might be very costly. Jada couldn't just borrow another ten thousand when Rick Bruzeman demanded it. Her credit and her income wouldn't justify it. And Bruzeman was smart, not patient. Michelle doubted he'd wait long.

But what else were poor Jada's options? A bad lawyer at a lower price? Some kind of legal aid program? Michelle shook her head. She looked down at her watch—in her new alcove she couldn't see either clock on the wall—and saw that it was just touching three. She got up to stretch her legs and get another mug of coffee when she heard the altercation at the door.

She sighed and stretched and kept walking. Almost every day at bank closing time, some bozo arrived who just had to—*had to*—make a deposit or a withdrawal before the bank closed. And every day, their security people waited and waited for that moment so that one of them, making six bucks an hour on his feet all day, would be able to tell the rich suburbanite that he or she was out of luck. Michelle looked up at the clock and glanced behind her toward the door. The clock said exactly three and the guard was pushing, actually *pushing*, the door closed despite the fact that some guy in brown shoes and a dark suit had inserted his foot between the two glass doors. Michelle didn't know the guard; he wasn't either of their regulars, but he was pushing pretty hard. The tellers didn't even bother to look up at this kind of thing anymore, and the rest of the people on the floor seemed engaged in other activities.

But the man's foot was being crushed. The guard had put all of his weight against the door. Something had to give, but Michelle couldn't decide if it was going to be glass or bone.

"Stop it," she snapped out to the guard. "Stop it. You'll hurt him and the bank will be sued." The guard turned to look at her, and just for a moment, moved his shoulder back from the door.

It was enough to allow the customer to slip in. He limped toward her. She smiled, waiting for his thanks, but as he reached her he only asked, "Where's the manager's office?"

God, she thought, *I let him in, saved his foot, and he's going to sue us anyway, or at least complain.* "Is it really necessary to see the manager?" she asked with a smile. "Maybe I can help you."

"Your name Jada Jackson?"

"No," Michelle told him.

"Then I don't have to talk to you," he said, and moved past her toward the glass office wall at the back of the floor.

Michelle continued her slow walk over to the coffee. But she did keep an eye on the obnoxious guy. She saw him approach Anne, and Michelle poured her coffee while Anne buzzed into Jada. But as Anne did that, the rude guy walked past her desk, opened the office door, and walked right in! From where she stood, Michelle could see Jada turn a surprised face to the now-open door, while Anne sprang up from her chair in protest.

Michelle abandoned her mug and walked as quickly as she could toward the little scene. As she got to the doorway she could hear the man ask Jada if she was Mrs. Jada Jackson. Michelle was about to call out to her, to say, "No. Mrs. Jackson isn't in," but it was too late. Jada had already nodded her head and the process server—because that was what he was, and Michelle knew she should have realized it—reached into his inner coat pocket and pulled out a large envelope.

"These are for you," he said to Jada. "Consider yourself served." Then he turned and limped past Michelle and back toward the door. Michelle couldn't tell if he was limping because his foot had been crushed in the door or because he had a limp. But she turned back to Jada, who had already opened the envelope and was staring at its contents.

"Oh my God. Oh my God," Jada said—maybe it was closer to a moan—and sank into her seat. "It's a determination of temporary custody," she said, looking up at Michelle. "*He's* gotten temporary custody and *pendente lite.*" Michelle shook her head.

"But you haven't gone to court yet. You—"

Jada kept looking through the papers. "*He* went to court. *He* did. Clinton, the king of procrastination, went to court already." She looked back down at the papers. "Where the hell was Bruzeman? How did this happen?" Jada asked. "He expects me to pay child support and alimony while he keeps the children."

"That's ridiculous," Michelle said. "That is absolutely ridiculous. The court can't do that. Can it?"

For the second time, Jada took her eyes off the papers and looked at Michelle. "Yes, it can," she said. "We were going to get there first and try to do *this* to *him*. At least that's what I thought Bruzeman was doing." She looked back down at the documents in her hand.

"You know what Frank told me?" Michelle asked. Jada shook her head. "He said the post office had to recall their latest stamps."

"Why?"

"Because they had pictures of lawyers on them and people couldn't figure out which side to spit on," Michelle said. "Has Bruzeman cashed your check? You better put a stop on it."

"I better do that *and* get another lawyer. I can't believe this," she added, and she looked as if she really couldn't. "I have to pay for Clinton to keep my children away from me?" She shook her head, as if to clear it.

"It's insane," Michelle said. "Absolutely ridiculous. Your kids can't get along without you, and Clinton ignores them most of the time. You don't have to pay that, do you?"

In a sort of disembodied, floating kind of voice, Jada answered. "No. I don't have to pay it. I can just not pay and be thrown in jail for contempt of court."

21

A momentous meeting for all

Jada sat perfectly still in the passenger's seat beside Michelle. She was perfectly still, except for her hands, which were in her lap shaking. Jada knew that the trembling was an unbearable combination of fear and rage, but the knowledge didn't stop the tremors. Half an hour before, back in her office, she'd tried to sign a memo Anne had brought into her. The shaking had started then. She'd turned her back on Anne, but even so she could barely hold her pen and her signature had been unrecognizable.

The rest of her felt turned to stone, so cold and heavy that she was surprised the springs of Michelle's car didn't groan when she ponderously got into the bucket seat. Now she sat immobilized—except for her shaking hands—while Michelle tried to distract and comfort her. "Because it's a *better* approach," Michelle was saying. "I mean, it's important to get the best, but you tried with Bruzeman, and Clinton beat you to the punch. Anyway, these people have got to know what's what with women. I mean, the word 'women' is in their name. I wonder if all the clients are women? I wonder if all the lawyers are women."

Michelle was babbling, but she knew that after Jada had been served with the legal documents she had gone into some kind of frozen state.

Michelle had helped her cope. She'd taken Jada into the copy room with a stack of papers as if everything were normal. Had told her to lock the door, though it was against the rules; had taped an OUT OF ORDER sign to the door, and then had made a couple of calls on Jada's behalf. Now they were rolling along the Cross County Highway on their way to some legal aid place.

"Okay. So, anyway, they're going to know what to do about this because they've probably seen it a hundred million times. And they'll tell you what lawyer to go to instead of that dick Bruzeman. Plus, you won't have to pay that ridiculous retainer." Michelle stopped talking abruptly, then turned and glanced at Jada. "Oh, I'm sorry," she blurted. "It's just that I feel so bad and I don't know what to do to help you. You want me to be quiet?"

Jada shook her head. She couldn't speak, though. She couldn't believe that Clinton had gone as far as he did. Here was a man who had done next to nothing for years, yet who had now managed a kidnapping, a legal coup, and a supreme revenge effort, secretly, swiftly, and incredibly effectively. Jada thought she'd known the man she was married to, but this behavior was new—and very, very frightening. What else was he capable of ?

Michelle was keeping up a line of chatter and what she must have thought were comforting little clichés. They were maddening. "It's always darkest before the dawn," she said.

"Except when the morning brings tornadoes," Jada answered.

"Oh, come on. It's got to get better than this. Every cloud has a silver lining." Michelle was focused on the road as if at any moment the highway might plunge a thousand feet, or disappear into quick sand. Every few minutes, though, she'd pull her eyes off the obviously untrustworthy road and murmur encouragement to Jada. "Hold yourself together. Just keep yourself together."

Jada was trying. She lifted the papers in front of her. It made her dizzy, even sick, to read them, but she had to keep looking. Her future was in her lap. Phrases jumped out at her: *"Serving as major bread-earner," "unavailable to the children daily and on many evenings," "over-involved with her job," "ambitious for herself to the exclusion of her family responsibilities."* Her hands began shaking again uncontrollably, blurring the words.

The creased white papers on her lap felt like some kind of blanched tarantula, each fold revealing another frightening leg, another sting. Jada wanted to fling them off of her knees and stamp the lying, hurtful papers to death on the floor of Michelle's car, but she knew that, like the brooms that the sorcerer's apprentice chopped up, more of these tarantula papers would simply spring forth. Jada couldn't help but let a little moan escape her lips.

"It'll all be all right," Michelle said, as soothingly as she could. She sounded as if she was talking to Jenna, or even Frankie, but this wasn't some kindergarten insult.

"Don't you understand what he's saying here?" Jada asked, her voice harsher than she meant it to be, but not as angry as she felt. "It will *not* be all right. He's actually trying to say that I am an unfit mother. That my work took precedence over my children. That I was the bread-earner because I put my career first and now I have to continue to support him and the children, even though they moved out."

"That's ridiculous," Michelle cried, and swerved into the right lane. "Jada, you're a wonderful mother. You are the one who took care of *everything* for them. I know that. They know that. This is just some kind of mistake, some legal thing. You know how awful legal mistakes can be. I know, too. But we're fixing ours. And this will be fixed. I know it. They'll be able to straighten it all out at the clinic."

Jada shook her head and stared out the window. She guessed she was glad she didn't have to go back to Rick Bruzeman, but how good could a free clinic be? When one of her babies was sick, she went to a private physician every time. But over this, this most important issue in her life, she was going to go to some damn clinic?

What, really, did Michelle know about anything? She was a white girl who let her husband take care of her. She didn't understand about how tough life really was. Could any white woman really know about the prejudice that Jada constantly ran up against, about the fear she'd inherited from her immigrant parents about lawyers, authority, and the courts? Jada could understand how the police could break into an innocent citizen's life and ruin it, but could Michelle be trusted to see how easy it would be for Jada to be misrepresented, to be cataloged as a useless, ineffectual, even a bad mother. And how practical was Michelle's judgment? Michelle had brought her in to Bruzeman, after all; in a way, she held Michelle responsible for this, though that wasn't fair. It was obvious that Clinton—for the first and only time in his life—had gotten the jump on her, and no matter who she hired, he wouldn't have been faster than this Creskin lawyer had been. Jada glanced over at Michelle. She was trying to help, but sometimes Jada thought the gulf that separated them was too wide and deep to bridge.

As if reading her thoughts, Michelle touched her knee and begged, "Just try it." Then they pulled into the parking lot. "I heard from Ruth Adams that this place got her sister out of a lot of trouble." Michelle parked, and in the silence, Jada felt like putting her head on the dashboard and weeping. Instead she forced herself to touch her lapful of white tarantulas, lifting them all by the edge of the paper.

"I just noticed this place," Michelle said. "I mean, Ruth had told me about it, but it was a while ago and I'd forgotten. I guess I didn't really notice it until about a week ago." She opened the door, and Jada silently followed her into the lobby. "I like the idea of legal services for women." Michelle had to inquire about the location of the office, and after they walked up a dozen stairs they were there.

Jada sat in the waiting room beside a tiny Asian woman in a Chinese jacket who was rubbing one of her hands against the other, over and over and over again. On the other side of Michelle was an older woman with a black eye. *Fine,* Jada thought. *I'm here with the obsessives and the battered wives.*

O Lord, forgive me and grant me compassion for them, she thought. *I guess I don't deserve to be anywhere else.* Despite how hard she had tried to keep her family together, and her marriage going on some level, she'd failed. She'd made all the wrong decisions and she was as pathetic as these other miserable, frightened women. *My pride was false pride,* she admitted to God. *Me, a church-goer all these years.*

She sat slumped on the bench and let Michelle deal with the receptionist. Twice Michelle was called to the front and twice she came back with other questions. Then, after both of the other women had disappeared down the dark hallway, Jada's name was called and Michelle patted her on the shoulder. Jada thought for a moment about leaving Michelle behind. She didn't want her friend to see her collapsed into the defeated pool of misery she was about to turn into, but somehow she needed Michelle to stay with her, to comfort her, and to testify to this attorney so that whoever she met with now wouldn't give her the condescending looks she'd received from Rick Bruzeman. Or, worse, believe that any of these disgusting allegations could be true.

As Jada stood up, she gently circled Michelle's pale wrist with her dark index finger and thumb and led her down the hall. She didn't ask. She only raised her brows. Michelle smiled and actually seemed pleased.

The receptionist opened a door and the two of them found themselves in a tiny, maximally cluttered office. There were two empty chairs surrounded by files and there was a young woman—younger than either Jada or Michelle, it seemed—sitting in a chair behind the small, messy desk.

The woman stood up. She had dark, wildly curly hair, small but bright eyes with long lashes, and a wide mouth painted an odd salmon color. "Hi, I'm Angie Romazzano-Wakefield," she said, then extended her hand to shake Jada's. Jada didn't need to have her hand shaken or to be sociable. She just put the white tarantula into this little girl's palm. Then she collapsed into one of the seats, only to find the back was sprung and hit her unevenly in the shoulders.

Michelle began to speak. Jada noticed her voice was high-pitched, almost breathy. "This is the most unfair thing in the world," she said. "My girlfriend has spent the last five years keeping her family together and then her husband, who hasn't earned a dime in all that time, has an affair, disappears with their children, and wants alimony *and* child support. He can't do that, can he?"

The hyphenated girl was looking through the paper tarantula. "It seems he has done it," she said, and shook her head. She looked through the papers, awkwardly turning them as she read. Finally she looked up. "He'd done worse. He's requested temporary custody, and there are more than hints at unfitness as a mother, while he presents himself as a stable and domestic influence in the home. Is that so?" she asked Jada.

Jada's eyes filled with tears of rage. Before she could choke out any answer, Mich spoke for her. "Look, my girlfriend took a job as a teller, making no bucks, so that she could put milk and eggs on the table. They ate macaroni for months. And in the last five years, she worked her way up to branch manager." Michelle looked at Jada, who looked away. "Nobody helped her. Nobody wanted her in that job. She was just too good to ignore. But she was also home every night. I saw her. She defrosted chicken, she made Spanish rice, she made sure that the kids ate broccoli, for God's sake. Mine won't. Jada even took them to church, all dressed up and scrubbed." Michelle stopped and the small room was silent. Jada looked at her friend with gratitude; someone was sticking up for her. "Meanwhile that jerk of a husband of hers, he sat on his hands all day long, except when he was playing around with somebody. Then he grabs the kids and is gone. And she hasn't seen them since. It would kill me. She's stronger, so she's just going crazy. Wouldn't it kill you?"

"I can't even imagine it."

It was her tone of voice, the real compassion that Jada heard in it, that started her falling apart. She took a deep shuddering breath, let it out, but her next one rattled and disintegrated like a junker car on a race track. Then she was wailing, gurgling, and coughing. She never cried, so she wasn't any good at it. She put her hands up to cover her face so that neither of them could see her anger, her terror, and her shame.

The lawyer girl reached out, and didn't pat but actually grabbed Jada's hand. Her own hand was surprisingly strong and hard. "Listen," she said, "*you* didn't do anything wrong. *He's* behaved dishonestly and then he found a smart, remorseless lawyer first. This can all be corrected. I can't save your marriage, but the clinic *can* save your children and better settle your divorce."

Jada looked up and wiped her eyes with her knuckles, realizing as she did that it was exactly the gesture Kevon used. "But right now I can't see the children, right?" she asked. "Right now I have to give them up." She reached over to the tarantula papers. "And all that money. Almost everything I make. And he can be with his girlfriend, an unemployed slut, while I have to work to support my family, which he's stolen."

The lawyer—Angela Something-Something—moved her hand to Jada's wrist and squeezed it even harder. To Jada it felt good, as if she were pulling Jada back to a world she could live in. "Look, he's making allegations here that simply are not true," she said. "It's nasty, but it's not serious. In fact, it's typical. And we have allegations of our own. The only problem is that he moved first. So, for the moment, he has a leg up. But, of course, that makes his crotch a little more vulnerable," she assured them. "Meanwhile, I'll immediately get visitation for you. Maybe for as soon as tomorrow. We've got some very good friends at family court and I'll speak to the judge and have a discussion with your husband's lawyer."

"I'd like Frank to go over there and have a discussion with Clinton. Wearing a pair of brass knuckles," Mich said. "I just never imagined—"

As the lawyer shook her head, her long curls flopped around. "No, no, no," she interrupted. "We have a lot to do here that's effective. *And* legal. It's just going to take some work. The clinic staff will petition for custody, we'll have testimony and fiscal proof about your forced employment, your competence. We'll have witnesses to confirm your involved motherhood status. We may have to get psychologists to talk to the children, and we may also have to find someone to testify about your husband's relationship with"—she looked over the papers— "Tonya Green."

She paused, glanced across the desk, and Jada no longer felt that the woman was weak and incompetent. She trusted her, even if perhaps she shouldn't yet, since talk was cheap.

"Each one is a small step," the woman was saying, "but pulled together, they *will* make a compelling case." Jada looked up. This girl sounded calm and trustworthy. *Oh, Lord,* Jada thought, *maybe this woman is the way out of this nightmare.*

"I'll petition for visitation today," the lawyer said. She looked up at Jada. "I promise I'll get you your children back."

"So you'll take the case? You'll take care of everything?" Jada asked and was shocked to hear how childlike she sounded.

"Well, the clinic has to present each incoming case to the board to decide about its disposition, but I think a custody and support case as extreme as this would certainly be the kind of thing we want to help with."

"I don't want someone else to do it," Jada said. "If the clinic will take me, I want you."

"Well, I'm not the most experienced—"

"I don't care. You're the most caring," Jada said.

Then Michelle knocked Jada gently with her foot. Jada looked over to her friend, who was mouthing something, but Jada didn't get it. Michelle kicked her gently again. When Jada still didn't respond, Michelle raised her voice. "Fees?" she asked. "How much will this cost?"

"Yeah, what about fees?" Jada asked, remembering Bruzeman's retainer. God, she couldn't . . . "I know this place is called a clinic, but it's not free, is it?"

"We have a sliding scale. But outside expert testimony, filing fees, and court charges are usually the client's responsibility. Though we do have a fund . . . for special situations." Angie paused and tried to smile. "Look, you have a lot on your mind right now," she said. "You pay what you can afford and if you can't afford anything, we'll still represent you. The clinic is underwritten in its work. That's why we can afford to be here at all." Angie smiled and stood up. "Look, can I get you two a cup of coffee?"

Jada took her other hand and wrapped it around Angie's so that Angie's fingers were trapped around Jada's wrist. "Thank you," she said. "Thank you, thank you, thank you."

Standing, Angie looked even younger—she must have been five years younger than Jada, but now Jada didn't wonder if she was any good as a lawyer or whether she could get a judge to listen to her. She was a little dynamo, and she had compassion. Suddenly Jada was grateful to Michelle for bringing her here, and ashamed of her earlier thoughts about "white girls."

"Come on," Angie was saying. "We have fresh danish. I love to talk war strategies over pastries. There's almost no situation that can't be improved by carbohydrates."

Jada saw Michelle smile.

But at the door, Angie paused. "No joke, Mrs. Jackson. You'll see your kids in the next forty-eight hours."

As she left the room, Jada herself managed, for a moment, to get some of the grimness out of her expression.

22

In which Angela decides how much square feet one girl needs

Angie had decided she better find her own place to live. After her lunch with JoAnn Metzger and her own client load had grown, she felt pretty confident that she'd be able to live on the modest salary they promised. The question was where should she live. And how.

Angie had never really lived alone. She'd spent her college years, and then her time in law school, bunking with roommates. After graduation she shared another woman's apartment for only a few months before she moved in with Reid. But she knew it wasn't right for her to continue living at her father's, she knew nobody here to share a place with, and there was no room for her at her mother's. She wasn't exactly sure how to go about it—where she wanted to live or exactly what she could afford. But she knew she didn't want a roommate and she knew she missed her things. She had a bunch of stuff in storage she was paying for—well, her dad had been paying for—and it was time for her to pull herself together. She certainly wasn't going back to Marblehead.

At the office, she asked Bill.

"Well, where exactly do you want to live?" he asked. "I mean, there's a *h-u-u-g-g-e* difference between White Plains and Scarsdale and it ain't the nine miles between them." He told her about the garden apartment he and his boyfriend had and gave her the name of his broker. "He's an evil queen, but he knows his real estate."

He also told her which paper had the best listings, and that day at lunchtime Angela bought one and sat alone in the corner at the counter of the Blue Bird Coffee Shop, the real estate section spread out in front of her.

CUTE AND SUNNY, read one headline. COZY ONE-BEDROOM, UTILITIES INCLUDED IN RENT, GREAT VIEWS, GREAT CLSTS. A DEAL AT $1200. Angie opened her eyes wide. Twelve hundred dollars was a deal for a one-bedroom apartment around here? She looked farther down the long column. COZY GROUND FLOOR STUDIO. QUIET, FACING BACK, SMALL PATIO. $600. NO DOGS. She was just circling it when she heard a voice behind her.

"Forget it," he said, and Angie turned to see Michael Rice, the attorney from the clinic, there.

"Looking for an apartment?" he asked.

She nodded, not sure whether she welcomed his interest or not.

"That first one you marked is way overpriced and the second one is gonna be the black hole of Calcutta." He indicated the stool next to her and raised his brows in a mind-if-I-join-you? expression.

Angie reached over and gave the stool a little spin. Michael sat down and leaned in toward the paper. "I just got finished doing this," he said. "And I know the language of real estate ads." He looked at the second one she'd circled. "Let me translate," he said. "'Cozy' means way too small. 'Quiet' and 'ground floor' together mean very, *very* dark. Sometimes ground floor isn't dark, but only if it says 'south facing' or 'light flooded' or both. Plus, if the rent's that cheap, you're not going to like the neighborhood. Got it?"

Angie looked up at him and smiled, partly amused and partly bemused. "I'm not sure I've gotten the whole language down yet," she said. "What about this one? 'Fabulous four. Sunny, cheerful. Great views. Laundry room, gym. Dining room could be used as extra bedroom.'"

Michael shook his head. "That means transient high-rise. Near the train, 'cause that's where the majority of the big buildings are. Lots of commuters to New York. Plus, they didn't list the rent, and when they don't include the price, it's always way expensive."

Angie nodded. "Did you write real estate ads in your previous job?"

"Maybe in one of my previous lives," Michael joked. "Riverside penthouse, just steps from the Nile. Great view of pyramids, won't last long."

Angie laughed. "Doing this is hard," she said.

"No, reading the ads is hard," he told her. "It makes choices seem so confusing. Once you get out there and look, you know right away what's out of the question because it's too grim, and what's out of the question because it's too expensive. So then you see what's possible, and you find a broker who actually listens to you, and then . . . something comes up."

Angie smiled and just then her grilled cheese arrived. "You make it sound easy," she said as she folded the paper and put it away.

"Oh yeah," Michael laughed. "Life is easy." Then he got up and went to stand at the take-out counter. "I've got a hot case back at the office," he said, "or else I'd join you. But you might want to call the broker I used. She's a chatty old thing, but she knows her business. Esther Anderson. She's listed. Give her a ring." He picked up his food and waved as he left.

To her own surprise, Angie felt a little tug of disappointment. *Hey, he's probably married,* one part of her brain told the other part. *So what?* the other part said. *I was just thinking of a lunch. At a counter. Yeah,* the first part of her brain answered. *That's what Lisa probably said.* Angie was about to reach for her grilled cheese and side of cole slaw when she suddenly felt sick to her stomach. So sick that, after a minute, she had to get up, get to the ladies room, and throw up into the sink because she couldn't make it all the way to a stall.

So, Angie began a new social life: at the end of her business day, she would meet or be met by one of a variety of brokers and drive to apartments all over the area. Instead of letting it feel like work, or the desperate scramblings of a woman newly alone, Angie decided to make it fun. It was a theater event—the cast was the broker, and sometimes the co-

broker, the set was the apartment or the condo or occasionally the little
house she went to look at.

Sometimes the cast was a little flat, a little boring, but every now and
then she'd hit someone like Mrs. Louise D'Orio, a woman who believed
that lip lines had nothing to do with lipstick application and that hats were
always appropriate. Mrs. D'Orio—"Call me Lou-Lou. All my friends do"—
would go through a space commenting on *everything*, from the window
treatments to the shelf paper. Mrs. D'Orio also explained how everything
should be, where Angie should put cup hooks for her mugs and which out-
let would be the best one to plug the coffeemaker into.

But Michael's suggestion was the best. Esther Anderson was terrific.
Angie knew that she was too chatty and would bug the shit out of her
mother, but underneath the compulsive talking and judgments, Angie
liked the woman's basic honesty. "You could do better than this, dear,"
she would say. Or, "This one's definitely not for you. It wouldn't have
worked for Mr. Rice, either." Or, "This would work if only it had more
closet space. You have to be able to put your stuff someplace and don't
start with those armoires. I tell you, they don't work."

It was in the apartment without enough closet space that Angie
became suddenly dizzy and then very, very nauseated. What was it with
her? Her emotional instability had gone to her stomach. She gestured to
Mrs. Anderson and then rushed to the bathroom, where her retching
noise had to be clearly audible. She flushed the toilet a few times,
washed her mouth at the sink, and then had to wipe it on her sleeve
since there wasn't even a sheet of toilet paper left in the abandoned bathroom.

Angie tried to think about why she felt so sick. She had really been
taking the apartment hunting gently; her father didn't want her to move
out and her mother was willing to help in any way she could. But it still
felt scary and lonely. Was she so frightened to live alone that it made her
puke? She shook her head, patted a little water on her face, and wiped it
with her other sleeve. She didn't feel flu-ish and she had no other symptoms. But maybe she should go to a doctor.

When she came out and joined Mrs. Anderson, the woman was looking through a kitchen cabinet below a bookshelf. "You couldn't put wine

here," she said. "Heat rises from the steam pipes. You'd have vinegar in a month." She stood up and turned to Angie. "Was it something you ate, dear?" she asked.

"I don't know."

"Maybe it's nerves," Mrs. Anderson told her. She put her hand on Angie's shoulder. "At least you know it's not morning sickness. It's not morning."

In the car driving back to her father's, Angie felt sick again, but not sick enough to throw up. What she felt was sick about the possibility that she might be pregnant. She tried to work backward, tried to figure out the last time she and Reid had made love. It was painful to think about, but she remembered the night before their anniversary, or was it the night before *that*? As she drove through the darkness she tried to count forward on her fingers, and tried to remember the last time she'd gotten her period. She hadn't come to her dad's with anything, not even a toothbrush, much less a tampon, and he certainly didn't have any at his house. *So,* Angie thought with anxiety tightening her neck and chest and even her throat, *since I haven't bought or borrowed any Tampax, I haven't had my period since . . .* She tried to count backward, but simply couldn't.

Of course, she told herself, she was nervous and upset. Of course she was. She knew that. That could make her skip. She also told herself she should stop at the next CVS or Rexall and pick up a home pregnancy test. But she kept driving.

Because if she was pregnant, what in the world would she do?

23

Consisting of milk, cookies, and vomit

Michelle stopped on her way back from dropping Jada at her car in the bank parking lot and did a quick grocery run—just for some skim milk, dog treats for Pookie, a head of lettuce, and a few vegetables because Frank liked them fresh. Everything looked picked over and tired. She put some produce in a bag, then stopped at a pyramid of apples, choosing one near the top. She knew they were waxed, and hated for Jenna to eat them, but her daughter loved apples. As Michelle was about to add another to the bag, she noticed that the skin which looked so red, so perfect, collapsed under the pressure of her fingers like a puffball mushroom collapsing. She realized she hadn't had time either to bake or stop at the bakery, so she threw a bag of Oreos onto the checkout counter as a guilty afterthought. She should at least have gotten Fig Newtons, but she weakened because the kids loved these.

She drove a little faster than she should have on the way home, but that was justified because it allowed her to pull into the driveway before the kids were dropped off by the bus. She'd just gotten placemats out and put some Oreos on Frankie Junior's favorite plate—the one with pictures of Peter Rabbit that he'd had since he was a baby—when the children walked in the door. Pookie went nuts, wagging not only his tail but his entire butt and doing a little dance of welcome. All of a sudden Michelle was so glad to see them that she felt like doing a dance. Instead she hugged Jenna a little more tightly than she meant to.

"*Mo-o-m!*" Jenna said, dragging out the syllable in the new pre-teen voice of annoyance she'd recently developed. She pushed Michelle away, but she did it with good humor. "I got a B on my spelling test," she added to show there were no hard feelings.

Michelle stopped the automatic question ("Why not an A?") that her own mother would have asked and instead gave her daughter a big smile. "That's great," she said while she helped Frankie take his turtleneck off. "I know you studied hard for it. Good girl. Daddy will be proud."

Jenna nodded. "If I hadn't messed up 'neighbor,' I would have gotten an A-. *Shouldn't* neighbor be spelled N-A-B-O-R-E?" she asked, aggrieved.

"If the world was fair, but it isn't," Michelle said, then straightened Frankie's dark, dark hair. "How was school for *you*, sweetie?" she asked her son.

"My snack was good," Frankie shrugged, then made straight for the kitchen table and climbed into his chair. That was positive for now. Obviously, things had calmed down and his pants had been dry. "Oreos! Two snacks! This *is* a good day," he said, already reaching for the cookies.

Michelle had to smile and felt such gratitude that it made the troubles she and Frank had gone through, at least for the moment, seem small. She had her children, she had her marriage, and whatever it took, they would get through their legal problems. For a moment she thought of Jada, probably alone now in her kitchen, and then she couldn't help but push the dark thought away. She'd think about it later, call her later, maybe invite her over.

"Can I have juice instead of milk?" Jenna asked as she took her seat at the table.

Michelle shook her head. "Juice *after* homework, if you want it. Right now you need the calcium." She poured out the glass of milk, as well as a cup for Frankie. Then, remembering herself for the first time in about a week, she found her packet of vitamins, took three Rolaids, and began to swallow them all down with the skim milk.

"You know what happened that was terrible?" Jenna asked, and Michelle nearly choked on the last mouthful. Had there been another emotional atrocity on the school bus or in the classroom? Things seemed to have really calmed down for the kids. Thank God, people forgot things quickly: there was always a new scandal in the paper, and Frank, as he predicted, hadn't been charged with anything. But that important legal distinction didn't prevent cruelty to her kids. "What?" she asked her daughter. What fresh hell was this?

"Mrs. Blackwell gave us so much math homework and almost all of it is word problems for the weekend." Jenna looked up at her mother. "Do you hate word problems?"

"I really do," Michelle said with more enthusiasm than usual. She kept the smile of relief to herself. "But your daddy is good at them," she reminded her daughter.

Jenna nodded, then dawdled over the cookies as she always did, separating them and licking off the cream before she ate them. Frankie grabbed and crunched down more than his share until Michelle stopped him.

"Can I play with Kevon today?" he asked.

Michelle shook her head. She couldn't explain about Kevon's disappearance now. She thought again of Jada, all alone, and put the thought away. "Uh-uh," she told her son, "but you can watch whatever video you want, and then play with Daddy. He's home early."

At least he should be. His truck had been parked outside. Where was Frank, she wondered? Usually you couldn't be in the house with him without knowing his whereabouts—whether you wanted to or not. He was always playing music or nailing something together or watching a ball game at top volume or yelling on the phone.

She turned to her daughter. "Jenna, stop playing with those cookies and eat them. I want to see you at that table with your math in front of you when I get back down here." Then she took Frankie by the hand and led him into the family room. Macy's had already delivered the new couch, and with the books back on the shelves along with the two lamps she'd picked up at the lighting store near the bank, the room actually looked good again. She made a mental note to stop tomorrow at Pier 1 and get some throw pillows in cheerful colors—maybe blue and yellow, she thought—because the kids loved to lounge on them and all the old ones had been destroyed. So had Pookie's wicker dog bed. She'd get one of those, too. She hoped Bruzeman got back every cent and more for them when they sued.

"Okay," she explained to Frankie, "you get to be the first to sit on the nice new couch and you can watch one video—whatever you want—before dinner." Frankie grinned up at her, made his selection, and she popped in *Fern Gully*. Then she went down the hall to search for Frank, Pookie padding along behind her.

He wasn't in the shop he'd built himself at the back of the two-car garage. Then, when she first put her head into his office, she thought that he wasn't in there because the room was dark and quiet. But as she was about to turn away and close the door, she heard a rustle and jumped. She turned back. This room had also been savaged by the cops, and they hadn't really fixed it yet except to right the furniture and clean up the broken bits and torn papers.

Pookie made his welcome noise as he approached a darker part of the darkness. Now, in the light she let in from the hall, Michelle could see the dog was greeting Frank, who was sitting in the dark at his desk, absolutely still in the torn and battered office chair—the one thing the cops hadn't ripped up any worse than it had been torn before. Frank had always liked it just as it was. He'd taken it from his old bedroom at his mother's house and carted it to their first apartment, then to the duplex they'd lived in, and finally to their own home.

Seeing him there, sitting in it in the darkness, one hand clutching the worn plastic arms, the other absently stroking the dog, filled Michelle with a sick feeling. He'd been so strong through all of this. Was he finally feeling the terrible strain? Despite her obvious presence in the doorway, he didn't even turn to acknowledge her. As she adjusted to the dimness, Michelle could see that her husband's eyes were open, so he wasn't sleeping.

"Frank?" she whispered, not because she was afraid the children could hear her—the office was down a long hall behind the dining room, close to the garage entrance—but because she was afraid to speak any louder to him. He seemed in some kind of daze, some faraway state. "Frank?" she whispered again.

Very, very slowly he swiveled the chair away and then toward her again. But his eyes didn't follow the movement. For a crazy moment she thought of the Jesus picture that used to hang in her mother's living room, wherever they lived at the time. The eyes followed her wherever she went, making sure, as her mother warned her, that she dusted even under the furniture and behind the books. But this was the opposite. Frank's body and face were directly in front of her, but his eyes had stayed focused somewhere beyond the window, though the shade was closed.

Michelle was frightened, and as usual, her fear froze her. She was afraid to either close the door and be alone in the darkness with Frank or turn on the light and reveal anything more to herself. But even across the room she could feel her husband's pain, as palpable as the new couch their son was sitting on upstairs.

"What is it, Frank?" she forced herself to ask. "Are you okay?" She thought of Jenna and Frankie, looking forward to their evening with Daddy. It didn't look as if he was up to it. Exhausted as she was from her afternoon with Jada, she would comfort him if he had to, finally, break down over this. And she'd cover with the kids.

"What is it Frank?" she repeated, her voice gentle.

"An indictment's going to be handed down," Frank said, his own voice low and dead. Michelle wasn't sure for a moment what he meant.

"They've indicted the police?" she asked.

"Not the police! They've indicted *me*," Frank said fiercely, as if she were an idiot. "They've indicted me, Michelle."

She couldn't help it—she took a step or two backward until she was leaning against the bookshelves. "But for what?" she asked. "And how could they indict you? I mean . . ." Her brain was spinning.

"I don't know. There was some kind of secret grand jury. Believe it or not, it's legal, Bruzeman says there was probably some kind of investigation going on for months. The prosecutor must have convinced the judge that they had substantial proof and a need for confidentiality. It's been convened this whole last week."

"But didn't *anybody*, didn't Bruzeman know? Our assemblymen? Your county friends? Anyone? I mean—"

"If they knew, they didn't say," Frank admitted, his voice harsh with anger. "What were all those lunches, those campaign contributions for? Bruzeman—" Frank tried to calm himself and ran his hand through his thick hair. "I have to trust him. He's the best in Westchester. As long as I can pay him, he's trustworthy. But I . . ." He stopped again and this time Michelle heard the panic in his voice. Which panicked her.

"What does this all mean?" she asked.

"Nothing. It means nothing."

"Don't tell me that, Frank. Don't say it means nothing. An indictment—it must mean something." Her wide mouth trembled. "I'm not a child, Frank. Don't treat me like one. Don't protect me. Were you trying to pay someone off to get the thing to go away? Are you trying to find out what the DA thinks he's got?"

"We tried both," Frank admitted.

"So what happened? You told me they had nothing. You told me there would be no indictment. But there is. So what's going on?"

There was silence between them for a little while. Michelle could feel the blood surging in her head and hear it inside her ears. She didn't think she took a breath until he answered.

"The indictment will be handed down soon, maybe Monday," he said. "I'm going to be accused of being some kind of mastermind of a cocaine and amphetamine distribution ring."

Michelle gasped then, so loudly Frank heard her and looked away.

"Bruzeman found out about it just in time to warn us, but not in time to prevent it." Frank shook his head. He looked at her again. "I'm innocent, Michelle. You know that."

"But—" She stopped. It was best to say nothing, but she couldn't in the end. "But Frank, you promised me this wouldn't go any further. It's been a mistake, hasn't it?"

He swiveled the chair toward her. "Of course, it's been a mistake," he said. "Do you think I'm some kind of a drug dealer?" he asked. "Would I be spending my days freezing my ass off on roofs with bozos working for me?" He stuck his arms out in the room between them. "Would my goddamn hands be chapped and cracked and bleeding if I was dealing drugs instead of fixing shingles?" He dropped his arms and turned away, lowering his voice. "I can't believe you'd ask me that," he almost moaned. "Did they find anything here? Am I driving a new Mercedes, or an eight-year-old Chevy van? Do we have a million dollars in a bank account you haven't told me about? I can't believe you'd ask me," he repeated, his voice low.

Tears rose in Michelle's eyes. She couldn't believe *any* of this. It was *all* a mistake, *all* wrong, and yet it could ruin them. How could she—how could *they*—be picked out of the universe and be tortured in this way?

"How can all this be happening?" she said out loud. "How could they have a secret grand jury? I never heard of that. How could . . ." She wanted to ask how he could turn so ugly on her, but it was stupid to even bring it up. He was beside himself, and she was . . . well, she wasn't even sure what she was, except suddenly very sick to her stomach. The vitamins and the skim milk were churning.

It took another ten seconds for her to know that she wouldn't be able to keep them down. She ran to the door, out into the tiny hall, and managed to get into Frank's shop where she heaved painfully once or twice before she vomited onto the cement floor, as close to the drain as she could get. She gasped and heaved again, and then yet again, holding her long hair up, away from what she was spewing. She felt Frank's hand on her back. She couldn't move or speak, even to acknowledge his presence. Instead she stayed crouched in her position, ready for a dry heave. But none came.

Slowly she straightened herself, wiped her wide mouth with one hand and her watery eyes with the other. She hoped the children hadn't heard. She turned to look at her husband. "My God, Frank, what are we going to do?" she asked, and she knew her voice sounded younger, more childish than Jenna's.

He put a hand on each of her shoulders. This time he looked at her directly, his deep brown eyes melting with pain and sorrow. "I'm not guilty, Michelle. You know that, don't you?" She nodded, trying to pull some air into her sensitive nostrils. "So we just fight it," he said. "We stick together, we try to protect each other and the kids, and we fight it. An indictment isn't a conviction. I don't know why they're out to get me. But I swear to you, they won't."

He put his arms around her. She averted her head so he wouldn't smell her sour breath. "What will it cost?" she whispered. She thought of the ten thousand dollars that Bruzeman had asked for from Jada. How much had Frank already had to give that slimy little . . . ? "What will it cost, Frank?" she asked.

"Don't worry about it," he said. "I can take care of that end. You just take care of the children." He pulled himself away from her enough so he could look her in the face again. "You just take care of Frankie and Jenna and me, baby. Can you do that?"

Although she wasn't sure if she could, Michelle nodded. He grabbed her and held her tight against his chest. Michelle stretched her long arms around his back and tried to hold him as she nodded, her sharp chin on his shoulder. They stood there, in the slight chill of the shop, while the sour smell from the drain slowly filled the room.

"We'll beat this," he said. "I promise you we will. And I'll protect you." His voice broke a little, and more than anything else, that felt heartbreaking to Michelle. "Just stick with me now," he begged. "Please, Mich, stick with me now."

24

Wherein Jada's body is cleansed but her spirit is broken

Jada sat in the full bath, the hot water still trickling in. She was a shower kind of girl, in and out quickly, but in what now seemed like the only safe spot in the whole, empty house, the only solace she could find was in this ceramic corner of the bathroom. It was only here, in the tub, that her hands stopped trembling, though her mind continued to race.

She supposed her behavior was bizarre; she'd probably taken four— or was it five?—baths today. But she felt drawn to the tub; she would sit in it, keeping the water as hot as she could bear, until her lethargy lightened when anxiety descended and wouldn't let her sit still any longer. So she'd get up, towel off, dress again, and attempt some minor household task—which she'd leave unfinished—or flip on the TV, only to find herself, an hour or so later, drawn back up to the bathroom, once again turning on the taps and filling the tub.

Luckily, she hadn't been in the tub when her mother called last night for their ritual once-a-week long-distance call. Hearing her mother's warm voice, Jada found comfort, but she had spared both her parents any of the details of what was going on. When Mama had asked to speak to the children, Jada had said they were playing at the neighbors. Lying felt low, but she knew Jesus would forgive her. The one thing Jada *didn't* have to worry about was her mother asking about Clinton—the story with him never changed.

Jada loved her mother but didn't want to worry her. She also didn't want to admit just how very right her mother had been. Yet, hanging up, she was swept by regret that she hadn't been able to be honest with her. Her mama only wanted the best for her, Jada knew. How could she be so proud, so pig-headed, as to not confide in her blood family? Pride was her downfall.

Her only rationale was that once the lawyer got this into family court, once she'd seen her kids, she would have issues she could face and share. Once she had the children back, she'd truly be delighted to change the locks, to get Clinton out forever, to mentally adjust and go on as a single mom. And her mother *wouldn't* judge her harshly, though none of the islanders or any member of their church approved of divorce. Jada knew her mother wouldn't even mention that she'd always known exactly how trashy and low Clinton was. Though last night Jada had been grateful that she'd had some human contact, someone to talk to while she waited for her chance with the children, the call had had a very painful backlash.

The water felt good. She was, after all, an Aquarius; it was an air sign, but she always felt it should have been a water sign. She raised her knees a little bit so she could settle the back of her neck against the tub. Exposed above the water, her knees looked like two dark islands in a sea of foam. They reminded her of the Caribbean, where Nevis and a few other places rose straight and dark out of the aqua sea. Jada suddenly wished she could be with her parents, home again. Not this place, but their home in Barbados, where she actually had never lived but had only visited. Home there, safe with her mama and her babies.

Last night had been the longest in her life. She'd walked from room to empty room, turning lights on, shutting them off, and moving on. The empty children's rooms frightened her, the kitchen seemed abandoned, and the living and dining rooms too big to sit in alone. Her bedroom was worst of all. She could never get back into the bed she'd shared with Clinton. She'd slept fitfully on the sofa, woke up at five, and then this morning had stretched out endlessly. But at noon today, she reminded herself, she would see her children.

The Romazzano-Wakefield woman over at the legal clinic had managed somehow to get through to the family court judge and had set up temporary visitation. Jada had stopped the check to Bruzeman and closed the loan file. It seemed that a free lawyer was as effective—and certainly more comforting—than a cold, expensive one. It was hard to say with an attorney, but Jada felt that Angie's NUP was a good one. When she'd gotten the call that she could see Shavonne, Kevon, and Sherrilee—if only for two hours today and another two on Sunday—she had been so grateful. Angie Romazzano had done it speedily, and although Jada didn't like the limits—two hours was an extra insult and ridiculous—it had been heaven to know for certain she'd see her babies.

She soaked in the hot water and it occurred to her that she still hadn't cried all of her pain out. She wasn't a weeper. But then she wondered whether her need for the constant drip of hot water into the tub was some externalized form of tears. She'd been dry-eyed and awake all last night and this morning—except for the brief catnap she'd managed on the sofa. The only sounds all that time had been the drip of hot water.

Well, that and the phone; once the lawyer with the news, and then two calls from Michelle to check up on her. Michelle, bless her heart, had called twice, inviting her over for dinner and then later, past eleven, just to check in on her. Michelle had sounded more upset than Jada was, but then she was more emotional. She'd even suggested she stay with Jada in her place for the night.

"Frank can watch the kids. Just so the silence doesn't get to you. You know me, I'm never silent," Michelle had tried to joke.

But though Jada had truly, deeply, appreciated the invitations, she didn't have the strength for company. She had to get through this part alone. After all, alone might be the state she was in for her entire future.

She glanced now at her wristwatch, languidly curled over the side of the tub, and realized she'd better get ready. She rose from the water with a shiver and wrapped herself in the still-damp towel she'd used from her last bath. Jada walked into the bedroom, avoided looking at her bed, and opened her closet door. *What do you wear when you get to visit your legally abducted children?* she wondered. She pulled down a pair of Gap khakis and went for one of her Equadorian sweaters. Both were easy to shrug into but looked cheerful, as if she'd made an effort. She was about to try and tame her hair when the phone rang for the first time that morning.

She rushed to it, with every unspeakable horror running through her head: Clinton refusing to let her see the kids; her lawyer calling to say the judge had changed his mind; one of the babies sick and in the hospital. Her hands started to tremble again, but she managed to lift the phone off the hook, then fumbled to get it to her ear.

"Hello," she said, and her voice was raspy. She realized she hadn't spoken aloud in hours and hours.

"Jada?" Michelle's voice asked. "Are you sick?"

"Only mentally," Jada told her.

"Do you want me to drive you over?"

"No. I can make it to my mother-in-law's on my own," Jada said. "But if you want to, you could follow to make sure that I don't shoot Clinton or his mother."

"Have you got a gun?" Michelle asked.

Even in her pain, Jada felt her heart expand toward Michelle, sometimes so gullible, but always so kind. She thought of the bitches who had sent back Michelle's brownies and decided that if she *was* going to go postal, Jada would take them out, as well. "No, I don't have a gun. How many female suburban bank branch managers do you know who pack a weapon?" She didn't even get a giggle from Michelle, but she knew Michelle was taking this almost as hard as she was. "So while I'm asking questions, what do I say to the kids? I don't know what Clinton's told them. And what do I *do* with them? I don't even have time to bring them back here if I have to return them to Yonkers. I mean, the round trip would use up my two hours."

"Jada, what you do is you tell them you love them. That this will be over soon," Michelle said. "Just like I told my kids. You tell them that this fight that Daddy and you are having will be over soon. And it wouldn't hurt to find out about their daily routine. Has he taken them to a new school? Who's cooking? You know."

"Right," Jada agreed.

"Did you pack some extra things for them for the meantime?" Michelle asked. "You know, favorite T-shirts or slippers or like that?"

Jada nodded, then cleared her throat and managed to tell Michelle she already had done that during her night wanderings.

"But I hate to take even one more of their things out of here," Jada admitted. "It makes this even less their home and that place—wherever they are—more."

"Oh, Jada, that place must be so empty for them without you. And your house must be . . . hell. You must be so scared."

"You have no idea," Jada said. "To be in danger of—"

"I do, Jada. I really do."

"Oh, Lord, it's almost noon. I gotta go." Jada hung up, put on her Reeboks, and checked in her purse for the car keys, the house keys, Kleenex, her lipstick, change for parking meters, money for lunch, gloves, and lip balm. She picked up the bag of things she'd packed for the children, then, armed with everything but an actual revolver in her old Coach bag, she went out to the garage and got in the car.

Clinton made her wait almost twenty minutes before he came out into the cold, ushering Shavonne and Kevon, and holding Sherrilee. For some reason Jada was unwilling to get out of the car and stand beside him, perhaps because she might do him violence if she did. Instead she leaned across the passenger seat in the front, threw open that door, and twisted to unlock and open the door behind her. She was unrolling her window an inch as Shavonne rushed into the front seat, slamming the door behind her, while Kevon scrambled into the back over the baby's carseat.

"You're late," she said to Clinton. "I'm not going to bring them back until twenty after four." As she spoke, she saw his mother, a hulking dark shape descending the rickety stairs. Clinton didn't say a word. She tried to read his face to see if there was guilt or shame written on it, but it was as blank as a brown paper bag. He put Sherrilee into the baby seat and closed the door. Meanwhile, Shavonne had climbed across the front seat and had her arms around Jada's neck. Shavonne, who had disdained PDAs—public displays of affection—for the last year or more. Jada cupped her daughter's head with her hand and kissed her hard on the cheek. "Hey, kids, I'm taking you for a treat," she said.

"Two hours and they're back," Clinton said, and as if to emphasize what he was doing, he looked at his watch. Jada said nothing at all. She just hit the accelerator and tried to burn rubber as she pulled the Volvo away from the man who was ruining her life.

"I want nuddets! I want nuddets! I want nuddets!" Kevon chanted for the sixtieth time.

Jada turned into the parking lot and pulled into a space. She took a deep breath.

"But do you want sauce, do you want sauce, do you want sauce?" Jada sang back. *Might as well join them,* she figured. Sometimes go with their flow.

Kevon smiled, delighted. "No, I do not. No, I do not. No, I do not!" he sang back at her, then giggled.

"I ain't eating no McDonald's," Shavonne said.

"I'm *not* eating *any* McDonald's," Jada corrected. "And yes, you're going to." Jada was amazed at Shavonne's language. She'd begun speaking Ebonics overnight. Tonya's influence?

"Ha! You're eating McDonald's," Kevon crowed.

"You're a poop with a fart for a brain."

"So? So . . . you're a doody mouth. Mama, she's a doody mouth."

"Tattletale. Fart brain."

"Okay, now. That's enough of all that. Calm it right down," Jada said, shocked at their vocabulary and the intensity of their bickering.

"Oh, Mom. Will you get some honey sauce? Then I can have some of Kevon's."

"They're *my* nuddets," Kevon said.

"They're not even nuddets, stupid," his sister informed him. "They're *nuggets*."

"No, they're not, no, they're not. And they *are* mine. Aren't they *mine*, Mom?"

Jada, who was struggling to get Sherrilee into the McDonald's high chair, assured her son that when she got the food, it would be his. Poor Kevon: his sister always knew more, always corrected him, and was almost always right. Is that where men's resentment of smart women, of powerful women, began? Jada wondered. But they didn't all have sisters who were six years older. Clinton didn't. "Sit down, honey," Jada told her son and he clambered onto the yellow laminated chair beside her.

"*I* want to sit next to Mommy," Shavonne said, raising her voice. Annoying as their bickering was, Jada was grateful for the small indication of affection.

"You can *both* sit next to me," Jada declared before there was war, "but then Sherilee has to sit across from me and we all have to help her."

"Oh, she don't eat nothing. She just throws it on the floor," Kevon said.

"She *doesn't* eat *anything*," Jada corrected firmly. Since when was Kevon using double negatives, talking street talk? Was that what a few days in funky Yonkers had done to his speech? If her boy started speaking Ebonics, Jada decided she would have to kill Clinton *and* her mother-in-law. "Shavonne, you watch the baby while I get your Happy Meals."

"Okay, Mom," Shavonne said, self-satisfied.

"Kevon, you watch our bags and see that no one takes them." She glanced over at the line and pulled a Sesame Street coloring book and some Crayolas out of her bag, just to be sure to keep them busy. "And there's also a contest, with a prize, to see who can fill in their picture best. Now I'm going to get lunch and I'll be right back." She kissed Kevon on his head as she passed him.

"Kiss me, too," Shavonne said, and Jada had to smile. She did it, of course, though she noticed Shavonne's hair didn't smell fresh. When had it last been washed? she wondered. Sherrilee was still drowsy from the car, but for good luck, Jada kissed the top of her head, as well. It, too, smelled . . . well, not exactly bad, but certainly not fresh. She was more uncomfortable than ever. Couldn't Clinton even keep the children clean?

She joined the short line at the fast food counter. The kisses and fight over seating were unusual. The kids were bothered by all this—they usually, especially Shavonne, avoided affection.

She looked around and sighed. She hated feeding her kids this stuff, but it was a big treat to them. They loved it. And they seemed hungry. What was Clinton, or her mother-in-law, serving them?

Thank God the restaurant wasn't too crowded. It was an off-peak time. Actually, Jada had planned all of this badly. She had been a little lost about what to do with them. It had been too cold to take them to a park and Jada also knew she couldn't bear the screaming at one of the indoor kids' gyms, so she'd just walked them through part of the Cross County Mall and shown them the Santa's Village already on display, though it wasn't even Thanksgiving. The kids had been excited by it, but all Jada wanted was to get them home and crawl into bed with the three of them, read them a story or tickle them, or just watch some television holding them tight. But there was the time limit, so it was the mall and McDonald's—such public places. She still hadn't had a chance to really talk with them; she didn't know how to start, and still wasn't sure what Clinton had said about this abduction.

"Next," the older woman behind the counter barked, peering through thick bifocals. Jada rattled off her order, then after a pause, added a decaf coffee for herself. She couldn't eat. She hadn't eaten anything in two days. No wonder she was so exhausted. "Are ya sure you're done now?" the woman in her McDonald's uniform asked nastily, and Jada felt as if she almost was.

She turned to make sure the children were all right. Sherrilee was awake now, tearing up her coloring book page, at least one piece already in her mouth. Kevon was standing on his chair, getting the most leverage he could out of a crayon he was pressing onto his picture, while Shavonne, of course, was daintily working on a page still in the book. Jada watched them until her order came. Then she brought the bag full of saturated fats and starch and sugar to her waiting babies.

"Okay," she said, summoning the energy to try to keep it cheerful. "Let's see what you got done. Remember, there's a prize for the best job."

"Mine. Mine!" cried Kevon. "Look at this!" He had colored Big Bird—and most of the rest of the page—in Caribbean turquoise.

"Great," she said. Jada put down the brown collapsible boxes of food. "Let's take the crayons and the coloring off the table for now. Let's eat." She handed round the food and cut one plain burger into bite-size bits for Sherrilee while the other two tore into their boxes and bags. They ate, thankfully, in silence, and Jada, too sick to her stomach to even watch them eat, sipped her decaf and checked her watch. Only twenty-eight minutes left. She couldn't believe that she was not savoring this time with them. When they went back to coloring, she was ashamed to find herself relieved.

"That's stupid," said Shavonne. "Big Bird should be yellow." Even though she had recently turned twelve, she still—secretly—liked to color. Just like Jada, Shavonne was a good girl and didn't go out of the lines. Jada looked over at Shavonne's neat rendering of Bert and Ernie.

"It ain't no Big Bird," Kevon answered. "It's Aunt Tonya."

Aunt Tonya? *Aunt* Tonya? Forget the "ain't." Now Jada had to deal with "aunt"? For a moment she felt she might lose control, tear the page of the coloring book off the table, and scream at the top of her lungs. Instead she clenched her fists in her lap, then laid three more french fries out for Sherrilee, and calmly turned to Kevon. "You don't have an Aunt Tonya, Kevon, honey," she said, and at least in her own ears her voice sounded close to normal.

Kevon continued mashing the crayon into the paper. "She's our baby-sitter," Kevon replied, still coloring. "Daddy said so."

"I'm not no baby," Shavonne said. "I don't need a baby-sitter. Do I win the prize, Mom?" Shavonne looked at her mother and Jada thought there may have been a flicker of pain or doubt in her daughter's eyes. The pain went straight to Jada's heart. "Mrs. Green," Shavonne said. "I call her Mrs. Green. You know, from church. She baby-sat." Shavonne looked away.

In a bid to secure the prize, her daughter looked with contempt at her little brother's page. "Isn't it Big Bird, Mom?" Shavonne asked, looking back at Kevon's paper. "Anyway, Mrs. Green isn't that color, she's dark. She's *real* dark brown."

"Her dress was this color," Kevon said. "And she gave me two Matchbox cars. Wanna see?" He shoved his hand in his pocket. Sherrilee chose that moment to choke on a french fry and Jada was up, around the table, and at her side in a moment. She lifted the baby's little arms to the ceiling and Sherrilee coughed and swallowed, then pulled one hand away from her mother's and directly went for another fry. No Heimlich needed. Jada gratefully bent down and inhaled the slightly stale bread scent that came from her daughter's hair and kissed the top of her head. She slowly walked back to her seat.

"Who's taking care of Sherrilee?" she asked as neutrally as she could. She knew it was wrong to pump the kids for information, but felt almost desperate.

"Aunt Big Bird did," Kevon said and laughed, giving her the look he gave her when he was naughty.

"I miss my stuff," Shavonne said. "My blue sweater, and the knapsack with the cats on it. But I can get it when we go home."

"Yeah, let's go home now," Kevon agreed. Sherrilee, finished with her lunch, reached her arms out to her mother and Jada smiled, rounded the table again and picked her up, putting her on her lap. Kevon, feeling left out, got up from his swivel chair and rubbed his head against his mother's shoulder.

"I brought you some things," she said. She opened the bag and took out Shavonne's slippers. Her daughter looked up; the little V between her eyebrows, one that exactly replicated Jada's own, appeared.

"I don't need those *now*," Shavonne said. "I can wait until we go home. I'll put them on then."

"I'm tired," Kevon said. "Can we go home now? Can I play with Frankie?"

And it was then that Jada realized that her children didn't have a clue. That Clinton, once again, had failed not only her, but them. They thought they were getting in the Volvo and driving back to Elm Street. One more responsibility, the most heartbreaking one, had been laid on her shoulders. What could she tell them? What should she? That their father was a selfish man who didn't care about their best interests? That right now they were a pawn in a stupid grown-up game?

Jada looked at the three messy faces of her beautiful babies and her shoulders sagged. She cupped a hand over Kevon's lovely round head. "Listen, sweethearts. Daddy wants me to take you back to him. You're going to go back there for right now."

"I don't want to," Kevon said.

"No, Mom. I don't like Grandma's," Shavonne added. "Why do we have to visit her now?"

Hadn't Clinton told them *anything*? Jada reached her hand out from around Sherrilee's back toward Shavonne and took her daughter's wrist. "Listen," she said, "Daddy and I are having a kind of fight. A big one. And he wants you to come back and stay with him there."

"Well, I don't want to," Shavonne said and Kevon put his head down and began to cry. Shavonne snatched her wrist away from Jada. "I don't want to. Grandma only makes us bologna sandwiches and I don't like Mrs. Green. I don't like her house. Let's go home."

Her daughter's voice had risen high and several people turned to look at her, not that Jada cared about any of those strangers. She only cared about her kids. But how could she explain? How could a six-year-old, or a pre-teen, or the baby understand visitation privileges and contempt of court? And she had only nineteen minutes left before they were due back. "Well, I have to go away for work. When I come back, we'll all decide, okay?" Shavonne narrowed her eyes. "Let's get into the car," Jada said. "We can talk for a little bit in the car."

"I wanna go home," Kevon wailed, and so Jada lifted him on one side while she cradled Sherrilee on the other.

"Take the bags and let's go," she told Shavonne and started toward the exit, hoping her daughter would follow her out the door to the Volvo.

25

Court and spark

The files had become, if possible, even higher and messier since Angie had moved "temporarily" into Karen Levis-Thomas's office. Angie figured that was appropriate, since *she* was higher and messier than she had been before she committed to this work. Not higher in the sense of a buzz, just higher in energy. Her mother, annoyingly, had been right: Anger did work as a high-octane fuel. Except for brief slumps of overwhelming self-pity, Angie had lost her lethargy. Now, most of the time she was so furious, not to mention so busy, that unwinding and sleeping at night had become difficult.

The staff at the clinic were great, and Angie actually enjoyed the joking, kibitzing, and other camaraderie. The other women were great and the two guys who worked there—one gay and one married—were just as dedicated as the women. Bill, the paralegal, was a riot, always there with a lawyer joke or a Mallomar to get you through a tough afternoon. And Michael Rice, the middle-aged married attorney, was really sweet, as well as smart. As a Yale graduate, he also should have been a snot-nose, but in Angie's non-Ivy opinion, he wasn't.

It was also a pleasant surprise to find how much she liked working with her mother, not that she got to see her often. Between depositions, fundraising, and office administration, Natalie was even busier than Angie. But she managed to check in with her every day, in person or on the phone, and Angie found their exchanges very comforting. Perhaps she hadn't been able to return to her old room, but working daily with her mother let her return to the womb at least in some psychological way.

The work load was incredible, all of it either bleak or rage-producing or both. That was good, as far as Angie was concerned. It kept her mind off her own pathetic life and allowed her to focus on people—women— whose problems were a lot more serious than hers. Angie knew it was an escape from her own pain, but what was so wrong with escaping? Didn't they make movies and television just to provide some?

Now she took out the Jackson vs. Jackson case. Of all the horrible, ter- rible injustices, for some reason this one bothered Angie the most. It was just another messy divorce with custody rights used as leverage—some- thing Angie would have considered beneath her back in Needham—but perhaps because she felt that she had clicked with Jada Jackson the first time they met, or perhaps because she had felt a little envious of her obvious closeness with the blond friend who'd brought her in, Angie liked Mrs. Jackson.

She hadn't thought about Lisa, her own "friend" at all. She absolutely wouldn't let herself. If their friendship had ever actually existed was a real question. Lisa could have simply used her as an accessory to the affair. If Angie even began to think of the things she'd said to Lisa about her feelings for Reid, and if she thought for a moment about what Lisa had possibly passed on, she'd die of humiliation. Luckily, Reid would probably just dump on Lisa eventually—but thinking about that was let- ting her mind wander dangerously, she realized.

She returned her attention to Jackson vs. Jackson. She'd been horri- fied by the direction Mr. Jackson's attorney, George Creskin, seemed to be taking. When she'd gone over the file at their weekly case discussion meeting, both Michael and her mother had raised their eyebrows. Apparently Creskin was notorious, a real operator. "What do you call a George Creskin who's been flattened by an eighteen-wheeler on I–95?" Bill had simply asked.

"A good beginning," the rest of them had said.

"New low in slime bags," he said. "Lucky Angie."

Unlucky Jada Jackson. The woman was coming in less than half an hour and Angie was going to have to explain her strategy. Clinton Jackson had filed a motion to show cause, and requested only temporary custody, temporary alimony, and temporary child support, but in addition he'd filed a motion to vacate and a motion for allowance to prosecute. It was such a complete barrage, such a totally relentless going-to-war mode, that Natalie had given a warning to Angie. "Be careful here," she said. "I've only seen women pull this kind of scorched-earth thing and when they do, it's usually with a restraining order."

"A restraining order against the husband?" Angie asked.

"Yeah. Because he beats her or the kids or both. There's no restraining order here, is there?"

"Oh, come on, Mom. That woman doesn't beat her children. She couldn't beat her husband."

"No, but he could say she did." Natalie looked over the papers briefly. "This guy wants the house, the kids, an allowance, child support, and he wants her to pay his legal fees. Is this woman rich?"

"No, she's a bank manager. He's just a cheating, unemployed guy who's been living off her for years. This thing is a total set-up, and it's absolutely the worst kind of punishment for a woman. This case stands for everything that can go wrong for us. The guy was a bread-earner who lost his income, forcing his wife to take a job outside the home."

Natalie sighed. "I hate it when they do that," she said. "Okay, let her know how hard it is going to be to get this leech unglued. Family court will definitely get a social worker involved in this one." Natalie shook her head. "The poor woman. He'll try to bleed her dry. Take her out to lunch, Angie. Get the petty cash from Bill. Mrs. Jackson isn't going to get any more free lunches for a real long time."

"I saw the children. Thank you. Thank you so much," Jada Jackson said, sitting in the chair just inches from Angie's knees.

"Hey, it was standard operating procedure. I just filed for visitation and got a family court judge who was willing to work late on Friday."

"But you have to help me get visitation extended. Two hours is ridiculous. And the kids want to come home. Their grandmother's is no place for them." Jada Jackson paused, looked out to where the view would be if the windowsill weren't stacked so high with papers and files, and then forced herself with visible effort to look into Angie's eyes. "I think he's taking them over to his girlfriend's," she said. "Or else the girl-friend is staying at his mother's. I don't know, but it can't be right. It shouldn't be allowed. I mean, somebody has to watch Sherrilee all day and I can't believe he'd give my baby to his . . . his lover." She bent her head for a moment, gaining some self-control and then turned back to Angie. "How soon can you get me the children back?"

"Mrs. Jackson, it's a little more complicated then that," Angie began. "When your husband filed his complaint he also made several motions to the court. You've looked at the documents?"

Jada nodded. "I didn't understand it all, that's why I'm here. But I just know we have to get it all thrown out. I don't mind about a divorce. I want one. He was cheating on me and probably had done it before. I earn a living and I pay for the mortgage and I take care of the kids. I just want my children back and he can have the divorce. No problem."

"Well, there seems to be a very big problem," Angie said. "He's asked for temporary custody—"

"But that was just to punish me," Jada said. "He wasn't interested in the kids when we were together. This was just his way to be really cruel. But I know Clinton. He doesn't want responsibility. He wants irresponsibility."

Angie picked up the document in front of her. "An irresponsible man," she said. "How unusual."

Jada grinned a little. "Yeah," she said. "I'm sure you don't see that in your practice."

Angie nodded, but knew she had to get into the pain-inducing expla-nation of all this legalese on the pages before her. "Listen, Jada . . ." She paused. "May I call you that?" she asked. Jada nodded. "Jada, here's the thing. He's asked for temporary custody, but he's going to go for perma-nent, and he's also asked for child support and alimony."

"I know. But that's just because he jumped the gun on me, right? We get that fixed up in a hearing. I mean, the judge would have to understand how unfair that was. I've been supporting the children and him, but just to keep us together. I'm certainly not going to do it if we're apart."

"The judge may think differently," Angie said as gently as she could. "There's established precedent here. You are the bread-winner of the house, and he is the homemaker."

"Homemaker? I spent more time picking up after that man than I did picking up after the children. The only thing he made in my home was trouble. He didn't help them with their homework. He didn't supervise their television. He didn't clean, he didn't—"

Angie wrote down some notes, but then held up her hand to stop Jada's rant. "I believe you. But the court will see a woman who left the house every morning at quarter to six—the complaint says you did that. Is it true?"

"Yes. To take a walk with my girlfriend. And then I came back and gave the kids breakfast and got them on the school bus."

"Well, not surprisingly, the complaint doesn't mention that. It says that your long working hours left the children virtually motherless, that you verbally abused your spouse and your children with constant nagging, and that you had consorted with a possible felon whom you invited into the home."

"What? Oh my God, Michelle."

Angie watched as her client's strength and dignity drained out of her. Angie felt awful, as if she were the person attacking this woman. She leaned over the desk. "Look," she said. "This isn't the truth. This is just what he has filed. We fight this, that's all. We fight it and we win."

Jada's face had turned an unpleasant shade of grayish brown. "Can you win?" she asked Angie.

"Well, you're going to have to help me. There are going to have to be a lot of depositions, but I'm going to do every single thing I can to make sure we win. We'll have character witnesses on your behalf, we'll call in your minister, we'll bring up your husband's infidelities, his job history. Unfortunately, we're working against a semi-notorious attorney. This George Creskin is a real piece of work, but we're going to do it."

"How much will all this cost?" Jada asked. "I mean, we were already—*I* was already stretched to the limit financially with the three kids and the house."

Angie took a deep breath, wondering why she would ever take this job. "It's a little worse than that," Angie said. "I've taken your case before our board and we will represent you for minimal fees. But I'm afraid George Creskin doesn't feel the same way."

"You mean Clinton's lawyer?" Jada asked. "What do I care about him?"

"Well, one of these motions is a show cause motion."

"Yeah, I saw that. Isn't he allowed to?"

Angie withheld her smile. It wasn't funny. It was tragic. "The allowance to prosecute means your husband wants you to pay Mr. Creskin's fees because he himself is indigent while you are employed."

Jada stood up and slammed her hand down on the desk. "That can't be right!"

"It certainly isn't right, but it is legal."

"So I have to pay his lawyer's bills?"

"No, not yet, but he's asking the court that they direct you to. It's another motion we have to have denied, along with the temporary alimony and the child support and, most importantly, the custody."

Jada tried to pace in the little space available. "This is some kind of visitation on me. Like God did with Job."

"I never really understood that story in the Bible," Angie admitted. "I thought it was mean that God would let Job be tortured like that, just as a game."

Jada turned to Angie. "I don't know if God played a game, but Clinton certainly is. You should have seen my children this weekend. Kevon's socks didn't match. The baby didn't have a hat, my eldest hadn't done any homework and spent three days watching television. He's torturing me, but he's also torturing the children. How do we stop this? What do we do next?"

"Well, there's one more thing I have to tell you before we put together our strategy," Angie admitted. "This motion to vacate, do you understand what he's asking?"

Jada looked directly at Angie. "He wants my house, doesn't he?"

"Well, he wants you to leave the house so that he can move into it. With the children. For continuity for them."

"And who else is he going to move in with? His mother, who lives like a pig and washes her sheets once a year if they last that long? Or with Tonya, his girlfriend, who has already slept with half the men in our congregation? I won't let her in my house. I'd burn it to the ground first."

"Look, we have plenty of time before we have to start setting fires," Angie said. "What you're going to have to do, though, is pull together a huge pile of information. You're going to have to fill in a thousand forms. I need you to disclose your assets, your liabilities, and all the financials about your house and any of the holdings you have. Then we're going to have to file counter motions and prepare complaints. We'll also have to be ready for a social worker interview, which can sometimes be tricky. It's going to be a lot of work and I'd like us to move quickly. Both for your sake and the sake of the children."

Jada was wringing her hands. "Look, Angie," she said. "He's not a really terrible man. Not really. Maybe we could just give him the house. That's what he wants. He built it. Of course, he never finished it, but he built it and maybe he'd finish it for Tonya. Get me my babies and give him the house. That's a trade I'll make."

Angie looked down at the paper. "I don't think George Creskin would allow that, even if your husband would go for it. There's a real aggressive strategy laid out here. Creskin's been known to rack up big bills, and to take a house in lieu of payment. But listen to me. We are going to combat this roach—well, both roaches—and we're going to win. It's going to be fine. But until it's fine, it'll be bad and worse." She looked up at Jada and realized what a very beautiful woman she was. "Are you strong enough for this?"

"Oh, honey, I'm just as strong as I have to be."

"Great," Angie said. "So let me take you out to lunch."

Jada looked surprised. "You don't look like you can afford much either."

"I can't, but the clinic's got petty cash and I got a chit for it burning a hole in my pocket." She stood up.

"Could my friend Michelle come, too?" she asked. "She's waiting in the car. She's been with me throughout this whole mess."

"Of course," Angie said. "If you don't mind if we talk a little bit about all of this in front of her."

Jada snorted. "What do you think she and I do every minute of the day?"

Angie nodded. "I'm going to the ladies' room to wash up," she said. "Why don't I meet you in the reception area?"

Angie did have to wash up, after she performed another pregnancy test and spilled urine all over the fingers of her right hand. This was the fifth test she'd done. She'd tried two different brands and both had given her the same result, but she was still hoping there was a mistake. She wrapped the indicator in a paper towel along with the box and packaging and stuffed it into the bottom of the wastebasket. Then she washed her hands carefully, tried not to think about what this meant, and went out to join Jada Jackson.

As Angie and Jada walked to the car, Jada briefly outlined Michelle's own legal problems. "Believe me, she's not judging. In fact, she's shell-shocked."

Angie thought of the world of pain out there sitting somewhere above the ether and waiting to descend; maybe more shit was falling because of the hole in the ozone, she thought. It was allowing universal troubles to flop in their hands like bird shit from the stars.

When they got to the car, Michelle, the very tall and leggy blond Angie had met, had to be woken out of her trance by more than a couple of hard taps on the window. She raised her arched brows then, and fumbled for the door lock, getting out the car still clutching a wet tissue in one hand.

"Angie's invited us to lunch," Jada said in the cheeriest voice she'd used since Angie met her. "Let's see if I can choke down anything more solid than consommé." Michelle shrugged, but Jada took her arm and they began walking across the parking lot with them. "I haven't been able to eat solid food since Clinton took my kids," she told Angie.

"Why don't I get stricken with that?" Angie asked. "I had to buy this in a size ten and now I'm having trouble zipping it." Of course, she knew why her waist was disappearing, but she preferred denial.

Michelle looked over at Angie briefly, but her eyes flicked away. No denial there. In that moment Angie saw a world of fear and pain. What kind of trouble was the woman in?

They got a booth at the diner. Angie had only thirty dollars from the kitty and maybe another nine dollars of her own money, but she figured if she watched what she ate she could cover it. These two wouldn't be ordering lobster, and if they did, in all good conscience she'd have to warn them that even the tuna salad at the Blue Bird was suspect.

Jada and Michelle sat opposite her. When Jada turned to ask Michelle what she was having, the nagging feeling in the back of her mind that she knew this woman finally connected with the synapse in her brain that had been reluctant to fire. "You walk together," Angie said. "You walk past my house every morning."

"Which one is your house?" Jada asked.

"Well, it isn't my house. It's my dad's house on the corner of Oak."

"Oh," Jada said, and turned to Michelle, who was wiping off her empty water glass. "She's the mistress."

She turned back to Angie. "We knew an older guy lived in there alone, but when we saw you in the window we figured you were his young chippie."

"Nope. Just his not-so-young daughter. He already had a young chippie after my mom. She took him to the cleaners." Angie picked up the menu. She looked at the lunch specials and felt that she could eat them all, beginning with the stuffed flounder, cole slaw, and parsley potatoes, and ending with the home-style meatloaf, mashed potatoes, and onions. She had to do something about this eating; she'd be a pork barrel in another month.

Jada put her menu down as if the weight of it exhausted her. "Yeah, we've been walking together for four years, right, Michelle?" Michelle nodded and put the glass down, but picked up her fork. "That's why Clinton is charging me for being a bad mother."

Michelle turned her full attention to Jada. "What?" she asked.

"Angie just explained to me that Clinton wants full custody, the house, alimony, child support, and for me to pay the legal bills that will get him all that. Because I've been a neglectful mother, doing all those irresponsible, mad, fun things like working at the bank and getting in a little cardiovascular exercise. That and the orgies, pony-rolling, pedicures, and endless martini parties."

"What the hell is he talking about?" Michelle asked, holding a knife in her hand.

"What the hell is pony-rolling?" Angie wanted to know. "Because if I gain another five pounds I think I'm eligible."

"I haven't a clue what it is," Jada said, "but it sounded decadent, didn't it? It all goes together with my decadent lifestyle. You know, the one all of us neglectful mothers indulge ourselves in—driving ten-year-old used cars, wearing the same four suits to work all the time, deciding which monthly bill won't get paid this month, and listening to James Brown while we vacuum. There may be hell to pay, but I don't regret a minute of it."

The waitress came over and Jada ordered tea, Jell-O, and the soup. When Michelle asked for a BLT, Angie was safe to hit the meatloaf special. Once the waitress had left, Angie decided to try to cheer up the natives. "Hey," she said, "why are dogs better than men?" The two women looked at her. "Because dogs feel guilty when they've done something wrong."

Even Michelle laughed. "I thought it was because dogs never bring strange bitches home and sleep with them in your bed," Jada said.

"Yeah. And dogs never request custody. Or alimony," Michelle added.

"Dogs don't get arrested," Jada said.

"Boy. You girls are good at this game," Angie told them. "We play it in the office all the time. My favorite one so far is, 'Dogs are better than men because they're happy with any video you rent.'"

"Dogs aren't threatened if you earn more than they do," Jada said bitterly. "They don't try to ruin your life."

Michelle lowered her voice. "Jada," she said, "this is horrible. He can't be such a miserable prick to you. He can't." Angie could see Michelle's eyes getting watery as Jada deftly patted her hand.

"Believe me, Mich, I'm taking it seriously," she said.

Angie looked at the two women, both with troubles that more than equaled her own, and felt envious. How nice to have such a supportive friendship. Angie couldn't prevent herself from thinking again of Lisa. How stupid could she have been? Why couldn't she find a trustworthy friend the way Jada Jackson had? Perhaps her hunger showed on her face, because when Jada looked away from Michelle, she stared at Angie for a long moment.

"Why don't you join us in our walks?" Jada asked. "It might be good for your weight and good for your head," she said. She turned to Michelle. "You wouldn't mind, would you?" Michelle just shrugged; it wasn't a formal invitation, but it wasn't a veto, either.

"I'd like to," Angie said. "That would be great."

"Well, don't count on greatness," Jada told her. "Mostly we just talk about men, dogs, and survival."

Angie began to laugh. "Girls, I can see you and raise you," Angie told them.

26

Another walk, another talk

On their morning walk, Michelle listened while Jada raged about her children and Clinton. "What did you finally tell them?" she asked, truly horrified.

"That Clinton and I were having a fight and that I was going to be away for work. That Daddy thought their visit would be fun."

"Did they buy it?"

"Are you kidding? Kevon started crying. He said he hated 'Aunt' Tonya. Aunt! Can you believe it? She's an aunt and I'm Princess Di's half-sister!" Jada paused. "Shavonne gave me a look . . ." Jada went silent, and Michelle knew only too clearly what receiving that look of betrayal and mute anger had felt like. She'd already seen it on Jenna's face, and after the Russos' next wave of notoriety, she'd see it again.

"You should have blamed Clinton," Michelle said.

"Not now. I'll wait until the legal ax falls on him. Then, when the kids are back home, I'll explain. Except not about the affair. That's not their business." Jada shook her head. "I had all I could do not to break down and cry like Sherrilee when I left them," she admitted.

But despite her sympathy—or because of it—Michelle couldn't bring herself to talk to Jada about the ax that was about to fall on her own neck. It wasn't fear that Jada would turn on her and consider her and Frank guilty. It was weirder, colder, as if a mental garage door had shut somewhere in her mind—and until the newspapers, television, lawyers, and court battered it down, Michelle was pretending there was nothing behind the door. It must be a gift she'd inherited from her mother, she thought bitterly as they trudged around the bend of Oak Street. She turned to her friend. "I thought of another reason why dogs are better than men," Michelle said.

"Because dogs don't criticize your friends?"

Michelle smiled. "Good one. But I think dogs are better than men because they don't care if you shave your legs or not."

"I think dogs are better because if they go crazy you can just put them to sleep," Jada said. She didn't sound as if she were joking.

"Jada, it's just awful. Are you going to work today?" she asked.

"Are you kidding? Work is all I'm good for," Jada said bitterly. "I'm a damn wage slave. And I need the job to keep sane as well as pay the bills."

Michelle wondered for a minute if that was a dig at her, since Jada knew that she and Frank didn't have money problems. But she let it go. If she had a sin, Michelle thought, it was pride. And she just couldn't tell anyone, not even Jada, about this until she absolutely had to. It made her feel a lot farther away from her friend than the yard between them. It made Michelle feel alone in the universe. "Look, I have to go to see Frank's lawyer this morning, so I won't be in until about noon. Can you cover for me?"

Jada nodded. "You're caught up on stuff?" she asked. "Because I do have to take heat from Mr. Marcus. He didn't like the newspaper stuff. But he's manageable."

"I'm up on everything," Michelle told her. "I got your loan through, and had it deposited in your account."

"But I don't need it now. Thanks for doing that for me. It wasn't exactly . . ."

"Bank policy?" Michelle asked. "Screw bank policy."

"Lord. I wish I'd never . . ."

"Did you stop payment on that check? Somehow I feel like Bruzeman's not the kind of guy who gladly refunds your money," Michelle said.

"I hear you. I did. Hope he doesn't sue me for it, not that he did anything to earn it." Jada sighed. "You up on everything else?"

"I only have one client who might call, and I'll check in."

"Fine," Jada said as they got to her house. She stamped her feet in the cold. "If there are any new applicants, I'll just have Anne give them the paperwork. Of course," Jada added with a grim smile, "she'd snitch to Mr. Marcus in a second to get a chance at your job. Not that I'd ever let her have it."

They parted without a good-bye, Jada grim and Michelle grimmer, both facing an almost unbearable day. Michelle's first hurdle was getting the kids up and off to school. Then she walked Pookie quickly, fed him, and brought some coffee up to Frank. Both of them dressed in silence to see Rick Bruzeman.

Michelle was ready first and went down to the kitchen, where she started to scrub the counter, being careful not to get her cuffs dirty. When her husband joined her, he sat on one of the stools at the center island. She had just wiped it off and noticed the coffee ring that his cup bottom made. She wanted more than anything to wipe it up, but instead she forced herself to take a seat across from him.

"Frank, how could this happen?" she asked. "I mean, if a person accuses you of something, if someone's jealous, or vengeful . . ." She paused. Frank was looking down at his cup. "The thing is, I can understand how the police might just push in here, but I don't understand how they could indict you. I mean, they didn't find anything."

"There isn't anything to find." He sounded defensive, or insulted. His tone implied that she was stupid.

"I know that, Frank. But I don't understand," she said in a voice she thought was submissive, not threatening. "Maybe I am stupid, but what I don't get is how they can put you on trial based on nothing but someone's accusations."

"I don't know either," Frank said bitterly. "They're just out to get a guy whose last name is Russo."

Michelle couldn't stand it any longer. She reached across the island, lifted Frank's cup, and swabbed away the coffee blot he'd been playing with. She got up and went to the sink, washing her hands twice after rinsing out the sponge. She almost jumped when Frank came up behind her. "You don't doubt me, do you, Mich?"

Michelle shook her head. She didn't doubt her husband, but she did doubt Bruzeman, the prosecutor, the court, and their ability to pay huge retainers to Bruzeman and to cope. "We better go," was all she said.

They had to take separate cars, since Michelle was going on to work. In the silence of her Lexus, she let the mental garage door close again on all of it. She needed the silence, the emptiness. She didn't play any music; there was just the road and the driving. For a brief minute, Michelle wished she didn't have to take the exit that led to Bruzeman's offices. She wanted to sail straight along the highway for days, her mind empty, the road ahead clear. She sighed and threw on her blinker, following Frank's taillights onto the exit ramp.

Bruzeman made them wait, just the way he had when she'd brought Jada in. Frank, never good at waiting, paced and became angrier and angrier. "First the little bastard tells me we're going to sue the cops and the county and make big money. Then he drops the news about this bullshit indictment like it's a Valentine," he spat. "Now he makes me wait? He makes *you* wait? After the money I'm already paying him? Just who the fuck does he think he is?"

Michelle watched Frank as he pulled himself into something close to a rage. She knew it was his way to deal, just like the garage door was hers. "It's only been fifteen minutes," she told him.

"You know what the guy charges per hour?" Frank snapped. "Fifteen minutes is a hundred and twenty bucks' worth of waiting in his world." Just as Frank muttered something about whether the prick would charge him for it or not, they were met and ushered down the hall by the secretary. Frank walked into Bruzeman's office as if he himself had built it, and sat on the big leather chair, rather than the sofa, leaving Bruzeman, who had only just hung up the phone, nowhere to sit but the other side of the couch. Michelle held on to the arm of her side as if the sofa were one of the Titanic's lifeboats. She was afraid she was going to go under.

"Well, the news isn't good, Frank. But—" Bruzeman began.

Frank wouldn't let him continue. "How the fuck could a secret grand jury be called without you knowing about it? Without us doing something?" Frank almost shouted.

Bruzeman raised his eyebrows. "What would there have been to do?" he asked. "Frank, I told you from the get-go that there was a good chance of an informant. I mean a heavy-hitting informant. Otherwise the cops couldn't have gotten the search warrant."

"But they didn't find a fucking thing. I mean . . ." Frank had calmed down a little, but Michelle still sat hunched and frightened.

"If they hadn't found anything, which of course they didn't," Bruzeman said in his slimy voice, "they wouldn't have arrested you and your wife, if the informant or even a cooperating witness already didn't have strong evidence. When I got your bail, I told you that."

He had? Michelle wondered if that were true. Neither Bruzeman nor Frank had told her that. "You also told me we'd have this cleaned up in a week and twenty-five thousand dollars," Frank said.

"Witness?" Michelle asked. It was the first word she'd spoken. She'd kept her head down, literally and figuratively, but now she turned to Bruzeman at the end of the sofa. "A witness to what?" she asked him.

"To these allegations," Bruzeman said as if she were a slow child, and turned back to Frank.

"But what did he witness?" Michelle asked. "What could he say he witnessed?" She could imagine a neighbor or a competitor of Frank's making some kind of angry anonymous phone call or sending a note. She could easily imagine one of the carpenters or roofers who Frank routinely fired for incompetence turning on a dime, complaining to the state unemployment office or dropping hints to the IRS. They had been audited three times, but they'd been fine. No fines or taxes due. The thing was, Michelle knew that people like that didn't convince a judge and grand jury that a man should be put up for trial. "Who's the witness?" she asked.

"It's my understanding it's a sealed indictment," Bruzeman said.

"What does that mean?" she asked.

Bruzeman raised his brows. He didn't even look at her, but directed himself to Frank. "Frank, we have a lot to cover and I don't think it's time for a legal lesson for your wife right now. I have word that this is going to break to the press this morning, so . . ."

"This morning?" Frank asked. He looked at his watch. "We only have two more hours before it's not this morning any more."

"My point exactly," Bruzeman agreed. He finally turned to Michelle. "*You're* not in any jeopardy," he told her, as if that were the only reason she'd asked. "Apparently the informant retracted any accusations against you, or whatever he said didn't hold. So you're completely out of this." He smiled. "That means you'll be able to testify on Frank's behalf. We'll prepare you for that. But right now I just wanted to prepare you for the indictment that's about to be handed down. Frank and I will do what we have to here."

Michelle realized she was being dismissed. The man's arrogance was unbelievable. She felt sorry for his wife, if he had one. Jesus, she felt sorry for his dog.

"Here's my point," Bruzeman was saying. "If you're approached by anyone, just give no interviews. Your only statement is that your husband is innocent of all charges and that you and the children stand behind him as a good father, a good husband, and an innocent man." He got up and handed her a typed sheet that said those things, as if she needed them written down. She looked over at Frank. He was white, as pale as she had ever seen him. Michelle felt more questions bubbling up, as if her throat were filling with foam, but she rose as Bruzeman had.

"You want me to go now, Frank?" she asked her husband. Frank nodded and didn't move from his chair. Michelle let go of the arm of her life raft and stepped away, out into the waves.

Driving to work, she had a little bit of time to think about the children. If it got bad again, if there was newspaper coverage and a lot of talk, maybe she'd have to think about different schools for both of them. But where? There were a few private schools nearby, but they were expensive, and anyway, what good would that do Jenna? The children there would probably be more, not less, aware of gossip, and she'd be a new girl as well as visible because of her father's upcoming trial. Jenna liked her current school and her classmates . . . well, as much as any twelve-year-old could.

Private school wouldn't help. Kids there were even hipper, and more cruel. Plus, they'd moved here for the good public schools. And they didn't have money now for tuition, along with all these extra expenses.

Michelle changed lanes, getting ready to take her right at the bank exit, and wondered how bad it would be for Jenna and Frankie if she just left them where they were. It wouldn't be easy, she knew, not if the trial got the kind of publicity that Bruzeman predicted. Perhaps . . . The thought came to her mind, but Michelle pushed it away. Then it made its way back.

Boarding school. A really good boarding school might be the best choice for Jenna. It would separate her from the local media circus that might evolve, and have other benefits as well: a better sports program—she was really into soccer and the swim team—and more focus on academics. It would probably help get her into a better college, too. Of course, the idea of getting along without her daughter, or breaking up their home so early, was heartbreaking to Michelle. But boarding school might be a good choice for Jenna now. That still left Frankie, and she couldn't let him go.

Michelle almost missed the turn into the parking lot of the bank, which was already busy. All the employee spots were, of course, filled. It had begun to rain, a cold misty dampness, and Michelle had to park in the farthest corner from the bank entrance and walk across the already puddled tarmac without an umbrella or boots. Her hair and her neck were wet by the time she reached the bank door.

Thank God she didn't have to greet anybody—there were too many customers and everyone was busy. That was a small relief. So she just crossed the lobby and ducked into the employees' break room, where she hung up her coat, grabbed a cup of coffee, and tried to do something about her miserable wet mop of hair. There wasn't much she could do, but she put a barrette in it and decided to let it go for the day—along with everything else.

She'd have to take it easy, she told herself. Nothing was perfect, and nothing in *her* life was going to be perfect, or even acceptable, for quite a long time. She took one more sip of the coffee to fortify herself. She'd have to face whatever came.

It was eleven-forty when Michelle slipped into the alcove where her desk waited for her. Despite Jada's warnings, she didn't seem to have been missed. She figured she wouldn't take a lunch break and make up for some of the time. She sorted through the phone message slips on her desk, had time to review one application, and then looked up to see a red-headed, bearded man in a windbreaker standing at her desk. "Can I help you?" she asked.

"Yeah," he said. "I'd like to take out a loan."

Michelle nodded. "You've come to the right place."

"Yeah? I tried earlier but you weren't here," the bearded guy told her.

"Have you filled in any forms? Do you have an application?" Michelle asked. He shook his head. She pulled out several packets. "Are you talking home equity, mortgage, or personal?" she asked.

"Well, I'm not sure." He sat down opposite her. "Maybe you could tell me the differences." He smiled a pleasant smile—almost too pleasant. Was he flirting with her? Not likely, on this worst of bad hair days.

Michelle tried to smile back. Then the phone rang and Michelle nodded an unspoken apology to him and picked the receiver up. Jada's voice came across the wires. Only a few dozen feet away, she sounded far away, almost ghostlike over the phone.

"Michelle. It's hit the papers again," Jada said without a preamble.

Michelle felt her breath leave her body. She immediately wanted one of the pills her doctor had prescribed, but couldn't take one in front of this client, sitting before her and watching her very attentively.

"There's been an indictment handed down. Did you know? And security tells me a news truck just pulled up outside."

"Outside where?" Michelle asked Jada.

"Outside here. In the parking lot. And we should probably expect another few."

"You're kidding!" Michelle said and was more aware than ever of the red-headed man's eyes on her.

"We can keep them out of the bank," Jada told her, and Michelle had never been so grateful for the plural, "but they'll swarm on you when you leave. Did you park out in the back?"

"No. It was full," Michelle said. Her client was leaning forward on his elbows, reading her memos upside down. She turned the papers over firmly.

"Well, you can take my car and I'll take yours," Jada suggested.

"You mean leave now?" Michelle asked. She looked over at Jada through the glass of her office.

"Better sooner than later," Jada suggested. "You might get home before they get you."

"They'll be at my house by now, too," Michelle said, and tried not to panic. "I'm going to have to face them eventually."

"Yeah, but tomorrow there might be someone else in a lot bigger trouble. They can torture them instead of you."

"I'll be all right," Michelle said, though she didn't think she would be. Then she saw Mr. Marcus's big shoulders and bald head moving among clients across the floor. "Marcus is here," she whispered.

"Oh shit. He's seen the reporters then. This isn't good," Jada said, and hung up.

Michelle kept the phone to her ear another ten seconds or so just to pull herself together. Then she smiled, said good-bye to the dial tone, and looked across her desk at the red-headed client. He had been scribbling on one of the forms she'd given him, but she had a feeling that he'd also been listening. Of course, she was paranoid and she knew it. "I'm sorry," she said. "Now, how can I help you?"

"My name's Howard Mindel. You're Michelle Russo?"

Since her name was on the little slide thing on the front of her desk, he didn't have to be genius to figure that out. She smiled and nodded. He extended his hand and she shook it. "So what kind of loan, and approximately how much do you think you're looking for?" she inquired, though what she was really thinking about was breathing—getting air in, getting air out.

"Have you worked here long?" Mr. Mindel asked. Michelle's smile got stiffer. Was he trying to chat her up, or was he now questioning her abilities? She didn't need a complaint to Marcus, now of all times.

"I'm sorry about the interruption," she said. "I've been a loan officer for three years," she said.

"Do you like it?" Mr. Mindel asked. Michelle narrowed her eyes. There was something off-balance about this guy, but he didn't seem mentally disturbed or challenged. And this wasn't a pick-up attempt, either.

"What can I do for you?" she asked.

He leaned forward, way too far across the desk. "Give me an exclusive interview, Michelle. The rest of the press is going to cream you.

You give me an interview and we'll have it on page two and three of *The Sentinel*. If you make it an exclusive, I'll give it the best slant I can."

It took a moment for Michelle to react, to realize what was going on. That he was just the advance guard of journalists about to crucify her and her family. It took another moment for her to realize that her desk trapped her in the alcove, since he had pulled his chair to the side where she slid in and out. "You're a reporter?" she asked, her voice low and breathless. She had to get some air.

"I'm Howard Mindel," he repeated, as if that meant something to her. Maybe she had read his byline, but she couldn't remember. She stood up, and in two big steps was past the desk by pushing hard against his chair. So hard he had to grab the desk corner not to topple over, but she was past him and already walking to the employee lounge.

But as she crossed the floor and got to Anne, the door to Jada's office opened and Mr. Marcus stuck his bald head out. "Mrs. Russo?" he asked. "Would you step in here for a moment?"

Michelle could see Jada's stricken face over Marcus's big shoulder. And so she walked with as much dignity as she could, into Jada's office, trying to get enough air into her lungs so she wouldn't pass out.

"Sit down," Jada said.

"Is that necessary?" Mr. Marcus asked.

"Yes," Jada snapped at him. "And as you leave, would you close the door?"

Michelle, feeling sick to her stomach, still almost smiled, imagining his look of surprise. Jada was pushing him, but Michelle could see now Jada herself had been pushed. Her face looked gray. The door closed behind Michelle. She tried to take a deep breath.

"Look," Jada began, "he wants you out, but I've pointed out to him we have no grounds. And if you make a fuss, threaten a lawyer, I'll just back off and tell him—"

She was a good, good friend. Michelle had never thought too much about her job here, but realized now how much she'd miss it. "Forget it, Jada. I know this is B.O., not your choice," she said. "I'm resigning."

"Mich, you don't have to—"

"It will make it easier for both of us," Michelle said. "God knows we have enough on our plates. And you need this job. Don't get Marcus really pissed."

"He's . . . expletive deleted."

"Yeah, well, I'm deleted, too, as of now," Michelle said.

27

Dealing with a social failure with the social worker

As Jada drove past Michelle's house, she caught herself averting her eyes. She made herself pray for forgiveness. She couldn't have prevented Michelle's firing for long—Marcus and the board were adamant, and the newspaper and television coverage since then had been brutal—but she had accepted Michelle's resignation with relief. She was going to continue being a loyal friend as long as Michelle would have her friendship. The irony that Michelle had gotten Jada her first job at the bank, and that then she had been asked to fire Michelle wasn't lost on her. She sighed.

No good deed goes unpunished, she thought. Michelle was too good a person to resent her for what had happened, but if she did later, Jada wouldn't blame her. Jada knew her own guilt was probably the more likely way to end the relationship. Her mother often said, "Just feel a pinch of guilt and add an ounce of procrastination and you got a recipe for failure." Jada would *not* avert her eyes from Michelle's house. She was calling Michelle twice a day and was making sure that they took their walk, despite some of the still unspoken awkwardness between them.

Jada had, of course, read the papers and seen the stuff on the news. The point was, even though Frank had only been indicted, the papers—

and everyone else—were treating him as if he were guilty. Jada remembered that security guard who'd found a bomb at the Atlanta Olympics. When the police turned the hero into a suspect, his life had been ruined. But he'd been innocent. The nation owed him an apology.

And if there was one thing Jada was sure of, it was that Michelle was totally innocent. She couldn't be sure about Frank, God forgive her, but if he'd been up to anything, Michelle certainly didn't know. She shouldn't have resigned. She'd done it to take the heat off Jada. It made Jada grateful, and she wondered again if the bank could legally fire Michelle because her husband was charged with a crime.

Jada pulled into her driveway and was annoyed to see that a car was already parked there. Damn it! That meant that the court-appointed social worker was already waiting. Jada looked at her watch. It wasn't four o'clock yet, so she wasn't late, but even the set of the shoulders of the woman inside the car seemed already affronted. Jada didn't even have time to smooth her skirt or check out her lipstick, so she just threw open the Volvo's door and stepped out to meet this woman. She hoped she wasn't dealing with a bigot.

Jada had to bend to look into the car. A light-skinned black woman, her hair pulled back tightly and hanging behind her in braids, looked through the glass at her, eyes already narrowed in assessment. Jada decided not to smile. Angie Romazzano had explained how important this meeting was, not that Jada needed that reminder, but Jada felt that kissing-up would only make things worse. Neither of them moved. Finally Jada raised her brows and, reluctantly it seemed, the woman got out of the car. She was short and dumpy.

She looked up at Jada and held her hand out. "I'm Mrs. Elroy," she announced in a voice that made it clear she was from the islands, but which ones? "Department of Social Services," the woman continued. "You must be Jada Jackson."

Jada nodded, placing the light accent and disturbed to hear the woman's Jamaican lilt. It was funny about islanders. You would think that people from the Caribbean would feel they had something in common, but they usually didn't. Jada decided immediately it was best to keep her background as quiet as she could.

"It's raw out here," she said. "Shall we go into the house?"

"Well, you'd have to invite me in, raw or not," Mrs. Elroy said. "I'm state-appointed to inspect the house."

As if she didn't know, Jada thought bitterly. It was going to be one of those. Jada knew she would have to stand it, but she almost couldn't bear the idea. "Well, let's go in the kitchen door," she said as brightly as she could manage. "I'll make you a cup of coffee or tea."

"I don't drink while I'm on duty," Mrs. Elroy said, as if she were some kind of police officer and Jada had offered her a double malt whiskey. They entered the kitchen and Jada took off her coat, hanging it on one of the hooks beside the door. She held out her hand for Mrs. Elroy's coat, but the woman shook her head until her braids wiggle-waggled. She didn't put her bag down, nor her briefcase.

"Why don't we start with an examination of the house," she said. "Then we can move on to the interview."

Jada just nodded. She'd been up half the night straightening, dusting, and vacuuming, but she knew already that it was most unlikely her housekeeping would measure up.

Mrs. Elroy took copious notes as she toured the house. Jada was very tempted to look over the short woman's shoulder at the clipboard she held, but knew it was best not to try. She wanted to explain about the plywood floor in the kitchen, the boarded window in the hall, and the tiles left stacked but not installed in both bathrooms. *See how lazy he is?* she wanted to ask. *See how he never put up my bookshelves or finished my kitchen floor?* But Jada kept her mouth shut. Mrs. Elroy—in between note taking—asked only a few questions about the house and the children's rooms, then led Jada back downstairs as if it were her house and Jada was an unwelcome guest. Jada silently took a deep breath and decided that she simply had to turn this thing around.

She excused herself for a moment and took another half of the little orange pills that Michelle had given her. She could do it, she told herself, and returned to ask Mrs. Elroy if she would like to sit in the living room; she almost repeated her offer of a drink, but stopped in time. Mrs. Elroy merely shook her head again and moved to one of the dining room chairs—the one at the head of the table.

"We'll sit here," she said, making it clear who was, and was going to stay, the boss.

Jada took the seat beside her. She noticed her hands had started fluttering again, so she pulled the chair as close to the table as she could and tried her best to smile at the social worker. Mrs. Elroy, however, didn't look up. She was busy sorting through some papers and finally pulled a printed sheet out of a file and placed it on top of her note-taking clipboard.

"I have some basic questions I need you to answer," she said, as if Jada didn't know that either. The woman must have been a first-grade teacher at some time in her life. That, or a passive-aggressive sadist in a house of pain. Madame Elroy, Queen of Discipline. "After that, I will have some more specific ones, ones relating both to the current situation of the children and to your fitness in the past."

Fitness? Jada said a silent prayer for strength and merely nodded. With a woman like this, it was best to be as submissive as she could manage. Jada wasn't good at submissive, but to save her children she'd do whatever it took.

They went fairly speedily through a lot of the basic information—full names, birth dates, school and grades, as well as information about Jada herself: her education, her work history, her salary. Mrs. Elroy raised her brows when Jada named her annual compensation. Instead of being proud of what she had achieved, for some reason Jada felt like hanging her head. She also wondered what Mrs. Elroy made, and knew it was significantly less. How angry was she about that?

"So, Mrs. Jackson, you began your career as a teller when the children were how old?" Mrs. Elroy asked.

Jada told her. "And of course, I wasn't even pregnant yet with Sherrilee," she added.

"And what hours were you working on your business career while your older two were at school and home without you?"

Jada didn't like the way the question was phrased. "Mrs. Elroy, I *had* to work. It wasn't a career. It was a minimum-paying job. I didn't want it. But my husband wasn't bringing in a dime. We were in debt. We had maxed out our MasterCard on groceries. I was afraid we might lose the house. It wasn't that I *wanted* to work. I just *had* to work."

Mrs. Elroy didn't take a single note. "And you *had* to move up from teller to branch manager?" she asked. She didn't wait for an answer. "Let's just stick to the questions, to my key questions, shall we?"

Jada wanted to do more than talk back. She wanted to slap the woman up-side her head. She was sure her hands would stop shaking if she did that. But this was too important to mess up.

"I only worked until three o'clock when I was a teller," Jada said. "After my promotion to head teller, I had to work a little later, but Clinton was always home." Jada paused for a moment. She didn't want to make it sound as if Clinton had been a house-husband. "He never did much with them, but at least the children were being supervised. And I took the promotion because the extra money was so important. Our tax returns would prove that."

"So when did you get your *next* promotion?" the woman asked, but to Jada it sounded more like "When did you get your next conviction?"

Jada went through her job history calmly, though she felt anything but calm herself. She was careful not to sound as if she were bragging. When Jada finished, Mrs. Elroy summarized it. "So in the last two years, despite your pregnancy and after the birth of you third child, you were working fifty to sixty hours a week." Jada had to nod. It did sound like a conviction.

"*And* doing the cooking and most of the grocery shopping and *all* of the cleaning," Jada added. "*I* was the one who supervised the children's homework. *I* supervised their television— or lack of it. I attended the parent-teacher conferences. I was the responsible parent."

Mrs. Elroy didn't take any notes and didn't respond to that. "With all of the difficulties you seemed already to be having," she said, "why did you have a third child—one you couldn't possibly be home to raise?"

Jada drew her breath in and hoped the woman hadn't heard her gasp. Was it legal for the social worker to pry like this? Wasn't that a question too much like "When did you stop beating your wife?" How could she— *why* would she—possibly explain about the way she and Clinton had avoided sex until that New Year's night? That she had been drunk. That she had agonized about having the baby, once she knew about the pregnancy. That, without telling Clinton, she'd made an appointment for an abortion. And that she hadn't shown up. Nor had she ever—even when she was exhausted from night feedings and returning to work—ever regretted her decision. Sherilee was an easy, loving, happy baby. She felt like a reward to Jada. What had Clinton already told her to poison the woman's mind? Jada, who never cried, felt her eyes fill with tears.

"I love my baby," she told Mrs. Elroy. "I love all my babies. And if you talk to them, you'll know that they love me. I've been a good mother. They need me."

"I *have* spoken to them, Mrs. Jackson, as well as their baby-sitter. I know how to do my job. And I have also spoken to your husband and your mother-in-law. I know your children are living in inadequate space, while you have seven empty rooms around you."

"But I *want* them here. I *want* them in these rooms."

"But you won't give up the house to them and your husband."

"What?" Jada imagined all the poison that Clinton, her mother-in-law, and God knows who else had poured into this woman's head. "Why shouldn't they be here with me?" Jada asked.

"Is it true that you consort with a known drug pusher? And that you let your children visit their home?"

"No, it's not true. My best friend has kids almost the ages of my children. They've been friends for years. Recently her husband was indicted—*not* convicted—for drugs. Anyway, my children have not seen them since he was indicted. And I believe he's innocent. And his wife, my girlfriend, certainly is."

"You yourself don't take drugs?" Mrs. Elroy asked.

"What?" Jada questioned. "Of course not."

"You wouldn't mind submitting to a urine analysis, would you?" Mrs. Elroy continued.

"Yes! I mean, no." Jada still didn't know what she meant: yes, she would mind, or no, she wouldn't submit—or yes, she would? She was too shocked by the question to say anything else except, "Is that what this is about? Is that what Clinton told you? That I'm a drug addict?"

"I'll do the questioning, Mrs. Jackson. So, you will submit a urine specimen."

"Yes. I guess so."

Mrs. Elroy checked a box on her form and nodded her head. "Also how long have you been under psychiatric care?"

"Psychiatric care?" Jada echoed. "Never."

"You *never* consulted a psychiatrist?"

Jada stopped and thought Clinton couldn't be saying all this. It was madness. It was so, so very mean—and clever. "I once went to a counselor—I think he was a psychologist—and he was a *marriage* counselor. It was years ago. I wanted Clinton to come. He wouldn't." Jada tried not to sound defensive, as if she'd been caught in a lie. "But I only went to the man two or three times, until it became clear that Clinton wouldn't participate."

Mrs. Elroy raised her bushy brows and made another note. She asked for the counselor's name and address. "I don't remember," Jada admitted. "It was years ago."

"So you refuse to give me his name."

"I don't remember," Jada repeated. "But I'll look for it."

"Fine," Mrs. Elroy said. Then she bent over, went into her canvas tote, and pulled out a small plastic container in a Ziploc bag. Calmly she handed it to Jada. "Just write your name on the side of the receptacle. Sign this release, fill the specimen jar, and return this to me in the bag, please."

"Now?" Jada asked, totally at a loss.

"No time like the present," Mrs. Elroy said, and rose. Jada reluctantly took the bag and stood up. She started to move out of the dining room.

"Where are you going?" Mrs. Elroy asked, her voice sharp.

"To the bathroom."

"That's not the way we do this. Which bathroom will you be using?"

"I guess the one off the kitchen," Jada said, now mystified.

"I'll have to tape the faucet," Mrs. Elroy told her, and took out a roll of bandage adhesive along with scissors. She followed Jada through the kitchen. Jada stopped for a moment to fix the paper towels. "Don't touch anything," Mrs. Elroy said sharply. "Not until we're finished."

She went into the bathroom first, and Jada watched from the doorway as she checked the room and the medicine cabinet, then taped the faucet and checked the toilet. "Please don't flush until you've returned the bag to me. Please don't touch anything until after you've capped the plastic bottle and sealed the bag."

Jada looked directly at the woman. "Why don't you just stay in her with me until I'm finished," she said bitterly.

"That won't be necessary," Mrs. Elroy told her. She passed Jada and waited while Jada went into the bathroom. Mrs. Elroy shut the door. It was only then that Jada thought about the Xanax that she had taken. My God, she thought, would that show up in her urine? And what did it show up *as*? She didn't know exactly what it was, and she sure didn't have a prescription for it. Did that make it illegal? She could imagine herself explaining to Mrs. Elroy, or to some judge, that her girlfriend, the one whose husband was accused of being a drug lord, had given her pills. Jada's hands began shaking so badly that the bag rattled, sounding as if she'd set a small crackling fire in her own lavatory. "I'm right outside the door," Mrs. Elroy said. It was all too much. Way too much.

Jada opened the door and handed the unopened bag to Mrs. Elroy.

"I couldn't do it," she said. "I'm just too nervous."

"I can wait," Mrs. Elroy said, and smiled for the first time since she'd arrived.

"No, you can't," Jada told her. "Our meeting is finished."

"I think I really fucked up," Jada said to Angie Romazzano. She'd gotten her on the phone immediately after that horror left the house.

"I'm sure it wasn't as bad as you think," the lawyer said. "I mean, you're bound to feel uncomfortable in these circumstances. Mrs. Jackson—Jada—you're a good mom and we can document that."

"He said, I *think* he said, that Tonya Green is a baby-sitter. And she believes it. Can *you* believe it?"

"Well, he wouldn't be the first man to be sleeping with his baby-sitter," Angie said. "Baby-sitters, best friends, sisters. Please, don't get too upset. We'll get everything in deposition that we need."

"But . . . but there was the drug test," Jada said, and her hands began to shake again. They shook so badly, the receiver of the phone actually bumped against one of her teeth.

"What drug test?" the lawyer asked, her voice raised.

Jada explained what had happened and there was a long silence at the other end of the phone. "I screwed up, didn't I?" Jada asked.

"I don't know. I think maybe I did," Angie told her. "Look, let me call a few people tonight and see what I can figure out. How about we meet early tomorrow? Before you go to work?"

"Before I go to work, I walk. Why don't you walk with us?" Jada asked. "You only live a few blocks from here. And I would hate to miss my walk with Michelle." There was another pause, but this one was much briefer.

"Fine," Angie Romazzano said. "What time should I be there?" Jada told her and Angie groaned. "God, I'll be exhausted."

"You think you're tired?" Jada asked. "I worked, then I had this interview with Mrs. I-Hate-You-Because-You're-A-Bad-Incompetent-Mother, and now I have to put on a happy face and pretend everything's fine." Jada took a big sigh. "What I really want is to see my kids more than anything, of course. But Lord knows I feel like shit. I don't want to break down in front of them. And I'm so afraid, afraid that . . . well, this wasn't a good thing."

"Don't worry, Jada," Angie said. "We'll get you your kids back. I promise."

That evening, after Jada fortified herself with a prayer and even considered a glass of rum and Coke, which she passed on, she finally picked up the phone and called her parents in Barbados. They had a little house not far from Crain Beach and Jada imagined her mother jumping when the phone rang in the evening island stillness. Jada had decided she wasn't going to tell them everything—if she did they'd be up there beside her, and right now she didn't think she could face them. They probably couldn't be of much help anyway.

It hurt her pride to have to admit to her mother that all of the woman's maternal instincts and prejudices had been right. She didn't want to upset her father, who had a mild heart condition and high blood pressure. Most of all, she didn't want to break down and cry like a broken-hearted child.

She wondered if the air down there was sweet with the smell of frangi-pani or night-blooming jasmine.

When, on the fifth ring, she heard the receiver lifted and her mother's voice saying, "Hello? Hello?" Jada was silent for a minute. Then she took a deep breath.

"Mama?" she asked, though she recognized her mother's voice. "Mama, you were right."

28

All girls get moving

Angie hadn't been able to reach her mother the night before, so in desperation she tried Michael, who was the clinic's specialist in marital law. He answered the phone on the first ring, and after Angie apologized profusely, she told him about Jada Jackson's meeting with the social worker and the unexpected request for a urine sample. "Is that usual, Michael?"

"No," he said. "There would have to be some real strong allegations about her. The husband, or George Creskin, is really playing hardball. And it's a no-win for your client. If she refuses, she looks bad. And she doesn't have to take it. But why *didn't* she take the test—humiliating as it was—just to prove how unsubstantiated his position is?"

"I don't know," Angie admitted. "But I'm going to meet with her tomorrow morning at six and find out."

"Boy, you're really throwing yourself into this." Michael paused. "Do you mind if I give you some non-legal advice?"

Angie didn't like advice, legal or not, but she liked the way he asked, giving her the option to refuse it. He really was a thoughtful, nice guy. "Okay," she said. "Fire away."

"This job can eat you up," he said. "You have to be committed but detached. I know that sounds contradictory, but it's the only thing that works." He paused for a minute and Angie was about to say thanks when he cleared his throat and continued. "These clients can break your heart if you get too involved," he said. "And it can destroy your personal life."

"Oh, that's okay," Angie told him. "I don't have one of those."

The next morning when the alarm went off, Angie felt that it was impossible for her to get up and go out. It was still really dark. But she forced herself to pull on the old Rangers sweatshirt (which she actually had thrown into the wash a couple of times since she'd begun wearing it) slipped into her father's jogging pants, and was sure to put on two pairs of socks along with her sneakers.

Trudging down the street toward Elm, feeling like a kid trussed up in snow pants, she thought about her conversation with Michael. She was sure he meant well. Her answer had probably sounded snotty to him, but it was true. She had no private life, except for the secret inside her. Aside from her trip to Marblehead, a couple of business lunches, some dinners with her mother, and the apartment hunting, Angie hadn't been out of her father's house. She didn't even make phone calls because she had lost not only her husband but her close friend, and she wasn't in the mood to tell her old college friends or law school acquaintances about the collapse of her life. Most of them probably knew by now anyway, though, thanks to the nasty grapevine—the one that always let classmates know when someone didn't get a partnership.

She had no close girlfriends, no hobbies, no home, and she was living off what was left in her checking account, the clinic's tiny salary—which was still a temporary per diem—and her father's unpredictable charity.

She had cooked her dad dinner the night before so she could prepare him for her move. As she expected, he had been grateful for her company and the grilled chicken, but he hadn't been glad about her relocation news. "It's not necessary," he said. "It's just an extra expense."

Angie suspected he was hurt and still recovering from the fact that she was working with her mother. Now, if she wasn't living with him, he was probably afraid he wouldn't see her. Her father was an odd man.

She knew that he loved her, but they didn't have much to share. It was odd thinking of her mom putting up with her dad for all those years, and odder still to think that he had broken up the marriage by cheating on Natalie. Not that it had done him much good; the second marriage hadn't worked and now he was stuck here alone without much of a life. Angela knew that he would both miss her company and be ashamed to admit it. Why was it that people who wanted to be with her were not the people she wanted to be with, and the people she wanted to be with didn't want a thing to do with her?

If I think about this, I'll go insane, Angie told herself. Then she realized that she was trudging through the dark on the cold street because she was moving toward the warmth she saw between Jada Jackson and her friend. She missed friendship—if she'd had any. Thinking about Lisa made her so angry or depressed she pushed the thought from her mind. She missed not Lisa, but having a real friend. Well, this walk probably was a bad idea, but it wouldn't kill her to get a little exercise, just this once.

When she joined Jada and Michelle, they were in the middle of the street just around the corner from their homes. They greeted each other silently and Angie turned around to walk back in the direction they were going, back past her father's house.

"We could just stop and pick you up on our way," Jada said.

"Yeah," Michelle agreed. "Jada always gets me. Except for those couple of times she couldn't get in gear. Then I got her. We could both get you and make sure you do the circuit."

Despite the cold, Angie felt warmed through by the offer. The kindness of inclusion felt so good it almost made her choke up. *Boy, you are really vulnerable,* Angie told herself. *Better watch out or you'll be rolling over and barking for treats. Remember not to lick their hands when we say good-bye.* They trudged for half a block in silence and then Jada picked up the pace. Angie figured she better get down to business. "So, tell me about this interview."

Jada shook her head. "It was unbelievable," she said. "I would say the woman was a bigot, except she obviously wasn't prejudiced against my husband."

"There's another five-letter word that begins with 'b,'" Michelle said. "She was just a bitch."

Angie asked for all the details, though it was obvious that Michelle had already heard them. They walked up a steep hill, then down it; around a bend, another long hill appeared. Angie was out of breath and out of shape and she wished she could take notes, but she kept up with the other two.

"Look, I'm checking into this. Don't worry. I'm sure we can get another social worker in, but may I ask why . . ." She paused. "Well, why you didn't take the test. Is there something I should know?"

She saw Jada and Michelle exchange looks. Then Michelle, who had been silent except for her bitch remark, spoke. "It's all my fault. I'm under a lot of stress, too." The woman looked deeply troubled and for a moment Angie thought she was about to spill her story. Then she watched as Michelle licked her lips and turned her head away. "Anyway, I went to my doctor because I was having anxiety attacks. He prescribed something."

"Yeah? So what's wrong with that?" Angie asked.

Michelle flicked a look at Jada, who shrugged. "She's my lawyer, Mich. I'm telling her everything. And I'm never taking those pills again."

Angie got worried. Was there some kind of drug problem going on? Oh Christ. Now that she had committed to this case, she'd find out that Jada was all the things Mr. Jackson accused her of.

"Look," Michelle said, "there's nothing wrong with them. They were psychotropics. Jada was so crazy from all this that I gave her a couple of my pills."

"Yeah," Jada said bitterly. "I was feeling like a psycho, but they sure didn't make me go to the tropics."

"The point is," Michelle said, "she was afraid they might show up in her urine. We don't even know what's in them."

"Well, what are they? Ecstasy?" Angie asked.

"Xanax," Michelle said, without even a hint of a smile.

"So what's the big deal?" Angie asked, deeply relieved. "Jada, with what you've been through, you probably need some anti-anxiety medication. Best to get a prescription, though." Angie turned to Michelle. "Can I have some, too?" she joked.

Michelle managed a weak smile. "I felt so guilty. I thought I ruined everything. You don't think it's too serious?"

Actually, Angie wasn't sure, but she shook her head no. "Half the women in America have prescriptions for Xanax or Valium," she said. "And the other half borrow them from their friends. It's no big deal." She paused, vamping for time, and hoped to give Jada some shred of comfort in what sounded like a vat of trouble. "I'm going to try to get another social worker assigned. It won't eliminate the first home visit, but it will add. And maybe it wasn't as bad as you thought."

Jada smiled for the first time that morning. "Do you really think you can get me a different social worker?"

"Look, if I can't, I'll certainly speak with Mrs. Monster and see exactly what she's planning to say."

"It's really good of you to do all this," Jada said. "I mean, a younger woman like you shouldn't have to be involved in all of this tragedy. You should be optimistic and enjoy your life."

Angie looked up at Jada and laughed. "Oh yeah," she said, "let me tell you how optimistic and pleasurable my life is. Let me tell you about my romantic first anniversary." She launched into the story and both women listened raptly as they walked along. She told them about the "older woman," the Soprano, and then finding out her friend Lisa *was* the older woman. She told them about the trip to Marblehead—all of it. All except the big secret. She was tempted, but she couldn't tell them.

"I can't believe it," Michelle said when Angela was done.

"I can." Jada snorted. The two women went on to criticize Reid, ranting on about him, and then they had a few choice words for Lisa.

Angela quickened her steps and marched along beside them. She realized she felt good. Well, if not good, then a little better. It wasn't just the walk, it was the company. She really liked Jada. Michelle, on the other hand, seemed kind of wimpy and distracted, but she was clearly a good friend to Jada and vice versa. Angie was just grateful that she'd been invited.

They came to the end of a cul-de-sac and began to turn around when Jada stopped. "Mich, aren't you going to hit the post?" Angie didn't know what Jada was talking about. She just looked at Michelle, whose head hung down limply until she shook it.

"Michelle, what's wrong with you?" Jada asked. "You *always* touch the post. Are you mad because of what went down at the bank?" Angie opened her eyes wider, but said nothing. "Or is it the reporters? Are they on you real bad?"

Angie knew a lot was up but decided to just keep her mouth shut. The three women stood there in the cold. The sky had lightened to silver along the eastern horizon, but long shadows still darkened the road. Angie stood very quiet. She could see the moon, a white sliver about to set. She looked at Michelle.

"Everyone in my family is dysfunctional now. Even my dog. He binges when we're outside and vomits in the house. He eats the neighbors' trash and ignores his biscuits. Everybody's life is miserable," Michelle said. "I didn't think it was going to be this way. I honestly didn't. I knew what Clinton did to you, but look at what happened to Angela," she said.

"And what happened to you," Jada added gently, and put her gloved hand on Michelle's thin shoulder. "It's not your fault."

Michelle shrugged away and started walking. Angela followed along with Jada.

"Oh yes it is," Michelle said. "I mean, what if I've been stupid? What if I've been wrong?" Angie could see tears in Michelle's blue eyes as she turned to Jada. Her voice dropped to a whisper. "What if Frank is guilty?" she whispered.

Angie still didn't say a word, but the penny had dropped and she put the pieces together. She'd read the paper and heard her father's comments. This was the woman from the drug bust down the street, the one who had made headlines. She didn't move, but for a moment she wondered whether her client was involved in a drug ring. Maybe *that* was why she hadn't wanted the urine test. Angie thought of what Michael had said, but looking at the two women Angie just knew that wasn't part of the equation.

Jada walked up to her friend and sort of bent her knees to put herself on eye level with Michelle. "Mich," she said gently. "It was always a possibility. Do you have a reason to doubt him? I mean, evidence or something?"

"No. Not really. I mean, I don't know. But they want me to testify, and I don't think I want to." She hung her head and now tears did squeeze out of her eyes. "I just don't think I want to. And I'm afraid to tell him and I'm afraid to tell Bruzeman," Michelle said, weeping.

Angie decided to take a chance and get herself involved. "Is it inappropriate of me to remind you that I'm an attorney and I might be useful?" Angie asked. Both women looked at her. "I know I'm not your lawyer, but do you know about your Fourth Amendment rights?" It was really cold, and Angie took a couple of steps forward. Michelle followed her as she shook her head. The three women continued walking and Angie pulled together her memory of constitutional law.

"The police searched your house, right?"

Michelle nodded again.

"Well, there is a particularity clause in the Fourth Amendment—it's because of the British searching any house they wanted to during the Revolutionary War. Colonists were furious. So when they drafted the Constitution, they made sure that a search couldn't be conducted unless there was a particular reason for looking—a strong indication that there was something or some reason to be searching for something particular."

"Oh, they were searching all right," Michelle said.

"They wrecked her house," Jada added.

"But the point is—" Angela almost shouted, stopping herself to think of her training in civil rights. "They couldn't be looking for just anything. There *has* to be probable cause."

"You mean some kind of proof against Frank? He's my husband."

Angela was careful not to say yes, though to get a search warrant the chances were pretty damn good. "Cops can be overzealous. District attorneys can be corrupt. But that Fourth Amendment law is pretty strong stuff. Samuel Adams said, 'Then and there the child liberty was born.'"

The three women walked on in silence for more than two blocks. Angie wondered if she had said too much. Finally Jada broke the silence. "Mich, I think you need a lawyer. I mean, a lawyer of your own," she added gently.

Michelle looked at her friend and Angie recognized the torture on the woman's face. She'd been there for the last weeks over Reid.

"Don't you understand?" Michelle snapped at Jada. "If I don't stick with Frank on this, our marriage is over."

"If he's guilty, it might be over anyway," Jada said.

29

Concerning buried treasure and other buried things

Michelle was cleaning. Not just at that moment, but constantly. She knew her behavior wasn't normal, but the situation wasn't normal and she was coping the best she could. Cleaning was better than drinking, certainly.

Aside from the daily bed-making, laundry, dishes, and dusting, she had already washed the walls of Frank's shop, dusted and rearranged all his tools, and even scrubbed the cement floor. She'd found a special product at the hardware store to add to her arsenal—a grease-buster that had worked so well on the concrete in the shop that she'd gone out to the garage and used it on the oil-stained floor there.

She'd then continued in the garage, stacking every old newspaper, rewinding the garden hoses more tightly than a surgeon's catgut, and going through every bottle of DW–40, can of motor oil, and jar of nails, wiping and dusting all of them, arranging them by size, and throwing away the ones that had solidified or gone unused for years.

She'd also sorted out the attic and had been through every single box of clothes and stored toys, and all of the old photographs. She'd washed and rewrapped the Christmas ornaments, laundered Jenna's and Frankie's old baby clothes, then ironed them and laid them all away again, this time packed in tissue paper. She'd made six boxes of items for Goodwill and taken them to the depository at the bank parking lot—but early in the morning, before there was any chance of seeing anyone she knew.

Michelle certainly didn't miss the bank. She didn't even miss going out. She was too busy cleaning. In fact, she never went out—except into the backyard—unless she absolutely had to. Then she pulled a cap over her hair and wore Jackie O. sunglasses no matter how gray the day might be.

Seeing people and being seen was not something she desired. She'd even stopped grocery shopping at the Grand Union in town and had begun driving two towns away. She went to a disgusting Price Chopper where the produce was inferior and the aisles were dirty but where she was certain she wouldn't run into anyone she knew; the checkout girls didn't even look up from their scanners when she ran her groceries by them. It was a relief, but also lonely.

She had no company during the day except the dog, and wanted none at night except her husband and her kids. Nobody called. Nobody visited. None of the women from the P.T.A., none of her so-called friends from work, no one at all. Except, of course, Jada. They still did their walking together every morning and Michelle thought she might go crazy if she didn't have that normalcy each day. Thank God for Jada, who was going through a living hell of her own. *Misery loves company,* Michelle thought, and for a moment she shuddered at the idea that their friendship might be based on mutual unhappiness. Then she remembered, with relief and nostalgia, what walking had been like only months before, before their worlds had separately disintegrated.

Michelle stood in her immaculate kitchen and looked around. Was there a smudge on the refrigerator handles? She took out the rubber bucket that she carried her key supplies in. Today she would clean out all the bedroom closets. Not merely reorganizing clothes and shoes, but the actual closets themselves, emptying everything out, vacuuming the carpet and the shelves, then washing down the walls, shampooing the carpet, and putting everything back.

She checked her supply bucket—two clean sponges, one for washing and one for rinsing; the foam carpet cleaner; the spot rug cleaner; the

Soft Scrub gel, which she liked to use for smudges on the walls; her rubber gloves; two brushes; Windex; Formula 409; and Pledge. She added the little tub of Brasso to polish the closet door pulls. She twisted her hair up into a knot, and then lifted the now-heavy bucket with one hand and the Dustbuster with the other. Her vacuum was upstairs, so she felt well armed.

Pookie followed her up the stairs, but he already knew to leave her well enough alone when she was in a cleaning frenzy. She looked at Pookie's wet brown eyes and they reminded her of Frank's. Dogs and men were the same—they never spoke about what was bothering them. Usually he'd find an undisturbed spot in the same room, lie down, cross his front paws, and lay his head attentively on them, watching her.

At the top of the stairs, they went into Frankie's room first and Pookie immediately jumped onto the bed. Well, Michelle thought, she'd need most of it to put Frankie's clothes and gear on, but Pookie would live with it or wind up under the bed if he had to. She liked having him there, cutting the silence with his breathing.

Frankie's closet took a little over an hour. It was an hour of, if not of peace exactly, then at least rescue from the crazy-making thoughts that wouldn't stop circulating in Michelle's head. While she scrubbed she didn't once think about Bruzeman, Frank, Jenna and boarding school, finding Frankie a therapist, or anything else. She just scrubbed in the enclosed space of the closet until everything looked and smelled so clean that her eyes smarted from the comforting but harsh scents of ammonia and carpet cleaner. It was the only reprieve from her own mind, the only time she wasn't terrified.

Michelle stood up outside the closet and looked at the pristine emptiness with something as close to pleasure as she'd felt lately. She took a deep breath and then, noticing the slight tarnish on the closet door handles, she took out the Brasso and carefully lathered it on, being sure not to allow even a bit of it to touch the high-gloss paint of the door. Michelle wiped off some of the Brasso and wished she had Simichrome instead, the polish that *really* worked, but she'd run out of the stuff and had to go all the way to White Plains to get it. This would just have to do, she told herself; so what if it just took longer and might need a second coat? She had nothing else but other closets waiting. She took out her roll of paper towels, tore one off, and tentatively began to rub the tarnish off the knob in a circular motion.

Somehow, it made her think of sex. She and Frank hadn't made love for a couple of weeks now. She'd woken up last night to find him on one elbow above her, watching her face with those wet, soulful eyes. She'd rolled under him invitingly, but he'd turned away. Except for after Frankie Junior had been born—a difficult birth—she couldn't think of when there had been such a long lapse between them. And it was funny—not in a *funny* way, of course—that she also couldn't think out whether it was Frank or herself who was holding back, and whether the reluctance came from exhaustion, misery, or something else all together. Michelle finished rubbing the door handle and moved on to its mate. At least the pair of doors nestled together. She and Frank were even sleeping on opposite sides of bed.

She sighed deeply, then coughed from the smell of the cleaning chemicals. Michelle moved both sliding doors apart so the closet was fully exposed to the air. To help circulation, she decided she'd better fetch the little fan that she kept in the upstairs linen closet, and set it up on the bedroom floor.

As she started to leave the room, Pookie, almost buried on the bed by Frankie's wardrobe, began to get up to follow her. "Stay," she commanded him and quickly returned, plugged in the fan, and trained its breeze into the closet. She couldn't hang up Frankie's clothes yet or they'd reek. She'd wait until everything in there dried and then she would rearrange his things. Michelle put her blonde tendrils up in a quick twist, stuck a hairpin in, checked her watch—it was already almost eleven—and turned to the dog.

"Okay, Pookie, we have another room to do."

Jenna's closet was another story altogether. She had an endless amount of dresses, tops, jackets, skirts, shoes, bags, belts, and other nonsense absolutely stuffed into her closet. When Michelle began the transfer from the hangers to the bed, Pookie was off it and under it in no time. Michelle took advantage of the space to arrange Jenna's clothes in categories on the spread.

Once again, as she'd done in Frankie's room, Michelle went into the closet and began on the walls. How did so many smudges get all over them? Michelle wouldn't allow herself to miss a single one. She thought of her mother and the house she grew up in, how her mother had let everything go, fixing things—whatever was wrong or dirty or broken—with a drink. Michelle would never, not *ever* let that happen. She wouldn't let *anything* go. She attacked a black heel smudge at the bottom of the closet wall with renewed vigor.

Jenna's closet was much bigger and dirtier than Frankie's. There was also an extra corner, a slight indentation where the closet went back another six inches because of a structural beam. She remembered Frank yelling at the wall boarder for starting to board over it and waste the niche. He was a stickler for quality. Well, she was, too. Michelle moved into the narrow space so she would wash the walls in the indentation and then get to the carpet. But as she worked her way down the wall to the bottom, she noticed for the first time how the tweed carpet there was frayed.

Well, she could get up and get her little scissors to cut it even, she thought, but first she pulled at it for a moment to see if the frizz was simply loose from wear or catching on the heels and buckles of Jenna's shoes.

Michelle tugged, and the carpet moved a little bit under her hand. Surprised, she pulled harder. She saw then that the fraying was a seam, not just a few loose loops of pile. She supposed the seam was because of the indentation in the back. She hated that, and so would Frank, though she supposed in a closet it wasn't worth the money to cut another huge swath if it was going to cause lots of waste. Still annoyed, she pulled at the seam harder than she meant to and this time the whole piece lifted up and away from the floor in her hand.

Great! Now there'd be sawdust, staples, dirt, and all the rest of it that might have been buried by the carpet layers when they'd stretched and nailed the rug. But when Michelle stared down at the floor beneath the carpet, it wasn't dusty. That wasn't normal. The floorboards weren't laid abutting one another in a running bond, as they were with the maple planking in the rest of the house. Instead, right before her, Michelle could

see a perfect alignment, a carefully crafted crack that went up one, two . . .
six boards. Michelle reached down with her rubber gloves still on and
began to pull at the exposed edge. Was there all kinds of grime in there?

She felt a wiggle, but couldn't get her fingers in, so she used the handle of her scrub brush. It worked as a lever, and as a single piece, the
wood lifted up.

Michelle suddenly felt dizzy. She dropped the piece of carpet and the
wooden cover to the open space exposed beneath the floor. Her skin
turned hot then cold with foreboding. There, very neatly wrapped in
newspaper, were four rectangular packages inserted between the joists.
Michelle picked one up.

Pookie, as if he could sense her changed mood, came into the closet
beside her and began sniffing—not just the carpet, but also the package
in her hand. Was it a book? Michelle carefully unwrapped the folded
paper in one corner where it wasn't held by the bakery string that tied it
up. As she bent the newspaper away, hundred-dollar-bills—still in their
wrapper—were exposed.

Pookie put out his head and began to snuffle at them. Without thinking, she pushed him roughly away. "No!" she said, and he slunk somewhere out of the closet, but Michelle could hardly think of the dog's feelings now. Her own were too frozen. She stared at the heavy package of
money in her hand. Pulling off her gloves, she ran the tip of her fingernail down past the money. They were hundreds, all of them hundreds.
And they were the old hundred-dollars-bills, not the new ugly ones.

Thinking of her first job in the teller's cage, Michelle tried to estimate
what she was holding in her hands, but then the dizziness came back and
she had to put the money down, get up, and almost stagger to her
daughter's bed. She pushed Jenna's clothes to the floor in piles and laid
down, drawing her knees up close to her chest. Slowly the dizziness
passed, but the fear took its place. Not fear—terror. She'd seen four
packages in the floor, and she estimated there were at least five or six
hundred bills in the first one. Over half a million dollars wrapped in
newspaper under floorboards and carpet, hidden in her eleven-year-old
daughter's closet beneath pairs of old Doc Martens and new platform
shoes?

Michelle felt suddenly so exposed, so endangered, that when Pookie jumped on the bed, she nearly screamed. The poor dog started and was about to bolt until she reached out to him and nestled him on her lap. She needed him and his body warmth right now more than he needed her. She patted his head and automatically pulled gently on his silky ears the way he liked. Everything else stopped. Everything except the dog's breathing and her own.

Then, almost like a video running behind her eyelids, she saw what her life with Frank and the children had been. Comfortable. Easy. They'd never worried about downsizing, about recessions, about turn-downs in the economy the way everyone else had for the last ten years. Unlike Clinton's, Frank's business had thrived. Michelle, who had never been greedy before, had spent whatever she wanted to and Frank had encouraged her. He'd bought her jewelry. They took vacations. He deposited cash in her checking account and she paid the bills without problems every month, month after month, for . . . for years and years. When she'd taken the bank job, Frank had mildly disapproved, and reminded her they didn't need the money. All the other couples in their neighborhood both worked, but . . .

Then the scene of the bust, fragmented, came to her, and the meet-ings with Bruzeman, and the promise from Frank that it was all a mis-take. The women at the bake sale. Getting fired at the bank, Jenna's tears, Frankie's wet beds. All of it kept flashing faster and faster at Michelle. Frank's face, and his promises, his protestations, her belief, her support, her loyalty. Her stupidity.

"Stupid," she said out loud, and it sounded like her mother's voice. Pookie jumped a little. "Stupid," Michelle repeated. *My mother was right. I am stupid. And Frank must think I'm stupid, too.*

But stupid as I am, Michelle thought, *even I know where all this money had to come from.*

30

In which Angela comes to her senses—mostly smells

Angie woke up and rushed across the bare floor to the bathroom sink. She was living in a state of siege. She was having all ahe could do to go on her walk with the girls each weekday morning, since she was sick almost every morning now. Then for the rest of the day, the smell of anything—even an apple sitting on the kitchen counter across the room—seemed to waft a strong odor that sent waves of nausea through her. In fact, her sense of smell had advanced along with her pregnancy, so that she could now detect soup or anything else being prepared in the immediate area. All meats had an odor of dead flesh; when Bill, the paralegal at work, had cheerfully offered her half of his turkey sandwich yesterday, she'd actually had to step quickly back, away from the innocent-looking white slabs of flesh he held out between two slices of bread.

Bread was about the only thing Angie *could* eat now. As she washed out her mouth, for some reason she thought of the biblical quote that "man doth not live by bread alone." But some pregnant women, even back then, surely did. Angie, in modern days, was foremost among them. Just another difference between men and women, Angie thought bitterly, as she took tiny bites out of a slice of Wonder Bread. She knew that the advertisements for the stuff from her youth weren't true—the spongy bread didn't build strong bodies in twelve ways. Too bad, since it was all she could choke down.

She thought of the tiny body growing within her and knew she should go to a doctor and probably be eating differently, but what was the point? She couldn't decide if she should continue the pregnancy for even one day more. But she also couldn't bear the thought of aborting the tiny life within her, of making the decision to do that all alone. She'd loved Reid so much, wanted him and a life with him, that thinking about ending this life, killing this dream was unbearable.

Keeping the secret was unbearable, too. She'd never let her father see or hear her vomiting, and Anthony, who was in and out on business all the time, hadn't said anything about her weight gain. Mostly she tried to avoid him. His protective love and anger wouldn't be helpful right now. He'd offer to beat up Reid and pay for the OB-GYN, but Angie had to make her decision first.

Angie got dressed and drove into work early. She'd left a note for her dad. She had chickened out at telling him about her apartment. Her mother had been bad enough, with offers of furniture, worries about the neighborhood, and requests for the floor plan. Anthony would be worse when he found out.

She got to work, poured herself a cup of hot water—coffee was out of the question—and sat at her quiet desk. She tried to work as much as she could—work took concentration, and when she focused on it she couldn't think about anything else, her own problems included. But she knew, deep inside her, that every moment that ticked by was one moment closer to the time when a decision would be made for her, even if she did nothing.

She was alone—yet not alone. She slept more deeply and with more exhaustion than she ever had in her life. The workload and the pressure to help her clients was enormous, but coupled with it was the energy drained from her body by this secret growing inside her.

Angie also got tired every afternoon—so tired that she twice had put her head down on her desk, waking up with a stiff neck to find she had drooled out of the side of her mouth and onto several of the files while she napped. Now she picked up the Jackson folder, marked with a blot from a previous nap, and began looking through it again. George

Creskin had gotten an incredibly early date for the custody hearing and Angie wasn't sure she could be prepared in time. Could she get a continuance? She'd have to ask Laura or Michael. For some reason—not just because she was spending her mornings walking with Jada Jackson, but because of the outrageous situation that the woman had found herself in—Angie felt this case was central to her. She got up and put the stained folder under her arm to go consult with Michael. Although his caseload was enormous, he'd already been kind about helping her—and she needed a lot of help.

He was working in his equally small but meticulously organized office at the very end of the hall. He looked up from his desk, capped his meaty pen, and swung his legs out from around the side of the modesty panel. "So," he said, "you're both mobile *and* awake." Angie felt her shoulders dip guiltily.

Michael raised his hand in a dismissive gesture and lowered his voice. "I stepped into Karen's—I mean, *your* office yesterday and you were asleep," he said and smiled. He had a nice-looking smile for a suburban father type. Angie had to grin back. "I warned you, this stuff can be really overwhelming," he continued. "I'm not good at sleeping, but I've been known to sneak out and go sit in a movie on an afternoon when it just gets to me." He put his hands behind his head in a sort of cradle and stretched back. Angie sat down in the seat clients usually used. She couldn't help but notice how Michael's belly pooched out when he stretched like that, as if *he* were in the earliest stage of pregnancy. She pushed the thought from her mind.

"I want you to look at this," she said, and handed him a copy of the social worker's report she had just received. "Is this report really pretty ghastly, or am I overreacting? Jada will be devastated."

Michael raised his brows again. "*Jada?*" he asked. "So, you're on a first-name basis?" Angie shrugged.

He picked up the document she offered him and began to read it. She had hoped the news wasn't as bad as she feared, but he raised his brows almost immediately. She took that as a bad sign. "Wow," he said after he'd skimmed through it. "Let's get in our own expert witness to counteract this."

"Good. You know one?"

"The best. Dr. Pollasky from Yale. A pal of mine. But . . ." He looked uncomfortable. "Look," he finally continued, thumbing through the report, "before we go through the expense of an outside expert, is there any chance that this woman is"—he looked down at the page—"unstable, a possible drug user, or any of the other crap listed here? I know she's your client, but there *are* children at stake."

Before Angie could reply, he went on. "Hmmm. No witnesses to any of that except her and him. He said, she said. The judge will usually rule for the mother, not that that's necessarily fair, but that's the way it is. Here, however, we have a very negative report from the social worker. Okay, she spoke with the father first and obviously was prejudiced but . . . Creskin has asked for and received an early date, claiming the kids are at risk. He points out the children are already in custody with the father, and a new caregiver is employed."

"The caregiver is his girlfriend!" Angela told Michael. "And she's being paid out of Jada's support money!"

Michael sighed and shook his head. "So she's giving testimony that the children were not cared for. And so will his mother. Where are her parents?"

"In Barbados," Angie admitted. "She didn't want them involved if she could help it. They're old, and they couldn't have witnessed much on a day-to-day basis. But I can get her friends to testify. A past PTA president. Her neighbor, Michelle Russo. Though there is a problem there . . ."

Michael was silent for a while as he looked through the file. "This thing about the drug dealer isn't good," he said. "Jesus, they've got news clippings and part of the testimony on this Russo guy and his wife. And she's a friend? The kids were in the Russo household? And then they were—"

"Look, don't jump to conclusions. The woman may be our next client. She hasn't been indicted. There was no extraordinary traffic in and out of the house. And the husband has only been indicted, not convicted, Michael. This is America."

"Tell it to the judge," Michael said. "In Dom Rel cases, if it looks like a rat, smells like a rat, and tastes like a rat, it's a rat."

Angie stood up. "I can't believe the injustice of it," she said. "This is a woman who did everything, *everything*, to keep her family together while her husband loafed and slept around. It's outrageous."

Michael nodded calmly in agreement. Then he smiled.

Suddenly Angie was furious. "Are you laughing at me?" Angie asked. "Do you think this is funny? Do you think *I'm* funny? Because I came to you for some help to win this case. With or without it, I'm *going* to win this case."

"I'm smiling at you because I like you," Michael said. "I used to be as fired up as you. As passionate." For some reason, Angie blushed. "I meant that in the professional sense, Angie," Michael said. "But you're what my kids call phat."

"What?" Angie said. Was she showing already? And who was he to call her names? He had a belly.

"P-H-A-T. Pretty, hot, and tempting," he said.

Angela could hardly believe it; she almost laughed out loud. This middle-aged, white-bread guy had used outdated rapper slang on her? But somehow she liked the compliment.

"Now sit down," he told her. He sounded so reasonable, so pleasant, that her anger evaporated and she did as she was told. "Look, domestic law is not about fair. It's about law. And sometimes it's not even about law—it's about manipulation and presentation and strategy. George Creskin has gotten a drop on us here, and he's obviously got a pretty good strategy. We need one as good or better, and it certainly can't be you explaining your view of fairness and expecting the judge to accept that." He paused and smiled again. "With me so far?" he asked, but not in an offensive way. Angie nodded.

"So the point here is that we have to come back in with our own witnesses, our own home assessment. We could also try to work through the kids."

"Jada insisted that was out of the question," Angie said.

"It's dirty pool," he said, "but the court will probably ask the two older children questions, and you can be sure that George Creskin is doing his best to prepare their views."

"They love their mother. They want to be home. That's what they'll say."

"Children with cigarette burns all over their bodies still report that they love the mother who did it to them, Angie," Michael said patiently. "Children love their mothers—at least, until their hormones kick in. And if I see Creskin's strategy, they will get to be home, if your client is forced to vacate."

Angie suddenly felt overwhelmed. She turned away from Michael, swept with another wave of fatigue so powerful she actually let her head hang for a moment while she resisted it. There was so much to do, so much to learn, and so little time. And she was so, so tired. Maybe she couldn't win this case. The thought frightened her and she raised her head with a snap. Michael was looking more closely at her.

"Look," he said, "this one is going to take some special resources. Maybe we send out an investigator. Look into this Tonya Green's background. How about the grandmother? Is she clean? And the husband, has anyone ever seen *him* smoke a joint? Has anyone ever seen him drunk? Has he ever hit her? If you really want to use everything you've got, and maybe even some stuff you might not have, you could dig in to make a case despite the lead George has on this. But it will take resources. Has she got any money?"

Angie rolled her eyes in answer. Michael made an I-knew-the-answer-to-that-one face and flipped through the rest of the brief. "Well, I think we ought to take it before the committee this afternoon. It's a real lulu, but I see your point about it being an extreme. If you're sure she's being railroaded, I'll stand behind you and we can see if we can squeeze some funding from the special kitty Laura guards."

"Funding for what?" Angie asked. "I mean, I am on salary now."

Michael grinned. "Yeah, but I bet it's not enough to pay for expert witnesses, psychologists to profile the kids, and a PI to check out Mr. Jackson and company." Michael stood up and stretched. He was taller than Angie thought, or maybe it was that she was sitting down. He took a few steps back and forth. "We also should see if we can get another social worker, and have a state-administered drug test for Mrs. Jackson. Or maybe a series of them." He put down the file. "You might also ask for one on Mr. Jackson. And it might not hurt to have me help on some of the testimony rehearsals."

"Would you?" she asked. "Would you have the time?"

He barked a kind of unpleasant laugh. "Oh, I got nothin' but time," he told her.

"You don't have to move, you know," Anthony said to Angie for about the fourth time. "I mean, there's plenty of room here."

Angie had been waiting for the other shoe to drop, but at least her father hadn't dropped dead when she'd broken the news to him that she'd found a place. He'd argued instead. Angie loved her father, despite his faults, despite his past behavior to her mother, but she couldn't live with him. Nor should she. He still saw her as a child. Wait until he found out she might be having one! She couldn't tell him that now. One blow at a time. And, Anthony being Anthony, he'd argued about money.

"You can't afford it. You don't need it. It's too expensive. It's a rip off. I can get one for you better and cheaper." The fact was, he'd miss her and he couldn't say he was hurt or afraid to lose her. "Really, Angie," he was repeating, "there's plenty of room."

Angie looked up from the box she was tying and smiled. "Too much room, if you want my opinion, Daddy," she said. "Why are you living here in the suburbs anyway? It doesn't make much sense for you."

"Are we talking about me or are we talking about you?" her father asked.

"Both of us," Angie said. She started to pick up the box and Anthony moved over to her side.

"I'll do that," he told her. She touched his arm. Gray was showing more and more in his hair, and his face had shrunken a little bit, so it looked as if his skin didn't fit smoothly across his head the way it once had. Time was passing, and he was getting old. Yet he still thought he could carry boxes better than his grown-up daughter.

She smiled at him, but there was sadness for him there. His life had not come together. After he and her mother had divorced, nothing had quite gone right. She wondered how disappointing his life was, how different it was from what he had expected or hoped for. And now hers might be moving that way, too, to the disappointment after the dream. Angie was suddenly flooded with love for her flawed father.

"Thank you, Daddy," Angie said. "Thank you for telling me to walk out of that restaurant. And thanks for letting me stay here with you. Now it's time for me to get myself together. But I love you, and I'll still see you all the time."

Anthony grabbed the box. "Of course, you will," he said gruffly. "What do you think? You're movin' to China? The apartment is only a couple of miles away."

"I know," Angie said. "Will you come next week for dinner? As soon as I unpack two plates."

"Sure," her father said casually, but it didn't fool Angie. All love, she thought, was so fragile. And so precious. "You sure you don't want me to come with you and help you unpack?" he asked.

"No. Mom's doing that," Angie told him.

"Okay, fine." He said it in that too-quick way that meant he didn't want to show hurt feelings. Angie sighed. He had made his bed, but that didn't mean it was a comfortable one. She'd made hers, and sometimes it felt like the rack. Angie, without looking around her, turned and walked from the room.

The place Michael's agent had helped her find was nice. It was the lower floor in a duplex. It was sunny, and the living room doors opened to a tiny patio. If the kitchen was nothing but a closeted wall at the side of the living room, that was made up for by the two bedrooms, both of which were a decent size. She didn't need the second bedroom, of course, but she might.

She had to blink quickly to clear her eyes, because the car behind her moved up to pass. She almost missed the turn onto Larkspur, but managed to brake and pull the left in time without cutting anyone off. The garden apartments were located at the end of a pretty street with nothing but private houses along it. She pulled up and parked as close to her apartment as she could, and saw her mother, Laura, and Bill were already waiting outside. As she approached them, Bill held out a bag.

"We got you coffee," he said, "but I wasn't sure if you wanted a cruller or a handful of Munchkins."

"I didn't know you were all coming," Angie said to him and kissed her mom.

"I didn't know you were moving," Bill said. He was a really nice guy. Angie enjoyed working with him. Maybe they could be friends.

Laura patted her shoulder and Angie reached into her pocket for her new key. "Well, let me show you what the largesse of the WLCC has afforded me," she told them.

"'In Xanadu did Kublah-Khan a lovely pleasure dome decree,'" intoned Bill as Angie threw open the door. She felt grateful that she didn't have to step over the threshold alone. She had been lucky, compared to a lot of people. She had a job, and now she had a place to live and some potential friends. She wasn't in the kind of trouble that Jada or poor Michelle were going through.

"Sometimes it's best to keep life simple," she said to Bill as all of them trooped through the three rooms. Then she wondered how simple she could keep it, if she were a single mother.

"They're here!" Natalie called out. "I can't believe they're on time!" It was the movers, and chaos ensued. Natalie became the boss, of course, suggesting everything from how the linen should be unpacked to which direction Angie should hang her clothes in her closet. At least Natalie had ordered a double mattress and box spring from 1-800-MATTRES and it had just been delivered when the movers left.

Thank God, Angie thought, that she had almost no other furniture, because Natalie would be putting it just where she *didn't* want it. God, she loved her mother, but she didn't want to have to tell her about her pregnancy. Natalie would cry, then she would take over, and Angie would be told what to do, what doctor should do it, and when. It was hard to stand up against her loving mother when Natalie was blowing at gale force.

She, Bill, and Laura were struggling to pull the boxes apart while her mother ineptly worked on putting together the rolling bed frame. "Can I offer a hand?" a man's voice asked. Angie peeked around the side of the mattress carton. It was Michael, dressed in a red sweater and corduroys, not even wearing a jacket despite the cold.

"Well, you got two," Bill said. "Why be stingy?"

Angie was really touched that Michael had showed up, too. He had his family and weekend chores, she was sure, but he took over the bed frame and made it stable, despite two screws missing from the packet. It was almost four o'clock when they were done. The space looked peculiar—not bad, but peculiar—since Angie had a few paintings hung on the walls, and a couple of good lamps but no chairs or a sofa. She had the Egyptian hippo that had been a wedding present, but no shelf to set it on. In fact, aside from the mattress and box spring, the only other piece of furniture she had was the little desk from her bedroom, the desk she'd taken from Natalie's when she first moved in with Reid. She didn't even have a chair for it.

Bill surveyed the rooms. "Very nice," he said. "Very ethereal. I like the simplicity, as if you're too spiritual to actually need to sit down."

"I don't need to sit down, I need to *lie* down," Angie said.

"Don't you want to go out to dinner?" Natalie asked the rest of them. "My treat."

Michael had taken off first, before she could even thank him, and Bill and Laura begged off. Angie suspected that it all might have been prearranged, but she was so grateful for their help that she kissed both of them on both cheeks. "Oooh, French kissing," Bill said, and then he left with a laugh.

Before she left, Laura stuck her head back in the doorway. "Angie, I just wanted you to know that we have a lot riding on this Jada Jackson case, so I've authorized more funds for it. I also contacted a friend of mine from the Yale Childhood Center to help against the social worker of Creskin's."

"That's great. Thanks, Laura," Angie said, but she couldn't help notice the tone of voice Laura had used. It meant: "Deliver on this." Well, she would. When Angie turned back to her mother, Natalie was looking at her with concern. "Are you sure you don't want to go out?" she asked. "Just you and me?" Angie closed the door.

"No," Angie said. "Really not. I *have* to lie down."

"Well, let me make up your bed," Natalie said. "I can go out for takeout." Angie knew she wasn't going to get rid of her mother without a fight, so she compromised.

"*I'll* make up my bed," she said, "and then I'll lie in it." It reminded her of her earlier thought about her dad and she almost smiled. "How about you get some Chinese in the meantime?"

"Okay. And to give you some time to rest, I'll pick up some groceries. You know, just the basics. Coffee, salt, Ben and Jerry's cookie dough ice cream." Angie laughed and gave her mother a hug.

"Thanks," she said, and made her way into the bedroom. After she heard the front door close, she didn't bother to put on sheets or a pillow. She just lay down, as tired as she had ever been. She wasn't sure how much of it was emotional, how much of it was from the pregnancy, and how much of it was simply the stress and strain of bending, lifting, and hammering, but it felt good to lie down.

She wasn't there long before Jada and Michelle rang the bell. Jada had a covered casserole dish in her hands, while Michelle held a plate of her infamous brownies. The smell from both mixed in her tiny hallway, but Angie tried to ignore her rising nausea. Jada looked at her closely. "Are you lonesome or scared in the new place, or are we just intruding?" she asked. Angie burst into tears and then vomited on the apartment floor.

Ten minutes later they were all sitting on her bare mattress. Jada had cleaned up the floor and Michelle had cleaned up Angie. She was grateful for these two women and their company and then, completely unexpectedly, she began to tell them the rest of her story: about her stupidity, and the sickness and other symptoms she hadn't noticed, and then . . .

Michelle took her hand. "Oh, Angie! This is just too much. You're pregnant. By him? The Boston shit bird?"

"Are you sure?" Jada asked.

Angie nodded. "And do you know what I keep doing? I keep buying home pregnancy tests. As if the last eleven haven't been accurate. It's nuts."

"I did that, too," Jada told her. "With Sherrilee. It was not the right time for me to be pregnant. Remember, Michelle? Everything with Clinton was already pretty much gone. I did not need to be pregnant."

"Man, those were some walks we took those mornings," Michelle said. Jada nodded, and Angie watched the two women exchange a look, a look with worlds of understanding and compassion.

"You never thought about . . ." Angie paused. "About ending the pregnancy?"

"I thought about it every day," Jada said. "I prayed over it. I also thought about suicide. I prayed over *that,* too."

"You never told me," Michelle said.

"I didn't have those thoughts in the morning, Mich," Jada said. "Only at night." Jada looked at Angie. "But I had my other two to think about." Jada paused for a moment, then took her bottom lip between her teeth. She shook her head. "Now I don't have any of my babies with me." She looked back at Angie. "I'm so sorry for your pain," she said, and that started Angie crying again.

Michelle rubbed Angie's hand. "I feel so stupid," Angie said. "This is such bad, bad timing."

Michelle sighed. "I *always* feel stupid. But doesn't a lot of what happens, happen at bad times?"

"Well," Jada said, "maybe it's God's time, not ours. And God always gives us choices."

Angie looked up, blew her nose on a Kleenex that Michelle handed her, and stared into Jada's face. The woman was in danger of losing so much. How could she believe that God was in charge?

"Hey," Michelle said, "let me make up this bed. You got sheets?" Angie nodded. "Why don't you take a shower?" Michelle asked. "Then you can feel fresh in nice clean sheets." She stood up, and so did Angie. Michelle looked around. "I'd like to wash down these walls," she said. "And the floor would look good after a real cleaning and waxing."

Jada shook her head. "Sterilizing the world again, Michelle?" she asked.

"Hey, I like to clean, okay? A false sense of accomplishment is better than none at all."

When Angie came back from the shower, she did feel better, though whether it was because she was about to sleep, because she was clean, or because she'd come clean was hard to tell. The two women helped her into bed as if she were an invalid. "Thanks for coming over," Angie said, almost formally. And all three of them looked at each other before they began laughing. "My mom is stopping by with some Chinese food. She should be here soon. You want to join us?"

Both Michelle and Jada shook their heads. "I haven't told her yet,"

Angie admitted. "I don't want to say anything until I decide what I'm going to do."

Michelle nodded, and Jada patted Angie on the shoulder. "It's up to you," she said. "It's between you and God."

"We'll help you either way," Michelle said, and Angie knew they meant it.

31

Frank gets tough

Jenna lay face down on the bed, her arms thrown like rags to cover her head. Michelle sat beside her. Her daughter had come in from school and burst into tears without speaking before running up to her bedroom. It took all of Michelle's self-control to hold herself back for almost ten minutes and give Jenna privacy to cry off some of her feelings. *After all,* Michelle thought, *even though I'm the only one she has to comfort her, I'm part of her pain.*

She had knocked on Jenna's door, walked in, and sat on the corner of her daughter's canopied bed. She put her hand on her daughter's back, in the place between her shoulder blades where, from the time she was tiny, she always liked to be rubbed. But Jenna jerked herself away from under Michelle's hand as if it were a branding iron. So Michelle just sat at the foot of the bed.

Since the indictment had hit, and all of them had been pictured in the newspapers and Frank had been on all of the local news programs (looking as much like a criminal as the media made most indicted people look) the children had fallen apart badly. Jenna came home from school either pale and silent or hysterical. And Frankie . . . Michelle took a deep breath and tried not to audibly sigh. Her son was too young to understand most of what was going on, but not too young to be hurt by name-calling and the fact that no one would play with him at school recess or after school. Plus, there was the loss of Kevon, who—as far as her son was concerned—had abandoned him personally.

Only Pookie could comfort Frankie, but apparently not well enough. Frankie had begun wetting his bed and woke up crying, cold and shamed when he discovered what he had done. She had thought that poor Jada was worse off than she was; her life was destroyed and her children, at least for the time being, had been stolen from her. But Jada at least had a chance to get it all back.

Poor Angie, on the other hand, had lost a man she loved, and to her friend who betrayed her. Worst of all was her pregnancy. *That poor, poor girl,* Michelle thought, and despite it all, she was using her time to help others. She had even helped Michelle. She pushed the thought from her mind. She didn't want to think about what she was going to have to do about Frank.

Michelle knew she had to think positively. She was going to the custody hearing and would get to see Jada and Angie triumph. But for her, for Michelle, there could be no triumph. Being with her children and watching them in pain was unbearable. Being with Frank and knowing he was guilty was unbearable. The thought of being without Frank, on her own, stigmatized and jobless, was unbearable.

Now Michelle reached out and touched her daughter's ankle. Jenna pulled her foot away but she did, at least, flip over on her back, push up on her elbows, and look at her mother. "Haven't you ever heard of privacy?" she asked. Michelle nodded. "Well, that's what I would like right now," Jenna told her. Then she burst into tears again and reached out and hugged Michelle to her. "I'm sorry," Jenna wept. "I'm just . . ."

"I know, sweetie. I know," Michelle said and stroked her daughter's long hair. "I know."

They were really falling apart, all of them, Michelle thought as she cleaned up after dinner. Frank had been out all day and had called to say he'd be late. The kids had eaten—not that either of them were eating much. She had had to throw away most of their macaroni, and almost all of the meatloaf she'd served with it. Now there was order and some quiet. No phone calls with Frank screaming obscenities

She went upstairs to check on Frankie, who only seemed to find comfort in his bath and his pajamas—at least when they were dry. He was playing in his room, some kind of game with action figures which took place mostly under his bed. His head was pushed into the low dark space there while his little rump in his blue and green flannel pajamas was up in the air. "Bedtime soon," she said, and he wiggled his butt and kept playing.

Downstairs, Jenna was sitting in front of the television screen playing one of the nastier Mortal Kombat games. She performed like an automaton, barely blinking at the screen as her character kicked and punched mayhem. Perhaps Michelle shouldn't worry as much about the hour or two Jenna did this every night. Maybe it was a healthy way to express anger, but what did she know? She trusted a man who had not only betrayed her but his children, a man who had bought their past by making a deal with a devil on the future. And the future was now.

Jenna hadn't even looked up. "I think it's about time to walk Pookie," Michelle said.

"Walk him yourself," Jenna said, and her tone of voice was eerie, like what Frank had used on the phone in Bruzeman's office. Michelle actually took a step back out of the room. She knew she should say something to Jenna, but she couldn't. Jenna abruptly got up and stomped up the stairs. Michelle picked up the remote and clicked the TV off. Then she turned and walked down the hallway and into the kitchen. She jumped when she realized Frank was sitting there at the table silent and staring. She would have to talk to him now.

With the overhead light on, the kitchen gleamed almost painfully white, Frank's bent head the only blot of darkness. In her cleaning mania, Michelle had gotten rid of every bit of clutter from the counters and windowsills; the starkness made the bottle of Dewars next to the sink and the glass in front of her husband on the table jump out at her like a warning sign. Frank rarely drank anything stronger than a glass of Chianti. Michelle, because of her mother, rarely drank at all. The bottle of Dewars and a couple of bottles of Peppermint Schnapps they'd received as Christmas gifts stood on a shelf over the refrigerator, rarely opened.

She pulled out the chair beside him, a chair she had scrupulously scrubbed with bleach just a few days ago, and sat down. "Frank," she said.

"What?" his voice was flat and dead.

"I . . ." She didn't know how to tell him about the money she'd found. She didn't know how to tell him that she didn't believe he was innocent anymore—that she knew he was guilty of *something*. She didn't know how to tell him that he'd broken her heart, that he'd ruined his family, that he'd destroyed her trust. She looked at him, her beautiful, dark, good, strong Frank and saw how weak he was. He had taken a risk, a terrible risk, and he had lost.

But he had taken the risk without telling her. Without her knowledge, though the risk was her risk, too, and one she would never have agreed to.

"We're gonna beat this, Michelle," Frank said, and Michelle looked at him. He'd said it before. She hadn't always believed him, but most often she had. Now, for the first time, she realized that she wasn't sure she wanted to. Proof of his guilt was now hidden in the spare tire well of the Lexus. For all she knew, Frank might have more evidence in the house, though she'd gone over every single bit of it again trying to see if she could find it.

She remembered what Angie had told her about getting the search warrant. Frank had known that there was plenty of evidence against him. He knew, even as she and the children were dragged out of the house, that he had endangered them, that something as dangerous as a ticking bomb was under the floorboards. But as she looked at him, despite her feelings, she couldn't just accuse him. She simply couldn't get the words out of her mouth: *Frank, I found the money. I know you're guilty, at least of something. How could you do this to us?*

"I spent the whole goddamn day over at Bruzeman's. I didn't see him. Not for a minute. Two associates made me watch a videotape—goddamn it, a videotape—on giving testimony. And then they asked me every question they've already asked before, and then they wanted me to watch the goddamn videotape again. I kept asking for Bruzeman and they kept telling me he was taking a deposition or some shit. He was probably on the golf course. He used to play golf with me sometimes on Wednesdays." Frank shook his head. "They want you down there tomorrow afternoon." He sighed, picked up the glass of scotch, swallowed a mouthful, and shivered. Frank didn't like liquor, either.

"I'm not going to testify, Frank." Michelle said.

"What?" Frank looked at her, really looked at her for the first time since she'd come into the kitchen.

"I'm not going to testify. I can't."

"What the fuck are you talking about?" Frank asked, his voice low. "Michelle, please. I have had a hard fucking day. A hard fucking week. At the end of a hard fucking month. Don't start with me."

Michelle thought of her day, of the children upstairs, of her feelings of panic and despair. But she couldn't talk to Frank. She also knew she couldn't testify. "I'm not going to testify, Frank."

He stood up abruptly, almost tipping his chair over. Michelle caught it, but Frank used his other arm to swing his sleeve across the table, past the blot on the Formica, against the now-empty glass that had held his scotch, which his arm flung across the kitchen into a bright whirling arc. It shattered with a pop against an upper cabinet and shards of glass showered the countertop and tile floor. Michelle gasped in surprise and more than a little fear. Frank paid no attention to the wreckage or her reaction. He was standing up, holding onto the edge of the table now and staring at her as if she were the one who had just done something crazy and out of control.

"Are you stupid?" he asked. "Is that it? Have you gone stupid on me? Is everyone I deal with stupid? Is that it?"

"I can't testify, Frank" was all Michelle could say. She expected him to ask why. She expected him to try to find out if it was because she was too upset or too frightened. She expected him to beg her to reassure him that she believed he was innocent. She even expected him to cry and try to hold her, to nuzzle her neck or to stroke her hair, and beg her to look at him and tell him that she still loved him. Well, she was ashamed to admit that she still did love him, but she wasn't prepared to tell him that now. She also wasn't prepared for what he actually did.

"What are you talking about?" he said with a snarl that she had never heard before. "Don't give me shit now, Michelle. No nerves, no headaches. You're going to testify, goddamnit."

And then he pushed her, hard against her shoulder. The force was so great that she lost her balance and was thrown from her chair. As she fell, it seemed that the corner of the table rushed up to meet her cheek, but it didn't stop her from winding up sprawled across the floor, her already injured cheek coming down hard on the immaculate tile. For a moment she didn't move. She felt nothing. Not for a moment, at least. Then she felt everything—fear, pain, shame, outrage. Her cheek and her temple began to burn. Then her eye began to throb.

In all their years together, Frank had never touched her except with affection or longing, tenderness or lust. She had seen him angry, but she didn't think he was capable of ever physically hurting her. Never. Now she lay stunned on the floor and knew she was wrong about that, as well as all the other things she'd been wrong about.

She felt something wet drip down her cheek past her nose. She sat up. Her right eye was already swelling and blurry, but she could see the blood on the floor. It wasn't a lot of blood, but it was very, very red. She put her hand up to her face and brought it away, looking down at it. It was slick with her blood, the palm and fingers and even the fingernail wells covered.

Frank took two steps toward her. She wasn't sure if he was going to shove her or kick her or help her up. But she didn't move. He could shoot her and it wouldn't make a difference. Instead, though, he hunkered down beside her sprawled figure. "Oh my God. Oh my God, Michelle. You're cut. The table cut you," Frank said as if his hand, his arm, his shoulder and brain had nothing to do with it. "Mich, I . . . I'm sorry. I think you need some stitches or something."

Michelle wasn't sure if he was sorry that he'd pushed or that she needed a doctor. She felt more blood drip from her chin and looked down at the floor. How often had she washed this floor, she wondered, as if it were the most sensible question at that moment.

Frank had moved away toward the sink. She heard the water running and he came back with a stack of paper towels, bunched and wet. He tried to daub at her cheek, but she flinched and he handed her the towels. She sat up to put their coolness against her face. After a moment, she pulled the towels away and revealed a gorier mess than she had expected to see. She let the bloody clump of papers fall to the kitchen floor.

Frank handed her another and peered at her cheek, though he avoided looking into her eyes. "It's not a big cut, Michelle. But it's deep. Come on. We better go to the emergency room." He went back to the sink and made another cold compress and brought it to her. Michelle took it and pressed it hard against her cheekbone, but let it rest only softly against her swollen eye.

"I'm not going anywhere with you," she said and turned her back on him. Dizzy as she was, she walked out of the kitchen, leaving the bloody mess behind her.

32

A trial—and bank—run

Jada and Angie had been at it for what seemed like hours. Well, actually it *was* hours, because Jada had arrived a little after eight in the morning and Bill had just come in with sandwiches for lunch.

Jada looked at her watch. Ten to twelve. Jada had had to skip work today and bow out of her morning walk with Michelle to do this. She didn't like to do either one, and of all mornings, she'd needed a walk today the most. She'd been surprised that Michelle seemed eager to cancel. "I was going to call you anyway," she'd said. "I'm just not up to it." It worried Jada, but she had a lot of other things to worry about.

Now, sitting across from poor Angie, Jada had realized that rehearsing for a court appearance was just like rehearsing for a play. Well, she supposed in a way it *was* a play. It wasn't about reality, but about a stranger—in this case, Judge Arnold D. Sneed—and his opinion of reality.

In the last few hours, Angie had been totally focused on the work in front of them. Jada had occasionally been reminded of Angie's own situation and wondered how she could do it. *I guess work can get you through some tough times, if you like your job,* Jada thought. Looking at Angie, she'd said a silent prayer for her, a woman alone with a sad past and a big decision in her future.

They had spent a long time carefully going through dozens of prepared questions. Angie cautioned Jada, who kept wanting to add things, to be sure not to offer any extra information. "You can be cross-examined on *anything* that we introduce, and by we, I mean both of us," Angie warned. "I'll protect you from unfair questions, but you can't make giveaway answers. The judge is going to award custody and make a division of assets at the trial. We don't have much time for discovery. I already tried to get an extension, but this guy Creskin is a real operator. He's forcing an emergency hearing."

Jada had merely nodded, and the two of them worked together, rehearsing for forty minutes at a time and then taking little coffee breaks, though Jada didn't drink any of the coffee. Angie kept focused on the work. Jada had been spending more time at the bank, too. After all, what else was there to do? Her empty, childless house was a misery to her. She couldn't read, she couldn't stand television and the shows her kids liked to watch. All of the unfinished work that Clinton hadn't done—that he would never do now—drove her more mad than ever.

She looked across the desk at Angie. Jada might have been wrong about Angie's NUP. She wasn't the spoiled brat she'd thought. What was her suffering like, alone in that small, empty apartment? Neither one spoke of it.

It was lunchtime and Jada looked at the ham and cheese sandwich she'd ordered as if it had come from another planet. She hadn't been able to really eat in . . . well, she couldn't exactly remember how long. Every now and then she forced herself to open a can of Campbell's Chicken 'n' Rice soup, and then she drank it right out of the can. She looked away from the sandwich.

"Maybe I better call the office," she said. As if all of this wasn't enough, she had to worry about her absences from work. She didn't want to tell Mr. Marcus anything more than she had to about her personal life. She looked over her sandwich to Angie. "You know what's pretty ironic?" she asked.

"Yeah," Angie said. "Just about everything I do know is ironic. But why don't you add your irony to my list." Angie smiled to soften her harsh words.

The girl had a really nice smile. Jada didn't just pity her, she truly liked her. "Well, I was going to say it was ironic that my husband—"

"Your future former husband," Angie corrected, just as her mother had corrected her.

Jada nodded. "My soon-to-be-ex-husband is trying to prove that I'm a bad mother because I work too much, while my boss may be trying to prove I'm a bad worker because I mother too much."

"Ho, ho, ho," Angie said with very exaggerated sarcasm. "What a funny irony, Jada. Let's throw it into the women's smelter with all the other irony we're trying to melt down." She gestured to the food on the desk. "Eat your sandwich," Angie directed. Then she paused and asked, "God, did I just sound like my mother?"

"You could do a lot worse than sound like your mama," Jada told her. "I'm not hungry. Can I use the phone?"

"You need privacy?"

Jada made a gesture at all the papers and notes that were already such an invasion. "You gotta be kidding," she said.

She dialed her office. Anne answered and read out a list of messages. Most of them were things that Jada could deal with tomorrow. She asked Anne to fax one document, had to give her the instructions twice, and then, just as she was about to hang up, Anne added a little bonus.

"Oh! I don't know if it's important, but I think that Michelle Russo called you," Jada's secretary said. "It sounded like Michelle, but she wouldn't say who it was."

Jada realized how much she truly disliked Anne and wondered if she could get her transferred or something. She thanked her coldly and hung up, then punched in Michelle's phone number. "Michelle?" she asked when she heard the hello, but it sounded like an unfamiliar voice.

"Jada, I'm sorry I called you at work. I didn't want to but . . . "

"I know," Jada said. Boy, it must be an emergency if Michelle, with all her pride, had spoken to Anne. "What's up?"

"When will you be done with your lawyer stuff?" Michelle asked.

"I don't know. In another hour or so." She looked over at Angie, who nodded.

"And then you see the kids?"

"Yeah, I pick 'em up after school. But I have to get them back to Yonkers by six. What is this about, Michelle?"

Michelle began whispering. "I can't talk about it," she said. "Not now, and not over the phone. But I have to ask a really big favor. Really big. And it will be okay if you say no."

"Okay," Jada said, trying to sound neutral.

"Really, you can say no, Jada. It's just that I have no one else to ask."

Little goosebumps rose on Jada's arms and the back of her neck. She had never heard Michelle sound like this. It was worse than after the bust. "Hold on a minute," she said. She turned to Angie. "Can we be done now?" she asked.

Angie looked down at her notes and the file. "Give me another half hour." She picked up half of Jada's untouched ham and cheese. "God, I haven't been hungry in weeks," she said. "Now, all of a sudden, I'm famished."

"It happens like that," Jada said, but didn't want to bring up the pregnancy or anything she shouldn't.

"You've got an emergency?" Angie asked.

"Apparently," Jada said, and spoke into the phone again. "I'll be at your house in an hour," she told Michelle.

"No. No," Michelle pleaded, her voice sounding breathless, almost panicky. "I'll meet you at the 7-Eleven on the Post Road next to the First Westchester Bank. You know the one."

"Yeah, sure," Jada said. "I can be there in forty-five minutes."

"Thanks, Jada. And remember, you don't have to say yes."

"I want you to open a safety deposit box," Michelle told Jada. Jada was leaning back in the driver's seat of the Volvo, parked beside Michelle's Lexus in the 7-Eleven lot. She was trying hard not to stare at her friend's profile. Jada knew how precious some boundaries were. "I need it to be in your name, and I want you to keep both of the keys." Michelle took a deep breath. "You have to hide them somewhere—not in your house or in the office."

Jada looked at her friend. She hadn't said anything about the sunglasses or the awful bruise under Michelle's eye. She hadn't asked why

Michelle, always perfectly dressed, with her hair beautifully tousled and her makeup perfectly applied, looked like something that washed up on a Barbados beach after a bad storm. But she figured she knew.

Jada had seen enough women beaten by their husbands, and enough violence in her old Yonkers neighborhood to know not to ask. But poor Michelle. Poor Michelle, who had not only worshipped Frank but had always depended on him. She looked like she was falling apart, and Jada was too good a friend to touch Michelle's arm and try to comfort her. She knew that Michelle was using everything she had to keep it together now, and Jada wanted to help her.

She wondered what Frank was really up to. She wondered what Michelle knew, or what she suspected. Jada was too wise in the ways of police and lawbreakers to believe that a bust and an indictment meant guilt. Frank, in her opinion, could be anything from framed to a Mafia hit man and she wouldn't be surprised. But she could tell Michelle was more than surprised. She was shell-shocked, and had been for days. Now, though, something had changed. "I have to ask you a question, Michelle," Jada said, her voice as calming as she could make it.

"You can say no," Michelle said quickly. "I totally understand. It was a lot to ask and it's okay, Jada. Really it is."

"Michelle, I'm not saying no. I just need to ask you if there are drugs in that bag. You know I'm not trying to insult you, and you know I'll believe what you say. You understand why I have to ask that."

Michelle's lip trembled. "I know," she said. She reached across the seat of the Volvo and took Jada's hand. "I promise you, it's not. It's not drugs. But it's stuff I don't want Frank to have access to."

"Okay," Jada nodded. She knew she was taking a risk, but she trusted her friend. "So I'll drive alone next door to First Westchester—our biggest competitor, I might add—take out a large box, and come back to you here."

Michelle nodded, and when she did, Jada could see that the bruise wasn't just on her cheek, but that the eye behind her glasses was swollen and angry-colored. "Michelle, you don't have to stay there," Jada told her in a low, sweet voice. "You can stay with me."

"It was an accident," Michelle said. "It really was. And it won't happen again."

Jada didn't believe the first part, but something in Michelle's tone made her believe the second. Jada took a deep breath and let it out very slowly. Oh, Lord, there was a whole world of sadness out there, and at that moment it felt to Jada as if she and Michelle were drowning in it. *Keep us afloat, Lord,* she prayed silently. Then she let go of Michelle's hand. "Buy yourself some wrap-around sunglasses," she told Michelle. "I'll be back here in about twenty minutes."

When Jada picked up the children, they weren't interested in talking about school, Tonya Green, their grandma, or any other subject except going home. Jada, already worn out from the legal workout and the frightening episode with Michelle, didn't have her best coping skills available. All she wanted was to kiss them, hold the baby, smell Kevon's delicious boy-smell, and do Shavonne's hair. Touch them. Love them. But the kids had another plan. "Can we go home now, Mama?" Kevon asked the very second he climbed into the car.

Jada strapped Sherilee in beside him. Of course it wasn't possible, but she didn't want to spoil the few hours she had with them immediately. "Maybe later," she said, though she knew the maybe was a lie. There was no maybe about it. "Who would like ice cream?" she asked as she got into the driver's seat.

"I wanna go home," Shavonne said. "I don't care about ice cream."

Jada turned to her daughter. "Something very hard is happening now, Shavonne," she said.

"Yeah. You and Daddy are going to get a divorce, right?"

It was the first time Jada had heard one of the children say that. "Did Daddy talk with you?" she asked.

"Grandma did," Shavonne said, and then her face crumpled up in a way that was unbearable for Jada to watch. "I just want to go home," Shavonne said.

"Look," Jada responded, "I only have a little bit of time with you before dinner. I—"

"Let's have dinner at home," Kevon said. "I wanna have dinner at home."

"Hey kids, work with me," Jada told them. "We'll go home for a little while, but then I promised Grandma that you'd have dinner over there." Jada didn't add that she would leave them at that point, or that the court wouldn't allow them to stay with her, or that she was fighting to keep their home right now. She wondered if she was doing the right thing. Once she had been so sure of herself, so positive that everything she did was right. Now, between her morning with Angie and her strange errand with Michelle and this drive with the children to the house, she wasn't sure of a single move she made.

It was already dark when she pulled up to her mother-in-law's in Yonkers. Sherilee was the first one to begin crying, but with that encouragement, Kevon joined her almost immediately. "I don't want to go back there," Shavonne said. "Not even just for dinner."

"It's not going to last long," Jada said. "I have a lawyer and we're trying to get everything straightened out, so I'll just leave you here and I'll see you in two days." Jada turned to the backseat. "Shh, babies, shh," she said. When she turned back to Shavonne, her daughter's face was a mask of fury and betrayal.

"You mean we're not going back home after dinner?" she asked.

Sherrilee's wails had become overwhelming. Kevon was unbuckling his seatbelt. Jada was forced to get out of the car and lift Sherilee from the backseat, and Shavonne met her on the sidewalk. Then there were lights, and Jada looked up to see Clinton with the video camera and the spotlights on, videotaping them as if this were a happy Christmas morning. But Shavonne paid no attention.

"You lied," she said. "I hate you." And she ran toward the house and Clinton. Sherilee cried even louder, her little body stiff against Jada's. Kevon had put his hands up to his eyes to avoid the harsh light and perhaps to avoid looking at her. She shouldn't have taken them home. It had made it worse, not better.

She looked toward Clinton. "Stop that," she yelled. His mother was approaching her, her arms stretched out to Sherrilee. Kevon ran into the darkness, somewhere behind Jada's line of vision, and she was forced to hand her daughter over.

• • •

Jada paced from wall to wall, from the empty living room through the unfinished dining room and across the plywood floor in the kitchen. She couldn't sit down, she couldn't lie down, she couldn't cry, and there was no comfort anywhere. She kept walking, a sort of horrible version of one of Kevon's motorized toys that banged into walls, adjusted slightly, and moved forward until it banged into another wall.

This visit had destroyed her hope that somehow she could normalize the family or calm the children. She could think of nothing to do to comfort herself. Finally, in despair, she picked up the telephone and punched in the Caribbean number.

"Mama," she said. "I need to tell you what's going on."

33

Trial and error

Angie was getting dressed with a lot more care than usual. She'd even used some of her new salary to buy a pretty good suit (at discount, at Loehmann's, with Natalie's help). Not that she thought the new suit would help her win this case, but she figured it couldn't hurt, though having to buy a size twelve did.

Angie couldn't help it—she'd been working like a dog and eating like a horse. Her caseload was enormous; not only was she trying to handle Karen Levin-Thomas's ongoing cases, but she also felt that she should take her place on the sofa, interviewing new clients. That way, if and when Karen came back, she'd have her own client list, a better shot at a permanent job. Because, oddly enough, she really *wanted* to be on the permanent staff at the clinic. It seemed right for her. She really liked and respected the other staff members. She also liked the variety of the work. And she felt deeply for her clients' plight. She couldn't say any of those things about the job in Marblehead.

So she'd prepared for Jackson vs. Jackson with every moment of spare time she had, and to tell the truth, with time she shouldn't have taken from her other cases. She knew this was a kind of test by fire. The clinic would judge her by this performance. Thank God Michael Rice had helped so much.

She went into her apartment's tiny bathroom and looked at herself in the mirror. Not a pretty picture. There were dark circles under her eyes. They no longer looked blue, and her skin was mottled. Well, too bad. She brushed her wet hair back and decided to just secure it with a scrunchy. She didn't need to look attractive, just professional and honest.

She was so nervous that she felt sick to her stomach. Her face actually looked a little green. She decided she better pat on a little makeup. By now Angie knew the difference between this feeling and morning sickness. This was pure fear. She was afraid that she didn't have the experience, that she hadn't the background, the brains, or the contacts to do all she had to do today: secure Jada's house for her, win her back her children, and get her out from under the sword of alimony and child support payments that was dangerously suspended over her.

As Angie tried to put eyeliner on her upper lid, her hand trembled and she ruined it. She sighed, tore a piece of toilet paper off the roll, and wiped off the black stuff. She took a deep breath and managed to get something approximating a straight line on both eyelids. Then she put some blusher on and finished with a little extra mascara. She looked better, though still pretty wan. *Hey,* she told herself, *this isn't a beauty contest. You have a good, innocent, unjustly treated client. You've done a lot of research. You have hired expert witness and investigators. And you have help from Michael Rice. You are going to win this case. You* have *to win this case.*

She looked deeply into her own eyes in the mirror. "You *have* to win this case," Angie told her reflection.

Jada snagged the right ankle of her pantyhose on the wicker leg of a chair just as she was getting her purse and was ready to go. She threw her bag down on the table, rushed upstairs, and began looking frantically for another pair. She didn't have one. "Damn it to hell," she said, though she very rarely swore. And she certainly didn't want to do anything offensive to God today.

She didn't think she had any more stockings here. She knew she had a spare pair at work, but she wasn't going to show up *there* this morning, and she certainly wasn't going to show up in the courtroom with a run from her ankle up to—Lord knows how far it would travel. It seemed to be moving like a freight train. The problem was, it wasn't so easy to find pantyhose in her flesh color and her size. "Nude" wasn't nude on a black woman's legs. Plus, there was the problem of her height. Her father had always teased her, saying her legs were too long.

For a moment, Jada had a terrible longing to see her daddy. She hadn't wanted to frighten and mortify her parents with all this court business, but at this moment she realized just how much she wished they'd be there in the courtroom with her. Her pride and independence had gotten in the way.

She guessed her father had been right—about her legs and a lot of things. When she bought a normal pair of pantyhose, the crotch didn't make it past her knees. If she got a queen-sized pair (which she'd tried once or twice), then the crotch was better but she wound up with ankles looking like an elephant's—all the wrinkles of the world gathered around them like bracelets on a Hindu bride.

Jada knew she had more important things to do than worry about pantyhose, today of all days. It was just that thinking about *anything* was better than thinking about the upcoming trial by fire. She'd read her Bible, the story of Job, over and over again, hoping for some comfort from it. Why had God chosen her—and her children—for such trials? She had spent most of last night on her knees praying, or on her back, sleepless. She knew that her babies loved her and needed her, she knew that God loved her and her babies, and she hoped that in his mercy He would deliver them to her, using Angie Romazzano as His instrument.

Jada liked Angie, and she knew that Angie understood her situation and identified with her. Angie was a good lawyer, a smart woman, and dedicated. The problem was that she couldn't quite believe that other people could be as unfair and slanted as they were. Angela should try being black for a few weeks—then she'd get it. Jada had come to believe that there was almost no evil, no lie, that Clinton wouldn't stoop to. She just hoped Angie had stooped lower.

Jada threw an extra lipstick into her handbag, checked her hair one more time, and ran out the door. She was picking Michelle up. As if everything else weren't bad enough, Michelle couldn't testify on her behalf now, because of the "accident"—if it was an accident—and the indictment. If she had the time, Jada would be even more worried about Michelle then she already was. Right now, though, she just needed to get through today.

Maybe, Jada thought, if she stopped at CVS on her way to the court-house, they'd have something for her to put on her legs. She walked to the door and opened it, but before she stepped out into the cold, she looked back. The kitchen, unlike the rest of the house, was fairly orderly, and she wondered if tonight, or tomorrow, or anytime soon, she would be sitting around that table with her babies. She promised God she'd never complain about the bare plywood floor or the unfinished cabinets again. But she knew there was a chance that Clinton might be sitting here, in her house, with her gone and Tonya upstairs in the bedroom waiting for him.

Michelle was applying a little more pressed powder to the area under her eye when she heard Jada's honk. A lot of the swelling around her eye had gone down, and the bruise had quickly changed from purple to a sort of mallard green. This morning she'd tried to cover it over with layers of pancake makeup and face powder. She thought she'd been pretty suc-cessful, if looking like a Kabuki dancer could be considered successful.

Michelle looked at herself, swallowed a Xanax, and put down the brush. Though the day was dreary, she slipped on her sunglasses, new wrap-around ones she'd gotten at 7-Eleven. She knew that Angie and her team had given up the idea of calling her to the stand, but she was going to be there for Jada even though showing up at court terrified her. She gave herself one last look in the mirror as the horn blared again, then ran down the stairs to her friend.

She left Frank sleeping. It amazed her that he hadn't awakened when she got up, or even when the kids went off to school. It had occurred to her that perhaps he *wasn't* sleeping; perhaps he was just lying there, feel-ing sorry or feeling angry. But she didn't care what he was feeling. Since the accident, she'd napped in their bed in the afternoons when he wasn't there, curled like a comma at the edge of a line of print. Then, in the evenings, she'd watch TV until he went upstairs and she could fall asleep on the sofa, wakened over and over by bad dreams.

Her mother had been the only one in her whole life who had physically hurt her—and only when she'd been very, very drunk. Michelle had always known cheating, lying, and beatings occurred in marriages, but Michelle had never, ever imagined that she would tolerate any of those. She'd picked Frank because he was safe, protective. Or so she thought. Now she'd experienced two out of three.

Frank had, of course, apologized to her later when they went to bed. He'd wept, and he'd put his arm around her. She'd stiffened and let him, though she didn't want to be touched. Then, to her total shock and surprise, Frank had wanted to make love to her. She'd been angrier than she'd been when he shoved her. The idea of him kissing her bruises and begging for forgiveness while he entered her was even now enough to make Michelle wince, hurting her eye. At the time, it had made her sick to her stomach. She had pulled away and then she had only stared at him, as best she could with her injury. "Is it okay? Are we okay?" Frank had asked.

"No, no, and no," Michelle had told him icily. "But I really don't want to talk about this now." And she'd slept pulled away from him. She'd kept up that wall of coldness between them since. The problem was, she didn't know what she should do. Walk out on him during this awful time? Try to talk it over? Listen to his lies? Threaten to leave?

And what if he realized that she had not only found the money, but removed it from the house? What would he do then? Would there be another "accident"? Michelle lifted her hand to her cheek.

For the first time in years, Michelle hadn't walked for the three days since her incident with Frank. She'd told Jada she'd fought with Frank and slipped. Jada had said nothing, which meant she was thinking a lot.

Meanwhile, Michelle knew the kids had noticed her eye, even though she'd smeared enough face paint over it to putty a window. Now, a few days later, she hoped she wouldn't shock Jada or Angie with her defaced face. She was sorry she couldn't testify, but she was doing the best she could. She ran toward the kitchen door and didn't even bother to leave Frank a note. She'd be home long before the kids, and she had to take

Jenna for a haircut late this afternoon. She walked to the door and closed up the kitchen behind her, ready to support her girlfriend simply by being there.

Jada thought Angie had managed the opening of the proceedings as well as could be expected. Creskin had immediately called Jada to the stand. He'd pounded her, but she'd held firm and her testimony sounded good. At least it had to her, and Angie had nodded several times. She kept her answers short, as she'd practiced. She talked about getting her job out of desperation. She explained her hours—and strongly insisted she did little overtime and almost no traveling. Creskin used some sarcasm, and started too many questions with "Isn't it true that . . . ?" but he was good. He pushed her too far on the drug stuff, and as Angie had directed her, Jada allowed herself to get angry . . . really angry. "I'm a Christian woman," she said. "I don't use alcohol or drugs." He pushed, but Angie objected and then it was over.

In cross-examination, Angie had been able to squeeze in a lot of the problems with Clinton, though then Creskin had voiced his objections whenever he could. Jada had been grateful to take her seat. Now Mrs. Jackson, Jada's mother-in-law, was called to the stand.

"So, how often were you invited to your son and daughter-in-law's home?" George Creskin was asking.

"Not often. I could feel she didn't want me there."

"Objection, Your Honor," Angie said, though Jada knew her mother-in-law was right.

"Sustained," the judge replied. "Please stick with the facts rather than the feelings, Mrs. Jackson."

Jada didn't like the big ugly courtroom and its harsh fluorescent lights. She felt like a long dark line, too tall, too thin, too dark. She was now sitting at the table with Angie and Michael Rice; her husband was at the other table with his smarmy counsel.

"Certainly, Your Honor," Mrs. Jackson said.

Jada liked Judge Sneed. He seemed businesslike, no nonsense. He'd have to see the truth in their story—Clinton's failure, her overcompensation. Her dedication to only one thing: the family.

Now, though, Sneed was looking down at her mother-in-law. Jada almost had to laugh. The woman had been costumed for her part. She looked like the savior of her people, the backbone of a family. Jada was actually amazed at how well her mother-in-law had cleaned up. She was wearing a bright blue suit, a pale blue blouse, and a hat—a *hat*—completed by a little veil. Jada had never even seen her hair decently combed, much less a hat on her head. Mrs. Jackson looked like some of the old-timers, or the choir singers at church, instead of the slattern she was.

This was a woman who had ignored her son night after night to go meet her cronies in the bar near the Yonkers train station. Clinton had had to cook his own dinner and put himself to bed from the time he was six or seven. And worst of all, this selfish, weak woman was on the stand because Clinton *wanted* her to be, and the woman was testifying that she, Jada, was a bad mother? Jada felt as if all of the rules of behavior were being broken and she should simply stand up in court and tell the judge, the bailiff, the stenographer, and everybody else about this ridiculous, insulting masquerade.

"What did you see when you did get to visit your son and grandchildren?" Mr. Creskin asked.

"Well, Your Honor—"

Judge Sneed interrupted. *"He's* Mr. Creskin. *I* am addressed as Your Honor," he told Mrs. Jackson. She looked up at him with an apologetic moue. "I'm so very sorry, Your Honor," she said. "I'm not used to this. Our family has never been in trouble before." Jada snorted as Mrs. Jackson turned back to Creskin, her head bowed. He repeated his question.

"Well, she didn't come home till real late. My son had to feed the kids and wash 'em down. He spent his life taking care of those kids. Then she'd come home, tired and cranky and braggin' on that bank job of hers. And sometimes she'd slap the kids."

Jada began to rise out of her seat, until Mr. Rice put a hand on her shoulder and pointed to the pad in front of her. *That's a lie,* she scrawled, and then added, *it's all lies.*

Angie leaned over to her and whispered, "Don't worry. We're going to discredit her as a witness. We've got her in a lie and her testimony will probably be contradicted. Don't worry."

Knowing that, Jada managed to stay calm during the next few questions. Then Mr. Creskin asked about the children's condition when Clinton brought them to her house. "Oooh, they was sad," Mrs. Jackson said.

"You mean sad because they left their mother?"

"No, I mean they were in sad condition. I don't think my granddaughter's hair had been combed for a week. And they was dirty. They was in dirty clothes and they needed baths. It was three o'clock in the morning. Clint had brought them over 'cause she was spendin' time till then at her drug house down the street." Mrs. Jackson looked right over at Jada.

"Objection, Your Honor," Angie rose and said, but Jada couldn't listen. She had to bend her head down so that the old witch in the witness box wouldn't see the pain she caused. Jada wouldn't give her the satisfaction. Lies. *All lies. Thou shalt not bear false witness . . .* When Jada could listen again, she heard the objection overruled.

"Please continue," oily Creskin requested.

"Oh yeah," Mrs. Jackson said, and Jada could see her lick her lips, either in nervousness or delight at the next bite she was about to take. "She and that woman—a white woman, no offense intended—they spent time together every day. You would think my daughter-in-law, a woman with a job and a husband and a family, would want to spend her free time with *them*. But, no. So anyway, on the night my boy brought the children over, she didn't even know they was gone. She was with her girlfriend. Past midnight. My boy and her, they didn't have a fight or nothin'."

Tears welled up in Mrs. Jackson's eyes and she took a cloth handkerchief out of her purse. It was white and spotless. Jada knew that the woman had never had a pair of panties that clean, and wondered if it was Clinton or Mr. Creskin who had bought her the damn hankie. Her mother-in-law took a moment to wipe her eyes. "My grandchilrun was sad and tired and hungry and dirty. And she didn't—"

"Who do you mean when you say she?" Mr. Creskin asked.

"Jada Jackson. She didn't even call or nothin' to find 'em. Can you imagine? I have an answering machine and I have messages from that night. And she didn't even telephone."

A lie. Jada wrote across the pad. *I called a dozen times. They didn't answer the phone.*

"Don't worry," Angie whispered. "We'll tear her apart under cross-examination. We've got the goods on her."

Angie stood up and pulled down her jacket. She had conducted only a few cross-examinations in her career, and she was nervous but confident. She knew the danger here was to act too aggressive, to appear cruel to this nice old lady.

"Mrs. Jackson, I know this must be very hard for you, but I need to ask you a few more detailed questions," she began. Cautiously, Mrs. Jackson nodded her head. Angie made a few bland inquiries about dates and times, and nodded as Mrs. Jackson answered them. Then she said, "Now, you've stated that when the children arrived with your son, they were in very bad condition?"

"Oh yes." She nodded her head vigorously. "They were dirty. I could smell the little one."

"And you say their clothes were dirty?"

Mrs. Jackson nodded.

"I'll need you to answer that aloud," Judge Sneed directed. Angie looked up at him for the first time and tried a very small smile and a nod. She got back nothing, except to see Sneed look at his watch and turn back to Mrs. Jackson.

"Yes," Mrs. Jackson said very loudly. "The clothes was dirty and they was crying."

"Now, didn't you testify that your son had been taking care of the children? Could we read back Mrs. Jackson's testimony?" Angie asked the stenographer. "It was something about her son spending his life taking care of the children."

It took a few moments for the court stenographer to locate it, but then she read it back. "'My son had to feed the kids and wash 'em down,'" the stenographer read tonelessly. "'He spent his life taking care of those kids.'"

"Thank you," Angie said, and tried to keep the smugness she felt out of her voice. This was going to be easier than she'd thought. "So if what you said was true, none of the children was dirty or hungry. Unless it was because your son *wasn't* taking care of them. So which was it?" Mrs. Jackson looked upset. *Good.*

"They were dirty. Their mother—" she began.

"According to your testimony, this doesn't concern their mother. Was your son being irresponsible, or were the children well taken care of?"

"Objection, Your Honor. Miss Romazzano is badgering the witness," Creskin said.

"Objection sustained. But there is an issue here," Judge Sneed said to Angie. "Lighten up, counselor."

Mrs. Jackson took out her handkerchief and used it to wipe her upper lip. That was good, Angie thought. She wanted to see the old woman sweat, not cry. "If the children were dirty and hungry, why hadn't your son cleaned them?"

"I told the truth," Mrs. Jackson said. "They *was* dirty. But my son, he had been busy. He had been lookin' for a job. So maybe just then he wasn't doin' *everything* for them."

"I see," Angie said. "And how long has Clinton Jackson been looking for a job?" she asked, trying to keep her voice flat.

"Oh, he's been lookin' hard for a *long* time."

"So how long has he been jobless?"

Angie saw Mrs. Jackson's eyes move from side to side as if she actually saw the jaws of the trap closing. "Well, he'd pick up some work now and then."

"So, sometimes he's working and *can't* take care of the children?" Angie asked, her voice raised in doubt.

"No. He's always takin' care of the chilrun," Mrs. Jackson said, ruffled as an old turkey buzzard. "He just hasn't had a regular job since his company kinda went down."

"And exactly how long ago was that?"

"Oh, I don't know. About four years ago . . . or maybe six."

Angie knew she had to be careful, but she thought she could go for a little more juice right there. "Well, which one was it? Was it four years, or six years? That's a long span."

"I think . . ." Angie saw Mrs. Jackson's eyes flick over to George Creskin when she paused, as if she were getting Morse code from over Angie's shoulder. Whatever the dots and dashes for *Shut up* were, Mrs. Jackson received them. She closed her lips as tightly as she'd closed her hankie-filled purse. "I fail to remember exactly," she said with great feigned dignity.

Angie kept herself from smiling. Now was the time to pop the big question. "Mrs. Jackson, do you have a drinking problem?" She allowed herself to look behind her at Creskin, waiting for him to jump up and object. But, oddly, he didn't.

"No! Who said that? Who lied and said that?" Mrs. Jackson demanded, indignantly.

Judge Sneed looked over at Creskin. "Counselor, are you permitting this line of questioning?"

"Yes, Your Honor," Creskin said, the odd little smile continuing. "My witness has nothing to hide."

The judge again looked at his watch. "Well, let's see where this goes," Sneed said, but Angie could tell he was as impatient as a commuter on a bus line. She'd cut to the chase for Judge "Speed," and use some of the expensive investigative stuff they'd paid for.

"Mrs. Jackson, have you ever been arrested?" Angie shot a look over to Creskin to see if she'd had surprised him, but his little smile had turned into something more concerned and impassive. Angie thought that she wouldn't even want to play poker opposite this guy, then remembered that she was attempting something a lot more risky than a card game. She turned back to Mrs. Jackson, who was now wiping her forehead with the handkerchief.

"I think I once did," the old lady admitted.

"You *think* you got arrested? Wouldn't you remember?"

"I mean, yes. I did. But I'm not proud of it."

"Weren't you arrested for drunk and disorderly conduct? *And* for resisting arrest?"

"Yes," Mrs. Jackson whispered. *Bingo,* Angie thought.

"We can't hear your response," Judge Sneed said, but he didn't sound too concerned.

"Yes," Mrs. Jackson repeated louder, directly at Sneed. "But that was a long time ago, Your Honor. I just once got into trouble."

"Oh, I think it was more than once," Angie corrected. "Don't you also have two citations for driving under the influence?"

There was a very long pause. The courtroom was silent. Mrs. Jackson opened and closed her purse and the loud click in the quiet room sounded like the slam of a car door. "Yes," Mrs. Jackson admitted, "I used to drink. It was wrong and I hated it, but I couldn't stop."

Angie didn't need any more. Mrs. Jackson was finished. "So you may have been wrong when you—"

"I haven't had a drink in four years. God saved me. I know what I did was wrong, but I have not had a drink in years, since God stepped into my life. I was saved."

Angie couldn't be more pleased. Their detective had done a good job, and Angie was prepared. "So, if that's the case, why did you appear at Alcoholics Anonymous meetings at the River Street Baptist Church in April and May of this year and admit to dozens of witnesses that you were drinking again?" Angie stared at Mrs. Jackson and saw her face collapse in on itself. A handkerchief wouldn't help her now. Angie, momentarily, felt sorry for the woman. But then the judge spoke up.

"Miss Romazzano," he said. "From this bench I have *directed* people to attend twelve-step meetings in various anonymous groups. Do you know why they are called Narcotics or Alcoholics *Anonymous*?" He put the emphasis on the last word. "It's because what goes on in those rooms is privileged information. Those programs do a world of good. If you had plans to use information gleaned from those meetings, you can forget about it right now. That undermines not only the well-being of people making a huge effort, but also undermines this courtroom. I will not allow testimony in that direction. Give it up, counselor. Now." He looked at his watch yet again. "We'll take a short recess now. Back in ten minutes. I want you all back here in ten."

"All rise," the bailiff said, and they did.

34

Consisting of liar, liar pants on fire

"How was I supposed to know that Sneed wouldn't allow a witness to testify about Mrs. Jackson's binges? Or that AA was sacrosanct to him?" Angie asked her mother as they gulped coffee in the hallway of the family court building. Natalie and Laura and Bill had showed up for the last—and worst—fifteen minutes of questioning. Now they were clustered in the wide hallway of the courthouse. Angie didn't feel quite so confident now about either the case or her job security.

"Well," Natalie said tartly, "some of us happen to know that he's in AA himself, and has been for over twenty years. Although there have been a couple of well-publicized slips." Natalie sighed. "You could have asked."

"It didn't even occur to me," Angie admitted.

"Michael," Laura said. "*You* should have known it."

Michael nodded. "I did know. I just didn't know his witness policy. AA isn't a priesthood, after all." He shook his head. "I don't think there's a chance of discrediting Mrs. Jackson now," Michael said, moving them forward. "Here comes our client. Let's be optimistic. You did a really good job with the beginning of the cross anyway." Angie was grateful that Jada was with Michelle in the ladies' room and hadn't heard this, though she was sure that Jada knew perfectly well that they had blundered.

Then Jada and Michelle came out of the rest room together and joined their group. "I just can't get over the lying she did," Jada said. "I can't get over it. It isn't fair."

"Fair? They're so far off base they aren't even in the stadium. We just saw Tonya in the bathroom, fixing her eye makeup as if this was an appearance on *Oprah*." Michelle took Jada's hand and Angie was tempted to take Jada's other one, but instead just gave her a quick pat on the shoulder.

"Don't worry about it," Angie said. "Your mother-in-law contradicted herself. I think we're fine. And Creskin's gonna call Tonya next. We'll take her apart."

"We better get in there," Michael said. "Judge Sneed's a nut about punctuality, so let's not be late."

"Oh yeah," Laura agreed. "He once gave me eleven minutes for an entire cross in a wrongful death suit. But I won." She looked at Angie. "The bailiff said he's leaving tonight for his vacation place in Fort Myers. You better not dawdle."

"What?" Angie asked. "This has to wrap today? But I have six witnesses. And before that, all of Creskin's to cross."

"Do it fast," Laura said.

"This isn't the trial," Michael reminded them all. "It's only the *pendente lite*. It's not the final word."

"No. Just temporary custody and purgatory," Jada said.

"There's not much room for maneuvering. And no chance for a continuance," Michael said.

"Rocket Docket rides again," Natalie said, throwing away the rest of her coffee. "Let's not be tardy," she added, and led the way back into the court room.

From her seat in the middle of the courtroom, Michelle looked at Tonya Green as carefully as she could from behind her sunglasses. Despite her primping at the mirror during the break, the woman was a mess. She was wearing a too-tight turquoise dress and every bulge of flesh showed. How could Clinton have picked that woman over elegant, tall, slim Jada? Of course, Michelle could see—even with her puffy eye—that Tonya Green was being presented as a caregiver, not a girlfriend. Too bad she dressed like a slut. The creepy lawyer—Michelle couldn't remember his name—was questioning her only about her role as a sitter to the kids.

"What was the most surprising or disturbing thing about the children when they first came into your care?" the creepy guy asked Tonya.

"Well," Tonya said, leaning forward, her heavy breasts shifting under the cheap fabric of her dress, "they wouldn't talk for three whole days. It was the worst I've seen in children in ten years of doing this."

"Why do you think they didn't speak?"

"I think it's because they were afraid of her. Their mother. That she'd punish them. They don't like her." Michelle saw Angie rise and heard her object, though she couldn't hear what else was said by the judge and the creep. Then Tonya responded and said, "They never mention their mother. None of them cried for her. And little Kevon—I call him my angel—he curl up on my lap after two days and he say, 'Would you be my mommy?'"

Michelle felt sick to her stomach. If one of her children had ever . . . But, of course, Kevon hadn't done that, either. Of the three children, Michelle knew Kevon was the mama's boy. But Michelle thought of what it must be like to be Jada at that moment, and the pain she felt for her was almost unbearable. She wished she could get up on the stand and tell people, tell that judge, what she had seen and what she knew about how Jada supported them, monitored them, and loved them day in and day out over the last seven years that she'd known Jada.

Jada must be dying, Michelle thought, but Michelle felt as if a part of her were dying, too. *I'd rather be bacon burned in the pan than face this,* Michelle thought. *At least bacon can wiggle and spit and curl up.*

Although she'd seen plenty of trial scenes on television and in the movies, she had never before been in a courtroom. The thought of being in one with Frank, the thought of being on the stand, harried and hounded until she talked herself into some terrible corner, until she admitted the truth about what she knew, about what she had found, made her sick enough that she nearly had to leave the room. But she forced herself to focus on what was happening in front of her. She and Jada had gone into the same booth in the ladies' room and she'd just silently held her friend while she trembled. She might be needed again.

It amazed Michelle that people weren't telling the truth. That Mrs. Jackson could lie like a rug, that the miserable adulteress on the stand was talking about how the children loved her. Tears rose in Michelle's eyes, though the bruised one hurt when she cried. This wasn't a trial, they'd said at the break. It was a *pendente lite* hearing, but that must have been Latin for crucifixion. Even when Jada won—and she *better* win—Michelle knew her friend would always carry the pain of this. Michelle tried to focus on what was going on next. Angie was up and cross-examining Tonya.

"So, Mrs. Green, you say you have been a child care provider for a long time."

"Objection, Your Honor. Asked and answered. The witness has already testified she's been doing this for more than ten years."

"Oh yes," the woman said.

Michelle thought that the judge didn't like Angie. Was that possible? Did it matter?

"Do you have any training in child development or child care?" Angie asked.

"Objection, Your Honor. Let's remember Mrs. Green is not on trial here. What's the relevance?"

"The relevance," Angie said, "is to judge her competence and comparative experience."

"Overruled. She will be providing child care to Mrs. Jackson's children."

Michelle thought it was bad to have an objection overruled, but she wasn't sure. "New York State requires child care providers to be licensed. Do you have a license?" Angie asked next.

"Oh yes," Tonya Green smiled. "I got it right here in my bag. And I also got a insurance policy in case anything might happen to the children, Lord protect them."

Angie seemed flustered. Tonya took out papers and waved them. "Bailiff, let me see those," Sneed commanded, and they were brought to him.

"Your Honor, could I have a glass of water, please?" Tonya asked. The judge nodded and the bailiff brought it over. Angie waited while Tonya took a drink, then regained her composure.

"So how many children have you taken care of in the last ten years?"

"Oh, quite a few."

"Please give me their names."

There was a pause.

"Your Honor, in the interest of time, I think we could provide such a list later," the creep lawyer said. Michelle bet Tonya had never baby-sat anyone.

"Fine. Continue, counselor," the judge told Angie. Michelle hoped that she had something good set up to nail Tonya with.

Even Michelle, from rows backs, could see that Angie was surprised by the fact that the list wasn't needed then and that Judge Sneed let questioning continue. So was Michelle.

"So would you not think that children snatched from their home in the middle of the night, missing their mother, might be silent for a few days? Could that not be homesickness? Or trauma, based on your experience?"

"Oh, homesick kids, they always cry for they mama. These kids never did that."

Michelle watched as the gross woman in the witness box shifted in the chair and continued to fan herself with a folded piece of paper. It wasn't hot in the courtroom, at least not to Michelle, sitting on a middle bench in her coat and sunglasses. Good, she thought, let her feel she's on the hot seat. Michelle wanted Angie to burn Tonya at the stake. "Do you know the name of the children's pediatrician?" Angie asked. Tonya shook her head. "Well, what would you do in case of illness?"

"Take them to the hospital," Tonya said. "Or call 911." She said it as if she was proud of the answer, but Michelle couldn't believe how stupid it was. She used to call her pediatrician twice a week. She hoped the judge knew.

"What are their favorite television programs?"

"Oh, they watch television *all* the time," Tonya said with a big smile of relief.

"You allow them to watch TV all the time?"

Tonya's smile faded. "No. No, I don't. Not at all."

"So what programs do you allow? Which are their favorites?"

"I don't know."

"Mrs. Green, you are being paid for your services. Yet you don't know the children's doctor, or their TV preferences. Exactly what are your services, then?" Angie didn't give the woman a chance to answer. "Isn't it true that on the night of November fifth, November eighth, and other nights Clinton Jackson left your home at three A.M.?"

"I don't remember that."

"Mrs. Green that was only a short time ago. And you don't remember? Just like you don't know their doctor, or their favorite television. There seems to be a lot you don't remember or know."

The big woman shifted in her chair, drank more of her water, then moved forward to the railing. "Oh, now I remember about Mr. Jackson. He came over to talk about the children. One time I think it was because Kevon woke up cryin'. And the other time, maybe it was to get the book that one of them needed for school."

"And he arrived at eleven-thirty and didn't leave until three A.M.? Before you answer, I'd like to point out we can provide a witness for this, Mrs. Green," Angie said in a warning voice.

Michelle felt her hands clench into fists. *Yes!* Now this was going the way trials in the movies went. Michelle hoped Jada was enjoying this.

"Well, one time I remember we talked about the children a real long time because he was so worried." Tonya paused. "And I think one time he was so tired he might have fallen asleep on the sofa. He was right in the middle of a sentence and was just so tired he fell asleep."

Bullshit, Michelle thought, and gritted her teeth. From the back, Jada looked so strong, so upright. And Jada was such a good mother, such a good woman, and so good-looking. She had to listen to this nonsense? This woman on the bench, with her ridiculous outfit and her huge drooping breasts was . . .

Then it occurred to Michelle that the judge, or for that matter any man, wouldn't take seriously the idea that Clinton would give up sleeping with lovely Jada for a cow like Tonya Green. That was why she dressed so badly and looked so unattractive. *This isn't reality,* Michelle thought. *It's theater. Just like when any punk maniac goes postal and takes out half a restaurant, but then shows up for his trial in a nice dark suit, his hair carefully parted to the left.*

"Mrs. Green, isn't it true you're having a sexual liaison with Clinton Jackson and have been for many months?"

Then everything seemed to happen at once. Tonya made a moaning noise as if she were having sex with Clinton at that moment. Her water glass fell and smashed. The greasy lawyer was yelling, and Angela either repeated her question or asked another, but Michelle didn't hear it. Tonya didn't answer, but instead drooped over the railing, dropped her fan, and slumped forward. Clinton's lawyer stood up, then ran to the front of the courtroom.

"Your Honor, Mrs. Green suffers from high blood pressure and migraines. I'm afraid that—" Tonya Green slumped farther forward, and only the railing of the witness box kept her from falling to the ground. Angie and the other lawyer both ran forward to her. "I think she's fainted, Your Honor," Mr. Creskin said.

"Bailiff, get the nurse up here right away," the judge directed.

"We'll break for lunch until one-fifteen. If the witness has recovered, we'll continue then."

Michelle saw Tonya lift her head as the court clerk and bailiff helped her down from the stand. And then, as Tonya Green was helped out of the court, Michelle could swear she saw the greaseball lawyer wink at her.

"All rise," the bailiff called, returning from the hall. They all did, except Michelle, who sat on her bench demonstrating both meanings of contempt.

35

Consisting of major performances

"It's not going very well, is it?" Angie asked Michael Rice. He shrugged. Angie was only happy that Laura and her mother had left. "How the hell did Tonya have a license, when we checked on licenses?"

"Hey, Angie," Michael said, "Creskin is using every trick in the book. You established that she didn't know dick about the kids. And that that husband was making night visitations. So she faints, with a migraine. Most judges wouldn't put up with that, but Judge Speed here is always impatient, and apparently his flight leaves at six tonight. That isn't going to help us. He doesn't want it good, he wants it fast."

He smiled at Angie. "Look, this isn't the Supreme Court. He hears these Dom Rel problems all day long, every day. Unlike you, this isn't his first case, and he doesn't have an attachment to the plaintiff. Makes it harder, doesn't it? When you're so close to it?" He didn't wait for an answer, just patted Angie on her arm. "We're doing okay."

But Angie knew she wasn't. "You knew about Sneed's alcoholism." If only she hadn't pushed that with Mrs. Jackson.

Michael sighed. "Yeah. My wife was in AA for a while. I used to drop her off at meetings and see him."

Angie didn't know if she was supposed to say she was sorry or not. She took a bite of her tasteless turkey on rye sandwich. Even if it had been good, from a restaurant instead of the canteen here in the courthouse (where the flavor had been hydraulically removed), she wouldn't have been able to taste it. She could barely swallow.

"Look, Angie, we're almost done with his witnesses. Then you can call up our child care expert; our social worker, the one who knows the other old bitch is biased; and maybe recall Jada herself. She did really well this morning."

"I don't know if I should call her. She's melting and I don't blame her."

Mike looked up. "Here she comes," he said. "She looks plenty strong to me."

Michelle and Jada were coming down the hall to join them. First they'd gone to the ladies' room again to patch up their makeup. Angie knew she should do that, too, as well as do something about her hair, but she'd wanted to review everything while Jada was gone. Now it was time to comfort and prepare her client.

Jada sat down and coolly crossed one of her long legs over the other. Angie noticed there was a run in her stocking, but said nothing. Michelle was the one who spoke up first.

"Can you nominate any of the witnesses for Academy Awards?" she asked. "I just saw performances that were incredible." She sat down next to Jada, but leaned around her to peer at Angie. She looked frightened, but spoke anyway. "I'm sorry about my face, but if you want to call me, I will. Of course I might wind up fainting, too. But Jada is *so* dedicated, such a good mom. She could tell you every toy that Shavonne ever played with. She's got the doctor's phone number memorized, and could reel off Kevon's allergies alphabetically. I can testify to all of that."

Angie nodded and smiled. She thought of the horrors of George Creskin's possible cross-examination of Michelle—*And exactly when was your husband indicted for drug dealing, Mrs. Russo?*—and merely nodded. "I think we're in good shape," she said. "Michael has a doctor from Yale, an expert in child development, who we have retained to testify. And we have an expensive drug expert from the city."

"Is that legal?" Michelle asked. "I mean, if you pay him, doesn't that mean he's biased?"

Angie shook her head. She didn't have time for this sort of conversation now. "No, it's standard procedure. Everyone has expert witnesses if they can afford to. Expertise is expensive, but we can't afford not to have big guns. And that social worker . . ." Angie thumbed through her file. "Mrs. Elroy. Well, we can neutralize her because one of her coworkers has volunteered to testify about how biased she is, as well as how many complaints have been registered against her."

"Uh, Angie, could I talk to you for a minute?" Bill asked. He'd stayed when her mother and Laura had to leave. She nodded, then realized he wanted to speak to her alone.

Angie followed him across the crowded lunchroom. The path he was taking was as twisted as the way the hearing was going. "What is it?" Angie asked when Bill finally stopped in front of the water cooler. Typical drama prop, Angie thought.

"Mrs. Innico hasn't shown up yet."

"Call the office and—"

"I have. No word, and she doesn't answer her phone at work, her cell phone, or at home."

Angie didn't want to show her panic so she took a cup and filled it with water. "There's still time, Bill. I have the other witnesses to present first. Keep me updated on it." Angie gulped down the water as if it were a shot of liquor, crumpled the cup, and threw it in the trash with the perfect arc of a professional basketball player. *Breathe,* she told herself and turned and went back to her client.

Angie tried not to show her fear to Jada and Michelle. "I think we're in pretty good shape," she said. She looked Jada in the eyes. "The only question is whether you testify or not. You did great this morning, but if I call you to the stand, then you'll have to testify again and take his cross-examination." Angie tried to smile at Jada, who looked exhausted. "There's a shiny quarter in it for you if you do," Angie tried to joke.

Michael reached over to both women. "There's one turkey sandwich and one ham," he said. "Actually, you can't tell the difference by taste, only by color. The pink one is the ham. But the macaroni salad isn't bad."

"Oh please," Michelle said, turning her head away.

"As my mother would say," Angie told Jada with a forced smile, "you have to eat to keep up your strength."

"You're the one who's got to be strong," Jada said.

"We're counting on you," Michelle added.

Angie looked down at the disgusting food. "Two cannibal wives were having dinner together. So one says to the other, 'I hate my husband.' The other one looks down at their plates and says, 'So just push him over and eat the noodles.'"

"I think I once saw an Alfred Hitchcock show like that," Jada said. Michelle didn't say anything. It was Michael who groaned and stood up.

"Okay. Let's go in and let the Amazing Creskin pull his last trick. Then it's our turn."

Michelle was slumped in her seat when Anne Cherril, Jada's bitch secretary and Michelle's old coworker, walked into the courtroom. Michelle couldn't believe it and slumped further down. Was Anne there to gloat, or to be supportive of Jada? Michelle knew she had nothing to be ashamed of, but somehow she didn't feel like being seen by the old witch. She hadn't expected this, but she *really* hadn't expected what happened next: Creskin called Anne Cherril as his witness.

"Objection, Your Honor." Angie was up and really firm. Her vice was almost raised. "This witness is not listed, and there was adequate discovery time to inform us. I must insist on her not being called, or request a continuance."

Michelle watched as the judge looked at Mr. Creskin. "Counselor, you know better than to spring a surprise on this court," he admonished. *Good*, Michelle thought. *I hope he gets the judge good and mad.*

"Your Honor, this was a witness I could only locate yesterday, and the well-being of the children as my only concern, I felt that you would want to hear any testimony that would clarify the Jackson domestic situation."

The judge seemed to pause and consider. Then he said, "Objection overruled."

Michelle couldn't believe it. Anne Cherril was going to be allowed to take the stand to talk about her boss? And talk she did. It was like a nightmare.

"Oh, nothing was more important to Mrs. Jackson than her job," she gabbled, bitter as old tea. Jada must be beside herself, Michelle thought. "She put in the hours, I'll give her that," Anne said, though she sounded as if she didn't want to give Jada anything—just take things away. "She was *always* at work. Sometimes those kids would ring up and she wouldn't even take their calls."

Michelle wished she had a gun. She'd shoot the woman. She really would.

"I felt sorry for them, I did," Anne went on. "Sometimes I talked to them myself just to give them someone to talk to." It went on and on. Michelle got so angry that more than once she let a noise escape her lips, a low moan. Anne's testimony was untrue, unfair, and biased, yet Michelle knew it was doing damage, big time. All those years of resentment that Anne had carried, all those years of jealousy as a black woman moved up the ladder ahead of her, spewed out in nasty little twisted factoids. "I don't have children of my own," Anne admitted when Angie began cross-examination, "but if I did, I would have given them a lot more time than I did my job."

Michelle shivered. She wondered which neighbors, coworkers, or friends would speak against Frank and against her at Frank's trial. And she wondered what they would have to say. She suspected some people Frank knew would have a lot more reasons than Anne had to testify against him. Poor Jada. It was all horrible. What would a trial do to Michelle and her family? She shivered and put her hand in her pocket. She took out another Xanax and slipped it under her tongue.

There was another surprise for Angie, and one worse than Anne Cherril. Creskin called a Miss Abigail Murchison. Angie searched the list of witnesses, panicking and again, but the name didn't appear anywhere. "Who the hell is she?" Angie asked. Creskin couldn't keep getting away with this.

Jada nudged her with a face Angie didn't like to see, and whispered, "Kevon's kindergarten teacher from last year. I tried to get her fired."

Angie objected and again was overruled. She grabbed a pen and began scribbling notes as Miss Murchison told how Jada showed up at school, was almost incoherent, completely out of control and irrational. "She appeared to be high on something," Miss Murchison said.

"Objection, Your Honor," Angie almost shouted. The objection was sustained, but the woman continued to do her worst: Mrs. Jackson had been vituperative; she had made threats against her; she had thrown books around the classroom. When it was Angie's turn to cross-examine, she asked for another brief recess. Clearly annoyed, Speed gave them only five minutes. She huddled with Michael and Jada.

"She's a nut," Jada said. "I don't think she ever taught a black child before. She used to make Kevon wash his hands five and six times after lunch and still say that they were dirty. She didn't have a single book for story time with a person of color in it, except for a copy of *Little Black Sambo*. God knows where she got *that* one from. Anyway, I went in to see her and I was damn mad. I *did* throw a book, but it was *Sambo*. I also took her in about a dozen other ones. And I did tell her I would do my best to get her fired if she ever made him wash his hands more than once."

"Did you see the principal?" Michael asked.

"Oh yes. She won't show up. She's a reasonable woman who doesn't ever want to get involved. But the situation eventually straightened up. I also sent a letter to her and the Board of Education. It's all on record."

Angie began to feel buried under the weight of all of this. She had two minutes left to make her strategy. She looked at Michael.

"With time," he said, "we could easily counteract all of this." He looked at Angie. "But we don't have time and Creskin has really played it dirty by keeping his shots surprises."

Just then Michelle approached them. "God, I can't believe it," she said. "Miss Murchinson! She gave my son trouble right after my legal stuff began. She let him sit in his clothes after he wet his pants. I can testify to that. Do you want me to? I will."

Angie looked at her watch. Oh boy. Creskin would make a carnival out of that: *So how soon after your drug bust did this happen? And would you show the court your bruised face and tell us how you got it?*

"We have to just move on with something better," she said. She and Michael looked at one another. Michelle leaned over Jada and hugged her, then said something awful about Anne Cherril.

"It's taking a big risk, but it might be all I have left" Angie said quietly to Michael.

"Michelle as a witness? He can only question her about what you bring up if she's your witness," Michael said. "But if he somehow manages to open up the drug stuff, he'll cook your goose."

"I hope my goose isn't already cooked."

In cross-examination, Miss Murchinson didn't exactly admit to being a bigot, but she was easily flustered. She did acknowledge that Jada had registered a protest with the principal and the Board of Education. Angie couldn't get her to admit that she read *Little Black Sambo* to the class— Miss Murchinson said she couldn't remember all the books she'd read the children—but she did admit that many parents, when upset about their children's problems, came to the school very angry. Angie also asked if Miss Murchinson had ever heard from the children's father, and she had to admit that she hadn't. Angie presented it all as a strength, an indication of Jada's commitment and involvement with her kids.

The social worker, Mrs. Elroy, was not as bad as Angie expected. Actually, she was terrible, but easy to take down if only she'd get a little luck. She bristled with outrage during Creskin's questions. Elroy's drug test request and some of her other testimony was damaging, but under cross-examination she harangued the court about how working mothers should not be raising children. How motherhood was a full-time job, blah, blah, blah. She clearly sounded more than a few cards short of a full deck, and when Angie pulled in Mrs. Elroy's colleague, she figured Elroy's credibility would be demolished.

Luckily, Judge Speed didn't have any patience for sermons on the box. Angie felt she'd done a fairly good job of neutralizing her, and had submitted as evidence the results of the daily drug tests that they had performed at the state laboratory. Still, Angie was acutely aware that Mrs. Innico, the witness from social services who would blow Elroy out of the water, even now had yet to appear.

Bill kept calling, and kept reporting that no one could reach the witness. Angie actually felt queasy, about ready to lose her turkey sandwich, because Mrs. Innico still hadn't arrived by the end of Mrs. Elroy's testimony. She would have liked to begin her witnesses with her, and the woman had promised she'd be there at lunchtime. Yet it was past two and she still hadn't made an appearance. When Creskin was finished, the judge gave them a ten-minute recess to prepare for their witnesses. Angie asked Michael what he thought was happening with Mrs. Innico.

"I think what's happening is what sometimes happens. Sometimes witnesses don't show. Just because it's important to you and your client doesn't mean that they don't get flat tires, or drunk at lunch, or miss a train, or need a tooth pulled." Mike shrugged. "Sometimes they just forget, or chicken out. She might get here. And we've got Anna Pollasky from Yale. She's fabulous, and she's sitting in the hallway. Why don't we lead with the big guns?"

Angie thought it over. "No. We go with Clinton Jackson. I have to nail the lying son-of-a-bitch to the wall."

Jada felt as if, bit by bit, she was turning to ice, or perhaps stone. From the moment early this morning when she'd walked into the courthouse and seen her husband, dressed in a new suit and wearing a pair of horn-rimmed glasses—the man didn't *need* glasses—she'd felt as if something beyond terrible was about to go on. But as the day had progressed, she doubted her own reality. She doubted everyone else's, too. Each participant in this charade was taking a view so different from reality that Jada had to close her eyes more than once, take a deep breath, and remind herself that she was not crazy.

After a meal that she couldn't eat, and after betrayals by Anne and that teacher from hell, Jada was beyond anger. She was frozen. For some reason, she thought of the TV shows her husband liked, the ones where actors played the parts of criminals while real police and FBI reenacted raids and arrests. Fictional shows pretending to be real life. All that had been presented during this endless day was a fictional show that had nothing to do with her real life.

When at last Clinton took the stand, he looked better than he had on the day she first met him. He was sworn in.

"Before I begin direct, I would just like the plaintiff to identify himself," Creskin said. In a strong voice, Clinton gave his name and address. More amazing was that under Creskin's questioning, she watched while Clinton became the Perfect American Black Man. He had his own company, he had built a house for his family in a fine neighborhood, and though he was undergoing some pressures in the marketplace right now, while dealing with the bigotry of both suppliers and prospective clients, he was confident he would survive. He spent all the time he wasn't out there looking for new contracts with his children. He provided all their care.

He and, he implied, their children had been abandoned by the wife and mother of the home. "Sometime I feel like she got something to prove against me. Or that she got a plan that we just don't fit into," he said, sounding sad.

During Clinton's testimony, Jada felt the ice melt in her chest and turn into something a lot hotter than molten steel. She just wanted to get up, throw herself across the table, and in three strides be in front of her husband's face. She'd slap it until those stupid glasses flew off and his lying mouth was silenced. But instead she just sat there. She couldn't take notes because her hands were trembling too hard. Every now and then, Angie gave her a small tap on the shoulder.

"Don't worry. We'll get him," Angie murmured. "I'll just get a few of the facts out now. Then I'll call him to the stand later and take him apart."

And that's what she did. Calmly, but as efficiently as a surgeon slicing into infected flesh, Angie opened Clinton up and pulled out all sorts of nasty bits. She asked his income for the last five years, year by year. It went from minuscule to nonexistent. She asked for the names of recent prospective clients he had given proposals to and he couldn't give her any. She even asked if he had a word processor, business cards, a pager, or any standard office equipment. Reluctantly, to each question he had to admit he didn't.

"In the interest of brevity, I'll dismiss the witness now, but reserve the right to recall him later," Angie said. She sat down while a far less cocky Clinton left the stand and almost shuffled to his seat.

Jada felt a little bit better and trusted that Angie could do even more dire things later. Next there was some discussion between the judge and George Creskin, and a large TV monitor was rolled in. "If it pleases the court, I'm about to show a video tape taken two weeks ago. Mr. Jackson's wife had two hours of visitation with the children and was returning them."

Angie stood up. "Objection, Your Honor. We were not made aware of this exhibit or its contents. We completely object to—"

"In the interest of brevity, Your Honor, I think we can agree a picture is worth a thousand words."

"Your Honor, there's absolutely no call for this and we strongly object."

"Sidebar, Your Honor," Creskin said.

"What's a sidebar?" Jada asked Michael. Angie got up and walked to the judge's bench. White people.

"We didn't know," Jada heard Angie whispering.

". . . sent it . . . didn't get it?" was all Jada heard Creskin reply. She looked at Michael for some reassurance and he rubbed her back with his left hand. ". . . faxed confirmation, sir," Jada heard, and saw Creskin hand over a piece of paper.

". . . problem with machine . . . but, Your Honor . . ." Now Angie sounded defensive. This couldn't be good.

". . . postal receipt right here . . ." Creskin snapped.

". . . we can't allow . . ." was the last she heard from Angie. Then the judge said something and her friend turned around and walked back to the table. Jada didn't like the look on Angie's face. Was it due to the new evidence, or because she had to stand so close to Creepy Creskin?

"If this was a trial, I couldn't allow this evidence to be submitted, but since it's only a *pendente lite* hearing and the defense has presented to me proof of mailing, notification, and the like, the defense may present this exhibit."

George Creskin, in a move rather like a technology magician, pulled out a small remote control and hit a button.

Jada watched the screen fill, and on it her own car pulled up to the front of her mother-in-law's dump. It must have been the visit when she took them to the house. Clinton had a close-up of Kevon hanging his head and crying, running toward the camera, away from Jada. Then there was a close-up of Shavonne, her face angry, pulling away from her mother's hands, refusing to hug her. The shot continued to reveal that even Sherilee was crying, but that was only because she'd just been woken from her nap.

Jada saw it all, but couldn't believe her eyes. "The children were crying because I told them I had to take them back to their grandmother. They had expected to stay with me that night," she whispered fiercely to Angie. Then, in a terrible insight that came far too late, Jada wondered if they'd been specifically told they were staying with her—told that so they'd be so upset. Could Clinton be that clever, that diabolical?

Angie, white-lipped, was nodding her head and took some notes. "We'll certainly get this disallowed," she assured Jada.

But as Jada watched, she felt like one of the martyred saints. She was having her heart torn out before her eyes. If the people in this courtroom actually believed her children wanted to run from her, she may as well be drawn and quartered. If the judge believed that, she might as well be dead.

When, at last, it was Angie's turn to call witnesses, she began very simply. "Your Honor, I'd like to recall Mr. Clinton Jackson to the stand." Clinton didn't look so crestfallen as he had after his last turn with Angie. That the man could be proud of the videotape was in itself a guilty verdict, but the judge wouldn't know that.

"So you've testified under oath that for the last several years you've been taking care of the children's needs at home, Mr. Jackson?" she asked. He nodded.

The court stenographer asked for a verbal response and he said, "Yes, I do," a little too loudly. Good. Maybe he was nervous, Jada thought.

"What is your eldest daughter's favorite dinner?" Angie asked.

Jada watched Clinton pause for a moment, caught off guard, and behind his fake glasses, she thought she saw a little spark of fear in his eyes. She almost laughed. It was such an Angie question, a woman's question, and Jada knew Clinton hadn't a clue. "Ah, Shavonne, she likes pizza," he said.

"You don't cook pizza yourself, do you?" Angie asked.

"No. I call out for that."

"So aside from what you call out for, what is Shavonne's favorite meal?"

He paused again, this time longer. "Meatloaf," he said. "Meatloaf and cream corn."

Wrong, Jada thought. He liked meatloaf and creamed corn. Shavonne liked macaroni and cheese with ham.

"And how do you prepare that for her?"

"Objection, Your Honor. This isn't a cooking lesson. Next we'll have the young counselor calling Betty Crocker as an expert witness." Creskin laughed. Jada hated the man so much she thought that the Lord might never forgive her.

"Overruled. But make it quick, counselor," Judge Sneed said.

"How do you make that meatloaf?" Angie asked.

Jada thought she heard Michelle giggle. Clinton couldn't make a cheese sandwich.

"Well, I put some meat in a long pan, you know, one of those pans."

"What kind of meat?"

"Like a chopped meat. You know, like maybe a hamburger meat."

"And do you put anything into the meat?"

Creskin audibly let his breath out, as if his exasperation was too much for him.

"No." Clinton paused. He seemed to reconsider. "Oh, yes, salt and pepper." He said it with such pride, as if he'd just won *Jeopardy.*

"And that's all you put into it?" Angie asked.

"Uh-huh. But I use real good hamburger. That's why they like it."

"And how do you make the creamed corn?"

"Well, I get a can of corn and I put some whipped cream in it. And then I stir it around until it's hot in the pot."

Angie could hardly believe it. Did the judge know just how ridiculous Clinton's "recipes" were? "And you've testified you make a lot of meals for the children?" she asked.

"Oh yeah."

"So what would Kevon's favorite meal be?"

George Creskin rose. "Objection, Your Honor. This information is irrelevant and—"

"Overruled," the judge said. Angie smiled. He did know how ridiculous Clinton was.

"You will answer the question," the judge directed.

"Spaghetti and meatballs," Clinton said. Then he smiled. "You know, all kids like spaghetti and meatballs."

"And how do you prepare that, Mr. Jackson?" Angie asked.

"Well, you get the box of spaghetti and you put it in a big bowl. Then you get those cans of spaghetti sauce—he likes the spicy kind— and you heat it. Then you pour it on the spaghetti."

Angie smiled directly at Judge Sneed. Then, keeping the smile on her face, she turned back to Clinton. "So, let me understand this. You take a box of spaghetti, empty it directly into a serving bowl, and then cover it with hot sauce."

"Yeah," Clinton said. "Then the hot sauce kinda makes the spaghetti soft and you're ready to eat. Even the baby loves that."

Angie shook her head in disbelief for both Clinton and Sneed to see. "Mr. Jackson, isn't it true that your wife does virtually all the cooking in your home? Remember, you are under oath."

"I cook for them. I cook for them all the time!" He paused. "Well, plenty of the time."

Angie turned to the judge. "Your Honor, against this testimony I would like to submit a dozen recipes for meatloaf. You will notice that in none of them is chopped meat the lone ingredient, because it wouldn't make a loaf if it wasn't bound with egg or sauce or bread crumbs. Most often creamed corn comes that way in a can. I also think you and the court understand that spaghetti must be cooked before it's served. Lastly, I would like to submit as evidence some interview results from the social worker, who found"—Angie looked down at the report—"that Kevon loves hot dogs with catsup, no mustard, while his sister prefers macaroni and cheese." After the exhibits were stamped, she turned back to Clinton. "Now, you've been home with them after school."

"Yes. *And* most evenings."

"So who is your daughter's idol? Can you tell me her favorite movie star? Or her favorite music?"

Clinton stared at Angie and now he looked angry. "I don't know," he admitted, then corrected himself. "I mean, there are so many of them, I'm not sure who's her favorite."

Jada watched her husband make an ass and a liar out of himself. And she enjoyed it. She could answer every question that Angie asked. She knew the name of Kevon's imaginary friend, and that her daughter loved Sonya Benoit, Leonard DiCaprio, and Puff Daddy. But Clinton didn't know a thing—and Angie was relentless.

"What are your daughter's grades like, Mr. Jackson?"

"She gets good grades. She's never had any trouble with grades."

"So they haven't suffered because of this so-called problem with their mother?"

Ha! Damned if he said they did, damned if he said they didn't.

"Well, maybe a little, but she gets good grades. I help her," Clinton lied. "She's a smart girl, I'm proud of her."

"I'm sure she is and I'm sure you are," Angie said mildly. "How does she do in math?"

Jada watched her husband's face take on that closed look he got when she caught him out and he knew it.

"Objection, Your Honor. We don't need to go into these tiny details or we'll be here all month." Jada watched as Angie threw a dirty look at Creskin, but she herself kept staring at her enemy in the witness box.

"Your Honor, with a moment more of this line of questioning, you'll see the relevance," Angie said.

"Objection overruled. Continue," Judge Sneed said. He looked at his watch.

"She's always done fine," Clinton said.

"Mr. Jackson, I have your daughter's report card, not only from this year but from the last *three* years. Would you read out her grades in math, starting with this one from two years ago."

Jada kept her mouth perfectly still, suppressing a smile. *Bless you, Lord,* she thought, *and thank you for putting this lawyer friend in my life.* Clinton was reading out the pathetic third-grade math scores that had kept Jada up at night, back when her nights were a lot simpler than they were now. "C, C, D, C, D, F," Clinton was forced to read.

"Would you call those good grades, Mr. Jackson?"

"No," he said reluctantly, and began to add something until Angie stopped him.

"Please read these." She handed him what Jada recognized as Shavonne's fourth-grade report card.

"C, A, A, B, A," Clinton read, though he almost mumbled it.

"Well, it seems that your daughter didn't always get good grades in math. Though you don't seem to remember that. Do you remember what happened to change those very poor grades to excellent ones?" Clinton looked over at Creskin's table, but Angie pursued it. "What happened?" she asked.

"I talked to her. I told her to knuckle down. I told her no Jackson's got failin' grades. So she studied harder."

"Mr. Jackson, do you recognize the name Allesio? Mrs. Allesio?"

"No," Clinton answered, as if afraid he was going to be accused of having slept with her. Jada almost laughed out loud again. All the preparation time she'd spent with Michael Rice and the others had been worth it.

"You never employed her?"

"No. I certainly never did."

"Well, I'm surprised at that. She's been Shavonne's math tutor for the last two years." Jada actually enjoyed watching Clinton's face drop. "No more questions, Your Honor," Angie said. She finally turned away from him and looked at the judge.

Surely, Jada thought, this man *had* to understand that it was she who had watched over her babies, who had cooked for them and took them to the doctor and gotten them tutors and confronted Kevon's bigoted kindergarten teacher. She had attended all the PTA meetings and nursed them when they were sick. He had to understand all of that.

"We'll take a brief recess." The judge looked down at his watch. "I want everybody back in this room in fifteen minutes." He looked at Angie. "Then, counselor, I want you to wrap this up."

He banged the gavel and the bailiff yelled out, "All rise."

"Your Honor," Angie began once court was again in session. "I would like to call Dr. Anna Pollasky to the stand as an expert witness."

Dr. Pollasky rose and walked from the back of the courtroom down the center aisle. She was a tall woman with a tremendous amount of presence. Her gray hair was cropped in a stylish but conservative bob and her grayish blue suit gleamed with authority. She'd written a dozen books on modern child care and had appeared on probably a hundred television programs. She stepped into the witness box, took the oath, and sat down.

Angie had to qualify her as a witness and went through a long list of Dr. Pollasky's degrees, accreditation, published works, and the positions she'd held both as a professor of child development and the current director of the Yale Center for Childhood Studies. She was an impressive woman with an impressive background. "I move to certify the expert, Your Honor," Angie said, and could almost feel how much she was going to enjoy wiping out the social worker, Tonya Green, and Mrs. Jackson's testimony with what would come next, but then George Creskin rose.

"I object to the expert witness, Your Honor."

"Object?" Where was the objection? Angie wondered. Judge Sneed asked the same thing as he raised his brows. It was clear that everybody knew who Dr. Pollasky was.

"May I cross-examine on this issue, Your Honor?" George Creskin asked. Sneed nodded, though he looked as surprised as Angie. "Dr. Pollasky, you testified you are a medical doctor licensed in the State of New York?"

"Yes," Dr. Pollasky answered calmly and surely.

"You're certain of that."

"Yes," she said. "Of course."

"And you're being paid to testify here today."

It was a stupid trick, if Creskin were doing this to make Pollasky deny she was paid. Some tyros did that, feeling guilty. Pollasky knew better, and Creskin should have known she would.

"Yes," she said. "It is customary to pay for a doctor's time. They also paid for my expenses to get here from New Haven."

Angie wondered what the hell Creskin was doing. It was the first time he'd looked foolish since the trial began.

But his objection was a lot simpler than that. Creskin pulled out a few sheets of paper. "I'm afraid, Doctor, that you are in noncompliance. You're not certified in this state." He put the papers before her, and handed copies to the judge and to Angie. "We inquired with the board and you are not licensed."

Dr. Pollasky, clearly confused, looked down at the papers. "But I have been licensed in New York for more than twenty years."

"But not now," Creskin said.

Dr. Pollasky was quiet for a moment. She looked over the sheets before her. "It seems my secretary forgot to send in the registration."

"Perhaps," Creskin said dryly. "Your Honor, I move to dismiss the witness. If she's not valid in the state, she can't testify." Creskin smiled familiarly at the judge. "It happened last Friday on the third circuit. Franko vs. Lapstone Oil. Judge Sullivan was presiding. Did you hear about it? Some guy they brought all the way in from Finland or something."

Angie knew judges, more than anything, followed precedent, even though she had no idea who Judge Sullivan was or what Franko vs. Lapstone Oil was about.

"Witness dismissed," Sneed said.

After that, Angie got the feeling she'd sometimes had in very bad dreams. It was as if she were in a terrible hurry, yet could only move in slow motion. She kept trying, but nothing seemed to work, and she could feel that Judge Sneed had lost interest and was losing patience, just as she could feel that she might very well be losing this case. Her drug test expert, a well-known New York technician, was dull and unconvincing, though accurate, and though the PTA president averred that Jada Jackson was an involved, carrying, competent mother, there was no drama, no strength. But Angie was afraid it wasn't enough, that *she* wasn't enough.

At last she finished with the last witness. Judge Sneed stopped drumming his fingers. She expected he would call a recess or announce that he would hand down his ruling in writing the next morning. But she had underestimated Rocket Docket. Nothing was going to interfere with his vacation. He lifted his head and looked at the two attorneys. "This was, let us recall, an emergency hearing," he said. "It was called and given priority based on serious questions about the children's welfare. It seems to me that there's no question here," the judge said. "The only interest I have are those of the children."

Yeah, Angie thought. *That and your flight to Florida.*

"At this point in time, Mrs. Jackson's apparent over-involvement with her work, her record of promotions, and hours speak for itself. The drug issue is also a troublesome one. I don't need to recess to make a ruling for the time being."

Oh my God, Angie thought, *I've lost it. I blew it.* She looked around the room, as panicked as an animal trying to escape a burning building. She could almost taste the ashes in her mouth.

"I grant custody, child support, and a reduced alimony to be determined subsequently to Mr. Jackson. In the meantime, I grant Mrs. Jackson supervised visitation"—he paused, as if considering—"twice a week, for two hours per session. Mrs. Jackson has two weeks to vacate the family dwelling before Mr. Jackson and the children can return." He raised his gavel. "Case adjourned."

"All rise," the bailiff said, but neither Jada nor Angie could stand.

RING TWO

Men are mostly dogs and marital diplomacy is all about pleasantly
saying "nice doggie" until you find a damn rock.

Nan Delano

36

Aftermath, geometry?

Angie lay as flat as her growing bulk would allow on the new mattress in her new bedroom staring up at her new ceiling. Unlike the one in her dad's house, this ceiling did not have infinity eights spackled over it. Instead it had some kind of blown-on texture that probably crumbled as you slept. As Angie stared at it, she decided it dropped off something you breathed in as you dreamed, and caused nightmares, or maybe a cancer that would only be discovered twenty years from now. Or, worse, birth defects. Angie put her hand on her belly. It was mounded, but the rest of her had never felt lower.

She couldn't get over how badly she'd failed in court. Failure, Angie reflected, hadn't been something she'd experienced much in her life. She'd done her preparation. She'd gotten her expert witnesses. But a combination of her inexperience and Creskin's sneakiness, along with the judge's peculiarities and the lousy laws, had brought her and her case down. She squirmed as she thought of how she'd disappointed Michael, her mother, and Jada. Now she had a professional failure she knew would haunt her conscience forever. But worse, she'd failed her friend. None of it felt good.

The phone rang and Angie swung her arm out like one of those claws that drop in an arcade. Whoever it was, this phone call could be no prize, but she'd never managed to get a prize from the arcade claw, either. A failed marriage and a failed career. No prizes for her anymore.

Natalie's voice was buzzing in Angela's ear before she had time to say hello. "I heard all about it. He's outrageous, that Sneed. We're going to have to start a campaign to get him off the bench. You had, what? An hour and a half to present your case? But it isn't like you didn't screw up. Sneed's outrageous, but you did screw up."

"Hello, Mom. It's nice to hear from you, too," Angie said weakly.

"I shouldn't have let you handle it. It was more complicated than we thought. And you couldn't catch a break. Michael told me about Dr. Pollasky's little forgetfulness. And the social worker who never showed. By the way, Bill finally reached her. Her dog was hit by a car."

"I feel like I've been," Angela said, closing her eyes on the deadly ceiling. "Not hit. Run over."

"Look, all this can be fixed," Natalie told her. "It'll take a little while, a little more money, but it's outrageous and we will pull together a request for the trial and—"

"Later, Mom," Angie said. There was a short pause. Angie held her belly with one hand, the phone with the other.

"You want me to come over?" Natalie asked. "I can pick up a couple of sardine sandwiches. Remember how you used to like sardine sandwiches?"

Sardine sandwiches were Natalie's favorite. Not Angela's. The thought of a sardine swimming in the ocean, much less swimming in oil on a piece of soggy bread, was enough to make Angie seriously consider heaving. "I think I just need some rest now, Mom," she announced, quietly but with deep certainty.

"Okay. Just know that no one is blaming you. Well, some people are, but I'm blaming Michael."

"Oh, Mom!"

"Just joking," Natalie said, and Angie, shaking her head, let the crane descend and drop her prize back in the cradle.

The idea of a cradle brought her hand back to her belly. She had to make a decision about this pregnancy and there was only one decision to make. She hated to think about it, but it was necessary.

The thing was, she loved children and had loved Reid. During the three years of law school, during their engagement, and at their wedding, she had looked at him and thought, "Yes. I want *him* to father my children." She'd loved him so much she wanted him to be a part of her, a permanent part, and the idea of a child, a mixture of them both, had thrilled her. But now . . .

Angie sighed deeply. She had ruined her life. She realized that, but she had the added burden of knowing the part she'd played in Jada Jackson's tragedy, as well.

After Judge Sneed had swept out of the courtroom, Angie had silently followed Jada, Michael, and Michelle through the hallways and into the parking lot. It wasn't until then that Michelle had asked, "What's next?"

"Nothing is next," Jada said. "Nothing."

Angie had, at first, tried to apologize. When Michelle had had to leave to get back to her kids, Michael had talked about an appeal, and then had taken Jada and Angie out and helped get Jada well and truly drunk. "I can't believe it. I just can't believe I won't have my babies," Jada had repeated over and over. Angela hadn't drank at all, but listened as long as Jada could talk.

Then she offered to drive Jada home. She'd turned to Michael and asked for his address, as well. "I live where you live," he told her, and laughed. Angie thought he was drunk or—worse—was making some kind of pass at her. But it turned out he lived in her garden apartment complex. "That's why I recommended the agent," he had mumbled.

So Angie was the designated driver and dropped off Jada at her darkened, empty home, then drove to the apartment building and watched Michael weave toward his own end of the complex. Exhausted, she had gone to bed, sober and sleepless and hoping she'd feel better the next morning.

But now it was the next morning, and she didn't feel better at all. Still, however bad she felt, she knew that Jada Jackson was feeling worse. She had to check on Jada, pick her up so that they could return to the parking lot where they'd left Jada's car. Then she remembered this was the day her father had planned to come over and help her "fix up the dump," as he had so graciously put it. She couldn't do it. She knew her dad would let her off the hook, but she also knew it would leave a big hole in his weekend plans.

She lifted the phone and punched in his number. He answered on the first ring, the way people who live alone often do. "Hi, baby," he said cheerfully. But when she told him they'd have to reschedule, she could hear the cheeriness leave his voice. First he tried to talk her into changing her mind, then he suggested that he could come over and help sort things out while she was busy elsewhere. She managed to tell him no and promised to reschedule.

Angie forced herself up and out of bed, showered, and dressed. The waistband of her leggings cut into her. It amazed her to think that there was a new life, her baby, there, under her navel. She pushed the thought away and threw a sweatshirt on, grabbed her purse, and walked out the door, though her hair was still wet.

The drive to Jada's wasn't long enough, because Angie knew she didn't want to knock on the door and have to face her client and friend. But she wouldn't, she couldn't, just leave Jada in that house alone. Angie took a deep breath. It was all so unfair, she raged to herself. Maybe she had not been a great lawyer. Maybe she hadn't even been a good lawyer, but George Creskin wasn't so fucking great, either. He had devastated her—and Jada, a good mother, a taxpayer, a good citizen. But despite Angie's mistakes, despite the Amazing Creskin's cleverness and experience and tricks, she was shocked that there could be such a total miscarriage of justice.

Miscarriage. As she turned onto Jada's street, her hand went to her belly again. Where was a miscarriage when you needed one? She grimaced. She didn't really want a miscarriage. She wanted a baby—or to not be pregnant right now. But if not now, when? She wasn't a kid anymore. It would take her years to ever trust a man again. And then? Then, maybe nothing.

But it was worse, much worse for Jada. None of this was fair, and Angie knew it was because Jada was a woman that these atrocities were possible. Playing fair, behaving well, working within the rules didn't work for women. The system was created by men, run by men, and benefited men. When women came out on top, it was either a happy accident or a triumph of will equal to climbing Everest.

Angie parked her car in Jada's driveway, walked to the kitchen door. She realized she was terrified. Here was a mountain Jada had to climb— or maybe it was a valley she had to climb out of. Angie wanted to help; after she'd taken Jada to her car, she'd offer to help her with packing.

Angie took a deep breath and rang the bell. She waited for a few minutes on the doorstep. No response. She rang again. After a few more minutes, she banged on the door as hard as she could.

Jada threw it open. "I hear you, I hear you," she said. "The bells don't work. He never fixed the goddamned chimes. Now he probably will, once I'm out of here." Jada spun around and walked through the living room. Relieved, Angie followed her.

Boxes were already spread across the floor, some empty, some partially packed. And colored paper, the kind kids used in grade school, was scattered across the coffee table along with magic markers, scissors, and tape. It looked like some kind of third-grade project, but Angie knew Jada's kids couldn't come to the house until she left it. "When did you get up?" Angie asked.

"I didn't go to sleep," Jada told her. "I just threw up, hosed myself off, and then got started." She gestured toward the coffee table. "I couldn't bear not to leave a trace of myself," she admitted. "Do you think that if I put notes in the kids' pockets and hide them in their drawers and stick them in their shoes and tape them to the inside of the closet doors, Clinton would find them all and take them all away?"

Angie pressed her lips together and shook her head. "I don't think so," she said, hoping she was right.

"I cleaned their rooms and prepared for them to come home over a week ago. Except then I thought that they'd be coming home to me." Jada sighed deeply and lifted up one of the heart-shaped bits of paper she'd cut. "Sherrilee likes sparkles," she said, pointing out the glinting border. "Of course, she can't read." She shook her head, then bit her lower lip for a minute. "You think Tonya might read this one to her?" she asked, her voice hard.

Angie looked at the construction paper heart and felt as if her own were breaking. *I am always thinking of you, my baby,* Jada had written.

"Oh my God, Jada, I'm just so sorry," Angie said, tears forming. "It's all my fault."

Jada looked at her and shook her head. "No, it isn't," she said. "But it isn't all *my* fault, either. I have to remember that or I'll go insane." They stared at each other.

Angie blinked her eyes to make sure they didn't tear. No one but Jada had the right to that right now. "There are still legal steps we can try," she said. "Do you remember Michael's suggestions from last night?"

Jada shook her head. "It's over," she said. "You know it's over and I know it's over. My house is disbanding. My family is disbanding." She looked down at her hand. "Even my hand is disbanding," she said as she pulled the wedding ring from her finger and threw it in the general direction of one of the boxes. "Our walks together are disbanding. You've moved. I know Michelle is still my friend, despite all of this, but now that she can come over here again, I'm moving."

"Where are you going to go?" Angie asked.

"I don't know and I don't care."

And then Angie had a good idea. "Why don't you come and stay with me?" she asked.

37

In which Michelle reflects and her friends mirror her

Michelle was carrying the bucket down the hallway, but it was so heavy and the water kept sloshing out. She had to get to the end of the hall to wash up the stain. All the stains had to be removed immediately, but each time she got halfway down the hall, the water had all gone and she would have to go back. Finally Michelle began to cry, and as she did, her tears filled the bucket. When she got to the end of the hall, she realized she was in a prison. Behind the bars, a dark figured loomed. The stains were on the floor and on the bars. With a lurch in her stomach, Michelle realized they were bloodstains. And then she turned around and looked up and realized the looming figure was Frank, bloody and frightening and chained to the prison wall. Michelle began to scream, but before the sound came out of her mouth, she woke up gasping.

She had forgotten the dream until she started coffee in the morning. Then it came back to her, making her shiver. Of course, the events at the courthouse had stunned Michelle in more ways than she had expected. She took down another mug, lined it up on the counter, and wiped down the place in the cabinet where it had been. She began to empty each cabinet, swabbing out the bottom and putting down shelf liner. It was a mechanical process, but it gave her time to think. The outcome of the hearing was, of course, unfair and shocking; if anyone was a good mother, if anyone deserved to be with her children, it was Jada.

But it wasn't only the injustice that upset Michelle. It was also the coldness of the whole process. None of Jada's mothering, her sacrifices for the kids, her piety, her values, the discipline she'd instilled in them, had come through. The wrong things had happened. Justice had not been served. The children had not been served. Watching the court help to wreck lives, to serve as a theater of lies, had made Michelle focus on Frank and his upcoming trial. At the thought of it all she'd break into cold sweats on the back of her neck and between her shoulder blades. So she'd started the cabinet project.

What would come out at Frank's trial, she wondered now, as she put the mug and all its sisters and brothers back in the newly cleaned and lined cabinet. What was the truth? She couldn't talk to him, couldn't ask. The two of them had managed to get through Friday night without speaking to one another, except for brief exchanges in front of the children. Then Michelle had gone to bed early and slept fitfully on a tiny sliver of their bed, not even waking when Frank came in.

She'd gotten up early, cleaned the house, dropped Jenna off at hockey, taken Pookie to the vet, and had just waved off Frankie as he left with his dad for his all-time favorite activity—a visit to the hardware store. Michelle didn't even bother to pull herself together before she put on her jacket and walked down the street to Jada's. She'd called twice last night, but Jada hadn't answered. God, she must have been suicidal.

She stepped quickly along the street to Jada's. She expected the house of the dead. But when she opened the kitchen door and walked in, Michelle was surprised to hear animated voices in the house that had been so painfully silent for the last weeks. She stepped into the living room.

Jada was on her knees, putting something into a carton, and Angie was taping another carton up. Since when had these two become so friendly? Had Angie stayed over? Surely comforting Jada was Michelle's job. For a moment she felt jealous. Then she told herself to grow up.

Jada raised her head. "Yo, Cindy! Just who I need," she said. "I found out there's one good thing about losing custody," she told Mich. "No more WAR."

"War? What war?"

"WAR. Worries About Reputation," Jada said. "I guess I can see you now whenever we have the time—without worrying about my rep. It's shot anyway."

"So's mine," agreed Michelle. "It's not the worst thing in the world. It saves on baking time—no more bake-sale requests."

"My reputation is shot, too, at least as a lawyer," Angie said, rubbing the tape on the box she had sealed. "First I walk out of my job up in Boston, then this." She looked at the crinkled strip she'd laid down. "Maybe I could try a career as a crate packer."

"You're not much good at that, either," Jada told Angie and added another strip of tape.

Michelle looked at the two women. How could they bear to go on? Jada's life was ruined, and Angie had helped ruin it. Michelle opened her mouth, but no words came out. How could Jada leave this home, a home that meant everything to her? Michelle wondered how she herself would go on living a few doors away, having Clinton and that woman as neighbors. No more barbecues in the backyard. Frankie might play with Kevon, Shavonne might still pick on Jenna, but Mich would never let them enter that house again.

She picked up an empty box, but realized she didn't even know what to pack in it. The other two seemed to be so organized, so in sync. But for Michelle there would be no best friend. No one to walk with. How was she going to deal with this? And how could Jada be coping so well? Michelle felt as if she were falling apart. Should she tell Jada again how sorry she was? Should she tell both of them how frightened she was about Frank's trial? Should she tell them . . . ? Just then Jada rose and came up to put an arm around her shoulder.

"I cried all night," she said. "Now I just have to do the next thing I have to do. You'll be okay, Mich," she said, as if reading her mind. "Frank will fight this thing and the two of you will go back to normal." Michelle looked up into her friend's eyes and she just couldn't stand it anymore. The secret she'd been carrying wouldn't stay a secret.

Jada, her friend, had the decency to think about her at a time like this, while Frank . . . Frank . . . "He's guilty," Michelle said, and both Jada and

Angie froze where they stood. "He's guilty," Michelle repeated. "It won't be okay." Saying the thought that had been with her constantly since her discovery in Jenna's closet was both terrifying and a relief. She sat down on one of Jada's mismatched dining room chairs and put her head in her hands. She couldn't look at them.

There was silence in the room for a few moments. Michelle could hear her own heartbeat and Jada's heavy breathing. "I'm so afraid. I really didn't think he would do anything bad," Michelle said to their silence. "Not really bad. When the cops came, I was sure it was payback for some business deal. Spite. Politics. That zoning thing. Even when he was indicted . . ." She glanced at them, then looked away, got up from the chair, and walked to the window, just so she'd have someplace else to look. "I know you think I'm stupid," she said. "You think I'm gullible. But I wasn't just having a Michelle moment. There was no way to know. No calls. No visits. Nothing. Nothing that involved us, ever."

She turned around and looked at them. "Frank loves us. He swore to me, I mean, he really did, that he was clean. He *made* me believe him. But then I . . . I found out . . ." She paused. Even with these two friends, she wasn't going to tell about the money. Not that she'd ever touch that cash. Blood money. For all she knew, it had come from teenagers or schoolchildren. She'd die before she'd have anything to do with that evidence. But she was afraid and ashamed to mention it, even to Jada and Angie. Would they understand?

"How long have you known?" Jada asked, her voice gentle. "I knew something was wrong with you, but I figured it was the pressure, the bullshit from the neighborhood. Or me. What was happening with me. I didn't know it was—" She stopped and then added, "I'm *so* sorry, Michelle."

Angie came up to the window. Michelle had never noticed how short Angie was. She looked down, into Angie's eyes. "You need a good lawyer, Michelle," Angie said.

"I have one. I mean, Frank has one."

Angie shook her head. "No, I mean a lawyer of your own. And a better one than I am."

"What are you going to do?" Jada asked.

"What can I do?" Michelle answered, and the feeling of being trapped started closing in on her again. Sooner or later Frank would find out the money was gone. What would happen then? If she had one of those Xanax pills with her, she'd take it right now. It became hard to breathe. How could she have come out of the house without one? Was she crazy? "What can I do?" she repeated. "I don't have a job, I have no family. Frank is the father of my kids. He's good to them. He's always been good to them, and he's good to me."

"Come on, Mich," Jada said, and Michelle recognized her voice was the tough one she used sometimes at the bank. "He pushed you around. Is that what you consider good treatment? Clinton is a lazy bastard and a lazy father. He's undependable and sneaky. He may have ruined my life, but he never hit me."

Michelle pulled away and tried to stand up straight. "He pushed me and I fell into the corner of the table," she said. "He was under so much pressure. He pushed me. Any woman can be hurt once."

"Any woman who's hurt once can be hurt twice," Angie told her.

Michelle turned away from them both. "No," she said. "Frank would never do it again. And he'd never hit me. He's so ashamed."

"Well, he should be," Jada said. "And is he ashamed of lying to you and ashamed of that evil stuff he's been up to?"

Michelle didn't have the nerve to tell them she hadn't discussed what she knew with Frank. They'd lose all respect for her. "Look, I'll be fine," she said. "I don't have to testify *against* Frank. And I won't lie for him. I'll just keep quiet and maybe . . . maybe it won't get too ugly."

"Sounds about as much fun as a visit to the Basketball Hall of Fame," Angie said.

"You ever been there, girlfriend?" Jada asked. "Clinton once made me and the kids go. Even Kevon was bored."

Michelle wondered why did Jada seemed so, well . . . cheerful? Was this the calm before the storm? Or the aftermath? "What are you going to do?" she asked. "Where are *you* going to move to?"

"I don't have much I have to take," Jada said. "Mostly everything here belongs to the kids, except for Clinton's tools that he never uses. For the time being, I'm just going to stay with Angie."

"Oh. Great. That's so nice for you," Michelle said, and at that moment she meant it. She turned to Angie. "And so nice of you to invite her."

Then Michelle's loneliness and her envy hit. What was she? Crazy? She had her own beautiful home. She had her children, and her husband—despite what he had done—loved her. How could she possibly feel envy for these two women, both in trouble and both alone?

38

In which boxes are packed and notes are hidden

It felt like dying to Jada, but dying without the possibility of the white light. She was outside her body, somewhere in darkness, watching herself perform. Angie's help and her generous offer of a place to stay, Michelle's revelation—none of it managed to bring her back to her body. They turned into the municipal parking lot where Jada could see her Volvo, abandoned since the verdict.

It was drizzling, and Michelle's windshield wipers were on slow. The noise was dreary. "Are you all right?" Michelle asked. "Can you drive yourself?"

"Considering the situation, I'm fine," Jada answered. She should ask Michelle the same question, but she didn't have the energy. Anyway, she'd always suspected Frank.

Michelle pulled her car up. "I'll follow you. Then I can take a load over to Angie's with you."

"Thanks," Jada said.

Jada nodded and slipped out from under Michelle's hand. The foggy rain fell on her, but she felt nothing. She made her way over to her car and opened the door. As if she were pulling her own strings from some other place, she raised her hand and waved to Michelle, then got into the car.

She wasn't angry, she wasn't sad, she wasn't accepting. She was past all that; she was some sort of robot, some kind of remote control creature that could pack and move and go to work but couldn't feel anything anymore. Which was a good thing, she supposed, because anything she might feel right now would be dangerous: murderous rage, crushing sadness, and the wish to end her pain. As she drove, on automatic pilot and with Michelle's car following her back to the house, Jada realized that she couldn't even pray. God felt further away from her than she felt from herself.

When she got back to her house, Jada saw that Angie had already filled her own car and had boxes and bags lined up on the slate walk (which Clinton had never finished paving). Silently, the three women put the now-damp remaining boxes in the back of the Volvo and then laid the clothes from Jada's closet, still on hangers, across the backseat of Michelle's Lexus.

"I'll try not to wrinkle them," Michelle said. Jada smiled and nodded but she didn't care. Michelle could burn them and she wouldn't blink. Sackcloth and ashes would do just as well, she figured, although Mr. Marcus at the bank might object. The corporate dress code did not include hair shirts or biblical mourning wear.

Their convoy drove through the wet, gray suburban streets. Jada was thirty-four years old and everything she had was contained in these few wet boxes and bags piled in just three cars. Not much to show from life. What had she been working for? Why had she worked at all? She sighed. She'd never been materialistic. She'd only wanted her children safe around her and a decent house and a loving partner. How had that natural desire spawned this bizarre result? She wondered if she'd been greedy, or if God was punishing her for some other sin that she hadn't recognized or acknowledged. Because, she realized now, she was being punished, and that this life, however it had happened, was as close to hell as she could imagine anything being.

They pulled up to the front of Angie's apartment building. Angie got out of her car and walked back to the Volvo. "I'm sorry," she said. "There's no way to park closer to my door. We have to schlep all this stuff across the sidewalk, up the path, and around to my apartment. When I moved in, it was really a pain."

"It's not so much," Jada said. "And I'm in no hurry. You don't have to help. I can do it myself if I take it slow."

"Don't be silly. The three of us will do it together," Angie said.

And they did. Back and forth, back and forth, through the rain, the three of them carried in all the bits and pieces left of Jada's broken life. As they did it, Jada realized that she could just as easily have piled them on the sidewalk and set them on fire, but she continued doing what was expected. Hadn't she always?

As they brought the last of the stuff in, the drizzle stopped, although the sky remained gray. "Perfect," Michelle said. "It stops coming down just when you're finished moving."

"Rain is good luck on a moving day," Angie said. "At least that's what my mother always told me."

"Was she wrong about anything else?" Jada asked.

"Just her marriage and mine," Angie wisecracked lamely.

Jada looked around. They had tried to stack all the boxes in Angie's small spare bedroom, and compulsive Michelle had already hung Jada's clothes in the little closet. But there were some stray bags and objects that had trailed into the living room.

"Do you want to put your mattress in here even though its damp from being rained on?" Angela asked.

Jada shrugged. She didn't care where she slept. The floor would be fine, but she knew she shouldn't say so. It was good of Angie to worry about her, even if it was futile.

Angie lifted up one of the remaining boxes from the hallway and started to carry it into the room, but her face went pale and she stumbled, dropping the box and spilling socks, a pair of sneakers, and a black pump onto the floor. The wet box tore, and everything else poured out. Angie stood still, still bent from the waist. Jada could see her lip film with perspiration. "Are you okay?" Michelle asked.

All at once Jada remembered her friend's condition. God, the three of them were a mess! "You shouldn't be lifting, not when you're pregnant," she said. "I forgot."

"You had other things on your mind," Angie said, and slid her back down the wall until she was sitting on the floor. Michelle squatted down next to her. "You want some tea?" Michelle asked.

"How about some sympathy?" Jada added, and also sat on the floor. The three of them looked at one another then and for the first time in twenty-four hours, Jada felt herself connect, felt herself drawn back into her body, into her life, by the two pairs of eyes she saw, each as frightened and haunted as hers must have been.

She shook her head. It was a strange feeling, returning to herself. "What a sorry set of suckers we are," she said. "Who do you think has been most ruined? Whose husband has been the most damaging?"

"Yours" both Angie and Michelle said at the same time.

And, for some reason, Jada began to laugh. At first, she laughed from her throat, and then it moved down to her chest and finally to her belly. Then Michelle began to giggle, and lastly Angie joined in. The sound bounced off the empty walls and ceiling, sounding odd and disorienting, as if they were in a fun house. All three of them laughed until Jada managed to wipe her eyes and shake her head. "Wrong. I think Frank is the worst."

For a moment Mich stopped laughing, and Jada was afraid she was going to begin defending the bastard again. "You may be right," Michelle said. Then she, in turn, looked at Angie. "Although we had some good years. So did you, Jada. Angie here just got good *months*." It was true, and so sad and ridiculous that they all began laughing again.

"I didn't even have good months, but I *thought* they were good months. Does that count?" Angie asked.

"Well, they say it's the thought that counts," Jada said. The three of them stopped laughing then and just sat there together on the floor. Jada knew it was a risk, but she felt compelled to say something she'd been afraid to and looked right at Angie—or rather, at her belly. "How many months?" she asked.

"Three and a half months," Angie admitted. "At least I think so." They were silent again, all three of them.

"I had an abortion," Michelle said. "I was pregnant by Frank in high school. I couldn't go that way."

Jada blinked. Michelle had never told her that. Not a word in seven years. "When I was pregnant the third time, with Sherrilee, I was going to go to the doctor. To terminate. I knew how bad the marriage was by then, and you know how tight money's been."

Jada couldn't believe she was telling this to anybody, much less to two white girls. But she thought, *I'm closer to them than I have been to most people.* Who would have thought that she would talk about this to middle-class girls who had never known an afternoon of suffering or had to face a really tough financial decision. *Gender brings us together more than race separates us,* Jada thought. *Maybe women should just line up with women and forget the rest.*

"I was afraid the bank would terminate *me*. I needed the job. But in the end, I realized I wanted the baby. I love my baby, but I certainly wouldn't want somebody else to raise her." She looked at Angie. "What do you want to do?" she asked.

"I think I want to call a clinic, but I'm afraid to make the call. And I'm afraid to go." Angie looked away. "But I'm more afraid not to." Angie put her head on her knees.

"We'll help you," Michelle said.

"Hell, we'll go with you," Jada said.

"It doesn't hurt." Michelle paused. "Well, not your body anyway."

39

A pregnant pause

When Angela woke up, she realized something was very wrong. There was a dull ache at the side of her head and for a moment she couldn't think. She hadn't been drinking, and it wasn't a normal headache. She felt around with her tongue and then sat up so abruptly she got dizzy. Something in her mouth was aching. Oh, perfect. As if she needed one more thing.

While she drank her morning coffee, she threw back a couple of Tylenol, but they didn't make a dent in the pain. She didn't have a dentist here and couldn't imagine what was wrong. Angela had only had a couple of fillings in her whole life. She had to call her mother to tell her that she wouldn't be in for a little while and to get the name of a reliable dentist in the neighborhood.

She had to beg to get the appointment and she could only beg because the pain was getting much worse. By the time she parked her car and made her way into the dentist's office, the left side of her head felt as if it might erupt with each step she took. She was seated in the dental chair in minutes and the technician laid the lead apron over her to do an x-ray. "Are you pregnant?" the technician asked.

Did it show that much? Angela wondered, and realized it was a standard question before x-rays were taken. When she said she was, the technician shook her head. "The doctor doesn't like to work on pregnant women," she said.

"But I'm in pain," Angela told her.

"I'll talk to him. He'll be in to see you."

Angela waited, her jaw throbbing. One more thing to worry about. Would Novocain affect the baby? Why was this happening now?

The dentist had nothing but bad news: Angie had an impacted wisdom tooth and it should be pulled, but her pregnancy complicated matters. He would make an appointment for the surgeon to see her. In the meantime he suggested she not take too many Tylenol because of the pregnancy. "But it's killing me," Angie said.

"The flare-up will come and go and the discomfort will vary," the dentist told her.

If he was feeling it, it would have been pain, she thought. "Your pregnancy complicates everything," he said.

"You have no idea," Angie told him, and left the office clutching the appointment card for the oral surgeon.

It wasn't as if the work went away just because she was miserable, Angie thought, looking at the stacks of files and pile of messages on her desk. Just because she had blown it on Jada's case, just because she had an appointment for an abortion for the following day, didn't mean that Angie was allowed to take a break from all the misery that had backed up or newly come in, needing attention.

Angie had told her mother nothing—well, nothing about her condition and how she was going to handle it. It was not that she was ashamed of choosing to abort, nor did she think that her mother would judge her. It just seemed the kind of thing Angie would rather confess to after it was over. Sometimes her mother's presence was comforting, other times it was overpowering. This time it was the latter. It just gave Angie one more thing to feel guilty about.

She finished interviewing a client about her late mother's estate property, which appeared to have been stolen by her stepfather. Next up was another estate client. Angela had been told the woman was waiting when Michael knocked and walked into her office.

"How goes it?" he asked. She only had the energy to shrug. He sat down in the chair across from her. "Losing a big one is hard," he said. He was so understanding that he sometimes seemed annoying. Angie just nodded. "How's the new apartment working out?" he asked. "Settling in?"

God! She thought of Jada's boxes scattered around and her complete lack of interest in painting or furnishing the place. "Pretty good," she said. "I'm doing it in kind of early squatter's rights."

She wasn't going to tell Michael that a client was living there now. After all, she already knew how he felt about "getting too involved" with clients. He did a good job, a dedicated job, but he was essentially uninvolved. What if she told him that a client was taking her for "a procedure" tomorrow? Angie sighed and looked down at her bitten thumbnail. Men were different from women. They could separate people from jobs and not feel for them. Work was only work.

Michael immediately disproved her theory. "I wondered if you'd like to go out for dinner with me tomorrow night?" he asked.

Angie looked up at him and actually blinked to clear her vision, as if that would alter what she had heard. Had he asked her out for a date? For tomorrow? "I'm busy," she said. "I won't be in tomorrow at all."

"Well, how about Thursday or Friday?" he asked, and then she was sure that he was actually asking her out. He was so pleasant-looking, and his brown eyes were so warm. She really liked him and she liked working with him. She liked talking with him. But what was he doing?

"I don't date married men," she coolly.

"I'm not married," Michael said. "If I were, I wouldn't ask you out."

Angie took a deep breath. She didn't need this right now. "Michael, you have two kids and you're married. I know you keep your private life private, but we do know the basics. Everybody here knows that," she said in a flat voice, the kind you would use talking to a not-very-bright eleven-year-old who was trying your patience. These men! They were crazy. Was this what had happened with Lisa and Reid?

"Angie, I have two kids and I have been divorced for six months, separated for over a year and a half," Michael explained, his voice as controlled as hers. "And if everyone doesn't know it, it's because I didn't choose to tell them."

Angie stared across the desk at him. Michael had gone through a divorce and separation in the last two years in *this* office and nobody knew? Bill, with his love of gossip and slight crush on Michael, didn't know it? Laura, the control freak, didn't know it? Angie's own mother, the Jewish yenta busybody, didn't know? How was it possible? It just proved how big the gap between men and women were, Angie thought. No woman could go through that kind of life change without talking to her coworkers.

Meanwhile, Michael watched her and then smiled. "To be technical," he said, "if I'm not mistaken, *you're* actually the married one."

Yeah, and the pregnant one, Angie thought. For a moment she almost laughed, though the laugh would have been a bitter one. This was amazing. For the first time in more than four years, since she started dating Reid, she had been asked out for a date—for the same evening she was having a D&C. What was wrong with this picture? God couldn't be a woman. This wasn't a woman's kind of joke.

It was horrible to think about, but Angie was really thirsty. She wanted to believe that she would have a more noble reaction, a more spiritual crisis, sitting between her two friends, waiting to be called in to have her uterus scraped. But Angie could only think of her thirst. Thank goodness her tooth wasn't throbbing. She'd been told not to eat or drink anything since midnight, and had come in early this morning with Michelle and Jada. Although all she wanted was for this to be over quickly, she had already spent close to an hour filling in forms, and then more than another hour sitting here with a roomful of sad-eyed teenaged girls.

"Are you okay?" Michelle asked for the third or fourth time, and reached over to give Angie's hand a squeeze.

"Not exactly," Angie said, trying to smile. She couldn't manage it. Michelle let go of Angie's hand and leaned over to the table in front of them. She'd already straightened out the magazines, arranging them in neat piles. Now she began sorting them by date.

An older woman was sitting in the corner quietly crying. Michelle, finished with the magazines, had already gone over to her, talked to her in a low and comforting voice, and returned outraged. "She wanted the baby," Michelle told Angie and Jada. "The amnio came back and there's something *really* wrong. She doesn't even want to abort, but it won't go to term. She's already started to bleed. And she's tried for years to have a child."

"This is horrible," Jada said. "You would think these clinic people would have a little more savvy. Mich, would you stop straightening up?"

"Oh. Sure. Sorry," Michelle apologized.

"I can't believe they'd let her sit here with all these high school girls," Jada said. "Don't they have *any* sensitivity at all? Don't they know some women have been trying to have the child?"

Angie put her head down and looked at her own belly. Reid was a lying, immature fool, but this baby was hers, too, conceived in love. She wasn't like the teenagers in the waiting room and she didn't want to be like the older woman. She *wanted* a child, she wanted to be a mother. Being around Jada and Michelle and their children had brought that home to her. And if it took years to meet another man she could love— or if she never did—she knew she could want and love this child, and take care of it. She was responsible. She'd lost her marriage, and she'd lost her first big trial, but she didn't have to lose this.

Angie lifted her head and looked around the room. They were a bunch of frightened little girls, aside from the broken-hearted woman who was losing the baby she wanted. But Angie wasn't a little girl. She might not be married, and she might not be settled, but she suddenly realized that she wanted this baby. It didn't make sense, and she certainly didn't want a connection to Reid, but she *had* loved him and the baby she was carrying was her baby, too. It wouldn't be convenient, or easy, or practical, but she wanted the baby. She had a job, and family, and good friends who could help her, and if they didn't, she could—she *would*—help herself.

She stood up. "Let's go home," she said.

Michelle looked up at her. "Are you all right?" Michelle asked.

Jada didn't say a word. She just stood up and put her arm around Angie. "I think she's going to be just fine," Jada said. She looked at Angie. "You mean this?" she asked. Angie nodded.

Michelle stood up, too. "You're going to have the baby?" she asked in a low voice. Angie nodded. "Oh my God," Michelle said. "Oh my God," she repeated, her voice full of joy. "Well, I can give you all the baby stuff you need. I saved everything. And I can sit for you."

"Maybe we can discuss these arrangements someplace else," Jada said dryly. "Someplace more appropriate." She looked at Angie again. "You're sure you're not just doing this out of guilt?" she asked. "Nothing to be guilty about, except not caring for a child you bring into the world."

Angie shook her head. She'd been afraid to consider her life with a child, but suddenly she couldn't bear to not have this one. It was a good thing she could take from her marriage, instead of only the heartbreak of her time with Reid. And she knew she could be a good mother. Day care, money, baby-sitters—all of the rest of it would sort itself out.

"Let's go," Angie said, and she picked up her bag while her friends gathered their coats and escorted her past the receptionist to the door. Just as they got there, a woman in a white jacket appeared from the inner sanctum and called, "Romazzano?" Angie didn't answer. She just walked out and let one of the others close the door behind her.

40

Containing something accidental and something on purpose

Jada was going to be late for work. She had managed to find everything she needed to get there, despite the fact that her clothes, her underpants, her shoes, her cosmetics, and her deodorant were all in boxes stacked one upon the other. The only thing she hadn't been able to find was her pantyhose, and that was why she was now frantic, ready to dump stuff all over the floor or steal a pair of No Nonsense from Angie.

Jada stopped herself at that. Anyway, the color wouldn't work. It was more than enough to take Angie's generosity and stay in her apartment. It was too much to take her intimate apparel also. Plus, Angie was probably five inches shorter and twenty pounds lighter than she was, and Jada wasn't going to spend the day hobbled by the waistband of a pair pantyhose stretched between her kneecaps. Pantyhose, she decided, had definitely been invented by the devil, or by men. Actually, she thought, they added up to pretty much the same thing. Men *were* devils.

She knew she could depend on women, though. Her mother, and her two friends, even though they were white. They'd stuck by her through some grim testimony. Black women who were close to one another used special words that they would almost never use with white girls.

"Sisterfriend" was one of those words. It was someone not blood related but as close—or closer—than a sister. Back in high school, Jada had felt that she and Simone LaClerk were sisterfriends, but she couldn't remember if they had used the term. She was certainly closer to Michelle than she had ever been to Simone (who had dissed her when she started dating Clinton because apparently Simone had secretly been hot for him). For a long time Jada had known Michelle was a sisterfriend, but hadn't thought she could ever get that close with Angie. Now she felt she was.

But that still didn't mean she'd wear her pantyhose. Finally, after ten more minutes of looking, she grabbed the only pantyhose she could—and they were the old pair she'd worn in court and had a run right up the back, from the ankle to the knee. But she was stuck with them. She slipped into her pumps and ran out the door, the keys to the Volvo jingling in her hand.

The car was her home now. She was going to get to see the children this afternoon after work, but the idea of sitting with them in the Volvo or driving to yet another mall or restaurant made her feel sick. How would she explain to them what had happened in court last? She didn't want to poison them against Clinton, but if she didn't make it clear that *she* wanted them and had to fight with Daddy to see them, they would be poisoned against her. Sometimes life was just too hard to bear. She felt as if the best solution—the only solution that would work for her—was to kill Clinton, or to get him killed.

As she drove through the morning traffic, she played with the murderous thought. If she killed him, she'd go to prison and then the children would have no one to raise them. But if someone *else* killed him . . . She thought of an old Hitchcock movie where a psychotic idly proposes to a stranger that each kills the other's wife. Neither would be suspect, because they'd have no motive, no connection to the victims. Maybe she could make a deal with Angie and go up to Boston to kill her bastard, while Angie could pull the trigger on Clinton. Of course, now that they lived together, they were too obviously connected for that to look like a coincidence . . .

Jada realized how crazy her thoughts were getting, stopped them, and prayed instead. But for almost the first time in her life, the prayer felt flat. She thought of the Bible's injunction to turn the other cheek, but she felt as if her cheeks—all four of them—had been lashed as badly as she could take. She tried to think of another comforting thought. Vengeance is mine, the Lord had said. Okay. But what was she to do? Be meek? The meek might inherit the earth, but her children were inheriting the dirt: Clinton and his lackadaisical supervision, Tonya Green and her feigned interest in them, which wouldn't last long, not to mention their Jackson grandmother's habitual lying and drinking. *Lord, protect my children,* Jada prayed. *Give me the strength to help them and love them.*

When she walked into the bank, she was in no mood for any of it. *How foolishly we spend our lives,* she thought. Not that she had ever been particularly interested in the work—it was only the paycheck she wanted. Now it was almost beyond her abilities to even pretend an interest.

She walked past Anne, picking up her messages as she did, and walked into her office. She returned calls to Mr. Marcus, two important clients with problems, and one of the consultants, who peppered her with a series of staffing questions that he'd already asked but apparently wanted to ask again. As she sat there, impatiently giving him the data, she tapped her foot. That caused the run in her stocking to creep up her thigh. It felt disturbingly like an insect moving cautiously under her clothes.

This was all unbearable. Pointless. Following these rules, playing by them, was absolutely ridiculous, she thought. "Look, Ben," she said brusquely. "I have a meeting now and I already gave you all this information once. I'm afraid you're going to have to search your records for it." She hung up, wondering as she did if he was asking the questions twice to see if she would change her answers. She shook her head, pulled out a sheet of blank paper, and began to write down a column of numbers. But this wasn't for the bank. This was for her.

If she paid the child support and alimony directed by the court, she would be left with less than three hundred dollars a week to live on. Out of that she'd also have to help Angie pay rent and gas money. And what about Clinton's legal fees? Apparently she was going to be expected to pay those, too, and she had a feeling that George Creskin didn't come cheap. Nor would he allow an installment plan. Jada tried to project and add in the raise that she was expecting and see where it left her, but it didn't leave her anywhere.

Then Anne buzzed her and told her that the afternoon meeting had been rescheduled from two o'clock to four. "Who rescheduled that?" she asked. She had the children to pick up at four-thirty. There was no way she was going to be late for them.

"Mr. Marcus," Anne said, and Jada wondered if there was a sneer in her voice. "He called at five to nine. I was here, but you weren't in yet. I didn't see anything on your calendar."

"Call his office," Jada snapped. "I tried him earlier but he wasn't in. Leave word that the meeting is at two o'clock today or four o'clock tomorrow, but it can't be four o'clock today."

Jada stood up, went to the window, and looked out at the desolate back parking area, the drive-through window, and the Dumpster. Her life was sort of like that—certainly desolate, she had been a drive-through for Clinton, who was going to make withdrawals from her for the rest of his life. She would be consigned to live in a dump, with nothing but garbage.

There had to be a better plan. When she'd spoken to her mother, Mama had first suggested prayer, and then that she get a really big knife and threaten to kill him. And Jada hadn't even told her mother the whole truth—only that they were thinking of separating and that he had another woman. Her father had offered to come up and "straighten the boy out."

Then both of her parents had suggested their other panacea for all problems—that she should come for a visit. As if her life were so flexible, she could take vacations whenever she needed some mental health.

Jada couldn't kill Clinton. God forgive her for even thinking of murder, but she also couldn't begin this kind of life.

Maybe she should do as her mother had suggested in their last phone call—pack up and go "home" to Barbados for a little while.

Except she couldn't go without her children. Like a trapped animal, she walked from the window back to the phone, picked it up, and punched in Michelle's number. "How are you, babe?" she asked when Michelle answered.

"Maybe not as bad as you," Michelle said. "Do you think drinking might help?"

"Oh yeah," Jada answered, her voice edged by sarcasm. "A nice Bloody Mary at eleven A.M. and one of your pills would be the perfect pick-me-up. You'd probably be out cold when the kids come home from school."

"I'm not worried about the kids coming home. I'm worried about *Frank* coming home."

On her end of the phone, Jada shook her head. When was Michelle going to give up on that lying bastard? "Listen, sisterfirend," Jada said, moving on to her own agenda. "I have a question to ask you. Honestly, how do you feel about kidnapping?"

"Who are we kidnapping? Clinton? Tonya? Judge Sneed?"

"No, who cares about any of them? I was thinking of my children."

There was a moment of silence. "Isn't that a federal offense?" Michelle asked. "Not that *I* would think it was wrong . . . especially if you got away with it."

There was another silence while Jada thought. "I'm only joking," she admitted. "How would I live? Where would I go? If I stayed here, I'd be arrested for contempt of court and kidnapping. If I joined my parents, Clinton would find me in a minute." She sighed. "It's just that I've tried to figure it out, and I can't see any way to comply with the judge and live any kind of life. It's not just the money. I'll have to watch my children suffer every day and slowly turn against me."

"I'm waiting for my husband to do that," Michelle admitted.

"Turn against you? Hey, *you* should be turning against *him*." But then Jada stopped and thought of the bruise on Michelle's face. "Are you afraid of him, Michelle?"

Before Michelle answered, there was a buzz from Anne. "Mr. Marcus on two," Anne announced.

When she hit the button for the other line, Marcus lit into her before she even had a chance to begin. About how she wasn't there when he called earlier, about how uncooperative she'd been with the consultant, and then about the meeting and its rescheduling. On and on. Jada listened as long as she could stand it. Finally she interrupted. "Mr. Marcus, if you schedule the meeting for four o'clock, you're welcome to have it without me. If you want me here, it's two o'clock today or any time tomorrow afternoon."

"Mrs. Jackson—Jada—I'm sorry, but I think you don't understand. This isn't a choice. In fact, you haven't been making the right choices for a while now." He cleared his throat. "I think it's time for you to consider resignation."

Jada froze. "Excuse me?" she said, but she'd heard him.

"Resignation, Mrs. Jackson. All that personal time you take. And Anne Cherril has kept a record of—"

"Of what?"

"Listen. It's best to make this a simple resignation on your part. Less embarrassing for you and the bank."

Jada couldn't believe it. "And if not, are you firing me?" she asked.

"Well, let's say I'd prefer your resignation."

"Let's say I'd prefer to tell you to go to hell. I'm not rolling over for you the way Michelle Russo did. I worked hard to get this job. I've done well. It's been demonstrated. And if you think—"

"I think you got an uncollateralized ten thousand-dollar loan that was rushed through improperly."

Jada felt her stomach sink, then the taste of bile in her throat. "I stopped the loan," she protested.

"Not the point, Mrs. Jackson. Not the point at all. You improperly used a subordinate to procure a loan you couldn't and shouldn't have received. And did so conspiratorially. In sworn testimony, wouldn't Mrs. Russo have to agree?"

"This has nothing to do with that, but you already know that," Jada said. Just one more example of an uppity black woman reaping what her portion was.

Mr. Marcus began to say something, but Jada wasn't waiting. She hung up. Then, without thinking anymore about it, she turned to the keyboard of her PC, typed, and then printed her resignation letter.

She'd give the people what they wanted. She wasn't even that surprised. Doing this job was insane if all it did was pay Clinton and Tonya's living expenses. What the hell. She signed the page and laid it on top of her desk. She said a quick good-bye to Michelle, then called Angie at work. "You," she said when she heard Angie's voice, "are a *very* lucky girl."

"Why is that?" Angie asked cautiously, not knowing if this was a joke or not.

"Because you have the perfect roommate," Jada said. "I'm depressed, single, and now I'm unemployed."

41

In which Michelle is both dazed and confused

Michelle was folding laundry, smoothing it on top of the warm dryer, when she heard Pookie begin barking. The barking was followed by impatient whining at the back hallway door. Then Michelle heard the sound of Frank's truck as it pulled in and she froze. For some reason— well, for a good reason—she was afraid of Frank. As he spent day after day with Rick Bruzeman or one of the other lawyers on the team, as his situation became graver, engulfing him, he'd become more and more short-tempered and unpredictable.

But his attitude wasn't really what she feared. Michelle knew that eventually Frank would notice her discovery of his secret cache of money. She didn't dare imagine the confrontation. The Xanax kept her from thinking about it too much. But so far, days had passed with nothing at all between them. Now, when the door outside the laundry room slammed open, Michelle froze without greeting Frank as he strode by in the hallway. Pookie didn't greet him, either. The dog sat down hard, then actually backed behind her.

Frank didn't call her name out, perhaps expecting to find her as he moved through the house. Or maybe he didn't expect to find her. She stopped and listened intently. Then she heard his feet on the stairs.

Pookie didn't follow him; instead, the dog stayed with her, his dark eyes questioning her, his head tilted at an angle. Both of them were listening. Michelle wondered if the dog was scared, too.

Michelle still stood there, one of Frankie's T-shirts held against her chest. She didn't know why she was so silent, nor why she wasn't breathing, until she heard Frank's bellow. This was it, then.

"*Michelle!*" he yelled, and he was clearly upstairs in one of the bedrooms—she could guess which one. His voice was so loud that Pookie actually jumped and ran into the small space between the cabinet and the wall. "*Michelle!*" Frank yelled again, and she heard him pounding down the stairs.

For a horrible moment, she thought about whether she could run out the door into the garage before he made it across the kitchen to her. But his truck was probably blocking her car, and the thought was insane. She had to stand up for herself and the children. She had to. She shouldn't have put this off so long anyway. It put her a little on the defensive, when it was he who had done wrong. Michelle realized she should have told him about finding the money immediately. She should have confronted him instead of waiting for this. Why did she make such stupid mistakes? Now it would be worse. Why did she do everything wrong?

She heard her husband in the kitchen, then the back hallway. She finished folding the T-shirt, turned, and put it on top of the dryer with the other folded clothes. Without turning around, she knew that Frank had come all the way down the carpeted hall. She actually felt him standing in the doorway, as if he had some magnetic charge.

"Where is it, Michelle?" Frank said.

Michelle turned around and looked at him. His right shoulder was leaning against the door frame, his left hand was stretched to the other side. It was a menacing position, as if he was blocking her way, as if he was trapping her in this domestic little corner of their house. *Don't get yourself crazier than necessary,* she thought, but Pookie whimpered from his spot beside the cabinet as if he felt the threat, too. Michelle didn't make a sound.

"Where's the money, Michelle?" Frank repeated.

For a moment, Michelle thought she just might try playing dumb. What the hell? Frank thought she was dumb anyway, didn't he? He'd been counting on her blindness, her stupidity, for years. But now she couldn't manage it. Her husband looked truly enraged, or maybe something worse. For the first time in her life, it seemed to her that Frank, her strong, fearless Frank, might himself be filled with terror. There was something glittering behind his dark eyes that she'd never seen before.

"Are you talking about the evidence?" she asked. "The evidence you hid in our daughter's room?"

"I'm talking about the *money*, goddamnit. Where's the *money*, Michelle?"

She tore her eyes away from his and turned back to the laundry basket, lifting out a pair of Jenna's jeans. Jenna liked to wear them wrinkled, but sometimes Michelle pressed them anyway. Now she gathered them by the seams and began smoothing them. She was afraid to tell Frank the truth and afraid to lie. It wasn't too late to say the police had come and taken the money, but what was the point? Frank would find out that it wasn't true. She would have to confront him now. She would have to tell him what he had done to her, how he had deceived her and broken her heart and destroyed their family. And how she knew he had done it all and lied to her as he did it.

"Do you know how pathetic I am, Frank?" she asked. "I still can't believe you're guilty. I know you are, now. Once I found that blood money, that stash of yours. And I had a dream about it, too. But I still almost can't believe it." She shook her head. Who was this man? "How could you do it? How could you do it to me and the children? Drugs, Frank. You jeopardized everything." Her voice was a shriek. "You ruined everything. How could you? And how could you lie about it all to me?"

She sensed him moving and turned enough to see Frank's body convulse for a moment and then he spread out in the doorway again and smashed his forearm against the jamb. The noise made her wince and jump, dropping the jeans on the floor. She bent down to pick them up, but then she realized Frank had moved, fast as a cat, into the room, and was crouched opposite her. His right hand grabbed her left shoulder, first squeezing it, then giving it a shake. "Why don't you ever trust me?" he asked.

She looked at him in disbelief. Was he crazy? Or did he think he could talk his way out of this, make believe it would all work out just fine? "Why did you lie?" she asked him.

"It's not drug money."

For a moment, Michelle was stopped by that, by his nerve. In her long nights of sleeplessness, she'd gone through every possible other explanation—savings, gambling winnings, untaxed profits, cash payments from clients, kickbacks from subcontractors. But she'd worked at a bank. She'd figured people's incomes and mortgages. No way any of those sources could possibly add up to over half a million dollars in cash. Not unless Frank was something *worse* than involved with drugs on the side. The only other explanation was that he was a hit man, or something even more awful, if there was anything more awful.

"Frank, let me make this perfectly clear," she said. "This is about how you lied to me and put me and the children and our home and our life at risk. I will not tolerate that behavior. If you had told me, you would have known I couldn't tolerate the risk. Not for any reason." She paused. "It was only luck that kept the police from finding that evidence. Do you know how *I* felt when *I* found it, Frank? Can you imagine how horrified *I* was, and how ashamed *I* am for believing in you? I *believed* you, Frank. I must have been crazy."

Frank shook her shoulder again. "Oh, you weren't so crazy when you were given the Lexus—all paid for, fully loaded," he snarled. "You weren't so crazy when we redid the kitchen, or put in the pool, or when you wanted a new piece of furniture, or when the kids needed school clothes, or party clothes, or birthday gifts. As long as I could pay for our vacations and the house and everything you ever dreamed of, you didn't think you were crazy then. You never asked me, 'Where is it all coming from, Frank?' No. I was Frank the Magician and I never, not once, said no to you. It was my job not to say no to you. You mean to tell me you thought we could live this well from roofing contracts alone?"

She began to cry, but she would not back down. He made it sound as if it were all her fault, as if she had driven him to this. "I got rid of it, Frank," she said. "I found it and I got it out of the house without getting caught and I got *rid* of it."

He pinched her shoulder in a painful clinch and rose up from the crouch he was in, making her rise as well. "You're hurting me," she cried, and tried to pull herself out of his painful grip. His eyes were terrifying—mad.

"I need that money, Michelle. What have you done with it?"

"I burned it," Michelle said. "I burned it to keep you safe. To keep the kids safe. Because if anyone ever saw that money, it was over. I had a dream you were behind bars, Frank. If anyone found the evidence, you'd be dead. Even your legal genius couldn't get you out of *that* trouble."

Frank stood almost stone still. "You did what?" he finally managed to ask, his voice low but more frightening than a shout. "For Christ's sake, Michelle. Tell me you're not that stupid." Tears sprang into Michelle's eyes, but he continued in a tone she'd never heard. "I need that money to pay the legal genius. You think Bruzeman would work one minute for free? I need that money to keep us going, to keep me out of jail. Please, dear Jesus, don't tell me you burned it. Even you couldn't be so fucking dumb. What did you do with the money, Michelle?"

His arm—the one that he had pressed across the door frame, lifted now to shoulder level as he pulled it back. Almost in slow motion, Michelle saw the hand coming toward her, but she couldn't believe it. It was happening so fast, and yet very slowly. For a moment too long, her brain didn't register the reality of what her eyes were seeing. So, a moment too late, she began to move her head, to tuck her chin in a little bit, but it was a mistake.

"I need the money," he cried, and his hand hit the side of her face just above her ear with tremendous force. She felt it move slowly. As if it were a rock wrapped in sandpaper as it scraped across her upper cheek and then hit her eye. She fell across the space behind her and bumped the back of her head hard against the dryer. Pinkie, now fully mended, cushioned the blow, and she strangled the stuffed toy as she tried to scramble away, but Frank grabbed her by the front of her shirt and lifted her up. Then he hit her again, this time with his other hand, connecting with her jaw. She felt a horrible popping in her ear and she managed to scream. He was going to kill her, or get her to give him the money. She closed her eyes and got her hands up to ward off the next blow, but before it came, Frank himself screamed.

Michelle opened her eyes and looked through her fingers. Frank was bending toward one side. Pookie's teeth were clamped on the back of Frank's thigh and Frank screamed again, stamped his leg, and awkwardly tried to hit at the little spaniel. As shocked as she was, Michelle knew this was her opening, her only chance. Still clutching Pinkie, she rushed past him, out the laundry room door, and into the garage. She could hear Frank cursing, along with Pookie's rare growl. She kept running. Behind her there was a high-pitched noise of pain, obviously the dog's, and a thud that made her feel sick to her stomach.

She ran out the door of the open garage. Frank hadn't blocked her car, and thank God she had the keys in her pocket. She got in the car and turned the ignition just as the school bus pulled to the stop across the road. Frank was running toward her, the dog behind him. "Pookie!" she screamed, and the little spaniel raced ahead and jumped into the car and onto her lap. She slammed the door shut. Breaking several laws at once, she backed into the street and across from the bus. She threw open the back door and screamed to Jenna and Frankie. "Get in the car!" she yelled. "Get in the car *now!*"

The two children looked at her and their faces froze in fear but thank God their legs moved and they scrambled into the backseat. "Lock the door!" she yelled to Jenna and Jenna did. Out of the side of the eye that wasn't swollen, Michelle could see Frank limping down the driveway. She put her foot on the gas pedal and tore out, burning rubber.

She wiped her cheek as she passed the familiar houses at full speed. She glanced down at her hand to see it was covered with blood, spittle, and tears. "Mommy, what happened?" Jenna asked. "Did you fall again? Where are we going? And what happened to Pinkie?"

As Michelle turned the corner, the bloodstained stuffed animal slid across the dashboard. She couldn't answer any of her daughter's questions.

RING THREE

꽃

Living well is the best earthly revenge,
but living well when your ex lives badly is heaven.

Nan Delano

42

Living cheek by jowl

Angie stepped out of the shower, dried herself with last night's still-damp towel, and put on a bathrobe. Normally she didn't bother with her robe, but since Michelle had shown up at her doorstep, bloodied and frightened, she and her kids were camped out in the living room—hence the robe. Angie never knew when one of the children would come ducking into the bathroom.

Angie decided she wouldn't put her makeup on in the steamy room because this was the time of morning when people lined up on the other side of the bathroom door like outdoor concert-goers at port-a-potties. Sure enough, as Angie opened the bathroom door, she came face to face with the battered Michelle, who had her daughter in tow.

"Do you mind if we—"

"Go ahead," Angie said. The truth was, she *didn't* mind. For the last two days the apartment had been more like a public campground, or maybe a two-ring circus, but for Angie it beat the hell out of lying on the mattress and staring at her popcorn ceiling.

Yesterday she and Jada had gone to a mall and gotten a few basic clothes for Jenna and Frankie. They'd left their house with nothing, and Michelle had kept them with her the day before. Angie was planning to drop them at school this morning, since Michelle was nervous about Frank showing up. Of course, Angie had already gotten an emergency restraining order, Michelle had had her eye checked at the emergency room, and Jada had baby-sat the kids, bribing them with some toys and books they'd picked up at the mall. Angie had moved her small television—her only television—into the living room. And the three women and the two children had spent Sunday night camped out on the floor watching the video of *The Nutty Professor*.

After Angie had gotten over the shock of Michelle's battered face, and the children had gotten over both that and their surprise at being spirited away from home, it had actually evolved into a peaceful, pleasant evening. It was only now, when Angie had to dress for work, the kids had to be off to school, and virtually everyone was tired and cranky, that Angie began to feel as if she were in the Marx Brothers' movie where a hundred people had to fit into Groucho's ocean liner cabin. Angie smiled when she remembered she'd been afraid to get her own place, thinking she'd be lonely. Right now, this joint didn't have wall-to-wall carpet, it had wall-to-wall beds.

She actually walked like Groucho as she bent from the waist and high-stepped over abandoned blankets, Frankie's sleeping form, the sleeping dog, crinkled paper towels, and a few abandoned water glasses to get to the far side of the living room, which served as the kitchen. She was desperate for caffeine. But once there she found that her coffeemaker's pot was missing. She thought for a minute; she remembered seeing it somewhere, but simply couldn't place it, so she added the coffee and the water to the bin on top, and put her lonely mug underneath the spout to catch at least the first cup.

She looked back at the sleeping bodies littering her floor. Kids were definitely a lot of work, but she liked them. It was cozy to see Jenna and Frankie cuddled on Michelle's lap last night, Jenna holding her stuffed toy.

Both of the children seemed so protective of Michelle. Frankie had made his mother promise over and over again that she would be more careful about "assidents." Jenna, who might have suspected this had been more than a slip into a door, just stroked her mother's forehead.

Angie put a hand up to her belly. She wanted that—and she would have it, too. She thought about how pleasant it would be to hold a warm, loving bundle up to her cheek or to her breast. They could watch her favorite Disney movies—*The Parent Trap*, *Pollyanna*—and then some of the PBS specials. It would be a while before they could lie on sleeping bags in the living room and share pizza, but it was something to look forward to.

A sizzling noise brought her back to the present. Her cup had runneth over. Angie replaced her mug with an empty cup, as spilling coffee hissed on the warming plate. Then she opened the refrigerator, but found there was no milk left. Kids definitely had a downside. God, she'd have to drink it black, and she *hated* black coffee. But she had to have *something* to kick-start her. She took a sip of the bitter black liquid, made a face that no one saw, and then opened a cabinet to see if there was something to eat. A box of Pop Tarts was right in front of her. She'd never had those in the house before. Jada or Michelle must have bought them—maybe for the kids. It was probably six hundred calories of empty carbohydrates, but Angie pulled one of those puppies out and had it in the toaster before she could count anywhere near that high.

Tomorrow she had to go to the OB-GYN and she'd have the client from hell come to the clinic, but today it was Pop Tarts. Pookie, the cocker spaniel, woke up and sniffed, then approached her—or the Pop Tart. She broke off a corner and gave it to the dog. So there was a trade-off to having no milk with these guests: instead she had tempting bad food at her disposal. Angela took a bite of her breakfast and a throb started just from the pressure of the food touching her tooth.

Angie wondered why every mother didn't weigh a thousand pounds, but if this tooth kept up, she wouldn't be one of the heavy ones. Then she picked up her legal papers, the two books she had been referencing, and her notes, putting them into her briefcase while she waited for the coffee to cool a little. In the meantime she went to the door to get the mail, which came very early at the apartment complex. Nothing much: two grocery circulars addressed to "Occupant," an electric bill, and her bank statement, but behind that lurked an envelope postmarked Boston. She dumped the other stuff on the card table and opened the last one with a shaky hand. She could see by the printed return address that it was from the law firm Reid was using to handle the divorce.

Inside was a request for her to make an appointment to meet with them and sign divorce papers. No surprise. But what *was* a surprise was that a court date was set for only two weeks away. Enclosed was a small handwritten note.

> Figured that faster was better. I'm sure you feel the same. And hope that you can get here because the court date was difficult to get. I don't think there are any details that I've overlooked, but I would so appreciate your full cooperation so both of us can get on with our lives.
>
> As ever,
>
> Reid

Get on with their lives? *Get on with their lives?* Angie had to read the note over a second time and then a third, sipping from the bitter cup and chewing on the sugary pastry. She wanted her child, and she wanted it free of Reid, so the faster he moved, the better off *she* was. But *he* didn't know that. She couldn't believe that he could be so cold or so obvious, this pathetically obvious.

But the most curious thing was his closing. *As ever, Reid.* Was he "as ever"? Had he *always* been so insensitive, so obtuse? When he was marrying her, was he "as ever" as this? She shook her head, trying to clear it. Jenna must have gotten out of the shower while she'd been staring at the note, because now she was gently kicking—if there was such a thing—her younger brother awake. What to do? Angela wasn't really used to children, though she knew she'd better get used to them in the next six months. "Hey, hey," Angela said in an authoritative voice, and to her astonishment, Jenna stopped. *Maybe I could be a good parent*, Angie thought. *Maybe I'm a natural.*

Just then Jada came out of her tiny bedroom looking frighteningly natural. She headed toward the coffeemaker, picked up the cup on the warming plate, and then almost screamed at the heat in the handle. Coffee flew everywhere.

"Wow! Ooh, man. Trying to get me disability?" Jada cried, shaking her hand out. Angie apologized while Michelle, who'd joined them all now in the one room, both mopped up the spill and wrapped some wet paper towels around Jada's hand. "Most accidents happen in the home," she reminded them.

"I had some mean dreams about home last night," Jada said. "Really *mean*. Clinton did not enjoy himself."

Angie handed Jada the papers from Boston. "I'm having some mean daydreams right now," Angie said. "I wonder if there's a scientist somewhere who knows the opposite formula for Viagra?"

Jada looked at the note, still waving her injured hand, and raised her brows. "Nice idea," she said. "You want to introduce it into the entire water system of Boston, or keep it neighborhood specific?"

"I haven't decided yet," Angie paused, "but I think something has to be done."

"Oh yeah! I can get behind that," Jada said. Then she began walking back to her room. "I have to get dressed now, though. I'll help with the female terrorism after I get myself a really high-paying job behind a deep fat fryer in some fast-food chain." As she turned to go into her room, she inquired over her shoulder, "Should I wear a power suit to apply for such jobs?"

"A power *jogging* suit maybe," Michelle called out as she shepherded Frankie into the bathroom.

It was chaos, but it was kind of fun to have all these people here. It was a little like dorm life. The teasing and the sharing.

"And save a job for me at the drive-through," Michelle added as she closed the bathroom door. Angela laughed out loud—something rare for her before ten A.M. She knew that Jada was going to go out job hunting and that Michelle had planned the same thing once her face healed up a little.

Jada pulled herself together quickly, and came out wearing something less than a power suit but more than a jogging suit. "I gotta do my face," she called out.

Michelle had the kids ready for school after a certain amount of squabbling about the whereabouts of some book and the mini-trauma of not being able to find Jenna's new pink socks. At last, though, they were ready to go. It didn't matter to Angie, since her car was sitting outside waiting for her. It was just interesting to watch the spectacle of modern morning motherhood.

"We're ready," Michelle announced. Angie handed her the car keys.

"Open the door. I'll be right out," she told her. Only then did she quickly gather up her own stuff. In the daylight, Michelle's face was shocking, the bruise on her neck an ugly purple. Angie thought of Reid. He'd never hit her, but he'd never loved her, not that those things should ever be combined.

She could be a good mother to his child, Angie thought. And she could enjoy it. If it was a girl, she'd teach her to be strong. If it was a boy, she'd teach him to be a better man than his father was.

In fact, all men should be taught to behave better than most of them had been. And it was up to women to teach them. She didn't think she was as frightened as she'd once been, but she was angry. Really angry. All these men: Clinton, Reid, and now Frank. All of them so needless, so selfish, so careless. "We should all get together and do something," Angie suggested out loud. Jada had came out of her bedroom, her face a perfectly done mask.

"About the coffeemaker?" she asked.

"No. About this idiot, my future former husband. About your idiot." Then Angie lowered her voice so the children just outside talking to their mother wouldn't hear. "And about Michelle's idiot."

Jada nodded. "Listen, if you've got an idea I'm willing to help out," she said. "In my dream last night, I remember there was a trash compactor and somehow Clinton's head fell in it. But in real life, you never see the trash get what they deserve. Still, if you want me to go and paint slogans on Lisa and Reid's garage door, I'll do it. Or if you want me to call the managing partner and rat them out? Or maybe the bar association?" She paused and laughed once, bitterly. "Oh, I forgot. They're lawyers, and there are no standards of personal behavior they can break. Anyway, if you have ideas, I'm willing to try. Remember I said that."

Angie nodded, then looked at her watch. She had to go. The morning had been very different from her usual ones, but not necessarily bad. She ran out and got into her car, waited while the kids said good-bye to Michelle, then listened to them bicker until she dropped them off. She watched them go into the school, then she headed for the clinic, thinking about all the wronged women she would see there and wondering, in a practical way, if there wasn't something that she, Jada, and Michelle couldn't do to change their own status quo.

43

In which Jada scans UPCs and gives customer satisfaction

The ridiculous thing was how hard it was to do a lousy, low-paying job. When Jada had taken her first job as a lowly teller, she had suspected that the Mr. Marcuses of the world did work that was both more interesting and better paying, but defintiely more difficult. Wrong. She'd had a management job, and despite the paperwork, it was a piece of cake compared to the back-breaking repetition and boredom of low-end work.

She had already tried for a counter job in a dry cleaner's and as a sales assistant at Payless, but had been turned down flat. Was it because she was black, and white girls in Westchester didn't want black fingers touching their clothes? *The black doesn't rub off,* she'd wanted to say. *If it did, some of us would be white.*

She figured it was best to go where she was expected to go—she had only to mention her experience as a teller to get a job as a check-out cashier at Price Chopper. Not that she didn't have to pay her dues. She wasn't scheduled for the top shift yet. She was on probation for a month first. But Mr. Stanton had eyed her and said, "I like your looks. A lot of your people shop here."

Jada wasn't sure who "her people" were—certainly not this big black woman whose baby was crying (though she seemed absolutely deaf to that) while Jada scanned in a big bag of chocolate kisses, an overpriced box of cereal with more sugar content than the chocolate, and a huge bag of onions. Weird, what people bought.

Jada found standing for the whole shift, scanning in item after item and managing not to fall over or fall asleep, really difficult. She'd already learned that busy times were better than slow ones, because when it was slow, she still had to stand there, staring at the headlines of the weekly tabloids, though she wasn't allowed to read them or anything else. Not that she cared what Jennifer Aniston's diet secret was, or Pam Anderson's. That was the hardest thing—just standing there and waiting.

It gave her time to think, which was not necessarily a good thing. What did she have to think about but how utterly meaningless her life was now? The court could do whatever it wanted with her, but it couldn't get blood from a stone. She was earning less than six dollars an hour, and she'd give it all to her children, but if Clinton wanted to keep the house for himself and Tonya, both of them would have to start working at a check-out counter, too.

For a moment Jada's stomach tightened. She compulsively went over her month's expenses against her month's projected income. She had insurance on the house, on the car, and the mortgage to pay. She had enough savings to last a little while, but then what? The phone and electric had to be kept up. The children had to be kept sheltered. And all of it in a house that she wouldn't even be allowed into.

She told herself she had to help with the costs to keep something stable for the children. Imperfect as it was, unfinished as it was, that was the house they had grown up in, and it *had* been a source of comfort. Well, she hoped it had. Perhaps she and Clinton had made a mistake and should have been in an area with more African-Americans, just for the sake of the children, but they were getting a good education. They had friends.

An old woman wheeled up her cart. Jada tried to look alert. She watched as the woman took out a box of crackers, one tomato, jellied fruit candy, and two boxes of pudding. As Jada started to scan the stuff in, the woman pulled out coupons, a couple of them almost as ancient as she was. One was for a brand of gelatin rather than pudding, and the coupon for the crackers had expired months ago. It had been cut from the newspaper sometime in the last decade and had become furry with age and folds. How long had the old lady been carrying it?

Jada gave her the discounts anyway, although at the end of the day she'd probably get it deducted from her own pay. She wondered where the woman lived, and why she hobbled off all alone. She said a little prayer for the old woman as she bagged the next client's groceries. Then she said a prayer for herself, begging the Lord that she didn't wind up as lonely and fragile as the old woman looked and to forgive her for not believing in Him.

Before Jada was half done with her shift, her legs ached all up her calves and to the back of her thighs, right into her hips. She wasn't used to standing for hours. Though she'd taken the job in desperation, it felt instead like failure. Not that she wished herself back at the bank, now that she'd been fired—the bank had robbed her of time with the kids, it had drained her mental energy, and it had exhausted her in a way she didn't like to admit. But this job was exhausting, too. Jada didn't mind working—she even liked it—but she had to figure out something more sensible, more well-paying, something that would give her more time to see her children, or better still, to get them back.

She scanned the aisles hoping for customers, anything to distract her thoughts. But it was the lull before five. She tried to keep busy by straightening up her counter, lining up the customer divider sticks just so. But her thoughts wondered. The visits with the children were breaking her heart. Sitting outside the school in the Volvo, waiting for them and being joined by Ms. Patel, the assigned social worker, was humiliating, but seeing the kids' confusion, disappointment, and pain was worse. Shavonne was deeply angry. On the last visit, she hadn't spoken at all for the first forty minutes they were together, and had kept her arms folded over her chest—exactly the way Jada's mother did. All of Jada's questions and comments had been met with stony silence.

Meanwhile, Kevon clung to her and told her long, disconnected strings of information that worried her even more. "You know what?" he'd ask, and she'd answer, "What?" He didn't have anything ready to say, so he'd blink a minute, thinking, and then repeat, "You know what?" To keep talking, he'd either repeat verbatim what he'd seen on TV the night before, or he'd tell her about a fight between Clinton and Tonya. "And Daddy said he didn't want no more take-out, and Tonya, she said she wasn't spendin' her day cookin'. So we had peanut butter," he'd say. Or "You know what? You know what? She doesn't know the name of *any* of the Jedi Knights. She said she did, but she didn't."

Or he'd ask Jada heartbreaking questions: "Do you know where my pajamas are? The ones that have the fish on them, with the little boats?" Or "How come you don't make my bed now? I don't like it all wrinkled. I can't sleep with all them wrinkles in the pillows and the sheets."

Jada would hold Sherrilee and rock her while Kevon held onto the back of her shirt and went on and on. Meanwhile, Shavonne wouldn't meet Jada's eye. Only Ms. Patel, who sat quietly, her face averted and shadowed by some personal sadness or the sadness of what she saw every day, reflected pain back to Jada.

But if the visits were painful, driving up to the house and dropping the children off was worse. Sherrilee began screaming even before they turned onto Elm Street. Kevon's monologue became almost manic. That was when Jada was temporarily grateful for Ms. Patel, who gently but firmly pried the screaming baby from Jada's arms and took Kevon by the hand and marched him up the walk. It was only then that Shavonne looked her mother in the eye. "Come back home," she'd said the day before. "Come back home."

And even though she swore she was never going to do it, never going to bad mouth Clinton to his own children, Jada had said, "Your daddy won't let me. I can't, Shavonne, because your daddy won't let me."

After Shavonne had gone into the house and Mrs. Patel had left, Jada had sobbed, alone in the empty Volvo. What she'd said hadn't helped her daughter. And the visits were so disturbing, Kevon's comments so upsetting, that she wondered about *everything* that was going on in her house.

A customer approached, a man with a full shopping cart. Distraction! But as Jada scanned in the groceries, she kept thinking. All three of them, poor Mich, frightened Angela, and Jada herself, had been bested, had been beaten—in Michelle's case, literally—by men and institutions that were supposed to protect them. Jada hadn't really believed such bad things could happen to white women, women with education and some money. One of the things she'd learned from this was how bad it was to be a woman—a woman of any color—at the mercy of any color man.

What had gone so wrong? Jada had always been strong, unafraid of hard work, and she'd followed the rules. But none of it had done her any good, nor had it helped Michelle or Angie. They were good girls, too, and look how they were living! The apartment was in chaos with all three women and Michelle's two kids in it, not to mention the damned dog. They were like desperadoes in a hideout, but they didn't even have the satisfaction of having committed some exciting, violent, successful crime.

Jada scanned in a wrapped head of lettuce and shook her own head. She could see what the others should do: Mich should divorce Frank and make a deal with the DA. Angela ought to figure out a way to punish that so-called "friend" of hers up there in Boston and get even with her husband instead of just slinking away. And she . . .

The register flashed a total, and the customer handed over two twenties. Jada had to input the amount so the register could automatically calculate the change to be given. As if she wasn't even capable of making change! Jada accepted the forty dollars from the middle-aged man who seemed to have bought nothing but meat products—sausage, bacon, smoked ham, and canned meat—and counted out the three dollars and forty-six cents that was his change. Melody, the housewife who worked as a part-time bagger, began to fill a paper sack with the packages. "I want it double bagged," he said. Melody nodded.

Jada turned her head to the next customer. *Keep busy,* she told herself. The shopper was a well-dressed woman with a bad face lift. Why didn't men cut themselves up with face lifts? Jada wondered. What had Angie said about punishing the men? About getting their own back or evening the score? Jada sighed. It was hard for her to see what her own future actions should be. If the other two could act *for* her, and she could act for Angie or . . .

That was it! She held a can of olives up in the air for a moment, suspended. The face-lifted woman stared at her, but Jada thought only of her two girlfriends. She could see what they should do. They had to work *together*. Not the way they were at the apartment, where she was bringing home the groceries, Michelle was cleaning like a maniac, and Angie was paying the rent. They had to work together against the system that had beaten them. They had to work against the structure that had crushed them. They should help one another to *do* something that would even the score, that would give them back their pride, or even their freedom. Give them what they wanted, what they deserved. She knew she deserved to be with her kids, and they needed to be with her. Jada stared at the keys on her register until they blurred in front of her. She had joked with Michelle about kidnapping her children, but maybe it wasn't a joke. Maybe with help from her friends, she could—

"Are the Kraft Deluxe dinners on special, or only the regular macaroni and cheese?" the face-lifted woman across the counter inquired with such intensity it seemed as if Jada's answer meant the extinction of the race, or at least lasting world peace.

"Just the regular dinners," Jada told her. "You still want these?" she asked, looking at the deluxe boxes. But the woman's decision didn't matter to her. Somewhere deep inside herself, Jada had come to her own decision.

It was time to try and even the score. By whatever means necessary.

"We're coming. Now don't try to change my mind. I said to your mother 'now is the time' and even she didn't argue. So don't you try."

Jada listened to her father's voice and wondered if the comfort he offered was worth the anxiety his plan would cost. She'd called him from Angela's phone, sitting with the portable in the bathroom, the only quiet place in Angela's apartment. "It's just a temporary thing," she lied. "At least I think so." She still hadn't told her parents anything close to the whole truth; if they thought it was an emergency at this point, what would they do when they found out that Clinton had the children and the house? On the other hand, what could be worse than things were now? And wouldn't it be something of a comfort to have her mama and papa with her?

"Don't tell me you don't want me there, because I know you do," her mother said.

"Of course I do, Mama." Jada would have to ask Angie to petition the court so that her parents could visit their grandchildren. What else was there to do to prepare for their invasion? Find a motel room for them, because three adults, two children, and a dog were the absolute maximum in Angie's apartment. And then what? Tell them that she was thinking of grabbing her own children and disappearing with them? Tell them she was so desperate that she was going to break the law? Maybe she'd better start preparing them for some of this.

"Mama, some things have changed since you were here," she began.

44

In which Michelle reveals her bruises to Bruzeman

Michelle had showered and cleaned up the apartment, and now she finished dressing, ready to go in and face the first part of her own plan. She'd been thinking, and Jada and Angela had been pushing her to think even harder. She didn't try and cover up the bruises on her face. Today she needed them to show.

She dressed and gathered her notes and papers, including the rewritten detailed list Frank had made her keep of all the things that had been broken or lost. Ha! She'd been more exacting, more precise, than a state comptroller, and all the time Frank had known he was guilty. She had always imagined a future very much like her recent past—the comfort of routine, of her beautiful home, the fun of watching the children grow, the love of her husband. It was what she had dreamed of and worked toward from the time she was six or seven, growing up with her drunken mother in those awful, cheap apartments. She'd wanted her own house, a steady husband, clean, smart children, good furniture, a new car. She'd had those things and loved them, and now she didn't really have another dream to replace them with.

Sometimes Michelle thought that because of the way she'd grown up, she was tougher than Jada and Angie. She hadn't had a real mother who took care of her, was concerned for her, or could help out now, so she had to do it all herself. But now, at a time like this, she saw she wasn't tougher—she was more vulnerable than both of her friends. She didn't have a plan B. And though she was trying, she couldn't really think of one. At least not yet. But she could try and clean up the mess she was in.

She pulled into the parking lot at Swaine, Copple & Bruzeman. She was glad to see that Michael Rice immediately got out of his car and walked across the lot to meet her. She and Angie and Jada had discussed all this, and Michelle—stupid as it was—felt better with a man to confront Bruzeman, that little bully.

Michael smiled at her, and didn't avert his eyes from the side of her face and the darkness of the bruises. "How are you?" he asked.

"Not as bad as I look," she said. "But pretty nervous."

"You did see a doctor?" he asked.

"Oh, it's nothing. I'm fine. I'm just worried about Frank and the children. About the whole situation."

"I understand," Michael said somberly. "Let's go upstairs and see what we can do."

This time Michelle wasn't made to wait. When she thought about it, she realized it was the only time. Perhaps Michael Rice carried some weight. Or, more likely, Rick Bruzeman didn't like battered women littering his reception area.

She and Michael were quickly escorted to Bruzeman's office; he was waiting for them at the door. He had his right hand already out, and put his left on Michael's elbow for that power handshake that scumbag politicians seemed to like to use. Then he turned to her, but she noticed, he didn't shake her hand.

"Well, Michelle, you look well," he said. Michelle didn't bother to answer. She just walked over to the sofa and sat down. Michael sat beside her.

Bruzeman pulled up one of his straight-backed chairs, took it, and crossed his legs, his right ankle resting on his left knee, showing the pattern of his designer socks. Michelle averted her eyes.

"I won't take up a lot of your time," Michael began. "We have a few simple requests."

Bruzeman smiled, as if there were no problem. "Of course," he said. "I'm always willing to listen."

"My client is not testifying on behalf of your client," Michael said. "If she *is* subpoenaed, she will testify for the state. Because of the violence that she's received at the hands of your client, she is suing for divorce and custody. If Mr. Russo agrees to grant her custody, we'll wait to sue until after the outcome of his trial. In the meantime, he's not to contact her or the children."

Bruzeman laughed. "Is that all? Mr. Russo will never agree. Don't you think that's a little harsh? And he needs his family now. It's not an easy time for Frank, as you must know, Michelle."

Michelle swallowed, thinking of Frank alone. For a moment she felt . . . well, best not to name it. She had to forget that feeling for now.

"I don't think it's harsh at all, considering the violence Mr. Russo visited on his wife," Michael said calmly.

Bruzeman stood up. "Oh, don't give me that! Everybody's tense. There are legal problems, money problems, who knows what problems? A little push, a little shove. Who knows who started it." He looked down at Michael, his position frozen, his face hard. He frightened Michelle. "I'm afraid these terms are totally unacceptable, Mr. Rice."

Michelle actually trembled at the tone of Bruzeman's voice. There was something powerful in his smallness, something coiled like a snake or a rat about to jump.

But Michael stood up. "I don't think *you* understand," he said. "We're not negotiating. We are explaining the new rules. If you'd like to know why these rules apply, you'll have to discuss it with your client. Michelle Russo has no doubt in her mind that her husband is guilty of everything charged. Count yourself lucky she doesn't go to the DA and explain why she holds that belief."

Rick Bruzeman shook his head, then took a seat again, but this time he didn't do the jaunty leg cross. He wrapped each of his small feet behind a front leg of the chair and leaned forward. He looked at Michelle. It was suddenly as if Michael had ceased to exist. She had to push herself not to avoid Bruzeman's eyes.

"Michelle," he said, "your husband loves you. You know that. And you know he loves the children. You can't, in good conscience, abandon him at this crucial time. You can't do it, Michelle." He paused. "He's on my private line now, patiently waiting, hoping to talk to you."

Michael moved between the two of them, as if his body could protect Michelle's mind. "That is totally inappropriate, counselor. My client will not speak to the man who beat her. We've made a complete statement to the police. We have a restraining order, photographs, a doctor's report, and we could press charges. In fact, we *will* press charges, if you push Mrs. Russo in this inappropriate way."

Michael turned to Michelle. "Forget about the phone," he told her, then he turned back to Bruzeman. "It won't be any easier to represent your client if he's already in jail for battery and spousal abuse."

Michelle stood up. She couldn't stand it anymore. "I'll talk to him," she said to Rick. She looked at Michael.

"You don't have to," he said.

"I'll talk to him," she repeated. "But everything you say is true." She turned to Bruzeman. "We're not negotiating," she said. "We're telling you where things stand. And now I'll tell Frank."

Bruzeman shook his head and then gestured toward the phone. "He's holding on line two," Bruzeman said. He raised his eyebrows to Michael. "Shall we give Mrs. Russo some privacy? I have a few things to discuss with you."

"Do you want me to stay?" Michael asked.

"No. It's really all right." She would be an adult. She would tell Frank the score. Michelle couldn't remember the last words that she'd said to her husband. He had been in such a rage when he discovered the money gone that . . . well, she didn't remember it all.

She reached for the phone, but hesitated another minute. He was the father of her children, the love of her life, the man she had slept beside and taken inside her body for the last fourteen years. Yet he was a stranger. He'd been dealing drugs, he'd been lying to her, he'd been living a double life. He'd been putting her and his children at risk and then he'd struck out at her and beaten her. If she lifted up the phone, she would have to remember that the man speaking to her wasn't the Frank Russo she had once known. She thought she could do that, although her hand was trembling as she reached for the receiver. She picked up the phone. "Hello," she said.

"Michelle? Michelle, is that you?"

Even hearing his voice was difficult. She took a deep breath. "Yes, it's me. What do you want?"

"I want you to stop this, Michelle. I want you to come home. You know I didn't mean it. I was desperate. I was crazy. I need you to come home, Michelle, I need the children, and I need you to bring back the money."

Oh yes, she thought. *The money.* There was always the money. He'd sacrificed everything for the money. It made her sick. She would never touch a dime of it. She'd rather starve first. She wondered what she had to say to this man. Should she tell him how he had destroyed her dream, how he'd ruined her past and erased her future? Should she tell him that the pain in her jaw was nothing—it was the pain in her mind and heart that mattered. She didn't think so. "Talk to my lawyer, Frank," she said.

"Please, Michelle. At least let me see you. Here, in front of Bruzeman, if you want."

"No," she said quickly.

"Then come home. Just to talk."

"Not yet."

As Michelle drove farther away from her morning ordeal, she began to feel a little bit better. She'd eventually see Frank if she had to, but it would change nothing. She still wouldn't testify and she wouldn't give him the drug money.

But meanwhile she needed some money of her own to live on. Some money and a plan.

Angie and Jada were trying to restructure their lives, but what about her? She'd thought for a little while about her own plan. So far what she had was a simple one. She was simple and she needed her life to be simple. She knew that now about herself. She wanted only to work and make enough money to support her kids and herself. She'd had the cus-tom-upholstered-matching-love-seat-and-sofa stage of her life. She'd had expensive window treatments and two sets of china. She'd had more throw pillows than she could count, and wall-to-wall wool Berber carpet. She'd had more clothes than she knew what to do with, more jewelry than she could wear at once, and her kids had had more toys, shoes, and outfits than were good for them. All of that would have to change.

Michelle's childhood had been one of such deprivation that she had confused affluence with love and safety. She might be excused for doing that once, but not for doing it twice. More than anything she wanted a simple life where the work she did—not pushing papers across a desk in a bank or anyplace else—but the physical work she did, would give her enough to put food on the table and a few dollars in a savings. And she also wanted to help some other women be able to achieve that goal.

The main thing was, she had to do something she was good at, something she was proud of. And, at last, she'd figured out what that was. She wanted her life to be clean, and balanced. She wanted to have a sense of accomplishment at the end of a day, at the end of a job. How proud could filling in forms or pressing a button and sending something to the print queue make her? That life wasn't for her.

Suddenly, she knew now what life might work. The idea must have been lurking there, in the edges of her mind for some time. She'd have to go to the newspapers.

She stopped at a Starbuck's and spent over an hour nursing a cappuccino grande while she worked out the wording she needed for the two ads. Then she headed for two newspaper offices and placed the ads, charging them to Frank's Visa card. Lastly, she stopped in White Plains, in a seedy part of town. She was careful to lock the car and made sure she parked it close to the door of the Gold Miner, a jewelry and pawn shop.

She walked across the wide sidewalk and entered. She'd never been in a pawn shop in her life, but she knew her mother used to make monthly trips to the Provident Loan Society, and sometimes to a guy on Third Avenue. But she wasn't like her mother, she reminded herself. She wasn't doing this to avoid life or buy booze. She was taking care of herself and her children. She wasn't a drunk. And if she'd been living in a dream world, if she'd been keeping her eyes closed to the facts of life, at least she wasn't doing it anymore. Most importantly, she knew that she had to do this, and most of her other plan, on her own. Jada and Angie were helping her, but this . . . this she had to do alone, because she'd done so very little on her own before. Frank had been her good parent, until he'd turned into a bad one. Now Michelle had to be independent.

An older woman, a surprisingly pretty blonde, came over to the counter. "Can I help you?" she asked. "Are you looking for anything in particular?"

"Oh, I'm not buying," Michelle said. "I'm selling." She pulled off her engagement ring, her wedding band, her solitaire earrings, and opened her purse. She took out the emerald ring that Frank had given her when they were in St. Thomas and the necklace with the two-carat diamond that hung from it. She'd managed to get into the house when Frank was gone to get her jewelry and stuff for the kids. "I'd like to sell all of these," she said. Then she took off her gold watch; a thirtieth birthday present, it had thirty tiny diamonds around the face.

The woman looked at the array on the counter. "Do you have sales receipts for these?" she asked.

Michelle looked her in the eye and shook her head. "They were gifts given to me by my husband."

The blond woman seemed to heave a big sigh. "Divorce, huh?" she asked.

Michelle wasn't in the mood to explain. She just nodded. "We see it all the time," the saleswoman told her kindly, took out a loupe, and began to look at first the ring, then the stone on Michelle's necklace. Next she took out a little calculator and began to add up numbers. Michelle stood there and waited as patiently as she could. She knew she would take whatever this woman offered, and she felt that money was hers. It represented her wages for keeping house, for doing all she had done during her years of marriage. And it would be the money that would start her in her own business, in her own career. Whatever the amount was, she had come by it honestly. It was clean money. She'd taken the gifts when she loved Frank, when they represented his love for her, but she didn't want them anymore. She would take the money and she would begin again.

The blond looked at her apologetically. She offered a number that seemed ridiculously low to Michelle. It was less than Frank had paid for her ring, much less all the other stuff, but it would be enough to get her started.

But should she accept their first offer? It never would have occurred to Michelle not to—at least not before. She looked at her jewelry. It was amazing to think how attached to it she had once been, and to know that now the only thing it represented was some comfort and security for her children. She wished she had more to add to the pile. Then it occurred to her to take off the earrings she was wearing. She placed them with the rest. "I want more," she said, and looked the woman straight in the eye.

"Well. Yes. Well, of course," the woman said, and named a higher figure.

Michelle nodded, and the saleswoman turned to the safe to take out the cash.

By the time Michelle got home, she was as limp as a three-day-dead sea scallop. As she walked up to the door of the apartment, Michelle felt good for the first time in weeks and weeks. Living with Angie and Jada felt a little bit like being in a camp bunk—not that Michelle had ever lived in one, and not that dorms allowed children and dogs.

But Michelle had never had a roommate except for Frank. Despite what they were going through, there was something nice about opening the door and finding who had been shopping, if anyone had started dinner, or what new outrage Jada or Angie had confronted at work. Michelle had bought filet mignon and was going to make her famous twice-baked potatoes as a treat. Unless, of course, Jada had already made macaroni and cheese. She was humming to herself as she opened the door.

"Mommy! Mommy! Auntie Angie got a party invitation and she doesn't want to go," Frankie said as Michelle got in the door. She put the groceries down on the counter.

Jenna was sitting on one of the dinette chairs, her eyes big. "Shut up, Frankie," she said. "It isn't a party. It's a wedding."

Michelle put down her purse and took off her coat. Had they gotten weddings and divorces confused? "I like to get invitations to parties," Frankie said. "So why is Auntie Angie crying?"

"Where is she?" Michelle asked. Jenna indicated the bedroom with a twist of her chin. Michelle knocked on the closed door, but didn't even wait for an answer before she walked in. It was worse than she expected. Angie was lying on the bed, her face buried in the pillow, and Jada was sitting next to her. Angie's sobs were muffled, but not enough for the children not to hear, so Michelle quickly closed the door behind her.

Jada looked up and shook her head. She held out an envelope addressed to Angie. It was cream-colored vellum and postmarked Boston. It looked like trouble. Michelle pulled out the contents. There was a small clipping from a newspaper announcing the engagement of Reid Wakefield III to Lisa Emily Randall. But it was worse than that. Because there was also a wedding invitation—an invitation to their wedding next summer. It was engraved, and even Michelle, who had sent photocopied invitations to her own wedding, knew engraving when she saw it. She moved to the bed and sat on the other side of Angie. "Holy shit" was all she could say. Then she thought about it for a moment. "Who sent this?" she asked.

"It's Lisa's handwriting," Angie said, coming up for air.

"I can't believe it," Jada said. "She's DAS as well as mean."

"Are you even legally separated?" Michelle asked, staring at the engagement announcement.

Angie raised her shoulders in a shrug at Michelle. "Maybe three hundred miles makes it legal," she said with a weak smile, wiping her face with the Kleenex Jada handed her.

"Maybe *I'm* dumb and stupid," Michelle said, "but how can these two shit birds announce their engagement if you're not even divorced?"

Angie shook her head. "It's not illegal," she said.

"Spoken like a true lawyer," Jada said. "It's not illegal. Just heartless, insensitive, immoral, and pathetic."

"I'm going to have to go up there to finalize it."

"I wouldn't if I were you. I'd never give that bitch the satisfaction of a legal wedding," Michelle declared. "Don't agree. Don't give him a divorce."

"Forget about it," Jada said. "It's Massachusetts, Cindy, not some fairy tale. Kennedys get annulments the way other people get mail. And since Reid's a lawyer . . . "

"Reid's a lying ugly male pig, but he's a LUMP with clout," Angie agreed.

"What does CLOUT stand for?" Michelle asked.

"It isn't an acronym, it's a way of life," Jada told her.

45

In which Angela drops her dead camel

A few hours later, the three friends were lying on Angie's bed, still talking over the horrors of this latest saga.

"Look, it's in bad taste, but I want this divorce to go through as quickly as possible, too. I mean, it's not like I want to get him back," Angie said.

"No, sisterfriend, but you ought to want to get back *at* him. Contest it. Delay it. Make him work for it. And make that little creep he's about to marry sweat it out for a year or two," Jada suggested.

"How did he get the case called so quickly?" Michelle asked.

"If the Wakefields' don't have connections in Boston, who does?" Angie asked, stretching. Her back ached and her jaw throbbed. "I guess I'll just do it. Get it over with. Put it all behind me."

Jada patted Angie's bubble belly. "I'm afraid you're putting it all in front of you dear. Have you thought of what he might say about a Wakefield the Fourth?"

Angie's eyes opened wide. "I don't really show that much, do I? I mean I know I *look* awful, but don't I mostly look fat?" She felt herself going cold with fear. "I don't want him to know anything about this. I couldn't bear it. I don't want to have to deal with Reid and his family for the rest of my life."

"Well then, you better get up there and move it along," Jada advised. "Who's your lawyer?"

"I guess I'll be my own lawyer," Angie said.

"Hey, forget about that," Michelle said. "What is that expression? 'A man who serves as his own attorney has a fool for a client.'"

"I'm not a man," Angie said.

"But you are a fool," Jada told her. "And you can't go up there alone."

"We could come," Michelle volunteered.

"I'd be willing to, but I'm not a lawyer, either." Jada looked at Angie. "Take Michael Rice, why don't you. He's not DDG, but he's kinda hot, in a slow-burning way."

"He's also VRD," Angie said, throwing the made-up acronym back at crazy Jada, who raised her brows. "Very Recently Divorced," Angie said. "Even I know enough to keep away from men who are newly separated."

"I think you should call your mother," Jada said. "And maybe your dad."

Angie laughed. "You don't understand," she said. "My parents aren't like yours. If I went up with them, we'd have to relive their divorce." Angie was silent for a few minutes. Jada had told her all about her mother and father and their visit. In a way, Angie was envious. Jada's parents might not be sophisticated in the ways of the law, but they were united and supportive. Not that her mother and father weren't support-ive—it was just that they got so involved in arguing with each other.

"You can't go up there alone, Angie," Jada said. "We just won't let you."

It could have been a very civilized event, Angie thought. Reid looked as perfect as ever and he actually smiled and came over to Angie as she arrived. "Thanks for responding so quickly," he said. Then her father walked into the courtroom behind her.

"Shut up, you son-of-a-bitch," he said. "If you say one more word to my little girl, I'll twist your nuts off."

"You shut up, Anthony," Natalie said. "Or I'll twist *your* nuts off. This is a court of law." Then she looked at Reid. "You have got to be one of the more pointless living scumbags in recent history," she said. "Get on the other side of the courtroom and stay where you belong until this is over. We're not doing this for your convenience, we're doing it for Angie."

Angie, Natalie, and Tom, the lawyer Natalie knew, sat down together. Anthony was resentful that he had to sit behind them and twice asked to come up to the table. Twice her mother denied him. The two of them had bickered all the way up to Boston. The only good thing about it was, it had distracted Angie from what was coming next.

But now she was here and could look across at her husband. It still amazed her how attractive he was, and how unaware he seemed to be of the damage he'd done. Unconsciously, Angie put her hands over her belly. Sitting across from the man she had married and planned to spend her life with, hearing but not hearing the lawyers drone, she thought of how very odd it was to be in the same room with the father of her unborn child. A man who didn't even know about the son or daughter she was carrying. Somehow all of it seemed surreal, a feminine Kafka novel.

Angie definitely didn't like the feeling of boredom combined with horror. It was kind of like what she'd thought the Basketball Hall of Fame might be like. The divorce proceedings didn't take long. Neither did breaking a bone or removing a tooth, but the sense of loss and the pain was just as acute. It was odd for Angie to be the client, not the lawyer. And it was equally odd to realize that love, or whatever it was that Reid had felt for her, could be there one day and gone the next. What could she count on?

What she could count on was that Anthony and Natalie began bickering the moment they all left the courtroom together. And the bickering continued in the taxi, at the airport, and boarding the shuttle. Angie finally turned to them. They were arguing about whether she should sit with Anthony or with Natalie, because the two of them didn't want to sit together.

"This one's an easy one," Angie said. "Thank you for your support, but I'm sitting by myself. I might as well get used to it," she said. Then, in silence, the three divorced members of the Romazzano family boarded the plane.

46

In which Jada gets her parents back

Even though Jada left early, the traffic to JFK had been backed up at the Whitestone Bridge and she was late getting to the airport. She parked and walked what seemed like miles to the baggage claim area for her parents' flight, but she realized she must be *very* late—the area was virtually deserted, with just a few forgotten or abandoned suitcases lined up in the center of the floor, her parents standing beside them with their own battered baggage, looking equally abandoned. Even from a distance, Jada was surprised at how much more gray there was in her mother's hair, how smaller and more stooped her father looked.

These people had worked hard all their lives, had been good parents, good church-goers, and good to one another. Now, Jada would reward them by letting them get a look at the shattered pieces of her and their grandchildren's lives. Perhaps this had been a terrible mistake on her part. She shouldn't have involved them.

But it was too late for an attack of conscience now. "Mama," Jada called across the empty terminal and rushed up to embrace the older woman. Jada was a lot taller than her mother, so she bent a little at the knee. It allowed her mother to reach around her shoulders and give her a proper hug.

"Oh, don't you look like a warm stove on a cold night," her mother said, reaching up to pat her face. "We thought maybe you'd forgotten us."

Her father, as always, stood a step behind his wife, patiently waiting for his turn. Jada kissed him and he smiled with pleasure, then hugged her, and looked up into her eyes. "I'm sorry for your troubles, daughter," he said.

Jada almost burst into tears at that, but wouldn't let herself. Oh, it felt good to be with people who had taken care of her, who knew her when she was four, and when she was nine, and when she was eleven, and when she was a very bad teenager. "I'm sorry I was late for you," she apologized. "There was some kind of accident on the way and the traffic was horribly backed up."

"Anyone hurt?" her father asked.

Jada almost smiled, remembering in a flash how different island people were. "I'm not sure," she admitted to her father.

"Well, let's say a prayer for them just in case," her mother suggested. They did, and then gathered the bags to go.

"Was it a good flight?"

"As good as being thirty thousand feet in the air can be," her mother told her.

"I'm afraid the car is parked way on the other side of the lot."

"That's all right," her daddy assured her. "We're used to walking."

But they weren't used to the weather. It wasn't a particularly cold day, but the temperature seemed to attack and diminish both of them. By the time they got to the Volvo, her mother was shivering and her father's face (he'd insisted on carrying both of the big bags) looked ashen. "Are you all right?" she asked him.

"Be a damn sight better when you put some heat in the car."

"Benjamin! You watch your language," her mother scolded. Jada got in and turned the temperature control to max heat. It would be too stuffy for her, but it was the only part of the Volvo that worked perfectly. Before they were back on the highway, her parents, like delicate plants brought into a hothouse, had bloomed again.

"Now tell us again, now that we're not paying overseas telephone rates, how all this here sad business happened to you," her father suggested.

Jada, watching the road ahead, hated the idea of letting them know just how bad it was, but that's why they had come, after all. And so she launched into the story, sparing them and herself nothing. Her father asked a few questions, but her mother was silent, though she let a few gasps and tooth-sucking noises escape her. The recitation got them past the BQE and the Van Wyck, past LaGuardia and almost to the Westchester county line. Then they were all silent for a little while, taking it in.

"Well, what I can't understand," her mother said, "is how your mother-in-law could let her son behave that way. Benjamin, I think you should go and box Clinton's ears. What all could make a man behave that way?"

In the rearview mirror, Jada could see her father shaking his head. "When you never had no daddy you don't know how to behave like one," he said. It was as critical as he ever got.

"No kind of excuse. A person can always learn," her mother said. "How he could take his two daughters away, his daughters who need their mama . . . ?"

"What kind of example is that for his son? Showing the boy how to be no-account trash?" Jada's father asked.

Her mother turned to her. "We will get to see them, won't we?"

Jada didn't have the heart to tell them that she didn't know yet, that she'd asked Ms. Patel and that her attorney—who was also her roommate—had called the judge to find out. She had another bit of news to tell them, as well. "I'm afraid you're going to have to stay in a motel," she said.

"Why is that? Clinton won't let us in the house?"

"Clinton won't let *me* in the house," Jada explained, and told them the last bit—about how she had lost her home as well as her job and the payments she was supposed to make. Both of her parents were silent for a moment.

"Why, that's just plain crazy," her mother said. "So where is it that you're living?"

Jada explained about Angie and the apartment. Also about Michelle, along with a brief rundown of *her* problem. "They both hooked up with LUMPS—Lying Ugly Male Pigs," Jada said. "And they're both white girls."

"Has everybody in this country gone crazy?" her father asked. "Clinton wants you to support him? And he takes away your home and your children? Don't these men know how to be men?"

"It doesn't seem so," Jada told him.

Jada's parents had settled into the inexpensive motel room. They had, thank the Lord, gotten to see their grandchildren, and now they were just finishing up the remains of a big Bajan dinner that Jada and her mother had cooked for Angie, Michelle, and her children. It was hard to imagine squeezing even two more people into Angie's tiny apartment, but that was one thing that hadn't bothered her parents, though Jada had to smile at their discomfort with Pookie.

Now, after cleaning up the dishes, both Angie and Michelle had retreated to the two bedrooms with the kids, leaving Jada in the living room with her parents. It was odd how over the last month or two Jada had finally become truly color-blind: her friends were her friends and the people who didn't wish her well were as often her race as any other.

"They're nice girls," Benjamin said with approval as he brought their coffee cups over to the sink and then settled himself, as best he could, on one of the tiny dinette chairs.

"They're good girls and they're good friends to you," her mother said. She said nothing, Jada noticed, about them being white. "I'm surprised, though, that the women from the church didn't rise to the occasion. Didn't any of *them* offer to help you out?"

"I think," Jada began, "they were . . . almost happy to see me fall. It proved that you couldn't do what I did. Not without being punished." It was the only way Jada could understand the little support she'd been offered. "And Tonya Green is a member. I think long before I saw this coming, she managed to put in a lot of bad words on my behalf."

"And they believed her? Well, if Reverend Marsh was still there, he wouldn't listen to some Magdalene woman," her mother said.

"But he's been gone a long, long time," Jada told her mother. "I don't even know this preacher very well. He's only been there two years, and with work and the children and all I haven't been as active as I once was. I didn't get to really know him."

Her mother looked up from her lap and—for the first time since she'd arrived—she criticized her daughter. "Well, *that* was a mistake on your part," she said. "How can you not know your preacher, and for over two years? Part of your work must always be helping the congregation. The poor will always be among us."

The words weren't said harshly, but even so they brought a sting to Jada's eyes. How could she explain to her mother about how busy she'd been? About how draining the job at the bank was, about taking care of the house, and paying the bills, and having to dress right, and tutoring the children and all the rest of it?

"The church will always help you," her mother said. "I don't want you to forget that."

Jada wondered about that in silence as she drove them back to the motel. Could the church help her? How? "I have to work tomorrow," she reminded her mother as they said goodnight. She'd taken two days off from Price Chopper but she needed the money—such as it was—and the job. "Will you be all right?"

"It will give your dad and me some time to talk and to think. This is some mess you have here, Jada. We'll see you tomorrow night?" Jada nodded. "All right, then," her mother said, and gave Jada another big hug. It wasn't an apology, or total understanding, but it comforted Jada. In fact, as she stood there, bent at the knees, she felt she never wanted to leave the comfort of her mother's arms.

"You have to bring the children back home," Jada's father said. He was speaking in a low voice, as if each table at the Olive Garden had microphones, listening to desperate grandparents' plans.

"They *are* back home, Papa," Jada reminded him.

Her mother shook her head. "They need to be back in the islands," her mother said. "They need to be around their own kind, their own kin."

"Well, over the school holiday, in the summer, I may be able to bring them down for a week or two. But right now I don't know if we could afford—"

"Jada, we're talking about sooner, not later. And we're not talking about a holiday. We're talking about a permanent move," her mother said.

Her father nodded in agreement. "We can help you. You could stay with us at first, if you wanted to. If not, we could find you a place and a job. Your mama could watch the children after school."

"Papa, you don't understand. I couldn't get permission from the court to take the kids overnight right now, much less permanently out of the country," Jada explained.

"Well, then you'd have to do it *without* permission," her father told her. "Certainly they can't go on this way. They need a sense of family and of home." Her mother nodded. "I don't like to say it, but Clinton Jackson never knew what he was doing and he doesn't know it now. He's hurting his own children. The man must be crazy. And if the court can't see it, well, you can, we can, the children can, and heaven knows the Lord can."

Her mother reached her hand out to Jada. "We have prayed over this, Jada. We have prayed and we know that you must render up to Caesar that which is Caesar's. But not your children. We want you and our grandchildren to get on the plane with us when we leave."

"Mama, I can't do that. I could never come back."

"Well?"

Her parents looked at her. She couldn't believe they were thinking of the same ideas that Jade had earlier. But did they didn't understand they were asking her to leave her country, her home, and become a law-breaker. Plus, there might be extradition. Maybe the courts or Clinton could remove the children. And she might be banned from the island, or jailed there, or here. "Mama, I don't know what the laws say. I don't know about schools for the kids. And I'm not a Bajan. I'd be a stranger on the island. And the children, for them it would worse. The adjustment to school alone would be—"

"You wouldn't stay strangers for long," her mother told her. "Not on Barbados."

For a moment, the idea of a tiny bungalow, endless sunshine, and her parents always nearby beckoned to Jada. But then she thought of the children and how big an adjustment it would be. They were American kids. The British-based school system would be difficult, at best, to adjust to. And there would be no work for her. Her parents, so conservative, so good, were trying to rescue her, yet their solution was not as simple as they made it seem. "Mama, I just don't think so," she said. "I could never come back here, and if the children did, if they had to, I couldn't visit them. I know you wish I were, but I'm not a Bajan. Neither are they."

Her mother and her father paused. Silence filled the room. "Well then, we want you to talk to Samuel."

Her father nodded. "Samuel," he said.

"Who *is* Samuel?" Jada asked. The way they said the name he sounded like some archangel from the Bible.

"Samuel Dumfries. He's a barrister. Very big man in Bridgetown. He's the son of the husband of my cousin, Arlette. Well, you remember Arlette, don't you?"

Jada just nodded. She didn't remember her cousin Arlette—who might actually be a second or third cousin, or the daughter of a third cousin, or just as likely only a courtesy cousin. But if she admitted *that,* it would take her mother fifteen minutes to work out the tortured relationship that "cousin" sometimes signified on the island.

"Mama, you forget I'm *living* with a lawyer. I'm afraid that there's no legal—"

"Samuel Dumfries is more than just a lawyer, Jada. He works all over the islands. He has clients here. He has work all the time in New York and Boston. He knows a lot of people, Jada. We think you must talk with him."

"All right, Mama," Jada said, out of fatigue rather than hope. "I'll talk with him."

But on her drive home Jada felt worse than ever. Samuel Dumfries, whoever he was, couldn't help in an American custody case. Jada sighed. Her parents loved her, but they offered no solution. It was silly to expect they would. It was hard for them to understand the complicated knot, the net, she'd found herself caught in. In a few more days they would have to leave, and Jada would find herself more lonely than she had been before. Her only hope was to comply as best she could with the court, hope that Ms. Patel would give good reports, and hope for a successful appeal. Jada didn't know why she felt so hopeless, so disappointed. She just knew that she did.

47

Consisting of a party, pasta, and plans

"Who wants stuffed shells?" Angie asked as she bustled into the apartment. "Who wants eggplant parmesan? Who wants garlic bread?" The place was spotless. Michelle must have been at it all day, polishing, washing, scrubbing, and folding.

"Hi!" Michelle said. "I was just about to start dinner."

"No need. I deliver," Angie said. Jada came out of the bathroom. Angie looked at Jenna and Frankie, not surprised that they hadn't clamored for the fancy stuff. "Oh," she said. "I guess you two wouldn't want spaghetti and meatballs, then."

"We do! We do!" Frankie cried. Triumphant, Angie put down the bag of take-out. She was good.

"I was going to make a casserole," Michelle said weakly, but Angie shook her head and then lifted a bottle of wine from the bag. "Who's up for a little Dago Red?" she asked.

Michelle, taken aback by the epithet, didn't have a chance to respond until Angie lifted a second bottle. "Here's some Jew Juice for me," she said, holding a bottle of what looked like rosé. Then she pulled out a third bottle of what looked like Chardonnay and gestured toward Jada with it.

"What's that? Black white?" Jada asked.

"You stole my line," Angie said, and Michelle decided not to be offended at the 'dago' stuff. "All for one and one for each," Angie said. "If you drink enough of it, would you consider extracting my tooth? It's killing me." Jada shrugged. Then she looked at the two kids. "*You* guys have Orange Crush," she added. "And you," she said to Pookie, "you've got a nice piece of rawhide al dente."

Her little dinette table was only big enough for two, but the kids sat at it and happily ate their meatballs while the three women perched on the couch and ate over the coffee table. Michelle had trouble chewing even the soft ricotta of the stuffed shells, but she managed to get a little of it down. Her jaw hurt, but the wine helped. When the news ended and Jenna had watched *Sabrina the Teenage Witch,* Angie suggested that tonight the kids go to bed in Jada's room while the three of them sat up and talked.

"Last night I had a dream. Reid was telling me something. I don't remember what he was saying, but he looked so gorgeous it was as if he was in the room with me." Angie stroked Pookie's ears and looked down at the dog. "You know another reason why dogs are better than men?" she asked, and kissed Pookie on top of his silky head. "Gorgeous dogs don't know they're gorgeous." Just then the dog started making weird noises.

"Uh-oh," Michelle said, but it was too late. Pookie upchucked. "Oh God, I'm so sorry," Michelle said. "My dog is bulemic. She binges out-side and then comes home and pukes."

"Better her than me," Angie said as Michelle cleaned up the mess.

Michelle kept watching as Angie filled her own glass with the rosé. Once the children were settled down, she returned to the living room and said, "Do you think you should be drinking that, in your condition?"

Angie looked from Michelle's serious face to the bottle. Then she laughed. "Alcohol-free," she said. "Jewish whine: how come I'm not drunk?" She laughed at her own joke. "But you two *need* alcohol to be free, so drink up. I have what might be called a modest proposal for you."

Michelle couldn't help but tidy away all the dinner things, pack the trash, and put the bag at the door. Then she joined the other two. By then Jada had finished more than half her bottle, though Michelle knew

Jada rarely drank. "Keep up with me," Jada said, and filled Michelle's glass. But now the wine seemed to be making her face hurt more—it throbbed, and all Michelle wanted was to lie down and try to sleep.

"Look," Angie said, oblivious to Michelle's mood. "I've been thinking. Every day I see women who are being wrecked not only by the men in their lives, but by the system. I'm doing what I can, but look at what happened to us."

"Train wreck," Jada said, nodding.

"The point is, I'm going through the system at work, but we don't have to go through the system if we don't want to."

"Amen, sister!" Jada put down her glass of wine so hard that some sloshed over the side onto the tabletop and splattered on her shirt. "Damn," she said. She tried to blot it off with her napkin.

"No. No, you need to soak it in—" Michelle began. Before she could finish, Jada whipped off the cardigan and handed it to her.

"I want it back, washed, and folded by tomorrow morning, Cinderella." Michelle got up to get a paper towel to blot it up, but Jada stopped her. "Sit down and listen up," she commanded.

Jada was the one who started talking then. "I stand at that cash register and I imagine all the things I'd like to do to Clinton. None of them are legal, and none of them are nice. But that's not the point. The point is what he did to me and how to fix it. I'm sick and tired of being a victim."

"And me?" Angie asked. "I'm busy counseling women while I'm a mess, and I'm giving advice? I'm telling them to work through the system? Look what it did for you, Jada! It gives me a feeling that Lorena Bobbitt might have had a point."

"It wasn't a point, it was a knife," Jada said.

Michelle just stared at the ring of wine on the glass tabletop. She didn't want to do anything to Frank. She just wanted him not to exist. She'd wished he'd never existed. Spending her life alone would have been better than the good years before this betrayal.

"My life as I knew it is over," Mich said.

The other two women were silent for a moment. Then, "Victim queen, victim queen," Jada sang. Angela joined in the chant. Then she stopped. "I want to be victim queen," she said.

"No way. Clinton has my children," Jada said.

Michelle laughed. "Okay. Don't bicker. You made me queen. Now live with it."

"Well, what I was thinking today," Angie said, "is what if none of us are victims? What if we do something about this? What if we help each other to even up the score."

"I swear I was thinking the same thing," Jada said. "All day long, I kept scanning in groceries and thinking of what to do. You remember that movie about the three women who got revenge on their husbands?"

Michelle remembered it. She hadn't bothered to see it in the movies, though Jenna had rented it over and over. "But that was a comedy," she said. "Anyway, it was just the movies. You can't do things like that in real life."

"Oh yes you can," Angie said. "I have a few ideas already. We'd have to brainstorm a little, do a little planning, but none of these guys are what you'd call Einsteins."

"More like beer steins," Jada said. "Bet you Clinton's sitting at the house knocking back a couple of malt liquors in front of my children right now."

Angie opened her briefcase and took out three sweatshirts. She unfolded one and held it open across her chest. "Operating Without Male Guidance" it read, and when both Jada and Michelle laughed, Angie threw each of them a shirt. "How about it?" she asked.

Michelle stood up and slipped the sweatshirt over her head, but it caught on her cheek. Her whole face ached. "Look, I don't want to discourage you two or be a party-pooper, but it's going to be hard enough for us to survive, to make a living, and to take care of our kids. Forget about anything more."

"Michelle, Michelle," Jada said, strutting around the room with her sweatshirt on. "Open up to the possibilities. Have another glass of wine. Once you open up to the possibilities . . . ." She paused. "*You* don't ever have to work outside the system."

"What do you mean?" Michelle asked, sitting down.

"The easiest way for you to get justice," Jada said. "Haven't you thought of it?" Michelle blinked and looked at her. "Turn him in," Jada said. "Turn state's evidence."

Michelle gasped. "I can't do that. I don't have to protect him, or testify *for* him, but I really don't want to testify *against* him."

"Oh really?" Angie said. "And why not? He's guilty and you know it."

"I don't give my own husband up to the police. I . . . I just couldn't. I mean . . . it's wrong. And I'm afraid. I'm afraid to even *meet* with him."

"Hey. Don't wig out. It was just a thought," Angie said.

"Well, I'd give him up in a minute, Mich. I'd do worse. Today I thought that if Clinton were dead, I'd get custody again. Maybe."

"Dead?" Angie asked, and her eyes opened wider. "I don't think we should move to physical violence. After all, I *am* technically an officer of the law. Plus, women's prisons are not as much fun as they seem in the movies."

"Yeah, but I'd like a scorched-earth policy," Jada said.

"Scorching is good," Angie agreed.

"Well, in your case, you should have it. What happened to you was totally, totally unfair," Michelle said to Angie.

"Oh, and you deserved what you got?" Jada asked Michelle, and very gently touched Michelle's face with her index finger.

Michelle paused. "So, what could we do? I mean if we were going to do something?"

"I don't have all my details worked out," Angie admitted. "But I'm making progress. And none of it's illegal. Not really."

"My parents have offered to help me. I don't know if they really can, but I do know my husband has to lose that house," Jada said. "No way justice is served if he has the house *or* the children."

Angie pulled a pad out from her purse. "Clinton," she said, writing it at the top of the page. "No house," she said, still writing. "And no kids," she added.

"Yeah, and no visitation unless it's supervised," Jada added bitterly.

"You want Tonya out of the picture?" Angie asked. "Remember, this is just a wish list."

"Honey, if he doesn't have a dime and a place to live, Tonya will dump him for someone who does. I couldn't care less."

Angie turned to a new page. "Reid," she said, jotting down his name across the top. "I'd like to see him exposed."

"What do you mean?" Jada said. "Like a flasher?"

Michelle, who had begun to sip her wine again, giggled and snorted some. "Get his dick in a ringer," she said, and then was shocked at herself.

"You know, that gives me an idea," Angie said, and wrote CRAZY GLUE on the pad. She paused, looking at the ceiling. "No. What I mean is, I'd like something bad to happen between him and Lisa, my ex-best friend, so that *he* gets dumped." She raised her eyebrows. "I don't want him back, girls. I just want him humiliated." She wrote DUMPED BY LISA, followed by CANCELED WEDDING? And then, SOCIAL HUMILIATION. "His parents hate any kind of scene, anything that isn't done appropriately or discreetly. They always hated me, but I only hated them back recently." She paused for a moment, then focused on Michelle. "But what do you want, Mich?"

"I had an idea, but now I can't imagine it working." She paused and wondered whether that were true. She supposed she could *imagine* things. She just couldn't make them happen. And she was afraid to tell her friends what she'd thought of. They'd probably laugh at her. "All I know is I'd like to live clean," she said. "Maybe really simple, but clean, you know what I mean?"

Jada nodded and patted Michelle's hand. Angie wrote FRANK at the top of a new page, but Michelle shook her head.

"I don't want to get back at Frank," Michelle said. "I want to get *away* from him. In real life and in my head. It's just that I don't know how to do it." Michelle's voice fell. "I've only ever worked twice, once as a salesgirl, and then I had the job at the bank. And I only got it because Frank did a lot of business there. I know how to take care of my kids and a house, but I don't know if I could support them and myself." She raised her head and her eyes flashed. "I just know I'm ashamed of every penny I took from Frank. If it was all . . . tainted." Her friends nodded.

"So, you've done *some* thinking, Mich," Jada said, being positive.

"Maybe to know what you do want, you have to figure out what you don't," Angie added.

Michelle almost smiled. It was a comforting thought. "Well, I know that when I work again, I don't want to work for a bank. I don't want to work for anyone but myself. It's not that I'm lazy, I just don't like to be bossed around."

Angie nodded and wrote MICHELLE at the top of a new page. Underneath it she wrote OWN BUSINESS, SELF-SUPPORTING, FREE FROM FRANK, and FREE FROM COURT.

"I also think I have to live somewhere else," Michelle added. "You know how I loved that house. But it was sick, and now it's all ruined. This town is no good for me or the kids anymore." Michelle sighed.

Angie wrote RELOCATION on the pad. "Good," Michelle said. "Okay, so you got some start out of me. But it's impossible."

She was angry all of a sudden. Angry at her powerlessness and fear, at what had happened to herself and her kids. "All of this stuff is pretty much impossible. Me as my own boss! A new place to live. Why bother to talk about any of it if we can't achieve it?" Michelle hunched her shoulders. "There's no way that I could have my own business." She laughed. "I never even had my own checking account. And talking about justice is fine, but when do women get that?"

"I think we could get it," Angie said. "It might take a little planning. It might take a little help, and a little time but I think we could do it." She pointed to her chest. "'Operating Without Male Guidance.'"

"I think it's possible, too," Jada added. "If we're willing to bend the rules or break them. It's too bad all of this would take some money," she added.

For the first time since they had focused on her, Michelle lifted her head and straightened her spine. "You know," she said slowly, "I might know a way around that."

48

If love is blind, why is lingerie so popular

"I don't know if I can do it. What's my name again?"

"Anthea Carstairs," Angie reminded Michelle.

"Who am I married to?"

Jada and Angie looked at each other for the answer. Then Jada's index finger pointed up. "Charles Henderson Moyers. I read about him in *Fortune* magazine."

"Only the richest, most secretive guy in the world," Angie told her. "Perfect!"

"What if Reid wants my phone number?" Michelle asked.

"Oh for God's sake, Michelle—I mean, Anthea," Jada said. "You can't get arrested over the phone. If you don't do it, I will." She reached for the phone.

"Well, what if he has caller ID?" Michelle asked.

"Then a big cop's arm will push out of the receiver and collar you," Jada said. "God, you're a wimpy white girl."

"Don't wig out. I know they don't have caller ID," Angie assured Michelle. "Andover Putnam probably still has rotary dials. When I say an old-line law firm, I mean *really* old-line." They were sitting in Angie's office, rendezvousing there because it was the only place Michelle wasn't ashamed to show her now yellow and green face, and where they could have some privacy because, as Jada had pointed out, "They don't give us a private office and phone use at Price Chopper."

Michelle looked over the piece of paper in front of her. For three evenings, the women had spent most of their free time plotting out how to make their plans, their desires, and their justice come about. This was only the very first step, Angie thought, the easiest one, and already Michelle wanted to wimp out. Angie took a deep breath, then waited while Michelle pulled herself together, touching the side of her face.

"What if I'm still swollen by next week?" she asked.

"You won't be. But if you are, it will just be a little more dramatic," Angie said. "He likes to rescue people. He also likes blondes. And big fees."

"Okay," Michelle said, "here goes nothin'." She punched in the number and asked for extension 239. She looked at the sheet of instructions in front of her. *Voice mail, hang up. Secretary, say it's an emergency.* But the phone was picked up and a man's voice said hello.

"Hello," Michelle responded, and tried to put an extra breath into it. "Is this Mr. Reid Wakefield?" she asked.

"Yes."

She nodded to the other women. Angie felt her heart thumping, her chest tighten, and even the artery in her neck move as her blood rose. "Mr. Wakefield, this is Anthea Carstairs," Michelle said. "You've come very highly recommended to me by a client of yours."

"Oh? That's always nice to hear. Who?"

"I'm afraid I can't disclose that information," she said. "I mean, he asked me to keep this quite confidential and said that you and Andover Putnam were especially good at keeping things in the family—as it were," Michelle was pleased with that last bit. "As it were," sounded classy.

"Well, I like to think *all* attorneys keep their client's work confidential," the jerk said. Michelle thought he did sound like a jerk, right from the get go, not just because of all Angie had told her. "We try to treat each of our clients as if they were special."

He was a jerk. "I have a very special problem. It involves my pre-nup and my inheritance." She paused. "I don't really want to discuss this over the phone. Would it be possible to come in and see you?"

"Certainly," he said. "But perhaps you could—"

"Listen, fees are no problem. Not even an issue." Oh, that sounded coarse. She looked on the sheet in front of her to see what she could add. "And Howard said that you could be most accommodating . . . "

"Howard Simonton?" Reid asked.

It was a name Angie had known from the firm. Big CEO with some big legal problem. "Oh please," Michelle said. "Just forget I mentioned his name. Promise me you will." He better. Howard Simonton had never heard of any Anthea Carstairs.

"No problem. Really," the jerk said, but his voice was full of new respect.

"Then maybe you *could* meet with me?"

"Fine. Of course. What would be good for you?" he asked. Michelle nodded to her friends. Angie was gesturing, but Michelle didn't know what she was trying to express. God, this wasn't charades!

"I think Tuesday would be good," Michelle said. "About four o'clock."

"Let's say four-thirty. How do you spell your name?" Michelle knew he had forgotten it. Thank God she hadn't.

"Anthea Carstairs," she said. "Spell it however you like," she told him and she hung up.

"*Woooo-hooooo!*" Jada yelled. "Honey, the silver screen missed out on a real talent when you decided to become a homemaker."

"Perfect. Perfect!" Angie agreed, dancing around.

Michelle felt good, almost cocky. She *could* do things. "Well, our next nominee for the Academy Award is none other than Angie Romazzano, who starred in *The Mistaken Honeymoon* and *A Woman Scorned*," Michelle said, and handed the phone over to Angie.

Jada laughed. "Now let's see her in a clip from her latest work, *Payback Time*." She did a perfect imitation of an *Entertainment Tonight* anchor.

"Okay, okay," Angie said. "I appreciate the support as well as your competitive instinct." She lifted up the phone and dialed Andover Putnam's number again. She felt her mouth go dry. Even her lips were dry. When the automated voice came on, she punched in Lisa's extension number. She could deal with voice mail or Lisa, but not with Donna, the secretary they once shared. That would be too much. Well, she would take this as a sign. If Donna answered, the whole crazy idea wouldn't work. But if Lisa picked up . . . She held her breath for a minute and then heard her once-best-friend-now-enemy cheerfully say her name.

"Lisa, this is Angie." There was a pause, and Angie wondered whether Lisa was going to hang up. She looked over at Michelle and Jada, both leaning in toward her, both wide-eyed with curiosity. "Look," Angie said. "I know we haven't spoken to each other, since, well, you know, but I feel very bad."

"I do, too, Angie," Lisa said, and Angie had to roll her eyes toward the ceiling.

Michelle and Jada looked at one another, then back at Angie, who took a very deep breath before asking, "Really?" Not that she cared. Okay, she told herself. Now it was time for the real bullshit. "Lisa, I feel like I didn't just lose a marriage. Obviously, that was on its way out anyway. But I also lost a best friend. That was tough." Phew. That was hard to get out, but she'd done it. Meanwhile her friends were acting up; Michelle covered her mouth with her hands and Jada stuck a finger down her throat and imitated gagging. *Victim queen*, Jada silently mouthed. Angie gave them both a cutesy smile.

"Angie, I'm so . . . surprised . . . and touched that you'd feel that way." Lisa was such a narcissist, she just might buy it. Or, who knew? Maybe she had a conscience.

"Well, it didn't happen overnight," Angie admitted. "But I've had a lot of time to think. I mean, maybe we could never be friends the way we were." Jada opened her eyes really wide at that and gave an exaggerated nod of her head. Angie paid no attention. She had to concentrate on Lisa. "But I would like to talk to you. And I have a few things I'd like to give you," Angie said.

Michelle flipped out her index finger. "Give her the bird," she whispered, until Jada covered her mouth.

Angie missed the first few words of what Lisa had said, because of the two of them giggling. But it didn't matter. Still, Lisa wasn't stupid, so Angie knew she had to be careful.

". . . and then to hear from you, just like this . . ." Lisa was saying.

"Well, I do have an ulterior motive," Angie admitted, and she almost smiled as she heard Lisa's silent alarms go off. "You know the last time I saw you, well . . . Reid . . . you know." Angie paused as if she were embarrassed. "Anyway, there were a few things I didn't bring back from Boston. Just small stuff, like a sketch book from Provincetown and, well, you know."

"Sure," Lisa said. She must have been remembering that day in the apartment, too. Angie smiled. Lisa wanted the divorce final. And then there was her avarice . . .

"Anyway, I also have a ring from Reid. I think it was a family stone. Anyway, he had it set at Shreve, Crump & Lowe for me, and I think you ought to have it."

"Oh, Angie," Lisa said. "That is just so"—now it was her turn to pause—"so *very* generous of you. I mean legally, I think—"

"Come on, Lisa. You know we're not talking legally. The ring doesn't give me any pleasure and it might give you some." Angie looked up and Jada was giving her the okay sign. "I'm working down in Westchester County now, but I can take a late afternoon flight up next week. I'll bring the ring. We could meet for dinner or a drink, and then go over to the condo and pick up my stuff. I'll fax you a list of it if you want. Nothing expensive. But I would like a pair of my flannel pajamas, and there's a journal I kept. Stuff like that. Would that work?"

"Sure," Lisa said, the greed loud and clear in her voice. "I'm booked up on Monday and Thursday but the rest of the week is open."

"Okay," Angie said. "Well, let me think about it and I'll call you back." She raised an eyebrow for her friends' benefit. "Ah, just one thing, Lisa. I'm really still angry at Reid. I don't want him to know about any of this. It's just too humiliating." She grinned at Michelle and Jada and gave them the nod. "It has to be a secret. Otherwise I won't come. Can you promise?"

"Absolutely," Lisa said, and Angie could almost hear the tinkling sound the imagined ring made in Lisa's materialistic little brain. "Fine then. I'll call soon." She hung up.

Jada stood up, and Michelle followed her. Both of them clapped. Then Michelle stuck out a hand and looked over at Jada, who did the same. "It's a two thumbs up," Michelle said. Jada nodded her head.

"The bitch bought it. Big time," she said.

• • •

"You know that old saying? When the going gets tough, the tough go shopping?" Michelle said. "Well, we got a lot of outfitting to do. Something to wear to Boston and some maternity clothes for you, little mama," she said to Angie. "And maybe some baby clothes, as well." She turned to her pal. "Jada, you're going to need a *lot* of luggage. I couldn't stand to see you traveling with cardboard boxes. And then there are the outfits for us in Marblehead."

"Speaking of which, it will be quite a drive for us," Angie told them.

"We'll have more time to practice our parts," Jada commented.

"And to get us in the mood, what do you say we start in the lingerie department?" Michelle grinned. "I don't know if Frank has canceled our credit cards yet, but it's time to find out."

"Michelle, you haven't won the lottery," Jada told her. "You shouldn't do it. Not for us."

"Really not for me," Angie said. "I have a job."

Michelle looked at both of them. "Hey, who took me in when I had nowhere to go? Who helped me with the kids? Come on. Don't be stupid." She looked at Jada. "I think we better buy your kids some summer clothes while we're at it," Michelle said, holding up a Visa card. "They'll call it 'cruisewear' and it will be a fortune, but I think you'll need it. Who knows how long this lottery ticket will last?"

They were in the mall until it closed. Michelle had not only outfitted Angie for her pregnancy, but had put together a complete layette as well. Good thing she did, too, because Angie didn't know a thing about it. She kept picking out the cute stuff that was next to useless once the baby came. Jada talked her out of most of it, but Michelle let her get the dry-clean-only tiny white woolen sweater and booties made to look like saddle shoes because they were so damn cute. Next all three of them almost died laughing when they went up to lingerie and Michelle and Jada tried on garter belts, push-up bras, and g-strings.

"Look at us," Jada said. "Angie, you are stunning, and Michelle, you are a fabulous blond bombshell, even if your roots do need touching up. And if I have to say so myself I'm a great looking brunette with good hair. But none of us is getting any."

"Some of us *might* be getting some soon." Angie giggled.

"Oooh," Jada and Michelle cried.

They giggled, and Angie began to lose patience with them—until she saw the color of Michelle's gold card.

"The best part is, it's all charged to Frank," Michelle said. "It's the only reason men are better than dogs—some men have charge accounts."

Jada had been talked into a great pair of leather slacks and a fabulous orange silk sweater—very seductive. "Perfect for you, Jenette," Michelle said, practicing Jada's cover name.

Michelle bought herself the most ridiculous little suit that anyone in Westchester—a county known for ridiculous little suits—could ever wear. Actually, the idea of wearing it almost made her giggle out loud. The other two did when they came out of the dressing room and saw her in it.

"God! I wish I could see what that looks like in the hallowed halls of Putnam Andover." Angie laughed.

"Too much?" Michelle wanted to know.

"Uh-uh. Perfect for Anthea Carstairs. Definitely a '*Glamour* Do,'" Angie told her.

Weighed down with their purchases, they decided to dump everything in their cars and then have a quick bite at Ruby Tuesday's before they went home. Michelle put a lot of the stuff into the trunk of the Lexus and joined her two friends at the booth they had already secured.

She slid in beside them. "Girls," she said, "this is a momentous day for me." Just then the waiter interrupted and they ordered—potatoes stuffed with various things, including potatoes, beers for two of them, and club soda for the fat one. The boy who took their order thought they were just silly suburban women. He didn't know they were anarchists.

"Okay," Michelle reminded them after the waiter had left, "I know what I'm going to do."

"You mean up in Massachusetts? We've been through that three times," Angie said. "But maybe we should run through it again."

"Later," Michelle said, and her voice had a ring of authority that made them both pay attention. She was impressed with herself as she looked at the two of them. "I have an announcement to make." She pulled a card out of her purse and slid it across the table.

CINDERELLA CLEANING SERVICE
Enchanting Housekeeping
Tiny feet, magic wands, but no prints

"Michelle! Oh my God!" Angie said.

Jada stared from the card to Michelle's face. "It's *perfect* for you," she said. "You're the Queen of Clean."

"Better than the other kind," Michelle grinned, delighted at their response. "And I'm not just going to do the cleaning," she admitted. "I'm going to start training some people as soon as they answer my ads. I'll begin by going to each house, even if I have to clean it myself. But then I'll go with my employees. They'll clean, but I'll check everything. I figure I can handle four houses a day. Maybe five, if I can get the right staff. What do you think?"

"I think it's great," Jada said.

Angie nodded her head, a huge smile on her face. "Unbelievable. Perfect. But you left off a phone number," she added, looking more closely at the card.

Michelle paused. "It wasn't a mistake," she admitted. She paused again. "It's because I'm going to have to move. You know I will." The three women were silent for a minute.

"It's okay. I want to put the kids in a different school in September. This is no good for them here. We'll adjust."

Their potatoes arrived and Michelle pulled her credit card from her purse along with scissors she had bought for the occasion. But she also pulled out three shuttle tickets and waved them in front of the girls. "A gift from Frank," she said, and handed them to Angie. "And now," she said ceremoniously, "I'm going to be responsible for myself." She cut the Visa card in half and then in quarters, and she pulled out her American Express and her MasterCard and cut them, too. She'd thought it might be frightening, but it actually felt satisfying, liberating. Soon she had a little stack of plastic bits arranged on the bread dish beside her. She lifted it up. "Thin mints, anyone?" she asked.

"Maybe a Martha Stewart mosaic," Angie suggested.

"Forget that bitch," she said, and hugged Michelle. "Congratulations, girlfriend," Jada said. "You go, girl!"

"Yeah," Michelle agreed. "And *you* pay for dinner."

49

In which children are taken by surprise

Jada had already received a call from Clinton and a letter from his lawyer about the late payments. She'd lied and told him she could make them up if only she could bring the children to her place. Reluctantly Clinton had agreed. "But otherwise I go to court," she'd said. "I got the law on *my* side!"

Jada couldn't describe what the last visit with her children had been like. She had gotten permission to bring the children to Angie's apartment, just so they would have a place to go that wasn't public. Of course, she still had to have Ms. Patel along with her. Jada, like the fool she was, had looked forward to having them indoors, to making them grilled cheese sandwiches or just sitting on the sofa and watching TV. She'd gotten two videos just in case. But when Shavonne, Kevon, and the baby had come into Angie's place, they'd sniffed around the sparsely furnished white living room like hostile cats. "Whose house is this?" Kevon wanted to know.

"It's not a house, baby, it's an apartment. And I'm sharing it with a friend."

"You like her more than us?" Kevon asked, and Jada had knelt beside him and held his shoulders.

"I love you," she said. "I couldn't love anybody more than I love you."

"So come back and be with us," Kevon said.

"I want to be with you more than anything," Jada had explained. "But your daddy went to the court and the judge decided it this way." She knew it wouldn't make sense to a six-year-old, but what more could she say? It didn't make sense to her. Ms. Patel sat quietly at the very edge of the sofa.

"I don't like this place," Shavonne said. "It's so small."

"I know. But it's bigger than the Volvo. And I can cook a little here. How about grilled cheese?" Jada asked.

"Okay," Kevon said reasonably, though Shavonne just shrugged her shoulders. Her son scrambled to a place at the table and Jada set Sherrilee down in one of the other chairs. She realized she should have a high chair, so she took off her scarf and tied it around Sherrilee's stomach, securing her to the seat.

"Grilled cheese, coming right up," she'd said. "And who wants a Barney glass?"

Sherrilee waved her hand and said, "Bah-ney."

"Who wants a Pocahontas glass?" Jada said, teasing.

"Not me," Kevon said.

"Oh, so I guess you don't want a Lion King one."

"Yes, I would," he said.

Out of the corner of her eye Jada saw Shavonne floating toward the table as if she were just a bit of dandelion fluff moving wihtout will. No matter what Michelle said about fats, they comforted kids and adults. Jada decided she'd have a grilled cheese, too.

She cut the crusts off and made squares and triangles out of the bread. It was only after the sandwiches, the milk, and the Mallomars that things fell apart. Sherrilee had gotten the scarf unknotted, scrambled down from the chair, out of the room, and into the little hallway leading to the two bedrooms. Jada was just putting in a video when she realized it and followed her a second too late. But Sherrilee had already gotten into the guest bedroom and scooped up Pinkie and a Beanie Baby from Jenna's pile. She came out carrying both of them. "Oh, look. It's the bunny," said Shavonne, and reached out for it.

"Mine," said Sherrilee, and pulled it and the other one into her chest.

"Are they both for her?" Shavonne asked, as if they were gifts.

"Mine," Sherrilee said again, and Jada tried to think quickly while she gently tried to pry the soft toys out of the baby's grip. But Kevon had jumped up, run down the hall, and was now standing in the doorway.

"Look!" he called out. "Shavonne! Come look!" Kevon ran into the room and moved immediately to Frankie's trucks. He sat down on the floor. Shavonne just stood in the doorway for a moment. Jada, holding the baby and the bloody, damaged rabbit, came up behind her. "Is this for us?" Kevon asked. "Is this our playroom?"

For a moment Jada felt paralyzed. Then Shavonne grabbed a closet door handle and pulled the door it open. She started to examine Jenna's dresses and shoes, hanging there neatly beside her mother's familiar clothes. "You're living here with some *other* children," Shavonne said, and walked out of the room.

"No! No other kids! *I* want this truck!" Kevon yelled, sitting on it with his knees almost up to his shoulders. He pushed with his feet. "Tonka, Tonka," he said.

It had taken Jada the next forty-five minutes to pry the toys away, get the kids together, and then try to explain that these were Jenna and Frankie's things. That Michelle and her husband were having a big fight and she and the children were staying here. "Then why can't *we* stay here?" Kevon asked.

Shavonne looked at him as if he were stupid. "Because *she* doesn't want us to," Shavonne said, and Kevon began to cry. Sherrilee picked up his wail, and in the end Jada had only gotten one of the Beanie Babies away.

She had tried the best she could to explain everything all over again, but she knew it was only words. Ms. Patel, who might have helped, sat silently, neither assisting nor being detrimental. But it was a humiliation to have anyone witness this. A humiliation, as well as a heartbreak. Jada had to herd the kids out to the car, and as they got into the Volvo to drive back to the house, Shavonne said, "I hate Tonya. She's a lazy slob. She doesn't fool me. And *you* don't fool me, either. I hate you, too."

• • •

Jada had been thinking seriously about just driving off into the sunset with the kids, but with the way the visits were going, the longer she put it off, the less likely she felt the kids would want to come with her. It wasn't that they preferred Clinton, or Tonya. It was just that they were so angry at her for abandoning them. But each time she thought of the hazards of trying to disappear with her kids, she became frightened. She saw what Michelle was up against with the criminal court system, and she wanted nothing to do with that trouble. Perhaps Barbados was the best idea. She decided that she would call the lawyer her mother and father had recommended. It took her a little while to find his name and number—she had jotted it down on the back of a receipt and stuffed it in the side pocket of her purse—but at last she found it and called him.

He took her call right away, though there were two secretaries who ran interference for him. "It's lucky you got me here," he said in a clipped accent. "I'm leaving Bridgetown this afternoon. But I'll be in the States next week. I wasn't planning to be in New York," he added. "Would it be possible for you to meet me in Boston? I think this is the kind of thing we need to cover in person, not over the phone."

Jada had to believe that it was some kind of a coincidence. She had never been in Boston in her life, yet she was going for Angie's caper. She didn't want to act as if she were a superstitious idiot, but perhaps God really did help those who helped themselves. They made a plan to meet and she thanked him.

"Oh, no thanks necessary, Mrs. Jackson. Let's just see if there's some way I can help."

"But it's *kidnapping*," Michelle said, her voice raised so that Jada had to shush her. Jenna and Frankie were sleeping in the other bedroom. Now the three women were sitting on Angie's bed.

"Don't tell me it's illegal to be with my own kids," Jada said, and now her voice was raised, but Michelle didn't have the heart to shush *her*. She tried to imagine what Jada must be going through, separated from her children but forced to watch Jenna and Frankie come home from school each day, filled with the same kind of news that Shavonne and Kevon used to bring home.

"I thought the plan was to appeal," Angie said. "Michael has really gone through a few channels to see what—"

"Forget about him and forget about it," Jada said. "It takes too long and we might not win at the end anyway. Meanwhile my babies are being hurt every single day."

"But I'm an officer of the court," said Angela. "I don't want to be a pussy, but a crime—"

"A crime is better than ruined children. When I picked up Sherrilee today, her whole body stiffened and she pulled away from me. That's how a baby lets you know how angry she is with you." Jada paused. "She may never forget this. She may never forgive this abandonment." She got up off the bed and walked to the other side of the crowded room. She had worked and worked on this plan. It wasn't without risk, but it seemed as if it would work, as long as the Volvo would.

She couldn't wait for another run at the court, so what else was there to do? "You don't have to help," Jada said calmly to Angie. "Neither do you," she said to Michelle. "But I'm going to do it anyway."

"You can't do something like this alone," Angie said.

"If you won't help me, I'll have to," Jada said coldly. "And I . . . there are organizations that assist women in my situation."

"Jada, they're strictly outside the law. You'd have to be underground for years. Maybe forever. And if you're caught—and you probably would be—you'd be criminally prosecuted. You'd go to prison," Angie said.

"Not if I leave the country," Jada said. "I'm thinking of going to Barbados with the kids."

Michelle took Jada's hand. "I'll help," she said. "I'll do whatever it takes. You need those kids back, and they need you. Whatever the risk."

Jada looked at her friend. And she realized just how far her friend would go for her.

"What if you fail?" Angie asked.

"It couldn't be worse than this," Jada said.

"Even if you fail, at least they'll know that you love them. That you wanted them," Michelle said. "Isn't that the most important thing?"

"Yes," Jada said.

Angie sighed. "I'm in," she said. She looked down at herself. "Do prison stripes run vertical or horizontal? What's the first step?"

"Calling my mother again," Jada told them.

50

Lights, camera, blackmail

"Do I look fat?" Angie asked, and both Michelle and Jada nodded. "Good," Angie said. She wanted to look fat rather than pregnant. She was starting to show, and she had put on weight even before she'd started showing. But as the costume designer as well as the script writer and director, she thought it was best for her to look as unattractive and non-threatening as possible in this scene.

She'd called Lisa to confirm meeting her. She'd pulled her hair back into a ponytail, and aside from lipstick, hadn't put on any makeup at all. Okay. What had she forgotten? She'd made reservations at a restaurant for dinner. She almost wished she hadn't gone to Michelle's dentist to get her tooth fixed, that way she'd be guaranteed not to overeat in front of Lisa. "Oh, wait," she said. "I can't forget this," and walked to the side of her bed and picked up the empty Shreve, Crump & Lowe box.

"I've got the ring," Michelle said. She was wearing enough makeup for both of them, Angie thought, and the Chanel-like suit she'd bought, which was tiny. But the part she had to play almost required one of those tiny versions—one where the knit skirt was very short and the jacket clung in all the right places. Two of the brass buttons were actually lined up over her nipples. But Michelle didn't look cheap and available—she looked expensive and available.

Michelle opened her little purse and took out a small Macy's bag. "Here we have it," Michelle said. "An heirloom hot off the jewelry counter. The best cubic zirconium money could buy." She showed it to Jada. "Does it look too new?" she asked.

"Nah," Jada said. "Tasteful. Very tasteful. Not too big for those old money people and not too small to be untempting. Just don't take it out in daylight," she advised Angie as she handed her the ring. "They shine like crystal then, and don't fool anybody."

Jada was wearing the low-cut orange sweater and tight black leather pants they'd bought for the occasion. She'd had her hair done and it was pulled back into a smooth chignon, anchored with what looked like a hundred small braids. She had orange lipstick on and had done something to her eyes, something with a lot of mascara. Whatever it was, she looked great.

"You should dress like that *all* the time," Angie said.

"I used to," Jada told her, "but I didn't think the bank would appreciate it. Of course, at Price Chopper it might make me employee of the week."

"What shoes are you wearing?" Michelle asked.

"I don't know. What do you think, girlfriend? The black boots or the stilettos?"

Michelle stopped and regarded her seriously. "Well, *I'm* going with stilettos—real killers—so just for a change, I think maybe the boots. Mr. Wakefield might like a smorgasbord."

"I don't want to look like a dyke."

Angie laughed. "Yes, you do," she said, and looked at her watch. "The kids are with Michael, we're looking good, so let's go. We've got to catch the shuttle."

Michelle sashayed into Reid Wakefield's office at Andover Putnam. She knew she looked good because the receptionist and four or five secretaries had really given her the once-over. She felt like Cinderella—after the fairy godmother's makeover. She was much more comfortable in jeans and a white shirt, but she could do this for her friend, and it was almost fun, in a Lana Turner sort of way.

She walked into Angie's ex-husband's office and smiled. He stood up and he was *very* tall, and *very* good-looking. He wasn't her type—she'd always liked small, dark men— but she could recognize this guy's good looks. His charms were certainly external, but she could see what Angie had found attractive. "Mr. Wakefield," she said, and extended her hand.

He leaned across the desk, a lot farther than he had to, and took her hand. Unless she was wrong, he also held it just a moment too long. Oh, this boy was trouble, no doubt about it. For a moment Michelle, almost felt sorry for his fiancée, but then she remembered that she was getting exactly what she deserved. "Shall I sit down here?" she asked in her littlest voice.

"No, please, make yourself comfortable on the sofa." He came from around the desk and sat down in the chair across from her. Not, she noticed, in the more comfortable easy chair beside the sofa, but the one where he could see her better. She crossed her legs to give him something to look at and then glanced toward the open door.

"I think we're going to need some privacy," she said, and he jumped up, crossed the office in just a few strides, and was back, the door safely closed.

"Mr. Wakefield," she said, "I have to confess that I've already told you a lie."

His smile wavered for a moment and one golden eyebrow rose, as if on its own. "Really?" he asked. "What was the lie? And why did you tell it?"

"I gave you a false name. I'm not really Anthea Carstairs. I only did it because I'm married to a very prominent man. I didn't want that to influence you before I reached you and got a chance to speak with you face-to-face."

Reid adjusted his own face. "Well, I don't specialize in matrimonial law, I do contract work mostly, and though I feel I wouldn't be easily swayed, I—"

Michelle leaned forward and said three words. "Charles Henderson Moyers."

Now both of Reid's eyebrows moved together up his forehead. Everybody knew about the Moyers family—the enormous wealth that came down from the long-dead father and the feud among his three sons. Their wealth was matched only by the tragedies they'd experienced. "The reclusive brother?" Reid asked.

Michelle nodded. "The richest. And the oldest," she said. "But I didn't mind that. We've been married for eleven years, Mr. Wakefield. And they were my best years. When a man is his age, it takes young flesh to move him." She lowered her eyes, just for a moment, as if it had been hard to say that. Surprisingly, none of it had been hard. Maybe she should have been an actress, Michelle thought, and then looked right back at Reid.

"Well," the lawyer said, and cleared his throat. "What exactly seems to be the difficulty now?" he asked.

"I signed a pre-nup and agreed that I wouldn't get a penny if I slept with another man. I've never broken my promise, Mr. Wakefield. Do you believe me?"

He nodded slowly as she kept her eyes on him, as if she were a snake and he was a mesmerized bit of prey. This was fun! Playing with this jerk was better than cleaning.

Michelle stuck the tip of her tongue out, just a quarter of an inch, and dampened her lips. She thought that maybe she'd gone too far, it was too much, but when he crossed his leg quickly, as if to hide himself, she decided it had been just the right thing to do.

"Charles wants a divorce," she said. "He's found another woman. That's all right with me, but not on his terms. He's accusing *me* of adultery and he wants to give me virtually nothing. After more than a decade."

Reid frowned. "But the man has billions," he said.

"And I'm innocent," she pointed out. "But the Moyers are notoriously strange about money. Remember when his daughter was kidnapped about fifteen years or so ago and he wouldn't pay ransom? They had to send him—gee, I think it was three of Meredith's fingers. And they came three *different* weeks. *And* she had been a violinist." Michelle shook her head. "Poor Meredith." She sighed.

Reid nodded his head. "I remember reading about that," he told her.

"Well, the Moyers have a way of forgetting their pasts. Meredith was his second wife's child. I'm his fifth wife. No children. And I think he's lining up this new one to be his sixth. Can you imagine? Not even divorced, and lining up your next wife?" Michelle asked, but Reid Wakefield III didn't notice her sarcasm.

"Wasn't it Fitzgerald who said the rich are different than you and I?" he asked.

Michelle didn't know who Fitzgerald was, but she smiled. "He was wrong," she said. "They're very, *very* different. Anyway, it's time for another change, and I honestly don't mind that, but I've played by the rules. I need help to make sure he does." She stared across at him again. She tried to use the look she'd used on Frank when she wanted to go upstairs. Reid nodded.

"Isn't it very warm in here?" Michelle asked. "Do you mind if I take off my jacket?" He shook his head and she shrugged the jacket off her shoulders, knowing that the little silk T-shirt she was wearing beneath it clung just perfectly. Worth every penny. She took a deep breath and pushed her breasts in his direction.

"To finish up my confession," she said, "there's something else I have to be candid about. I *have* slept with other women." She actually watched the man keep his face still, but he swallowed. It was a big swallow that moved his Adam's apple like a high-speed elevator, down and up. "I did it at first because *he* wanted me to. Then, about two years ago, I met a woman who . . . well, she was different. Charles had introduced her and set up the threesome the way he always did, but she was just . . ." Michelle stopped. She tried to show shame. Then she put her head down, counted to five, and lifted her head again, tossing her hair. "I'm not apologizing to you," she said. "I'm *not* ashamed." He nodded. "I'm just telling you this because that is what Charles is using as his leverage, as an example of my so-called adultery. But the fact is, I do love her."

She leaned across and touched Reid's knee. She could feel it, hot, through the fabric of his Brooks Brothers trousers. What else was hot in there, she wondered. Michelle made her voice almost break. "I think a woman has to love somebody or a part of her dies." Oops. That was *really* a Lana Turner line, Michelle thought. But it appeared that Mr. Wakefield had gotten over the shock. She wasn't sure if it was lust and greed that she saw in his eyes, or a combination of the two. "*I'm* not greedy, Mr. Wakefield," she told him. "I'd settle for a hundred million. It's nothing to Charles. Do you think your firm could handle this?" she asked. "Do you think *you* could?"

"Oh, I'm certain that we could."

She smiled and stood up. "Thank you," she said. "Thank you *so* much. I don't want to stay here too long. I never know when I'm being followed. That's why I used a made-up name. But I'm really Katherine. Katherine Moyers." She extended her hand and this time *she* held *his* with both of her own. "We'll have to talk about fees," she said. "I know that this won't come cheap, but I need to feel that I can trust you completely. That would be worth *any* amount of money."

He nodded. "I know that you can," he said. "I just have to make sure that *you* know that you can."

"Well, time will tell." She took her hands away. There definitely was a current between them. Some men were so easy, it was ridiculous, Michelle thought. She picked up her jacket and then turned to him again. "May I ask you for a very big favor?" she murmured.

"Of course." He nodded.

"I would like you to meet Jenette," she told him. "I mean, eventually she would probably have to testify. And I would just like her opinion of you. I have no family. I have no one else to trust about a decision like this."

"It's no problem," he said.

"*Everything* is a problem when you're Mrs. Charles Henderson Moyers," she said with a sigh. "I'm staying at the Four Seasons, but you can't come there. Do you know a bar where we could meet you, just briefly, when you finish work? Someplace quiet where we won't be seen by anyone from my crowd."

"Of course," he said, and Michelle saw he didn't have a moment of hesitation. He was excited by the idea! He gave her an address, and then he walked her all the way to the elevator, pressed the button for her, and helped her in it. "See you at six," he said.

And she nodded as the doors closed. When she got off the elevator, she went immediately to the pay phone near the restroom and left a message for Jada on Angie's home answering machine.

Angie sat quietly, trying not to show any nerves at all. She'd arrived early so she wouldn't have to reveal all of herself to Lisa at one time. Her face looked plain, and her dress did, too. She didn't need Lisa to see her weight and totally gloat.

Angie had made reservations at a Commonwealth Avenue bistro for the same time that Jada should be meeting up with Samuel Dumfries. Timing was everything. When Lisa finally came in, late as usual, and as tall and thin and blond as ever, Angie watched her look around the room, and, at first, pass over her. Well, she didn't look like the old Angie, and she didn't feel like her, either. She raised her hand and Lisa made a smile—even across the room Angie could see she wasn't genuinely smiling, she made one on her face—then came toward the corner table.

While Lisa, usually graceful, fumbled with the chair and her hello, her purse, and her coat, Angie felt how very pleasant it was not to have anything to feel guilty about. She didn't even feel stupid anymore. Anyone you trust, any friend or confidant, always has the option of betrayal. With the grace of detachment, Angie could observe the woman she considered so thoughtless. Lisa managed to finally settle herself, then glance at her, only to avert her eyes and pick up the menu. "It's good to see you," she said. "You look great."

Two lies in a single breath! Angie actually almost smiled. "I feel great," she said honestly, and thought of her child, the secret she was carrying.

"Really?" Lisa inquired, and for a moment sounded surprised. Then she recovered. "Well, that's great," she said. "You've found another job?" she asked.

Angie wondered if her "friend" was really interested, thinking about alimony, or just being competitive. "Yeah," Angie said. "I'm doing a different kind of work."

"That's great," Lisa said.

How many "greats" had that been in less than three minutes? Angie wondered. It was grating on her, so she smiled and said, "And I got a dog. A Great Dane."

"Great!" Lisa said again, and Angie couldn't help it—she laughed, but picked up her own menu to hide her face.

"Should we order?" Lisa said. "I'm just starving."

Angie knew what that meant. Lisa would order a salad with no dressing, and a piece of fish broiled without butter or oil. That was as hungry as Lisa ever got—for food, at least.

The waiter arrived and asked for their orders. They asked for a bottle of Pellegrino, along with the mango chicken and asparagus that Angie wanted, and—big surprise—the salad and fish for Lisa. Angie wondered what Lisa ate when she wasn't starving. She also wondered how she could have made a best friend of this woman. How had her judgment and taste been so clouded? But wasn't there a time when they *had* liked each other, or had Lisa been acting all the time? Did Lisa eat at home? Angie wondered if Lisa brought Ben & Jerry's to bed after sex with Reid, the way she used to.

"I told Reid that I'd be out late tonight," Lisa said, as if the name had floated between them. "I mean, I don't know what your schedule is, but I have plenty of time."

"Great," Angie told her, using the word on purpose. As if she wanted to spend more time than necessary with this woman. But timing was important. There was work being done by her friends while she sat here with her enemy.

"Anyway," Lisa went on. "I brought all the things you asked for. I thought I could save you a trip out to Marblehead. You know, I figured it might be . . . well, awkward or too painful for you."

Oh shit, Angie thought. Awkward? This was absolutely wrong, catastrophic, even. Why did something always go wrong? She *had* to get to Marblehead, and with Lisa, and in two hours, max. "Well, and I've brought something for you," she said in a voice she managed to keep calm. She'd have a whole mango chicken to think through. Lisa wouldn't defeat all their careful plans.

51

Taking tea for two

Jada felt weird walking across Boston Common. People looked at her. Was it because she was black? Or because of her get-up? She certainly wasn't dressed like a Bostonian, she thought. Leather pants were definitely *not* what most women wore in Boston. Jada got across to the other side of the park—that was apparently all the Common was—and after all those years of hearing about it, Jada was a little disappointed. She'd never been to Boston, and she'd expected more.

Now, though, she had to hurry to meet Samuel Dumfries, the son of the husband of her mother's cousin. What a way to find help, she thought! Only Bajans would bother to go through that much trouble, and when they did, the help given was usually incompetent. Still, she was desperate, and he sounded competent over the phone. What did she have to lose?

She walked out of the Common and by a corner that looked very familiar, but it couldn't be, since she'd never been in Boston before. Still, it was a place she'd been. She stood there for a second until it registered with her—it was the place where *Cheers* had been filmed, the place where everybody knew your name. *Fine,* she thought. Now she was confusing old television with real life. Except here everybody didn't know Jada's name, and that was a good thing, since she was about to perform lewd and lascivious acts, or at least pretend to, as well as meet with an off-shore lawyer to talk about illegal immigration. Jada shook her head. All her life she'd been a good girl, following the rules, behaving the way her mama told her to. How had it all come to this?

She crossed the wet street and walked into the impressive warmth, color, and gold-leaf grandeur of the Ritz Carlton. She expected nothing from this. She was only showing up because she had nothing to do until the caper with Michelle at six. When she heard Michelle's voice on the recording, she sounded all excited and put together. Good old Cindy. But now she had to walk across the Common and meet Mr. Dumfries for tea.

She smiled. When was the last time she'd been on her own, well-dressed and in a city where she knew no one? She couldn't remember. It made her feel adventurous suddenly, as if she weren't thirty-four but twenty-four. She strode through the foyer and hallway. She hoped she didn't look like a hooker—her walk had already proved to her that the hair extensions, boots, and leather did not exactly scream "Beacon Hill Matron." At the concierge desk, she asked where tea was being served and was relieved that she was given polite directions. No wonder they called classy things "ritzy." This was it.

It was easy to spot Dumfries. He was the only black man in the room, and he stood up when she came in. He was tall, but a little too thin for his frame—and he was very, very black. It couldn't have been easy for him on the island, where each shade darker usually meant a rung down the social ladder. Jada crossed the room and realized closer up that his skin had the kind of darkness that seemed to absorb light. His face was arresting—he had gray eyes, a light gray, and the whites of his eyes were very, very white. It made his face almost, well, spooky. He wasn't DDG, but he was a handsome man, and when he smiled at her, she relaxed a little bit.

"You are Jada Jackson?" he said.

She nodded. "You have got to be Samuel Dumfries."

He smiled again. His teeth were very white, too. "Sit down, please," he said. He didn't have an island accent. His voice was deep, but his enunciation was clipped, precise. It was actually quite British.

"Tea?" he asked, and she was surprised to see that he was already sipping a cupful. "It's India, not China, but at least it's properly brewed," he said.

"Well, thank goodness for that," she wisecracked. Samuel Dumfries didn't seem to get it. Jada thought of her Lipton tea bags at home. She'd forgotten how seriously some islanders took their tea. The English influence.

He shook his head. "It is amazing that there are only two or three places left in all of Boston where you can get a cup of brewed tea."

"That *has* always amazed me," Jada said, joking once again.

But this time he turned to her, paused, and said, "You're having me on, aren't you?"

"If that means I'm teasing you, you're absolutely right. But I'm not sure that I speak English."

He smiled again. "I think you're doing just fine," he said. "Sorry I was so thick. I wasn't expecting humor. I mean, your mother explained your situation and I . . ."

Jada wondered what the hell she was doing. Well, she knew what she was doing—she was flirting. But she hadn't done it in fifteen years. Why now? It must have been the leather pants, she thought, or maybe it was the hair extensions. She noticed him looking at her hair. It *did* look good. If she had an extra hundred and eighty-five dollars to throw away every month, she might keep it this way. "Mr. Dumfries," she said. "I know I have a serious problem."

"So I understand. Sugar?"

She blinked. Wow. Was Samuel Dumfries flirting with her? For a moment she thought he had called her "sugar." Then she realized he was offering her the bowl of sugar lumps. Well, she'd already taken her lumps from a man. "No. Thanks."

"Milk?" he asked.

"No," she said. She didn't give a damn about the tea. She never drank the stuff unless she had cramps. "Anyway, Mr. Dumfries, I don't know how much my mother told you. Knowing her, it was quite a lot."

Samuel Dumfries smiled. "Your mother has never had a reputation for being tongue-tied," he agreed. "It was quite a sobering story."

And she wondered how they'd told it, and how much of it he believed. Suddenly, she wished she wasn't wearing this ridiculous outfit and the hair. She wished the orange lipstick and the flirting had never happened. Because though she'd come to this table in Boston without hope, something about this man, some emanation, gave her the feeling that he knew how to get things done, that he was used to having power.

"Well, anything my mother told you is actually not as bad as the reality." So Jada launched into the facts and she went through an entire tea pot, a jug of hot water, four lumps of sugar, two Kleenexes, and a trip to the ladies' room before she was done. Samuel Dumfries listened through it all, nodding, asking intelligent questions, and looking at her with his strange gray eyes.

He handled the waiter smoothly, and though they were the only black couple in the place, and had stayed so long past tea time that they were the last ones there, he never let her feel rushed, nor beholden to the staff. There was a deep calmness to him.

"So," he said, when she was finally done, "what will you do next?"

"I'm going to be honest with you," she said. "I know you're an attorney, but I feel that I have to move against the law, or perhaps I should say beyond it. When my parents came to visit, they suggested going to the island; I had already thought of the idea but resisted. I've never even gotten a traffic ticket in my life. But now I'm sure that for the sake of my children, I have to get them back. And I can't wait for the court to catch up with what's right and what's good for them." She waited for his eyes to close with disapproval, or for him to actually tell her he wouldn't, *couldn't,* discuss it. But instead he nodded.

"One way to look at all common law is simple, as a code to settle property claims," he said. "The unfortunate thing about that is that while the law is a truly beautiful construction, human conception of what property is has changed significantly while the law carries remnants of the old patterns. Our ancestors were once regarded as property. Wives were. So were children. Instead of thinking solely of the children, the law here is based on precedents and property. That, and of course, fake and misleading evidence."

Did he actually believe her? All the wrong steps, all the slanted testimony, all the accidents of fate that made her sound at the worst an incompetent mother, and at the best, a poor judge of legal help, the victim of a clever man? "So, if I can get them on a plane to Barbados, what is likely to happen once I get there?"

They talked it over for a little while longer, until Jada understood that the situation would be far from ideal. As the light faded outside the window, so did her hope.

"But do you know the Cayman Islands?" Mr. Dumfries asked.

Jada shook her head. "You see," he said, "since you're not a citizen of Barbados, it would be difficult to find a way to block your husband there. But as an American in the Cayman Islands, a place where I do a great deal of business, if you had . . . well, a certain amount of cash on deposit, you might do very well. There would be the added benefit of no reason for your husband to seek you out there, and the economy is booming. Anyone with a banking background like yours could find work. I just thought that perhaps . . . "

Jada could hardly believe it. What was this guy's NUP? "You mean you might help? You don't disapprove of what I'm trying to do?" she asked.

"Protecting your children? Certainly not," he said. "Of course, I can't condone breaking the law, but I certainly know what it is to live with injustice. After all, I was educated in the UK."

Just then Jada noticed his watch, the thinnest, most elegant she'd ever seen. But she also noticed the time. "Oh my God," she said. "I have an appointment. And I can't be late." She'd expected nothing from this man, but somehow she had spent nearly two hours with him! It had seemed like twenty minutes. And she had been given some good counsel, support, and encouragement. Now, though, she didn't even have time to be gracious about it.

"I'm going to be late if I don't leave right now," she said. She stood up and he did, too. Awkward for a moment, she extended her hand. "I'm so happy to have met you. I'm going to think about your advice."

"Oh, do more than think about it," he said. "You will need some help." He took out a card and handed it to her. Jada had to leave, but she didn't want to break this comforting connection. "Why don't you give me your phone number?" he said.

She gave him Angie's number and picked up her purse. She hoped there was a taxi waiting right outside, otherwise she'd never make it. "Thank you," she told him. And, much as she disliked having to do it, she left.

52

During which Jenette and Katherine play hard to get,
while Reid is merely hard

Jada saw Reid come into the bar and knew, even before Michelle began to whisper, that he was Angie's husband. His eyes took a little while to adjust to the dimness; in that time Jada knew a lot about him. She could read it from his height, the blue suit he wore, that arrogant, light yellow Foulard tie, and the way he stood in the doorway. Michelle raised her hand and the movement turned his head toward them.

As Reid crossed the room, making his way among the mostly empty chairs clustered around the tiny cocktail tables, Jada had him pegged. He was one of those white boys who owned the world. They were the kind of men who were so high on the totem pole of power and prestige, that stooping to do a black woman didn't threaten their status, it was a forbidden treat. Blue-collar white guys rarely looked at her, but Jada could see how Reid Wakefield's eyes opened when he saw her. She wondered if a hundred and fifty years ago or so, his ancestors had bought black women at auction. Well, to be fair, she thought Angie had said they were all Bostonians for the last two hundred years. For all she knew, they were Abolitionists all the way back.

"Hello," he said to Michelle, and Jada reminded herself again that her friend was now Katherine and she was Jenette. "May I join you?" he asked, turning to include her in his smile, smooth as the skin inside a baby's elbow.

"Certainly," Michelle said, and Reid slid into the banquette seat across from Jada. She smiled at him, but couldn't make the smile move up to her eyes, so she half closed them.

"Jenette, this is Reid Wakefield," "Katherine" said, and Jada extended her long hand.

"I've already heard a lot about you," she said, deepening and softening her voice. She thought she saw Michelle's mouth twitch, and realized for the first time this could be a lot of fun, but she decided it was best to play it straight. Well, she told herself, as straight as a *faux* lesbian lure could play it. "Katherine says you've already won her trust, but in my opinion Katherine has always been far too trusting." She smiled, but made her smile cold.

"Well," Reid said in a corporate-lawyer-I-bill-by-the-hour voice, "I'd like to think that my reputation and my personality will gain your trust, too."

"Well," she echoed. "I certainly do know you by reputation. Otherwise we wouldn't be here." Did she see Michelle smirk again? She wasn't sure. She took Michelle's hand. What the hell. Might as well make the first move and see how he reacted. "Katherine needs someone who can take care of her," she said. "She deserves it. I know Charles better than I wish I did, and I know what he's put her through." She paused a minute to let the guy imagine a few of those scenes. Then she opened Michelle's palm and she kissed it, putting it back down on the table.

Michelle left her hand lying open like a blown flower, and the orange imprint of Jada's lipstick seemed to shine like neon off of Michelle's white, white flesh: SEX! SEX! SEX!

Jada looked across at Reid. He was staring at Michelle's palm, mesmerized. Jada allowed herself to smile. That old black magic, she thought. But it was more than the race issue. It was the lesbian thing. She had no idea why white men's fantasies so often seemed to center around two women, when they were so often inadequate even with one. Maybe it took the pressure off them. She couldn't think of anything less attractive then going to bed with two gay men.

Reid kept staring at Michelle's anointed hand. Jada thought it was about time to break the spell and give Reid a complete show, so she stood up and let him eye her. "I'm going to the toilet," she said. "I'll be right back." And she made sure that her stomach was pulled in and her ass was not just high but swinging as she crossed the room in her tight leather pants. *Fantasize this,* she thought. She'd let Michelle take the next shift. What the hell—she could use the time to actually use the toilet.

She strutted across the restaurant, passing the bar, aware that many of the men's eyes were on her. As she turned toward the ladies' room, a man looked up from his drink and eyed her. "Black is beautiful," he said, and she ignored him. "Hey," he said. "I'd love to get into your panties."

Jada looked him over. "Sorry," she said. "I already have an asshole in them." She moved on, smooth as silk, to the restrooms. As she sat down on the seat, she realized she was humming, and when she began singing, it was Cole Porter's brilliant lyrics. "'Do do that voodoo that you do so well,'" she sang, and then began to laugh, alone in the stall.

Yes, she thought. She was voodoo to a guy like Reid Wakefield. She could see the appeal of a black woman and a white woman together in bed for a man like him. It was breaking so many taboos at one time, and there was an aesthetic that made it particularly juicy. The contrast of the dark skin against the light, so that, arranged properly, two women could look like a photo and a negative of one another.

There was nothing personal about it; actually, it was impersonal. He was already interested. She didn't think it would be hard to get Reid more than interested. And she had to admit that after the years of Clinton virtually ignoring her, she was enjoying the attention. The *frisson* of sexual tension was something she'd almost forgotten about. But it would only be tension, and lots of it.

Angie could hardly believe it. Lisa had the nerve to ramble on, not only about her job and the people at work—people that Angie had been forced to abandon because of Lisa's underhandedness—but then she continued, and as Angie allowed her to get away with it, she began to talk about the engagement, her wedding plans, and even the honeymoon. It was unbelievable! Had she always been this insensitive, or was she spiteful?

"Reid wanted to take a week, but I said you can't go to France for a *week*," she was saying now. "It would be ridiculous. So we made it ten days, though I wanted two weeks."

Angie nodded. For their honeymoon, she and Reid had gone to Bermuda for five days, but she wasn't going to mention that.

When the waiter came to remove their plates, Lisa lifted a Saks shopping bag to the table and handed it over to Angie. For one crazy moment, Angie thought it might be a present. What gift did Lisa think Angie wanted from her? A gun to shoot her with? Arsenic for her drink? Or maybe it was a make-over bag: exercise clothes, cross-trainers, and gift certificates to a gym and cosmetic surgeon, so Angie could keep the next man she found.

Angie hesitated, then looked into the bag and recognized her own blue sweater, the one she'd left behind in Marblehead. Underneath it was the night-light she'd had since she was five—a figurine of a little girl bending over a duckling. There were also the photo albums she'd asked for, her high school yearbook, and some other stuff. "I have the rest out in the car," Lisa said.

Angie smiled wanly. This was not the plan. It was supposed to be a house call. And Angie, not Lisa, was supposed to call the shots. Why was she so easily outflanked by this narcissist? Was it her personality defect, or Lisa's? Angie tried to look at her watch without letting Lisa notice. She tried to think. There wasn't much time, so Angie was relieved when the waiter brought the bill. She noticed that Lisa didn't reach for it—a minor irritation in the face of this larger one. Angie took a look at the tab, and put out exactly half of what was owed, along with half a tip. Then she pushed it toward Lisa, because she sure as hell wasn't paying for this dinner.

"Oh," Lisa said, as if receiving a check at the end of a restaurant meal was a complete novelty. She fumbled in her bag and wound up putting crumpled bills and a handful of change on the table. Angie remembered now that like the queen, Lisa never carried much money.

Okay, she thought. She needed to get control again and get this show on the road. Quickly. When Lisa next looked up, Angie very obviously took out the Shreve, Crump & Lowe box. She saw Lisa's eyes widen. Only then did Angie stand, putting the box back in her pocket. Ha! "Well, let's go out to your car and get the rest of my stuff," she said calmly, but she was still panicked. She had to get over to the condo and she had to do it in the next hour. Considering the drive would take at least thirty minutes, it didn't give her much leeway. What if she couldn't get there? Everything would be ruined. Lisa would forever think she'd humiliated a poor, pathetic, broken Angie. A fat Angie. Angie couldn't help but clench her teeth.

Lisa, as if mesmerized, followed her out of the restaurant. Angie thought of *The Lord of the Rings*. *All* rings had a lot of power over women. They didn't have to be smithed in Mordor. She imagined herself as Bilbo and Lisa as sneaky Gollum. Easy image. Next she'd be hissing, *"What has it got in its pockets?"*

When they reached Lisa's car, Lisa flipped open the trunk and there was another bag of the cast-offs—oops, personal treasures—she'd mentioned: an afghan crocheted by Angie's grandmother, and torn leather-covered bookends that looked like real books. In the tiny light of the trunk, Angie looked through the carton. Lisa was smiling. "I tried to fold everything neatly," she said. "But you know me, I'm not good at packing." Angie wondered if Lisa's hand was itching for the ring.

"I don't see my diary here," Angie said.

"Oh. No? I tried to bring everything. There's that sketchbook or whatever I found on one of the shelves."

"No," Angie said. "I'm not talking about that. I mean my journal."

"You didn't mention a journal. That wasn't on the list."

It wasn't, and for just this very reason. It was Plan B. Obviously, a necessary one, with a girl as sneaky as Lisa. Angie turned from the trunk and looked at Lisa with a very woebegone face. "Did you read it?" she asked, her face a mask of desperation and embarrassment. "Promise me you didn't read it."

"No, no," Lisa assured her. "I didn't even *find* it." But it looked as if she now wished that she had.

"Oh. I can't believe this! I think it was right there on the bookshelf. I'm sure I asked for it," Angie said. "I *have* to have it back, Lisa. I'd die if anyone else read it."

"Well, I'll send it to you," Lisa said. "I promise."

Yeah! Like Angie could trust her word. Angie put her hand into her pocket, and silently took out the box. She flipped it open again. In the darkness, illuminated only by the trunk light, the ring gleamed. She fluttered the box just a little, to enhance the gleaming sparkle, and heard Lisa let out a breath that became white mist in the cold air. *That's it, Lisa. Here's the piece that will make you a Wakefield, the thing that will join you forever to your future in-laws from hell.* Angie figured thirty seconds was enough bait and snapped the box shut.

"Look, Lisa. This stuff might look like a bunch of junk to you, but it's important to me. I need you to respect that."

"Oh, I do. I do!" Lisa told her, the acquisitiveness in her voice almost as visible as the mist from her mouth.

"So the thing that *I* need the most is my journal," Angie said. They stood there for a moment, and Angie simply waited.

"Well, let's just go to the house and get it," Lisa said at last. Yes! As she got in her car to follow Lisa, Angie had to laugh out loud. Enemies were easy once you realized they weren't friends. Angie just hoped after Lisa put the damned ring on, the gold-toned metal of the shank of the ring would leave a nasty green line on Lisa's so-perfect skin.

53

Both a strip and a tease

Michelle got out of Reid's car and made sure her skirt was hiked up high—not that it wasn't already only the width of Santa's belt. But she and Jada had invested a lot of Frank's charge card in lingerie and great stockings. Now was the time to show them off. Reid was out of the car and running to her side for a look even before Jada pulled up in the rental car.

Michelle almost giggled as she stepped out of the car and felt him eyeing her. She was proud of her acting over drinks—in fact, though she actually drank almost nothing, she'd managed to make it look as if she'd consumed quite a bit, and was behaving so giddily she almost felt she actually had a buzz. And it had been exciting to drive with Reid because the man was so beside himself with lust. Michelle had spent most of the ride telling him how much she really trusted him, how important it was that no one saw her, and how long it had been since she'd been with a man. Blah, blah, blah. "Except Charles, of course," she had said. "But there is a reverse proportion to the size of his bank accounts and his . . ." She'd paused in a ladylike way, "personal proportions." Then she'd squeezed the inside of Reid's right leg.

Now, outside the car, Jada sauntered over to her. "I don't think it's a good idea for you to be seen here on the street in front of a man's house," she said to Michelle. "I mean, Katherine, that you must always remember Charles's pre-nup."

Michelle looked at Reid. "Jenette, he's not a man. He's my lawyer," she said, and giggled.

Jada turned to Reid and gave him an appraising look. "You have *really* caught her fancy," Jada said. "Shall we take our little love baby inside?" She could see that Reid's face was flushed. She bet that Michelle had been a perfect little tease.

Reid, dumb as a cocker spaniel in heat, led the way, opened the door; Michelle and Jada followed him into Angie's first home. The condo was nice, Jada thought. Young, rich, white kids lived well. Not like her and Clinton's first place in Yonkers. It was hard to imagine that she and Michelle hadn't known Angie when she lived here and thought she was safe and happy. All of the wood furniture was that fifties blond stuff that had become popular again, and the rugs and walls were light. "Can I get you ladies a drink?" Reid asked as he put down the keys, gesturing toward the sofa as he turned toward the kitchen.

"Oh, we're not ladies," Jada said, her voice deep. Reid turned back to look at her. "We're women. We're *definitely* women. But even Katherine is not a lady." She moved over to Michelle and put her hand on Michelle's long hair, stroking it. She thought she could see the white boy's jimmy move along the left side of his crotch. Hmmm. She looked down at her dark, dark hand on top of Michelle's light, light hair, but only so she could see what time it was. How long did they have?

"Well, I stand corrected," Reid said.

"Oh, is it standing?" Michelle asked and giggled. Then she threw herself back on the sofa, her legs spread, her arms akimbo.

Reid took a deep breath. Jada wondered if he was a religious man, because if he believed in any kind of God, he was thanking Him right now. "I'll be right back," he said, and walked into the kitchen.

Michelle and Jada looked at each other and began tearing off their clothes. "Don't touch me like that," Michelle whispered. "It was creepy."

"I just patted your head, Katherine," Jada said. "I did it for Mr. Rogers over there."

"Well, that's enough," Michelle told her. She'd gotten her jacket off and was sliding out of her obscene little skirt. Meanwhile, Jada took out a *Cosmopolitan,* laid it on the coffee table as planned. She had her orange sweater almost unbuttoned in the next minute, but for speed decided to just pull it over her head.

"Hey, listen," she whispered to Michelle. "Nothing personal, but the idea of touching your breast—or anyone's—makes me nauseous. I'm a Christian woman." She wiggled out of the leather slacks, revealing the orange silk underpants and garter belt holding up her stockings.

"Take off the boots," Michelle whispered, and shrugged out of her shirt. She was wearing a pink satin bra and matching hi-cut panties.

"What are you? The stylist for this shoot? Anyway, you leave your shoes on," Jada told her in return. "And don't touch me, either," she added. "I'll scream."

Just then Reid came through the swinging door, pushing it open with his back and turning around with a tray in front of him. When he saw the two of them, lingerie-clad beside the couch, he dropped the tray and everything on it. Jada had to laugh. Mr. Cool. "Oooh," she said. "Looks like you're going to have to pick up something more than us two ladies tonight."

It was amazing how easy it had been to get him half drunk, to proposition him, and to get him to invite them into his home. As they walked up the stairs to the bedroom, Jada shook her head. Men! She was still in her fancy lingerie, and the elastic of her garters slapped the back of her legs on each step. It was hard to believe women had actually worn these things for years. Pantyhose were bad enough.

She hoped Reid was enjoying the view, and wriggled an extra bit to be sure. She then tried to map out the next few moves. She was carrying her purse, which would have looked funny to anybody who didn't have a mind fogged by gin and lust. "Which door?" she asked, and Michelle, all pink and blond, stood at the top of the stairs and shrugged.

Reid passed them by and opened the door on the right. "In here," he said, his voice thick.

"Now, you're not married are you? We wouldn't want a man who would cheat," Michelle said in a teasing tone.

"No, I'm not married. Well, I *was* married, but she's living in New York now and the divorce is almost final." He ushered them into a large white bedroom.

Michelle immediately sat down at the edge of the bed. "So, we got you while you're still hot. Before all the other women could descend on a handsome, single, sexy lawyer." Reid had followed her and she moved toward his tie. He reached forward to kiss her, but she made sure that her face was turned just a little bit away. *Good move,* Jada thought. *He's the one we've got to pin, without a hit on us.* Michelle moved down to his shirt buttons while Jada opened her purse.

"How do you like it, Mr. Wakefield?" Jada asked, her own voice husky and almost secretive.

Reid pulled his eyes away from Michelle. He seemed fascinated by Jada, but almost afraid to be caught looking at her. White guilt. You know his great-grandaddy owned slaves. "I like it anyway you want," Reid said.

"I know ya gonna like it in a threesome," Jada said. "But do ya want it ribbed or fluorescent, or ribbed *and* fluorescent?" she asked, pulling out a handful of condoms. She put them all in his hands and lifted his thumb, putting it in her mouth for only one wet moment. *"You* decide," she said. *"I'll* apply." Then she turned back to her purse, put it on the floor beside the bed, and took out the body oil, the Polaroid and the little tube of Crazy Glue. Unlike the condoms, she left those three bits of paraphernalia on the floor.

Jada couldn't help smiling at this dumb white man. His eyes were glassy with forbidden lust. Guess it was true about white men, as well as black ones—their little heads did all the thinking and ignored the big one. Jada stood up. Michelle had gotten his shirt off, but . . .

"You still look overdressed to me," Jada said to Reid.

"Strip for us," Michelle suggested from her spot on the bed. She watched as Jada paraded around the foot of the bed in her gorgeous orange satin. She looked great, and so unselfconscious. What would happen when it was *her* turn? Michelle had never been completely naked in front of any man except Frank. Well, that was then, this was now. And the underwear wasn't any worse than a skimpy swimsuit, she guessed. It just *felt* different than a swimsuit. She forced herself to get on her knees and began untying Reid's shoes. "Do I have to be your geisha?" she asked, and batted her eyelashes up at him. Frank loved to see her kneel.

She pulled off Reid's shoes and then each sock slowly and suggestively. His feet were big, but she didn't feel like rubbing them, or any of his other parts, so she tugged at the cuff of his pants leg. As if he'd been mesmerized, and was deep in some kind of sexual daze, Reid unbuckled his pants in slow motion and unzipped his fly. That was the cue for Jada to wiggle up to Reid and tug at Reid's trouser legs. "Here," she said, "let Mama help. Mama wants to get to see how good you look, baby."

Michelle actually blushed, and wondered if that was the way Jada had talked to Clinton when they were in bed. It was funny: you knew a lot about your girlfriends, but you couldn't know what they were really like with their husbands. They spoke precisely about sex—but not with the feelings.

She felt Reid's rump rise, giving her the opportunity to pull down his trousers. She began to help Jada, and just hoped that his boxers wouldn't come off along with his pants. God, he had big, big feet. She *really* didn't want to see his thing.

He was actually wearing briefs, and to her relief, they didn't move when the trousers came off—although something inside them *was* moving. It wasn't dignified to think about, but Michelle had always imagined that movement looking like a hamster in a little laundry sack.

"Ooooh, nice chest, counselor," Jada cooed.

This guy was DDG. Too bad his NUP—or whatever Jada called it— was so screwed up. Michelle glanced at him again. His chest *was* nice— broad, flat and almost hairless. It looked like a swimmer's chest, Michelle thought, one of those Olympic guys. But Michelle couldn't imagine laying her head on it. For a moment it made her miss Frank's soft, dark hair. Well, she had no time for that. She had to get to work.

"You two are the most beautiful women I've ever seen," Reid said, his voice vague as if lost in a dream. At that, Michelle stood up. How dare he! What about Angie, or even Lisa. He was such a disloyal piece of work. She'd get him. She'd make him suffer, the louse. She put one foot back up on the bed, spike heel still on, then bent her head a little toward him and looked up at him through her veil of blond hair.

"Really?" she asked, and she saw the hamster move again. "Well, do you want us to tell you what we're going to do to each other? Or do you want to tell us what you're going to do to us? Or how about if you tell us what you'd like *us* to do to *you*?"

"Oh *maannn*," Reid groaned and pulled off his briefs.

Leaning against the bed post, Jada looked at Angie's husband's three piece combo and then at Michelle with a shrug and a little fluttered hand motion which meant, *So-so, nothing impressive.* Michelle made the little mouth she did when she didn't want to laugh out loud. Jada winked at her. She knew she couldn't laugh at this, of all moments—men were so sensitive about their size—so Michelle put her hands over her mouth. Then, when she was in control again, she moved her arms up over her head. She knew it emphasized her curves.

"Come over here," Reid said.

"Patience. Patience!" Jada said.

"Slow but steady. I hope we don't need to bind and gag you," Michelle warned. "We only do that to each other if we go too fast. Or if we're very, very naughty."

Reid's dick sprang up and almost did a little dance. Men and their machines. They so often lacked dignity. Jada looked at him as he motioned to her with his head. "Come on over here to the bed and join me. Please," he added, patting the mattress on his other side. That was better.

But they had to slow this down, Jada thought, or else it wasn't going to just *look* ungodly, it would *be* ungodly. "Well, before that . . . first I got some oil I want to put on you, baby," she said in her sexy voice. Well, it was her sexy voice or else she sounded like a black, female Austin Powers. So she switched to a Suzy Housekeeper tone. "But maybe I should first get a towel to protect the sheets," she suggested.

She took her time going into and returning from the bathroom, checking the time. She handed a bottle of oil to Michelle while she began to unfold the towel. She tried to think if there was anything she had forgotten, anything that could go wrong. The *Cosmo* was left downstairs, the timing was on the money, she hadn't gotten a call on her pager. It seemed all was in readiness.

"It's show time," Jada said, using the code term the three of them had created.

Smiling, Michelle walked up to Reid, who reached out and put his hands on her hips. Thank God, she thought, he didn't touch her breasts—she would have screamed and smacked him with the oil bottle. Instead, she took it and began to pour the oil over Reid's adulterous shoulders so that it ran down his back and chest. Then she decided to add more. He leaned back against her. Yuck! But "Ooohh," she crooned, pulling away. "I used too much. It was *too big* a squirt," she added with a leer, distracting him as much as she could.

Reid looked down at his glistening body. At that moment, Jada pulled the sheet from the upper corner of the bed, stripped it to the foot, and lay the towel down. "Rub on this, lamb," she purred. Behind Reid's back, she made a face at her friend.

Lamb to slaughter, Michelle thought. *Or maybe ram.*

Then Jada disappeared for a moment at the end of the bed. When she stood up, she turned to Michelle. "Don't get oil on his dickie-bird, Katherine," she warned, pouting. "*I* want to do that myself."

Michelle almost laughed out loud. Dickie-bird? "Why do you get it first?" she asked, pretending to pout. "I haven't had one in *sooo* long."

"Uh-uh-*oooh.* You women. You two girls. You . . ." Reid was breathless. "You're *unbelievable.*"

That, Jada thought, was the first accurate thing the jerk had said all night. She smiled and spread herself from the foot of the bed almost up to his lap. His eyes—appropriately in light of what was coming—were glued to her. Michelle chose that moment to put her face in front of his and rub it with oil.

"We're going to make you nice and slick," she said.

"Oh yeah," Jada agreed. "Slick. That's a good name for you, Mr. Wakefield. You're *very* slick now, honey." Hidden for the moment by Michelle, she popped open the cap of the Crazy Glue and in a single movement applied it all along one side of Reid's penis. Then she took her hand, asked the Lord's forgiveness, grabbed hold of the nasty thing, and pushed him on his side, holding his dick down—not against the towel, but the bare mattress.

Reid groaned, partly from the unexpected but longed-for touch, and partly, probably, from Jada's roughness. "Ummm. Ummmm. Ow. Ouch," Reid recited in a litany that quickly moved from intense pleasure to intense pain. "Wait! Ow! That hurts! Hey, what . . ." Just to be safe Jada slid the tube of glue along the exposed side of his penis, leaving a long thin line of wetness. She held his hip down with her own, giving the glue already applied the thirty seconds it needed to set.

Reid put his left hand up against himself just as she finished. Jada actually almost warned him not to. Well, what the hell, she figured, and squirted more glue as he held his rod but also cupped his testicles. Then, as he tried to pull his hand away, he nearly screamed.

"Oh, Sorry," Jada said, as she looked over Michelle at Reid's contorted face. Certain the glue was doing its super job, she ducked down, this time for the Polaroid. "Say cheese," she requested, and Michelle turned around with a feigned expression of surprise on her face. Reid's face was more sincere, though less photogenic at the moment. Jada shot off the first picture, which looked through the view finder at least about as sexually guilty as possible, short of showing actual penetration. But, Jada thought, they could do better. She pulled the film out of the camera, put it on the bureau to develop, and stood on the bed to shoot another one.

"Hey. Hey! No pictures. And this oil burns. Come on, girls . . . "

"Don't you like getting stung?" Michelle asked.

"I'm . . . I'm stuck," Reid said, just beginning to get a clue. He couldn't move the hand glued to himself, but anyone who didn't know that would think he seemed to be comfortably cupping one hand there. Michelle leaned in, giving Jada a big cleavage shot. Jada got the two of them in the picture, from chest to thigh. Then she quickly shot another, this one focused higher up on the bed, so she got the two of them against the headboard, their faces beside one another, Michelle's chest leaning against Reid, and his hand still around his private parts, the other reaching.

"Come on," Jada coaxed.

Michelle winced, then she put her hand gingerly over Reid's glued one. It was probably the only Johnson she'd ever touched except for Frank's. Jada nodded and snapped off another picture. The more intense look of "discomfort" on Reid's face made it seem—at least for the photo—as if he was almost ejaculating.

"Perfect," she cooed.

"What are you doing? What's this on my dick? I'm really stuck!" Reid cried. "And I told you I don't want pictures!"

"We *always* do pictures," Jada said, her voice reasonable. Then, to be as truthful as possible she added, "Every time I've done this, I do pictures."

Michelle actually laughed out loud and held her hand out for the camera, so Jada gave it to her and got onto the bed. Showtime! She squatted over Reid's trapped body without touching it, and turned to look over her shoulder at the camera. Michelle snapped off two more pictures, lining them up with the others on the bureau to develop. For a moment, Jada wondered how she—a church-going, God-loving Christian woman—had come to be crouched, glistening black and almost naked, over this white toad, but God was forgiving and the cause was a just one.

"What the hell *is* this?" Reid said. "I'm, I'm . . ."

"Trapped?" Jada asked.

"Cornered?" Michelle added.

"Ummm, maybe *'betrayed'* is the word you're looking for," Jada suggested, mock-helpfully.

"I tell you I'm stuck. I can't get this up," Reid said as he tried to lift his private parts from the mattress.

"You got a lot of problems, Slick, but getting it up didn't seem to be one of them," Jada laughed. "Now getting it off," she continued, "*that* could be a major problem in this particular situation."

"Something's wrong," Reid said. "You stuck me down."

"It was an accident," Jada sneered.

"Yeah. Most accidents happen in the home," Michelle added and giggled. Jada giggled, too, and it felt good to laugh. Reid pulled himself, then howled.

Mission accomplished, Jada thought. Now Angie just had to do her part of the job.

"What are you doing? What are the two of you doing?" Reid Wakefield III, her first naked white boy, whined. "I mean, is this some kind of sex game? Because I don't think it's funny." He looked at the laughing Jada and his face changed. "Or do you want to rob the house or something?"

It took the smile right off her face. *Yeah. There's always that. When in doubt, figure an African-American is going to rob you,* Jada thought. One minute she was his greatest wet dream and the next his most common nightmare.

"Well? Is that it?" Reid asked. "Is that what this is all about?" he demanded, with as much dignity as a naked man with his penis stuck to a bed could muster.

"Slick, baby, you don't have a clue," Michelle told him.

54

In which Angie serves the Older Other Woman dessert

Angie stood for a moment outside the condo—the place she had once thought of as her "starter home"—and tried to act unwilling. "He's not in there, is he?" she asked for at least the third time.

"No. He had a business meeting tonight—some kind of emergency." Lisa assured her.

Angie was dying to get into the place, but she had to play reluctant. Very reluctant. "Wait. You didn't tell him you were seeing me?" Angie asked. "You promised. He won't be here, will he? I don't want him to see me like this. I mean, fat and all."

"Oh, Angie, you're not fat," Lisa said easily, as if the thirty extra pounds Angie was schlepping didn't exist. Lies rolled off her lips as easily as frogs slid into ponds. Wasn't there a fairy tale about a princess who spoke and frogs and toads emerged from her mouth? And another, maybe her sister, who had diamonds and gems fall out instead? Angie couldn't remember, but there was definitely a toad, a liar, and a few *faux* gems already in *this* story.

Angie pulled back her mind to concentrate, and remembered how much she wanted this to happen, so she stood there silently while Lisa threw open the door. She followed Lisa into what had been her own living room, and Lisa seemed to have no remorse or concern at all. She flipped on a few lights, but Angie knew by the *Cosmo* magazine Jada had left that all was in progress. Show time. Angie concealed her glee, went right to the bookshelves, pretending to look through them while Lisa took off her coat, hung it up, and looked in the mirror on the back of the closet door to fluff her hair. Angie had never had a mirror there. It was a good idea. She hoped it made Lisa very happy. There was going to be lots of new things to see in the house in just a few minutes.

Angie heard a little noise, a murmur or a click of a lamp being switched on, and looked toward the stairwell. She kept running her hands over the books in the bookshelf though. "I don't see it here, Lisa," she whined, as if the journal wasn't in her coat pocket. "Maybe I should go upstairs. Maybe I might have left it on that shelf across the top of the armoire."

"Oh," Lisa said. "Yeah, maybe. I can't even reach up there." Together they moved up the stairs and through the dark hallway. There was a light coming from under the door of the bedroom. Angie stopped.

"Is he here?" she asked again, trying to sound both frightened and accusatory.

"No," Lisa reassured her. "He said he'd be late. And he would have said hello when I came in."

She strode up to the door and Angie had a moment to wonder again whether Lisa, in pure spite, was hoping he was there, to finalize Angie's humiliation. But she just shrugged and followed Lisa.

When the door was thrown open, the scene before them was better than Angie possibly could have imagined. The light spilled out of the room, freezing Lisa in the doorway. The shock of the scene, the colors, and the shapes were amazing: "Jenette's" darkness, her brown legs bent up in high triangles on either side of Reid's ruddy arms, the blond of his hair contrasted by Mich's slightly darker tones, and her pale, matte back behind Jada's deep glossy one. Even the orange and the pink of their bras and scanty panties added to the visual shock of it. This wasn't some black lace prostitute or a red garter belt joke. The entire scene was so totally unpredictable, so real and yet so incredibly strange, it was mind-blowing. Michelle was sitting on Reid's feet, while Jada, in the unbelievably tiny pair of panties, was sitting on his chest. Ha! Take that! Angie had expected it—but what was Lisa seeing? And what about Reid?

Golden Boy looked at Lisa with horror and comprehension, but it was when Angie stepped out from behind her that he turned a real fish-belly white.

Angie looked over his head to the wall. Taped over the bed were several photos, and more of them lay scattered on the floor.

"Oh my God!" Lisa gasped and took another step into the room. Jada jumped off Reid and stood by the side of the bed so that the view would be clear for Angie and Lisa. Her breasts were barely contained by the orange brassiere. The color made her mouth, her breasts, and her orange silk crotch stand out against the deep burnished color of her skin.

"Oh my God!" Angie echoed. It looked so real, and so very, very sordid. Ha! Oh yes!

Michelle now turned her head. Her hair floated like a princess's, and her finely chiseled, beautiful face and milk-white body looked like a pornographer's wet dream. "Oh my God!" she too said.

But Jada wasn't going there. "You all religious?" she asked. "Or do you want to join us?"

"Lisa! Thank God! I mean . . . I . . . you don't understand . . . I'm trapped here," Reid said. "I'm . . . stuck. I mean it. I'm stuck to the mattress."

"Hey baby, from what I hear, you've always been stuck on yourself," Jada said, laughed and threw a smirk at Angie.

Lisa's mouth opened and closed like a guppy's. Angela stepped out from behind her and moved closer to the bed for a better look. Reid, his hands still cupped over his genitalia, gazed at her, his face becoming a mask of shock—and something else she couldn't identify. Pain? Shame?

"Angie?" he asked, as if he doubted his vision. She just looked down at his package, and wondered just how much glue Jada had used. "I . . . I didn't know you were in town," he said. "I mean . . . I didn't mean to see you."

"That's obvious. Oh, Reid. I thought you'd promised to stop these sick games of yours." She almost laughed, and covered it with a choking noise. "I thought that maybe he was over all this." She tried to sound sincerely disappointed. "I better go," she said to Lisa. "I . . . I just better go."

She turned and walked out and down the stairs. Only then did she smile, the deeply satisfied grin of a happy consumer. After all, she had bought that mattress *and* the Crazy Glue that Reid was tethered to it with. She was pleased with both. Her grin broadened.

Jada had been right; the Polaroids were a really nice touch, and she knew that others had already been hidden in bureau drawers, in the desk, and even in the linen closet. If Lisa *did* hang around after this—which Angie truly doubted—she'd go batshit all over again when she found the photos.

As she walked across the living room, Angie could hear yelling up in the bedroom. She better move fast. She had one more thing to do, sliding the little journal she'd prepared onto a shelf behind another book. It was only then that she realized that now she didn't really care if Lisa and that idiot got married or not. They deserved each other. Her pain was cauterized, her envy gone. She walked out the door of her first home for the last time.

"You know, I think I *like* this underwear," Michelle said. "And I *definitely* like the orange lipstick on you, Jada."

"I should have put some on him," Jada said, "instead of just settling for the panties on his head."

"Oh yeah!" Michelle agreed enthusiastically. They were all pretty boisterous. "*And* a bra. To match his eyes. Why didn't we think of that before?"

Angie, sitting between them in the uncomfortably small shuttle seat, laughed. "As if what she saw wasn't enough for Lisa to chew on," she said. "A *ménage à trois*. Lesbianism. Adultery. Miscegenation. Plus a pinch of sadomasochism *and* cross-dressing?" Angie began to cackle. "Poor Lisa!"

That made Michelle and Jada crack up. They probably sounded as if they were drunk, but aside from diet Coke nothing had been consumed—except, of course, Reid's pride and Lisa's smugness.

The shuttle jumped and settled as it hit some turbulence, but though Michelle clutched the armrests, Jada just shrugged. "It's nothing," she said. "Just a mountain sayin' hello."

Michelle glanced nervously out the window and Angie smiled at her friends. "If we've got to go down," she said, "this is when I'd like to go. I'd smile all the way to the ground." Then she thought of the baby and changed her mind. She adjusted the belt across her expanding belly and wondered if she could go the rest of the flight without having to make yet another trip to the lavatory.

"It was unbelievable," Michelle said, over her fright flight. She turned her back from the clouds outside. "I felt so powerful. I ran the show. And it was so easy," she marveled. "We should celebrate. We should have done something really great."

"Yeah. We should have spent the night at the Ritz Carlton."

"I still can't believe we got away with it," Michelle said.

"Most men are easy," Jada told her. "I just loved it when you invited us over to *his* place." She turned to Angie. "You should have seen him slaver. I could have filled a bucket with his saliva," she added.

"So tell me again what happened at the very end?" Angie asked. "When I discreetly left the room so that I wouldn't witness their shame."

"Again?" Michelle smiled. "I have a feeling this may become baby's favorite bedtime story," she predicted. "Kind of like what happened on the day I was born." She made her voice sugary, like those recordings for very young children. "And then Auntie Jada handed the Bad Witch Lisa a magic bottle of nail polish remover. And she said, 'This has the power to break the spell. At least it's how we got it unglued last time.' And Auntie Michelle said, 'It burns a little, but he's into that. If you really want to, just blow on it.' The Bad Witch started to yell at the Wicked Prince. While she did, Auntie Michelle hid the other naughty, naughty pictures all over the castle, for the Bad Witch Lisa to find later. And then the two good Aunties disappeared, and left the Wicked Prince with his dick in a bind."

"Yeah. And then the Witch probably turned into a dragon and set the whole bed on fire," Jada finished. "But we were already on the way to Logan by then. And taken we all had to wait on line at the car rental counter."

"All stories end like that." Angie said. "Instead of happily ever after. I just wonder if she unglues him?" Michelle asked.

"I wonder how much it will hurt." Jada added.

"I always wondered why they called it Crazy Glue, but now I think I know," Michelle laughed.

"Oh, I thought it was Five-Second Glue," Angie said. "That would have been appropriate for Reid."

Jada put her palm up. "Uh-uh. No details, sisterfriend. I don't want to hear it. Yuck!"

Angie laughed. "God, it looked so kinky."

"And he didn't even get to touch us!" Jada gloated.

"Do you know the difference between sexy and kinky?" Michelle asked suddenly. Both of her friends shook their heads. "If you do it with a feather, it's sexy," Michelle said. "But with a whole chicken, it's kinky."

They all laughed. The flight attendant announced they were arriving in "the New York area". Passing them, she looked annoyed, as if they were laughing at her. The three of them calmed down. Then Jada said, "God, I wished we'd brought a chicken." Angie began to cackle, and her friends joined her. Jada shook her head. "Unbelievable," she said. "I really do feel so . . . so powerful."

"We *are* powerful," Angie said. "Let's not forget it." She paused and looked from one to another. "Thank you, both of you, for your help." She took their hands.

"Do we look like campfire girls at a seance?" Jada asked. "Or are we acting lesbian again?"

"Shut up," Michelle said. "This is a tender moment." She turned to Angie. "You're welcome," Michelle said. "He deserved every minute of it. And I hope Lisa finds the journal *and* shows it to him. Icing on the cake."

"I hope she publishes it. What was in it? Where did you hide it?" Jada asked.

"I put the journal on the bookshelf. If she ever finds it, I wrote about how bad the sex was with him. I even put in something about how his dad felt me up at the Christmas party. And how Reid's breath always stank in the morning. Plus, I made up this affair he had. The one with his friend from prep school."

"A girlfriend or a boyfriend?" Michelle asked.

Angie grinned. "A boyfriend, of course."

"What a bombshell!" Jada laughed.

"I didn't say his name. I just used an initial—X. But I was really graphic. And I *did* say he was one of Reid's closest friends. Let Lisa forever wonder. I wrote a really good couple of pages about finding him giving head in the men's room of the club the night Reid passed out there, too. *Very* graphic."

The plane was making its final descent as the three women laughed again.

"It was a good plan," Jada admitted.

"Well, one down, two to go," Angie told them.

55

In which Cinderella is delivered

Michelle went to open the numbered mailbox she had rented at Mailboxes, Etc. Not that she expected anything, she told herself. Don't get your hopes up. Her idea was silly, and her ads were probably stupid, so she'd waited more than a week before she came to check, each day telling herself not to bother.

Now, opening the tiny door reminded her suddenly of the other box—the lockbox full of drug money that Jada had trusted her about and innocently put in her name. Michelle had been having dreams almost every night about getting busted.

Despite all her fears and her bad dreams, Michelle had done nothing. Typical of her, she thought with disgust. Without someone to tell her what to do, it was almost guaranteed she'd do nothing. But Michelle felt that in her situation now, doing nothing was no longer an option. It wasn't just herself and Frank, but her children's future, and now Jada's and maybe even Angie's at stake.

Since the Boston affair she'd felt as if . . . well, as if *she* could, maybe, make things happen. Now she struggled with the mailbox key and finally got the lock to turn. She opened the little door, and to her delight, there was a pile of envelopes. Michelle started to pull them out, but realized they were actually so densely packed that she couldn't do it without tearing a few, so she stopped and just stared at the letters in front of her. They were all responses. Responses to the ads *she* had run.

She looked at the clump of mail for a moment, not believing her eyes. Then, with a whoop, she began to pull them out and tear them open. She stood at the counter of the mail drop, her fingers shaking, as she read them and sorted them by category. There were responses from people looking for work—people who wanted to be her employees! A few she saw right away wouldn't do, but there were lots of nicely typed—and several hand-written—intelligent letters. Once she had taken out the obviously crazy and one obscene one, as well as the two who had not included a phone number or return address, she had sixteen legitimate responses for help.

But even more unbelievably, there were five requests for her services, or at least people who were interested in hearing more about them.

These little piles of letters represented a whole new life. Michelle just stood there and stared. She'd had the power to get this kind of response? And on her first try? With only a few ads? Even if she never heard from any of these people again, she felt she'd already scored some kind of victory. What was even more extraordinary to her was that she'd done it, all of it, by herself. Maybe she'd still be cleaning, but she wasn't Cindy anymore and she didn't need a prince. She stared at the letters for as long as she dared to. They represented a new life—the possibility of a clean life, in both senses of the word. Michelle didn't have to be dependent on anyone. She could take care of herself and her children.

She hadn't advertised her services nearby but in northern Westchester instead; if all of this worked, she'd decided she would move even farther away from the scene of her husband's crime. Maybe all of this could happen. It was a modest enough hope—to be able to work and take care of her children. But that was all she wanted. Michelle wasn't interested in anything except self-sufficiency and peace. No more haunting dreams. She wanted to feel that she could provide whatever was needed and deal with whatever arose. And these letters—these precious letters—did more to make her believe that was possible than anything had before.

Time was passing. She didn't know how long she'd been standing there, but she looked down at her watch and realized she'd be late for

Michael Rice and the meeting he had set up. She stuffed the letters into her purse and then got into the Lexus—a car she now despised—and drove to the county municipal building.

As she got closer and closer, she lost all of that delicious feeling of lightness she had had and felt it replaced with dread and fear. Her chest tightened as if she'd tried to struggle into one of Jenna's leotards. She knew why—she didn't want to have to see District Attorney Douglas. He was the man who had ruined her life, frightened her and her children, and scarred them in a way they would never recover from. Now that she'd realized her husband's guilt, she felt that she couldn't really object to Douglas's attitude toward Frank, but Michelle was afraid to find out what his attitude toward her might be. Hostile, she was sure. But she had to find out if she was free to move away, to leave Frank and go undisturbed, as far as the law was concerned.

Michael was waiting for her and she could see by the expression on his face that it wasn't good that she was late.

"Let's go," he said, without any preamble. "It wasn't easy to get this time with Douglas and I don't want him to shuffle us off his calendar."

Michelle nodded meekly and followed her lawyer into the building and up to the fourth floor.

George Douglas was a big man—beefy, but not fat. His hair was sandy red and thinning, plastered in thin strips over a mostly bald head, and his skin was freckled all over. He came out of his office as soon as his secretary had announced them. "Rice," he said, and nodded curtly at Michael. "And you're Mrs. Russo?"

Michelle couldn't speak. He reminded her too much of her father, a man who had died almost twenty years ago but was the approximate size and shape of DA Douglas. If she wasn't already terrified, which she was, she would have been by this reincarnation. Typical luck for her. Where was it written that this man she already feared would also have to resemble another man she'd feared? For a moment, she was afraid that she couldn't cope, that she'd literally turn and run away. But there was nothing to do except take a deep breath and move forward as he ushered them into his office. His bald head glistened like his many plaques and trophies between the pomaded and carefully placed reddish strands plastered to his head.

"This is Assistant District Attorney Ben Michaelson and this is Stephen Katz," Douglas said by way of introduction. "Michael Rice. And his client, Mrs. Russo." He sat down heavily in a worn leatherette swivel chair, leaned back, and steepled his hands in front of his stomach. "So," he said. "What have you got to offer, Rice?"

"We're not here to offer anything," Michael said. "As I told you on the phone, this is an open discussion to determine how justice can best be served."

"Yeah, sure," Douglas said. And for a moment Michelle raised her head from the defensive position she had tucked it into and dared to take a look at him. "Well, if you want justice to be served," Douglas repeated, "here's what you can do—you can have Mrs. Russo wear a wire and give us a recorded admission of guilt from her husband. Better yet, you could let us know where his stash is, and who he was working *for*. We already know who he was working *with*, so I'm not interested in the names of his soldiers."

Michelle felt she might die, right there in her chair. All of these men were so tough and so quick to dispose of her, her husband, and the lives of her children. The most humiliating part of it was that she now knew Frank was guilty, and that they'd known before she did. She felt tears come to her eyes and she lowered her head again.

"Mrs. Russo is the mother of two school-age children. She's also innocent, and completely unaware of any criminal activity on her husband's part," Michael said. "I'd also like to remind you that though he's been charged, you still have no evidence and you're conducting this based totally on the testimony of men who may prove to be unreliable."

"Hey, Michael," Douglas said. "Am I mistaken or did you come here looking for a deal, just like they did?"

"No, we didn't. We just wanted to let you know Mrs. Russo plans to leave the county, and perhaps begin divorce proceedings."

"Oh really? How interesting. And this is just coincidental, having no bearing on Frank Russo's recent activities?"

"George, we're not on trial, and Mrs. Russo doesn't have to explain her domestic life to you or plead the Fifth Amendment. Just let us know if she's free to go," Michael Rice said. "You're not charging her."

"Not yet, but she's not free to go," Douglas said. "Now, if Mrs. Russo wants to turn state's evidence in return for a guarantee that she will not be prosecuted, we might be able—*might* be able—to work that out," he said. "But she'd be doing just the same thing as my other witnesses, so don't malign them, okay?" Michelle felt panic, but tried not to show it. "I only let someone walk if they can bring me in someone bigger, not someone who's irrelevant."

For the first time, Douglas turned and looked directly at Michelle. "Do you know something useful?" he asked her. "Can you tell me who he spoke to? Who he brought to your house? Can you tell me where shipments came from? What cousins does Frank have who might, just possibly, of course, be connected? Who does he know from Colombia? Have you taken a lot of vacations in Mexico, or Caracas? You're going to have to give it up, Mrs. Russo."

She looked at the disgusting man. She could tell him the truth. "If I knew any of that, if Frank had done any of that in front of me, I wouldn't be Mrs. Russo any more," she said. "All I want is to find out if you think I'm involved, which I'm not. And whether or not I'm safe to take my children out of this county. I'm concerned about my children and"— here she took a deep breath—"I have no proof if Frank's guilty or not, but I'm afraid he may be and that makes me frightened and ashamed."

"You're *afraid* he may be guilty?" Douglas asked, his voice full of false concern. "You're *afraid* he may be guilty? Let me tell you something. You know goddamned well that your husband has been playing the game. Either that or you are the most disloyal, disgusting wife I've run into in some time. You're telling me you're abandoning that son-of-a-bitch because he's run into trouble with the law and you don't even *know* if he's guilty? You're just *afraid* he might be. What kind of woman does that, Mrs. Russo?"

"I don't like your tone, Douglas," Michael said hotly. "I don't like the way you're talking to Mrs. Russo. We came here in good faith."

Douglas looked at Michelle and she forced herself not to look away.

"You know," he said. "I don't think that you're a bitch, but I *do* think that you're a liar. You're not afraid he's guilty. You know it. You know plenty, enough to make you want to get the hell away from the father of your children. Now, I'll help you do that, but you got to help me, too. If you came here in good faith, then give me something."

"Mrs. Russo has nothing to give you," Michael said. "She's innocent and she's been terrorized both by her husband and by the police. Come on, George. It's been brutal on her. And her children have become pariahs at school."

Douglas took his hands off his belly and put them behind his head. "Well, I'm hurting for them," he said, with what seemed like sincerity. "But you know what? I can't cry for all the women I see who for years prefer to keep their eyes shut. Who don't want to know exactly what their husbands are doing because, if they did, it might rock their boat. It might shake their world. It might even cut their income." He paused. "You live on a nice street, Mrs. Russo. You drive a nice car. I know that for a fact. We've looked at your tax returns, we've looked at your husband's business income. He's not stupid, I'll grant you that. But I don't think you are, either. I don't want to hear women tell me"—here he raised his voice in an unpleasant falsetto—"'I didn't know he was busting heads. I didn't know about the thirty phone lines and the fact that he was taking more bets than OTB. I didn't know who Lefty or PeeWee really were.' They know. They just don't *want* to know." Douglas shrugged. "What have you got for me, Michael?"

"What I've got is an innocent woman who wants some assurances and some help from the public servants paid to protect and serve her," he said.

Douglas stood up. "Mrs. Russo, if you *are* innocent and telling the truth, I'm sorry to tell you that you and your kids are about to unfairly be the recipients of a shitstorm of trouble. We're looking for everything we can grab until the trial. You can't leave the county. You got no guarantees that we won't tail you or pick you up or do whatever it might take to take Frank Russo down. You may be subpoenaed, even as a hostile witness. You've got a simple choice—give us something to help us and walk, or go through this with him."

56

Consisting of a confidence and a kiss

Since her return from Marblehead Angie felt *so* much better—almost lighthearted. Who knew she had so much spite in her? As she drove to work in her old clunker, she actually laughed out loud. She still couldn't think of the scene without smirking to herself. But it wasn't really spite. Somehow, whatever the outcome between Reid and Lisa, Angie felt that she'd gotten her self-respect back. And if she hadn't had the help of Jada and Michelle—or should she say, Jenette and Katherine?—she never would have been able to pull it off.

She giggled at that phrase. She'd wondered if Reid had been able to "pull it off," or if Lisa had left him right then and he was still attached to the mattress. If she had, Angie wondered how he'd get into his trousers. It was like that old joke about a guy with five penises—his pants fit like a glove. She guessed that Reid's trousers, if he was still stuck to the mattress, would have to fit like a sheet. She almost laughed out loud, alone in the car. What giddiness. If only she had thought to snag a photo or two for herself out of all those Polaroids. She'd also wished she'd had the presence of mind to say, "Oh, Lisa, I'm so very, very sorry." Just to rub her nose in it. But she hadn't. Well, she'd pulled it off as perfectly as she could, and she was deeply satisfied. She knew that she and Jada and Michelle would laugh about it for the rest of their lives.

Somehow she felt she could start living her life now. She'd make her job permanent, if there was budgetary approval. She'd start saving money for a new car, tell her parents about the baby, and prepare for it. She wasn't afraid of raising the child on her own. Somehow she felt prepared for anything life dished out.

She got closer to the office and the smile faded from her face. The only dark thing about these last few days had been sitting in the diner and watching Frank talk to Michelle. Because he'd never met her, she felt that she could take the risk of occasionally looking at him in her mirror, but even in reflection his intensity and anger was enough to frighten her. There was no doubt he was a good-looking man, and a sexy one. But there was also no doubt that he terrified Michelle. She prayed that Michelle wouldn't back off her resolve, especially now that they had the incriminating tape. Her friends had helped her. Now she would help them, if only they'd stick to their plans.

Angie had a few things she had to do today along those lines, and none of them would be pleasant. Most importantly, she had to inform Michael and the board that Jada was dropping her appeal. After the investment they'd made in Jackson vs. Jackson, Laura and the board would probably be disappointed. Angie still wished with all her heart that Jada would pursue a legal approach to her problems, but she of all people was in no position to insist on that. After all, the Marblehead caper was anything but aboveboard. Still, she worried that what Jada was thinking of was going way too far and might end in tragedy—for all of them.

Then there was another difficult thing she had to do—she had to face Michael and inform him about her condition. She didn't know why she had been putting it off; they'd barely spoken since he'd asked her out. She'd been busy, of course, but that wasn't the only reason she hadn't revealed her pregnancy. Maybe she was afraid that it would discourage Michael—and maybe she was afraid it wouldn't. But as she pulled into her spot at the clinic, she knew she had to say something.

Her morning was busy with appointments. She literally bumped into Michael in the hallway once, but he was with a client and she was on her way to meet one in reception. They exchanged looks, but not a word was spoken.

In the early afternoon, there was a staff meeting where she broke the news to all of them that the Jackson case was off the agenda. Everyone was disappointed, but Michael was the one who raised the most objections. "What's she gonna do?" he asked. "Just live with the situation? Pretend it doesn't exist? Forget about her kids?"

"I don't know," Angie lied calmly. "Maybe she's going to seek private counsel." She knew that reflected badly on both of them, but she just wanted this part of the board meeting to end. But Michael wouldn't give up. He brought up three alternatives to present to Jada, as well as a final scenario for good measure. The guy was certainly dedicated.

"Just bring her in. Let me talk to her," he said.

"I don't think she will. She's just not going to."

"She owes us that much," he said. In the end, though, he and the board had to accept the decision. Angie gave them the letter that she and Jada had drafted and they went on to other business. If Angie noticed her mother and Laura looking at her with what seemed like disappointment, she just had to hope she was wrong or imagining it. It had been a big case, bigger than she could handle. She hoped it didn't mean that when Karen Levin-Thomas came back that Angie would find herself without a job.

She was finally back in her office, filling in a restraining order, when there was a knock on the door. Angie knew it was Michael's knock. When she invited him in, she tried to mentally prepare herself for what she had to do. He looked uncomfortable. He ran his hands through his hair, which must have had the worst cut in Westchester. But a suit and a haircut could be fixed. "Angie, can I talk to you for a minute?" he asked.

"Sure," Angie agreed. "The county takes about a week to process these restraining orders anyway. What difference does a few minutes make?"

Michael didn't sit down. Instead, he leaned up against the wall, across from her desk. She had to look up at him. She wondered if it was a psychological maneuver to make her uncomfortable, or if he did it because he was uncomfortable himself. "Look, Angie, you don't have to avoid me. I'm really sorry. I never mixed my professional and private lives before. It's a testament to how much I like you, how much I enjoy your company. I'm sorry if you don't want to go out with me. Maybe I shouldn't have even asked you. I mean, you don't feel harassed or anything, do you?"

Angie almost laughed out loud, but restrained herself because she didn't want to hurt Michael's feelings. He was so very politically correct that only he could think about the possibility of harassment in their situation. He'd been so appropriate, so restrained, and so kind to her. "I don't feel harassed, Michael. I feel complimented," Angie admitted. "Frankly, I can't imagine what you see in me."

Michael didn't move or change his expression. "I haven't dated for a while, Angie, but I guess I remember enough from when I did to know that's just another way of saying you don't want to go out with me."

Angie shook her head. How could she tell him? God, she owed it to him, she had to get this out. And if she didn't, he'd see her "secret" soon enough—any day she was going to show in spite of her loose tops.

But still, it was hard to say. She thought, if things were different, she might actually want this man. Of course, it was far too soon to tell if she wanted anyone, and she didn't know him well, but she knew the things she used to care about didn't matter to her any more. Looks, status, and money were all the gifts Reid had to give, and they were empty. Michael Rice wasn't a handsome man, but he wasn't what Jada called TUFW— Too Ugly For Words.

Anyway, she'd had DDG and it hadn't worked. Michael certainly wasn't powerful in the world, and he was probably paid not much more than she was making, but he had integrity and compassion and a warmth that she'd never felt from Reid. She looked at his roundish face, his glinting glasses. "Michael, I just think it's best if we didn't let ourselves get involved now. I mean, there are things about me that you don't know."

"Well, there's things about me you don't know," he said reasonably. "I thought that was why you dated someone—to find out things about them." He shrugged. "I'm being stupid." As he started toward the door, he added, "Okay, Angie. Forget about it. I'm sorry I bothered you."

Oh, he had it all wrong. He thought it was *him*. How could she let him know that wasn't it? "Michael, I'm pregnant," she blurted.

He turned from the door. His face was calm. "Yeah. Of course you are."

"You knew? I mean, you know?" she asked.

"Angie, I watch you very closely. Men do that. And I've been married. I've watched my wife go through two pregnancies."

"You know?" was all Angie could repeat. "You know, and you *still* want to go out with me?"

"Yeah. Do you think that's so odd?"

"Yeah. I do, actually."

"Then I'm odd," he said. He began to leave again, then stopped and turned around. "Wait. You thought I didn't . . . Is that why you didn't want to go out?" His face softened, and he smiled. He moved back to the desk.

Angie felt like an idiot. "You still do?" she said.

As an answer, Michael leaned forward, put his hands on her desk, and kissed her.

57

Containing a date at the diner

Michelle brushed out her long hair. She needed her roots done, but what was the point? She'd lightened her hair for Frank, and he wouldn't see it, except for today.

Angie had thought this through so thoroughly that even Michelle felt safe. Angie had set it up as if it were a bank heist, or a security sweep for a presidential visit. Jada had gotten behind it, too. Still, Michelle felt nervous as she twisted her hair up. Marblehead had been nerve-racking but fun. This, though, felt dangerous, and not funny at all.

Michelle was waiting for Angie to start talking about possible sniper sights on rooftops, or for Jada to pull out Frankie's walkie-talkies so they could keep in constant contact. Angie had even insisted that they bring a man—she said she felt awkward about asking Michael, so she had convinced Bill to come. Frankly, Michelle didn't see much point in that. If Frank *did* go ballistic, which he wouldn't, there was certainly nothing that weedy Bill could do about it. All of it made Michelle feel even more nervous, and at the same time as if she might laugh out loud.

Michael Rice had contacted Bruzeman and started negotiations for support for the kids. The problem was that Frank kept insisting she should bring the kids home, that he'd support all of them as he always had. But Frank was a different man. It wasn't that he had hit her. It wasn't that she didn't believe he was capable of doing it again, under the right circumstances. It was just that it wasn't going to happen in a diner in Scarsdale. Not at one o'clock in the afternoon in front of a few dozen lunchers and as many service staff. "Look, we're just going to talk," she reminded Jada. "And only for a half an hour. Then I'm going to get up and go. That's it. Nothing else is going to happen."

"Fine," Jada said. "We'll make sure of that." Jada was going to sit in her car in the diner parking lot, watching Frank arrive and leave. Then she was to make sure he didn't follow Michelle. Meanwhile, Angie was already stationed in a corner booth, her back to the table where Michelle was sitting, Bill opposite her. His eyes would stay glued on Michelle as if she were Leonardo DiCaprio.

Michelle drove over to the diner alone, her heart thudding painfully in her chest. She didn't want to wear a wire, and it was good thing, because her chest felt like it was going to burst and the device would have been exposed. But once there, twenty-five minutes early to be sure they beat Frank in, she felt better. The one good thing about all the activity around this, as far as Michelle was concerned, was that it hadn't given her too much time to be nervous about actually seeing Frank. She was more nervous about him seeing Jada or the others. She glanced briefly over at the corner booth where Bill and Angie were sitting. Angie, totally in her *I Spy* mode, pulled out a compact and actually looked in its mirror so that she could see Michelle without turning around. Again Michelle almost giggled out loud. As far as she knew, Angie didn't even wear makeup that required a compact. Had she bought it purposely for this caper?

But the giggle died in her throat as Michelle saw Frank coming up the stairs of the diner entrance. She felt a pull at her chest, a tightening that pushed the air out of her. He came in the door and saw her immediately. He slid into the seat opposite hers.

It amazed her that he looked exactly the same. She didn't know what she'd expected, but his hair was just as dark and glossy, his skin as smooth, his eyes as beautiful. He was wearing a black turtleneck sweater—one that she had given him last Christmas. Michelle admitted to herself that she still loved him. She knew what he was, and she hated it, but old feelings died slowly in her.

He put both of his hands down flat on the table and she had to remind herself that they were the hands that had hit her. She looked up from them and back at his eyes. His eyes had always fascinated her. Now, if anything, they were deeper than ever—eyes she could get lost in.

"How are the kids?" Frank began.

"Okay." She wasn't going to talk much. They'd all decided that was best.

"What did you tell them?" he asked. His voice didn't sound defensive or angry, but oddly it didn't sound concerned either. That wasn't Frank. He adored the kids. He must miss them more than anything else. He was so calm, almost cold. Michelle knew him enough to know he was using a lot of control to achieve this apparent neutrality.

"I told them that you had to go away for a little while and that the painters were working in our house." She paused. "I don't think they want more information than they can handle."

"You're not going to tell me where you're staying?" he asked, and there was some feeling in his voice now. Michelle just shook her head. She'd get up if he pushed her. "So, they're okay," he said going back to neutral.

"Well, I guess as okay as they can be. They aren't asking any questions. That's a bad sign."

"It is?"

"Of course, Frank. They know something is up, and they know I don't want to talk about it, and they don't want to know about it. What hasn't gone wrong for them in the last few months?"

Frank looked out the window, past the miniature jukebox affixed to the end of the table. For a moment Michelle thought he was going to focus on Jada's Volvo, way to the side of the lot, but to her relief he was merely scanning empty space. Then he turned his eyes back to her. "Michelle, it's not too late to fix everything that's wrong. I promise you I can do it."

Again, Michelle felt an inappropriate giggle rise in her throat, but she certainly didn't feel like laughing. It was a kind of horror reaction, like the time her mother had told her about her grandma's death and Michelle had laughed out of nerves and . . . something else she still couldn't identify. "How can you say that?" she asked him. "How can you possibly fix this, Frank? I have a list that's twenty-two pages long. I don't think that it can be fixed. The only way to fix it is by making it never happen, and that isn't possible."

Frank stared at her and clutched the edge of the Formica tabletop. She couldn't help but stare at his hands—the hands that had made her feel so good, the hands that had hit her. She watched the skin under his nails go white with the pressure he used to clutch the table. "Look," he said, his voice lower but now more intense. "I can do it. I have a way around this with Bruzeman. I get off, we get the family back together, and I will never hurt you or the children again. Not in any way, Michelle."

For a moment she didn't know what he was saying. Then she realized that he really expected, or at least hoped, that she'd forget everything. That they were going to get back together. "Frank—" she began, but he interrupted.

"I made a mistake, Michelle. One mistake, and it led to a few more. I didn't see the way it would play out. I'm sorry. I thought I was protected. I thought you were protected." He paused. She wondered if he meant payoffs, or political pull, or pals at the police headquarters, or . . . worse. She watched his mouth moving, but couldn't hear him for a moment until she forced herself to focus. "It's not too late to be protected again," he was saying. "I don't want you out there alone, Michelle. I don't want the kids living in some motel, or some rental dump. I don't want you worried about money, or me, or anything else. I want what we had. And we can have it again, Michelle."

The intensity of his voice, the force of will he projected from his eyes, even the strength of his grip on the table, exerted his old force on her. No wonder she had adored him for so long. He was handsome, he was sexy, he was intense. He seemed so certain, he seemed so solid and focused. He seemed like the most trustworthy man in America. But she'd been polishing an apple that was rotten inside, she thought. It had been no Eden, no garden of paradise. The apple had collapsed like the one at Shop Rite all those weeks ago, and Frank wasn't Adam—he was the snake.

"Michelle, think about last Christmas," Frank was saying, "When I gave you the watch? And we put together the bunk beds? You remember dinner that night, and opening our stockings?" He let go of the table with one hand and dropped it out of sight. For a crazy minute she worried about a gun.

But Frank was simply taking a compass from his pocket. It was the cheap dime store one that Frankie had bought for him. Michelle remembered helping Frankie wrap it in red and green holiday tissue. Seeing it sitting there against the turquoise marble pattern of the diner table suddenly brought tears to Michelle's eyes. "Just stick with me, Michelle. Just wait it out," Frank begged. "You don't have to testify if you don't want to. You don't even have to come home yet. Just forgive me and wait for me to clean this all up."

Michelle tried to imagine being back in the house, cooking meals, picking up Legos, lying in her bed in Frank's arms. It had been the only kind of life she'd wanted. How could he dare tempt her with the idea she could have it again? How could he? "Frank, *you* ruined everything, *I* didn't," she said. "I—"

"Don't, Michelle," he warned. "We can have it all back. They still got nothing on me. Just hearsay. Some witnesses that Bruzeman will tear apart. No credibility. There's no evidence." He paused. "Just the money. That's why I have to have it back. And because Bruzeman and the judge will be expensive."

Michelle listened to what he was trying to tell her. The judge would be bribed? That his legal costs would be a half a million dollars? That he was afraid that she couldn't hide the evidence better than he had?

And then she wondered if somehow all that he promised was possible. If she gave him back the money—money she was afraid to keep, money she didn't want—*could* he make it all right? *Could* she forgive him? Could she ever trust him again? She knew the children would, and being back with their mommy and daddy would be the best thing for them. For a moment she . . .

"I'll spend the rest of my life making it up to you, Mich," Frank said, leaning forward, his voice low but strong. "I regret everything. My mother is beside herself. This may kill her. I've hurt everyone I love."

Michelle looked at his eyes, and wetness had made his long lashes clump together like tiny rays around deep brown stars. She felt like crying herself, letting him touch the place below her jaw that still hurt, letting him put his head against her neck and weep and beg her to forgive him and then take her to bed.

"Where are you keeping the money, Michelle?" he asked. "I need to know."

And then she took a deep breath and snapped out of the poisoned dream. She looked out into the parking lot to check that the Volvo was there. She let her eyes glance over at the corner table where Bill had a loaded fork halfway up to his mouth, but nodded slightly. She looked at her husband. "You'd say anything to get the money back, wouldn't you?"

"I *have* to get the money back. I won't get out of this if I don't get the money back," Frank snapped. "And you know it's the right thing to do. It's right for me, and it's right for you."

"I used to think you did know what was right for me and for you. But I don't anymore," Michelle told him. "I thought this meeting was going to be about how you hit me. Instead it's about how you need the money? You've lost your right to make decisions for both of us, Frank. I'm the one who has to make the decisions for me and the children. You kept me in the dark. You're probably lying to me now. How could I know?" She leaned away from him.

"Michelle," he said, and leaned in closer toward her. "I'm not negotiating. It's my money and I need it, and I need you to give it to me. I know the lawyer's creed—a client is innocent until proven broke. Bruzeman will leave me twisting in the wind. I want to get up from here and go get that money, my freedom, wherever it is right now. And if you don't agree, I'm going to implicate you."

"What?"

"I'm going to tell the district attorney how you were in on it, how you acted as a mule, whatever it takes," Frank told her. "I'm not going to let this fall apart under me. You have to do what I tell you to do."

Michelle could hardly believe it. Two minutes ago, she'd been thinking about what it might be like back in their home again, all together.

Now he was threatening her with prison? She didn't know this man, and she had to remember that every minute. Her children were better off without him, and even if she never slept with anyone again for the rest of her life, she'd still be better off as well.

She began to stand up. He reached for her arm, but she snatched it away. "There's a restraining order out," she said. "Don't forget that. Don't touch me. Don't follow me. I won't talk to you again. I won't talk to Bruzeman again. You can speak to my lawyers if you have to get in touch with me."

His face paled. "Michelle, I didn't mean it," he said. "Don't go. Hey, I was just—"

"Good-bye, Frank," Michelle said, and got up and walked out of the diner.

She was still shaking when she parked the Lexus at the clinic. Angie and Bill pulled up first. Angie rushed over to her side of the car. "Wow! You got out of there fast," she said. "Are you all right?"

Michelle nodded. Bill came up behind them, holding the tape recorder still partly covered with duct tape. He'd placed it under the diner table before she'd sat down and recovered it after Frank left. "We listened to it in the car," he said. "Holy shit!"

Michelle didn't have anything to say. "Are you okay?" Angie repeated.

"He didn't follow me, did he?" she asked.

"Jada will know," Angie said. "She should be here in a minute or two. But I think it's time for you to come in and talk to Michael about a call to the DA. Don't you think so, Michelle?"

58

In which bills collect, a light goes on, and money rolls in

Jada had gotten back from Price Chopper a little bit late. She'd had the opportunity to work two extra hours, and she'd grabbed it—not that the nine dollars in additional take-home pay would make much of a difference. The apartment was quiet now, giving her time to think and plan. She sat at the dinette table and went through the mail that Clinton had handed her the last time she'd picked up the children.

For the first time in almost four years, she was getting way behind on bills. She opened them now, wincing at the ugly red stripe or the rubber stamp of PAST DUE on most of them. Of course, the phone, the electricity, and the mortgage had to be paid, but how? Her first Price Chopper paycheck had been ridiculous—it wouldn't even cover the phone bill, since it appeared that Tonya had made a lot of toll calls to White Plains.

Jada jotted down everything outstanding and then pulled out her checkbook. She still hadn't gotten around to closing out her account at the County Wide Bank, but she'd noticed they had been very quick to reinstate their monthly charge and their charge per check since she was no longer an employee. Before all this had happened—back in the Pleistocene era—she'd managed to be a few thousand dollars ahead. But that was already gone, and even paying just the minimums on her charges would wipe her out very soon. And that wasn't counting alimony and child support.

She had ignored George Creskin's bill, except to send him a fifty-dollar check and a note saying that she planned to pay every penny, no matter how long it took. It hadn't worked. Now, it appeared, Creskin was going to put a lien on their—well, Clinton's—house. At the time, she thought it was funny, but now as she opened the last envelope, she realized how spiteful and stupid she had been.

In front of her was a letter from the Westchester Court System explaining that she was in contempt because of her late payments and her failure to pay legal bills. She stared at the letter. What more could she do? She was a working mother, putting in sometimes two shifts, at little more than minimum wage. Her children had been taken from her, and she was paying for their father's mistress to take care of them. Yet she was in contempt? Jada got so angry that she crumpled the letter up and hurled it across the room. Unfortunately, that was the moment Michelle walked out of the hallway.

"What's with that?" Michelle asked.

"I might be the first Deadbeat Mom in the history of our country," Jada said. "Cover of *Time*? *Newsweek*?"

Michelle picked up the letter, spread it out, and looked it over. She shook her head. "Almost dead," she agreed, looking sympathetically at her friend. "You can't do another graveyard shift, Jada. And beat . . . well, last night you fell asleep with a mouth full of food. It wasn't a pretty picture, let me tell you. But deadbeat, as in irresponsible?" Michelle shook her head. "The whole system is crazy." She handed the crumpled letter back to Jada. "Maybe Angie and Michael can help you handle this."

"Forget them. I told them already that I don't care about an appeal. The whole system is ridiculous." She looked at her watch. "Come on," she said. "If I'm going to beat the system, I'm going to need your help now."

She ran and got their jackets and they struggled into them as they picked up their purses and walked out the door.

"Come on, Pookie," Michelle called. The dog was more than ready.

"Oh please," Jada said. "Do we have to take the damn dog? I don't know how Angie puts up with it," Jada said. "Can't we just have a little freedom from that pooch?"

"Hey. Come on. Don't you like Pookie by now?" Michelle asked, and she seemed really hurt.

"Not really," Jada said. "I admit that he is better than Clinton to live with. He seems to be in touch with his inner puppy. But he's still a pain in the butt."

Michelle looked crushed. "I didn't know you really felt that way," she said. "I'm so sorry. Do you think Angie hates having the dog here, too?"

Jada shook her head. "I'm sorry," she said. "I'm just nervous. Pay no attention to me. I don't know what I'm saying. I don't mind driving with Pookie. Dogs don't step on the imaginary brake."

With Pookie in tow, they all got into Michelle's Lexus, and she drove, much faster than usual, over to the school. Jada searched through her big black bag to find the stopwatch she needed. "Wow," Michelle said, impressed. "Where did you get *that*?"

"I stole it from one of those efficiency experts when they were doing those studies at the bank," Jada admitted.

"You're kidding?"

"Uh-uh. It was just out of spite. I didn't know I would need it to commit a crime."

They got to the school just as the bus was pulling out. "Damn it," Jada said. "We'll need to get here earlier tomorrow. Maybe while the kids are boarding. I have to see where the best opportunity is."

"Well, it can't be in front of the school, in front of everyone," Michelle said.

"You never know," Jada told her. "Maybe a note on that court stationery, that they're being picked up."

"It might have worked if you hadn't crumpled up the stationery," Michelle agreed. "Wouldn't it just be easiest if I pick them up?"

"Only if you want to go to prison for kidnapping," Jada said.

"Not way up there in my priorities," Michelle admitted. "But I'd do anything I could for you, Jada."

"I know it. But I can't ask you to go to prison." Jada was busy taking notes, detailing each bus stop, and the time. "Are those the Brewster kids? I know Mrs. Brewster. Maybe the kids could get off there . . . "

The school bus lurched around a corner, causing traffic mayhem as it always did. They were only one of the many cars behind it, since it was illegal to pass a school bus. Jada kept jotting down each of the stops and the times for each one. None worked. She couldn't just board the bus and snatch them.

"If I leave when I have a visit with them, I have the problem of Ms. Patel," she said aloud to Michelle. "I'd be reported immediately. But if I pick them up off of the school bus, I don't have Sherrilee. I can't just go busting into the house and get Sherrilee."

Still, Michelle kept following the bus and Jada kept taking notes.

"I need to pray." Then, as if in answer to her prayer, the idea came to her. "Church!" she said.

"You want to go to church? Now?" Michelle asked.

"No. No, I mean it can be done from church. Maybe I can take them to church. I could do it from there."

Michelle's eyes opened wide. "There is a God," she said.

That evening Jada called Samuel Dumfries. She had spoken to him twice since the meeting in Boston, but hadn't had good news to report. Now she excitedly told him about the way she felt she could scoop up the children. "But I might need some help," she admitted. "I can't ask my girl-friends. It's just too dangerous. Perhaps my mom and dad—"

"Don't be silly," he said. "They're too old and it's too risky. I'll come up."

"You?" Jada asked. "Mr. Dumfries, I'm not certain I can pay your expenses, much less a bill."

"I'm not doing this for financial gain," he said. "I'm sure I can help you get to Barbados. As you know, the problem is that this will be the most obvious place for your husband to look for you. Barbados does present some significant legal questions."

Jada had forgotten how formally the man spoke. "Mr. Dumfries, it can't present more problems than I have up here," she told him. "I'm determined to do this and I want to thank you, in advance, for all your help."

"Well, there is a favor I need to ask of you," he said.

"Yes, of course. Anything I can do," Jada said, wondering what she could possibly do for him.

"Would you mind calling me by my given name?" he asked.

"Not at all, Samuel," she told him.

Michelle hated to be sneaky, but she didn't know any other way to help. She waited until Jada was off the phone—the apartment was so small and crowded that there was almost no privacy—and then she asked to use it next. Jada had spoken to her lawyer friend from Angie's bedroom. Now Michelle went in there, lifted the phone, and hit the redial button. When the telephone was answered by an official secretarial voice, for a moment Michelle couldn't remember the name of the remote relation that Jada had mentioned. Then part of it came to her. "Sam, please," she said, and after a moment of silence she was put through.

"Samuel Dumfries here," a brisk British voice said.

Could this be right? Michelle wondered. "Hello," she began lamely. "Umm . . . are you a relative of Jada Jackson?"

"What is this in reference to, please?" Sam said.

"Look, I'm Jada's best friend. My name is Michelle Russo. And I have a way of helping her, but I need to know the best way to do it."

"Why don't you discuss it directly with Mrs. Jackson?" the man asked.

"Well, it involves a lot of things. But mostly it involves money. Would a lot of money help Jada in Barbados?"

"Money is almost always helpful," Mr. Dumfries said. "But it would be most helpful if Mrs. Jackson had enough to go elsewhere. Why don't you explain a little more."

And so Michelle did.

59

It's in the bag

Michelle let Jada drive her in the Volvo. The whole bank thing was risky, but so was everything they were trying now. She figured it was best for her to not be very visible. She also had no idea if anyone from Bruzeman's office, the DA's, the police, or Frank followed her in the Volvo or not. And she had no idea whether or not she was putting Jada in danger. But she told herself this was necessary.

She sat back, as low as she could in the seat, hoping that no one would follow or notice them as they drove toward the First Westchester Bank. She tried to focus on other things than her fear: the passing scenery, the hum of the Volvo. "Isn't the motor making some kind of clunking noise?" Michelle asked. Just what they needed, for the car to break down while they were on their way back with the haul.

Jada listened. "I think it's going." She sighed. "If it's got balls or wheels, it's going to give a woman trouble," she said, and kept on driving until she pulled into the bank parking lot. She parked without saying a word. She had never asked Michelle a single question about the safety-deposit box, and Michelle was deeply grateful for that trust. She'd never had a friend as loyal, as strong, as funny, or as right-minded as Jada. How odd that her best friend in the world was an African-

American. What had Jada called her? Sisterfriend? That's what Jada was to Michelle.

She thought about all of her high school friends back in the Bronx, and how they'd been back-biters and gossips. They'd also all been bigots who talked about "spades" and "jungle bunnies" and a lot worse. But they were idiots, not fit to even know a person like Jada. Michelle glanced over at Jada with enormous affection—no, love.

It was sad to her that the very thing that would now bring them both freedom would also separate them. But the money was necessary. Michelle just hoped that nothing would go wrong. Because if it did, she'd never forgive herself.

"Well, in case you haven't noticed, we're here now," Jada said, breaking into Michelle's thoughts. "What do I do next?" she asked.

"You go into the bank and you close out the box," Michelle told her. She took out a zippered black bag and handed it to Jada. "You put everything into this and we're outta here."

Jada nodded, ready to go. But first Michelle took her hand. It was very warm compared to Michelle's, which felt icy. "Jada, I don't think there's anything dangerous here, but I'd be lying if I said there was no risk at all."

"It's not drugs, right?" Jada said. "I already told you I won't have anything to do with that. Not that I thought you would. Anyway, you already told me it wasn't, and I believe you."

"It's just that Frank may be watching me, or one of his people, or worse." She didn't say what "worse" might be—because having police in your life once made it awful to even consider twice.

"Michelle, you're helping me get back my babies. I don't know what's in there, in that box, and I don't wanna know. But you're willing to help me and that means a lot. I think if you hadn't stepped up to the plate, Angie might not have helped. And I . . . I just don't seem to have the courage to do everything alone." Jada squeezed Michelle's hand. "You know what I mean?" Michelle nodded and Jada smiled. "Okay. So I'm gonna go in, unload the box, close it out, and come back."

Michelle's heart felt as if it were fluttering in her chest, while at the same time there seemed to be a cue ball in her throat. She couldn't swallow her own spit. She also couldn't help but check the rearview mirror (for the twentieth time) to see if there was anybody following them. She tried to swallow again. If she got Jada involved in all this, what if Jada got arrested and accused of being part of Frank's crime? What if *she* did, just because she was here sending Jada in? Both of them would surely lose their children forever.

Maybe, Michelle thought, she should just abandon the idea. Maybe she should leave all that cursed money just where it was, away from Frank and unable to hurt anybody. That was probably the best idea—to tell Jada to put the car in reverse and get them out of there. She sat very still for a moment, considering the option. It wasn't as if she wanted anything to do with the money in there, sitting neatly stacked in its box inside the bank vault walls. But to make the deal with the DA, she had to have something to show him. This bad money could be turned to good. And maybe in more ways than one.

She glanced into the rearview mirror again. Hadn't that white Chevrolet across the lot been sitting there a long time? There was a man alone in the driver's seat. The car looked exactly like a plainclothes cop's car—stripped down, no special features. Was it a Cavalier? Wasn't that what Frank once told her that most Westchester undercover cops drove? Then an older woman with a really bad perm crossed the lot and got into the passenger seat. Michelle took a deep breath. She was getting crazy, paranoid.

"Michelle, are you all right?" Jada asked.

Michelle couldn't speak. She was that shook up. She just nodded. If anything happened, if one of Frank's people grabbed the money, it would just be gone. As long as they didn't hurt Jada. And if the DA's people did anything, Michelle would just tell them the truth—that she was getting the money to take to them.

"Make it quick, Jada," Michelle finally managed to say. "Don't bother to close the box out. You know how much time it used to take Anne to do that. Just pack up the bag and come back as quick as you can. Okay?"

"Okay," Jada told her. "But are *you* okay?"

"Yeah. I'm fine. I'm just a little dehydrated or something."

"Well, I'll be right back," Jada said cheerfully, opening her door and sliding her long legs out. She walked onto the sidewalk and Michelle watched her, counting every step. She looked down at her—well, Jenna's—Swatch. It was seven minutes after ten when Jada disappeared into the double doors of the bank. How long could it possibly take? Ten minutes? Fifteen? Michelle tried to swallow the cue ball in her throat and began to wait.

But not two minutes later, a police car pulled into the parking lot from Post Road and right up to the door of the bank. Michelle panicked—she didn't know what to do. Her mind raced. There was no point in running, and she supposed she shouldn't go into the bank, because if they were looking for her it would only make their job easier. Not that they wouldn't find her here. She remembered the icy feel of the handcuffs when they had taken her away.

She rubbed her wrists and slid farther down in her seat, shivering. She watched and waited. The cop on the driver's side stayed in his seat, but on the other side of the car, the door opened, a policeman got out, and walked to the sidewalk in front of the bank entrance. Then he made a left and walked past the dry cleaner's and into the deli. Michelle could hardly believe it, but in two or three minutes, he walked out again holding two coffees in one hand and eating a danish that he held in the other. Michelle could see crumbs all over the front of his uniform. He got back into the cruiser and Michelle watched, feeling as if her body had turned into liquid, while the police car pulled out of the parking lot.

After a few minutes she could breath again, and even move and think. She looked down at her watch—it was almost a quarter after. Jada should be in a booth by now. That is, if she hadn't been stopped inside the bank. Michelle found that she had been tapping her foot and stopped herself. She turned her head around and scanned the parking lot again. Surely, if there had been people inside the bank waiting for Jada to show up, they would have already come to get Michelle.

She glanced again down at her watch. Eighteen minutes past ten. Jada had been in the bank for eleven minutes. Well, eleven minutes wasn't long. Michelle was tapping her foot again, but this time she didn't even try to stop it. She would just wait, tapping as much as she had to.

She managed to wait until ten-thirty, but by then it seemed unbearable. If Jada was being detained in the bank, if Michelle had gotten her involved, she'd never forgive herself. And Jada would probably never forgive her. Michelle decided she had better go in to see what was happening, but as she put her hand on the door handle, she thought better of it. She might be the one they were looking for. Despite the cold of the handle, her hand was sweating. What good would it do if she went into the bank? If people were searching for her, she'd be spotted and that would get Jada in trouble. Meanwhile, if they had caught Jada, they would certainly be out any minute looking for her car.

Michelle, who hadn't had a cigarette since she was in eleventh grade (when Frank had made her quit) wished desperately for the comfort of a drag on a Marlboro. For a moment she even considered going into the deli and getting a pack. Instead she looked down at her watch—it was 10:34. Jada had been in the bank for twenty-seven minutes—almost half an hour.

Michelle was freezing, but even though Jada had left the keys in the ignition, she wouldn't turn on the motor and the heat. The fact was, aside from her foot tapping, she couldn't move. If Jada never came out of the bank, the headline in the papers tomorrow would read: DRUG KINGPIN'S WIFE FOUND FROZEN IN FOREIGN CAR, FOOT FALLEN OFF. The funny thing was that even though she was so cold, Michelle was sweating under her arms. It was that nasty, clammy sweat that ruined her clothes. This sweater would be in the garbage by the end of the day, if she lived through the end of the day.

A woman came out of the bank holding a little girl by the hand. In fact, it was the first person who had come out in the last half hour. Maybe there was a problem in the bank. Maybe the bank was being held up and everyone was a hostage. But then why would this woman be walking out? *Michelle*, she said to herself, *you're going crazy. Stark raving bonkerinos.* The bank doors opened again. Michelle held her breath, but this time it was only an old lady, one who took tiny steps down the slate stairs, holding the railing and avoiding anything that might look like ice or dampness.

Then, at last, at precisely six minutes to eleven, the doors opened again and Jada walked out. She was swinging the black bag, and it looked appropriately heavy. She walked down the steps, got up to the Volvo, opened the door, and stuck her head in. "Mission accomplished," she said cheerfully, and placed the black bag on Michelle's lap before settling herself into the driver's seat. The bag felt solid and heavy against Michelle's thighs. Jada reached for the ignition and had the car started just before Michelle burst into loud, wet sobs.

60

A boyfriend, a brunch, a broadcast

Michelle had cleaned Angie's apartment until everything gleamed—Cinderella had struck again. Jada had brought her some flowers from Price Chopper—two mixed bouquets of carnations, gerbera daisies, gladiola, and a lot of leaves. They looked cheery. Angie had just finished putting the quiche in the oven. Then she mixed the salad and added the dressing. She couldn't eat, so she had set the little table for two. Her nausea had passed, but she was now ravenously hungry, so she'd eaten once already. Later she'd eat the leftovers.

The apartment was unusually quiet. Her roommates and the kids had cleared out early; Jada had gone to a church service, and Michelle was killing time with her kids until she could take them to the first show at the movies. That ought to give Angie more than enough time, more than enough privacy, but she wondered whether she'd done the right thing at all.

There was a knock on the door. It was early—her mother was usually late and her father was a nut about getting to places exactly on time, so Angie was surprised. She went to the door and Michael was standing on the other side of it. He was carrying the Sunday papers and a big bakery bag. "I thought I had extrasensory perception," he said. "It emanated from here. Is there somebody craving both newsprint and empty carbo-hydrates?" he asked.

He looked cute. He was wearing a red sweater and one of those puffy sleeveless vests that Angie could never understand, because she needed seven layers and lots of long sleeves to keep warm. "Come on in," she said, but though she tried to keep the warmth in her voice, she felt the reluctance of her invitation. Her plate was full with the news she was going to have to drop on her parents in the next hour. She couldn't expect both of them to take it as well as Michael had.

Michael, she'd discovered, was attractive in a way she had never appreciated before. He was very sure of himself and very competent—at least in the things he was sure of.

He came in and his eyes briefly swept around the room. "Where's Coxie's Army?" he asked. "I brought enough for all of them. Are all your varied guests and roomies still sleeping?"

"No," she admitted. "They've gone out."

Michael looked over at the set table, took in the flowers and the guest-readiness of the place. "I think my ESP has just kicked in again," he said. His shoulders drooped. "You're about to entertain someone else for brunch." He handed her the bag and looked, for a moment, flushed and embarrassed. "Well, he's welcome to my crullers."

Angie smiled. He was jealous. It was so cute. It gave her a little *frisson* of pleasure, but not at his expense. "Michael, the table is set for two," she said, "because there are two guests, aside from me—my mother and my father."

"Do they break bread—or crullers—together?" he asked.

She could see that under the joke he was relieved. "No, not usually," she admitted. "This is what you might call experimental in nature. But since they're going to be grandparents together, I figured now was the time for them to hear the news. And hear it together."

"Whew. You know, two strikes and I'm out. First I think you're here with the gang. Then I think you're here with a lover. I don't think I'm going to set up that part-time business as a reader-slash-adviser, after all," Michael told her. "I might not have been attuned to all the music of the spheres. In fact, now that I am, I think I'll take a powder."

She walked him to the door, then she held on to one of the red sleeves of his sweater, stood on tiptoe, and gave him a kiss. "Thank you for the attention," she said. "But I'm afraid this morning is going to be fraught with difficulties."

"Well, it's the fraught that counts," he said. They both winced. "Give me a call if you survive," he said, and started to leave. Halfway down the walk, he turned back. "Hey, Angie?" he asked. "You told me about, you know, the pregnancy, *before* you told your mom and dad?" She nodded. He smiled. "Good," he said, and walked away with a jaunty step.

Some things were so predictable, they were ridiculous. Her father had arrived exactly on time with a big and ridiculous house gift—one of those ice cream makers which would take up at least half of her kitchen counter space and be used only once, if ever. "It took you long enough to invite me to the housewarming," he said, as if this were a black-tie party for fifty and she'd been holding out on him.

He walked through the whole place suspiciously, as if she might be hiding a poster of Fidel Castro on a closet door somewhere. Then he sat down on the sofa and wanted to know about the rent, whether utilities were included, how long the lease lasted, and every other useless financial detail about the place. She answered while she made raspberry ice tea. She knew he'd go on and on with his inquisition as long as she let him. Then the doorbell rang. Angie put the salad on the table and opened the door.

Natalie bustled in with two shopping bags filled with more delicatessen and prepared gourmet take-out than any normal family could eat in a week. "Hi, darling," she said, and Angie had time to kiss her before Natalie heard Anthony's grunt and looked over her daughter's shoulder to see her ex-husband. "What is this?" she asked, putting down her bags.

"This is my apartment," Angie said. "*He* is my father."

Anthony stood up. "You didn't tell me about this," he said.

Natalie got nasty and Anthony grew defensive. It took her ten minutes to calm them both down, get them to their seats at the table, and place food in front of them. She could get mules to brunch, but she couldn't get them to graze. They sat across from each other, ridiculously hostile, her mother glaring at her father, her father glaring at her. This was something important to remember about marriage: once you had children together, it was never over. There were kids' graduations, there were weddings and funerals and birthdays. There were all the events that brought families together, where you had to stare across a table at a person you never wanted to see again. *Ah yes,* Angie thought. She was glad Reid wasn't going to know about the baby.

Finally Natalie turned to Angie, about to remove the untouched salad. "This is totally inappropriate," Natalie said. "If I need to see him, which I don't, I can see him without your intervention."

"Yeah? Since when? I don't need to see you. Just because you need to see me sometimes doesn't mean you *get* to see me," said Anthony. "What am I? An exhibition in a museum?"

Angie couldn't stand it. They were like Jenna and Frankie fighting. No wonder she was immature. She got it from both sides of her family. "Look, this isn't about what *you* need. Either of you," she told them. "What you needed to do was break up our family, so you did it. Maybe that wasn't what I needed, but I understand. And even though you've both been there for me, you haven't been there for me *together.*"

The two of them looked at her as if she were ranting. Then both of them assumed guilty looks. Well, let them. Angie unpacked the bag her mother had brought, putting the artichoke hearts and the beet root salad on the counter, banging the little plastic containers one on top of the other.

"Look," she said. "I am grateful to both of you because you helped me through a really bad time." She put her arms around her father and kissed his cheek. "You gave me courage to walk out, Daddy," she said. "And a place to stay." She turned to her mother. "And you got me motivated, and gave me a job. And introduced me to new friends." She thought of Michael and smiled. "I want you to know that I am really grateful. But I'm really sad because we don't have a family left. America, I don't know, everything just . . . American family life is dissolved. There are no more family holidays, dinners all together at night, just a person alone in front of a TV eating take-out food. That's how you guys live, and it's how I was going to live, except for my friends."

"Look," Natalie began, "I don't think I have to apologize for your father's behavior—"

"Don't say it was me who broke up our marriage," Anthony interrupted.

"Oh, shut up. Both of you," Angie said. "I'm trying to say something *new*. I'm going to have a baby. I *am* having a baby, and Reid doesn't know it. Anyway, he's getting remarried. I don't have a husband, but I will have a baby. And I want the baby to have a family. You're it."

This was so weird, so not as she imagined it. Angie had thought this would be a session where her parents yelled at her, and instead she was yelling at them. Why did that make her feel bad? Perhaps because she felt like the adult, and she wanted the comfort of being their child. *Ah,* she thought, *get used to being the parent,* she said to herself. *It's going to start in about four and a half months and not quit till you're dead.*

Natalie stood up. "You're having a baby?" she asked. "Oh my God!" Anthony didn't say anything, but he stood up also and came over to hug her. The hug felt good. No yelling? No screaming? No cries that she was ruining her life, or throwing away all her education, or being unfair to an unborn child?

"When's the baby due?" Natalie asked. "I can't believe you didn't tell me before! What's the due date? Who's your obstetrician?"

Her father just kissed her and then hugged her again. "So now I guess I can't have anyone kill your ex?" he asked.

"Sure you can," Angie said. "'Cause he's not going to have anything to do with this. But you two are. I'm going to need help, and honestly, I think you need a little family connection yourselves." Angie looked from one to the other. "I know how impossible this seems, but I want you to try to be mature," she said. "Get along. Be grandparents. Is that too much to ask?"

Natalie walked over to her daughter, put one arm around her shoulder, and stretched the other one out to her belly, ready to feel it. "May I?" she asked. And Angie nodded her head. This wasn't the family she'd imagined, but it was one that she'd make work.

61

During which DA Douglas gets the dirt and the dough

Michelle did not want to go back to Douglas, that nasty district attorney, but she didn't really have a choice and she supposed that what he had said was more right than not. All of the insulting things he had ranted about women in her situation had applied to her. She had kept her eyes closed to a lot of what Frank must have been up to. So as the next part of her plan, she and Angie met with Michael Rice and made another appointment to see Douglas.

"You know, Michelle," Michael had said, "I feel that I didn't really prepare you for him. He was tough, and he's not going to be willing to see you again unless you've got some hard evidence. And it's going to have to be pretty compelling evidence."

Michelle had told no one about the money, not even Jada. The very idea of it terrified her. She had it hidden now in the Lexus but she knew if she was found with it she would be implicated in the drug dealing itself. And if it was stolen, or if she lost it, all of their plans would be threatened. She was haunted. Each night she woke up half a dozen times to check that the Lexus was safely parked and undisturbed. She almost asked Angie to park her old wreck on the street and let Michelle park in Angie's spot closer to the apartment, but she was afraid that if—for any reason—the police found the car on Angie's property, it would ruin her friend. They were all taking risks for one another, but it ought to be risks they agreed to.

The blood money was an awful burden. Michelle just wanted to get rid of it.

"I have compelling evidence," she told Michael, without going any further. "Make the appointment." She didn't like Mr. Douglas and it was going to be humiliating to see him again, to admit that he had been right and she had been foolish. It would be worse yet to be virtually assigning her husband to a prison term. But Michelle knew it had to be done. "Tell him I have evidence," she said, but she didn't respond to the question in Angie's eyes.

Michael merely nodded. "Is there some kind of deal that you want cut?" Michael asked. "If there is, tell me now. The only way you'll get it is before you produce evidence."

"I'll give him evidence. I'll testify only if I have to. The only thing I want is to be allowed to leave town, to leave the county, right away, and not return until the trial date. I'll give him my address, but I want it to be kept secret. I want full custody of the children and I want to change my name. I want protection when I return for the trial. That's it."

"I don't think there'll be a problem with any of that," Michael said. "Douglas can't guarantee custody, but if your husband—"

"My future former husband," Michelle corrected.

"Well, if Frank Russo is imprisoned, you'll get custody. I can assure you of that, and I'll handle your case personally. It's a modest request. You can actually get much more from Douglas."

Michelle shook her head. "This isn't about barter," she said. "And I'm not doing this to punish my husband. I just want to make things clean."

When they met this time, the district attorney was just a little more civil, probably because Michael had warned him to be. But Douglas's attitude was as arrogant as before, and his office just as spotless. Michelle wondered who polished all of the plaques and trophies that were on display, because each one glistened and not a single fingerprint defaced any of them.

Only Douglas himself was defaced. His shiny head still had his combed-over eight strands of hair. "Well, we meet again, Mrs. Russo. Mr. Rice assures me that today you won't be wasting our time," he said.

Michelle clutched her bag on her lap. This was her last moment for second thoughts, the last chance she had to possibly stop her husband from going to prison, to stop her children's father from becoming a jailbird. Against the brown leather of her purse, her hands were wet with sweat. She doubted that anybody in her Irish family had ever cooperated with the police for any reason. Well, what had that got them? Poverty and alcoholism for ten generations!

She went face-to-face with Douglas, forcing herself to look straight into his eyes. They were surprisingly blue, but small and buried very deeply in the flesh around his cheekbones. She could save Frank, she told herself, but she couldn't save her family, not unless she did this. And Frank was guilty.

"Well, Mrs. Russo?" Douglas asked. "What have you got?"

"I found something," Michelle said. "I found something that your officers missed."

Douglas made a face of disbelief, his lips pouted, his chin lowered. "We did a *very* thorough search of your house, Mrs. Russo."

"Well, you didn't find this," Michelle said. She took out the bundle of money and put it on the buffed coffee table between them. Michael Rice leaned forward.

"Drugs?" he murmured. Michelle didn't even bother to shake her head. Douglas stood up, and without even touching the bundle, went to the desk and punched in a number on his phone.

"I possibly have new physical evidence here," he said. "I need an officer, a stenographer, and a court clerk immediately." He turned around and sat back down in his chair. "What's in the package? Is it money?" Douglas asked. Michelle nodded. "So you opened it?" he asked. She nodded again. "Hundred-dollar bills?"

Michelle nodded once more. "I didn't look through all of them," she said. "I didn't know if I should even touch it. Fingerprints or whatever. You know, Frank threatened to involve me in this if I brought this to you. We have a tape of him doing that."

"So he knows you found it?"

Michelle nodded again.

"But he doesn't know you're turning it in."

"No." There was a knock at the door and two men and a woman joined them.

"Pick up Frank Russo. We have evidence," Douglas told one of them. "This is Mrs. Russo. I'd like to take her statement." The woman sat down and pulled out some kind of a machine. "I'd like to record it as well," he added, and the uniformed officer brought out a recorder, plugged it in, and set the microphone on the table in front of her, while the other man left, ready to give the order to jail Frank. Poor Frank.

Michael Rice spoke up. "I would like it to be understood that my client has been unaware, until this recent find, of any illegal activity on the part of Frank Russo, her husband. I would also like to make it clear that she gives this testimony and evidence voluntarily. In return she would ask the court for immunity, permission to relocate, and physical protection if required. There's already a restraining order in place against the man."

When the DA nodded, Michael said, "I would like to hear a verbal response to that, Mr. Douglas, just for the record."

"I don't foresee a problem with it," the DA agreed aloud. "No charges have ever been pressed against Mrs. Russo."

They discussed preliminaries for a few more minutes, which allowed Michelle to space out. This was it, then—the end of her marriage. Michelle looked down at the purse on her lap. Having Angie process divorce papers and the rest of it meant nothing. Once *this* happened there would be no turning back. And Michelle didn't want to turn back, not to a comfortable life built on lies. She clutched the bag to her. How many other lives had been ruined by money? So many that hers hardly mattered to anyone but her.

When Michelle looked up, Douglas and Michael Rice had finished and were both looking at her. "Are you ready?" Michael asked. Michelle nodded. She looked at the brown-paper-wrapped parcel on the DA's sparkling coffee table.

Douglas began his questioning. "This package in front of you is something that you've found, independently and on your own?"

"Yes," she said.

"Mark it exhibit two for now," he told the clerk. "And I've been told it contains money," he said.

She nodded. "Please state your answers verbally," the stenographer requested.

"Oh, I'm sorry," Michelle said. "Yes, I found this money. It's packages of hundred-dollar bills. At least that's what I think it all is."

Douglas picked up the package and gave it to the court clerk. "Could you please count this?" he asked. Then he turned to Michelle. "Where did you find this money?" he said.

"Under the carpet in the floor of the closet in my daughter's room," Michelle told him.

"Didn't our officers search your home, including the closet?" Douglas asked.

"Yes," Michelle agreed. "They wrecked my whole house." For a moment, her lip trembled as she thought about it—about the way her house had been torn apart, as her life had been.

She took a breath. "It was very well hidden. I didn't find it right away," she said. "You see, for days and days I was cleaning up the terrible mess they left." She told the entire story while the tape recorder rolled and the stenographer pecked away at her odd machine and the court clerk counted silently at the other side of the office.

Douglas interrupted her a few times, but now that he was getting what he wanted, he was surprisingly cordial. "Could this money represent savings?" he asked.

"No. I don't think so. We have a savings account."

"And it's money you didn't know about?"

"Yes. I mean, yes I didn't know it was there."

The questioning went on. Michael patted her hand once or twice, but Michelle felt confident, sure now that she was doing the right thing. It took more than two hours, and Douglas repeated some questions over and over, but Michael would remind him he'd already been there, and Michelle kept it simple, giving short answers as Michael had advised. She told them the truth, leaving out only the parts she had to—like the entire safety deposit box episode. Finally she was done. She felt like a limp rag by then.

"Mrs. Russo. I want to thank you for this," Douglas said, doing a fairly good impersonation of a human being. "You did the right thing. I know it couldn't have been easy for you." The clerk came over with the money, now wrapped in plastic bags. He handed a piece of paper to Douglas.

"Well, that's it," Douglas said. "The evidence we needed. I'll have to ask you to sign for it." He looked at Michelle. "Do you think there might be any more?" he asked.

"I didn't find any other hiding places in the house. But you can certainly look," she said, telling the truth. "Who knows?" And then they all rose, shook hands, and left the office.

62

In which Rice gets mushy

Angie had to make seventeen calls that morning to get permission for Jada to have her weekend visitation changed from Saturday to Sunday, in addition to permission to take the children to church. "My God," she complained to Bill after she'd finally gotten call-backs, returned other calls, faxed the documentation, received receipt of the documentation back, spoken to the court clerk, spoken to the judge's secretary, and finally confirmed it all with the supervisor of the Department of Social Welfare, "think what it would take if I was trying to get permission for them to be in a bump and grind show instead of just going to church."

"That would be no problem," Bill said. "Parents make little girls do that all the time. It's called kiddie beauty pageants."

Angie just shook her head. "Would you mind making copies of all of this? One for Mrs. Jackson, one for my file, and one for Mr. Jackson."

"Should I do one for Michael, Latoya, Janet, and Jesse while I'm at it?" Bill asked.

"Boring," Angie said.

"Me? Boring?" Michael asked as he walked into the room.

Bill, on his way out, passed him and raised his eyebrows. "You? The young—well, middle-aged—Lochinvar?"

Michael raised his brows in disapproval. "Loose lips sink ships," he said.

"I haven't said a word," Angie protested. Michael raised his brows higher. Angie shook her head, assuring him of her innocence. "You know, Bill has a kind of genius for office gossip. It's radar or something."

"He didn't know about my separation and divorce," Michael said dryly. "But he knows that we're an item."

"I take your point, counselor," Angie said rising. "But you only have two choices here. You can believe I'm lying to you or that I'm not." She moved closer to him and put her hand on his shoulder, the edges of her fingers against his neck. "Which one is it going to be?"

"Dinner," Michael replied. "Lobster, I think. And then we'll explore this loose lips business."

Angie actually blushed.

Dinner was great. Michael took her to an old house that had been converted into an inn. "Westchester is lousy with these joints," he told her as they were seated at a table next to the fireplace. They talked a little bit about work, and about Angie's mother, then Angie asked Michael a few questions about growing up. He'd been born in Minnesota. He was the oldest of three boys. The youngest had died of cancer just eleven months ago.

"With that and the divorce, it must have been a tough year for you," she said.

He nodded, rotating the brandy snifter in his hand. "I'd have to agree with that," he said. He looked into the glass. "Do you know that your eyes are exactly the same color as this Courvoisier?" he asked.

Angie shook her head. In the low light Michael looked almost boyish. And she could tell that he really, really liked her. "You know, it wasn't easy to let my wife leave. She's moved back to Omaha. She's got a teaching job at the university there and I let the kids go with her. I miss them a lot."

"I'm sure you do."

"What I'm trying to stay, Angie, is that it isn't only women who suffer in a divorce. Men sometimes do, too." He took another sip of his brandy. "I can't wait to see my daughters. I only let them go because it was best for them."

"That's being a good parent in difficult circumstances," Angie said, thinking of Jada. Michael smiled at her.

"Thanks," he said, then reached out and took one of her corkscrew curls in his fingers. "How do you make it do that?" he asked, and Angie had to smile.

"It just grows out of my head that way," she said. "It drives me nuts."

"It drives me nuts, too," he said and his voice was lower with insinuation.

His voice, sexy and deep like that, made her hold her breath. Suddenly Angie remembered looking at the hundred golden streaks in Reid's hair and asking *him* how *he* had gotten it like that. She let out her breath slowly. She wondered if, in every relationship, there was someone who adored and someone who was adored. She also wondered who had the better deal.

She took Michael's hand, gently untangling her hair from his grasp. It seemed to wake him out of his trance. "So, how many people are you living with now?" he asked. "Is it up to fifty yet? Do you have cats and turtles and hamsters, as well as girlfriends, dogs, and children? Do you have fiestas and grill goats on the holidays? Piñata parties? Chinese New Year? Do you sleep in shifts?"

"There are only nineteen of us," Angie joked. "That's nothing. And we don't do piñatas. We do Mardi Gras and the High Holy Days." She paused. "I know you don't approve of mixing business with social life, but—"

"Hey, I'm in no position to talk," he said, gesturing back and forth between them.

"Well, anyway, Jada and Michelle will be moving out pretty soon. They're getting on their feet." She would have liked to tell him about Marblehead and the rest of their audacious plans, but Michael was a man who believed in the law. She didn't think he would inform on them, but she was certain he would try to stop her from helping. Angie, though, had decided she would take the risk. She just wouldn't share it with Michael.

But when he wrapped her in her coat and helped her down the stairs outside the restaurant, she felt a pleasant tingling and hoped he'd invite her to his apartment for coffee. She also thought there might be other things she would enjoy sharing with Mr. Rice.

63

In which Jada sells out to Clinton

"No. No! *No!*" Angie shouted. "Look, we've gotten this far. I am not going to let you go insane." She glared at Jada. So did Michelle, if she could ever be described as glaring. They were in Angie's kitchen, just finishing their third cups of coffee. They were all pretty hyper.

"Honey, I have to agree with Angie. Everything else is all ready," Michelle said to Jada. "Don't mess it up. Your stuff is packed, the kids' new things are all waiting to go. We've got it stowed in my car. You even have permission to take the kids to church. How can you do this now? Samuel should be here any minute."

Angie took a deep breath. "Jada, you know how hard it was for me to agree to help with the kids' . . . disappearance. I just don't think that there's one more chance you can afford to take."

Jada looked at her two friends. "I'm not asking you to do anything," she said. "I'll do it all by myself. But I'm going to do it."

"Jada, it's illegal and maybe even dangerous," Angie reminded her.

"So is everything else I'm doing."

Angie got up from the dinette chair and looked at Michelle. "Your friend has finally gone completely crazy. I cannot listen to this any longer. I'm an officer of the court. I could be disbarred. And what about me? You two are going to be gone. But people might come around here, sniffing."

"What if they do?" Jada said. "It has nothing to do with you."

Angie made a hopeless gesture with her hands. She spilled some of the coffee on the counter. "Michelle, you talk to your irresponsible, vengeful, risk-taking friend. I have no patience." She walked down the hall and slammed her bedroom door.

Michelle looked at Jada, but Jada turned her head away. "She's making sense and you're not," Michelle said.

"Oh, don't be taking sides with her. You don't know what it was like to live in that house for all those years! Your house was perfect. My kitchen floor was still raw plywood. You know what it's like to try and keep that clean. And the garage door rotting off its track. And the upstairs bathroom never finished. And the guest room only framed in. The overhead light in the dining room was a bare bulb in an orange plastic construction cage. *Now* he's fixing that place up?" Jada stopped to take a breath. She put her hand on the counter, smearing Angie's spilled coffee. She'd spent years in that house, constantly troubled by the unfinished state of it, resenting Clinton, and yet paying the monthly mortgage. "I would *beg* him. I would buy the wallboard. I would drag it into the house myself. I even offered to pay someone *else* to finish up. He wouldn't let me. He was offended. You were living in House Beautiful, but I was always in a construction zone."

"Jada, calm down. Let's remember what's important. I'm leaving my whole house behind me. The carpets, the couches, the curtains. That's not what's important, Jada, and you know it."

"Don't you tell me what's important."

Michelle took a step back and Jada could tell she'd hurt her. She hadn't meant to. It was just that these white women sometimes were so damn sure of everything. And people accused *black* women of being bossy. Jada took a deep breath.

She had tried to think it through calmly, but each time she did, it seemed that this was the last piece of unfinished business she had to complete. She couldn't just leave the home she'd worked so hard to keep together, the home Clinton didn't respect but would now inherit. She walked over to one of the cots that they borrowed from Natalie and perched at the end of it. She looked up at Michelle, who had gone to the sink, and in her usual crazy way was washing the two mugs that had been left on the drain board. But Jada knew Michelle was only doing that to cover her hurt.

"Michelle," she said. "I'm sorry," but Michelle couldn't hear her with the water running. Hard as it was for Jada to apologize, she owed it to her friend. Jada got up, walked to the sink, and leaned over to look at Michelle. "I'm really sorry, Michelle," she repeated.

"That's okay," Michelle said. Jada hoped that was true and took her friend's soapy hands, rinsed them, and pulled her over to the cot.

They were already doing so much for her that Jada found it hard to ask for just one more thing—even if it was only understanding. But she wanted—*needed*—them to understand. "Vengeance is mine, sayeth the Lord" was a quote that Jada had wrestled with over and over again, but this felt so right—even if it was risky—that she felt certain she had to do it. "Just sit down and listen?" she asked Michelle. "I have it all figured. If you agree, I know we can get Angie to see it."

Michelle took a deep sigh. "Penis gluing, kidnapping, turning state's evidence, and now . . . this. Why don't we just join the mob?"

"Why don't you just listen for a few minutes," Jada said. "I'm telling you, I have it all worked out."

And she did have it all worked out.

Michelle, reluctantly, made the call to Clinton. Of course, Tonya answered (which was only one of the reasons Michelle had to make the call) but Michelle asked for Clinton. Though it was clear the woman was reluctant to hand over the phone, Clinton did, at last, get on the line. Michelle had been letter perfect.

"You know, I'm moving," she'd said. "All this trouble with Frank and all. Anyway, I thought you might want some of my furniture." Jada couldn't hear her husband's response, but if Tonya was listening on the extension—and she probably was—Jada was pretty sure about the response. "I have a sofa and a love seat I don't need. There's a lot of other stuff, too."

Angie joined them and listened to the phone call, shaking her head and rolling her eyes. She hadn't said she would cooperate, but she would. Clinton, the freeloader, jumped on the offer. Jada knew he was the kind of hypocrite who didn't want his kids to play with "a druggie's children," but he'd take the guy's furniture into his house and let his kids sit on it. And so it was arranged that Tonya and Clinton would come over to Michelle's on Sunday for the pick-up.

Michelle stood at the counter, making the arrangements with Clinton and sounding perfectly neutral, as if there were nothing unusual about offering her best friend's enemy a gift.

Jada watched and listened and then noticed something really different. Truly different. Amazing, even. "Angie, look at this," she whispered. "Do you see what I see?"

"I see a felony in the making," Angie whispered.

"No. No. Look at the counter." Michelle, just finishing her conversation on the phone, was standing before the mess of coffee cups and the smeared counter. *And she wasn't picking up a sponge.* "She's looking right at the mess and she isn't doing a thing about it."

"Oh my God," Angie said. "You're right."

Jada had made sure that Michelle was very specific about the time, and she made sure that Clinton understood that if he didn't get it then, he wouldn't get it at all. "I may not be there, Clinton," Michelle said. "But if not, if I'm already on the road, my lawyer will let you in and you can take the stuff." Michelle hung up the phone and looked over at her two friends. "What are you staring at?" she asked them.

"Michelle, do you want to wipe down that counter?" Jada asked.

"Oh, fuck it," Michelle said. "We have more important things to worry about."

"Unbelievable," Angie said.

Jada spread out her arms. "Cindy! Cindy, you've grown up."

64

During which Michelle is briefly behind bars

Michelle had to be sure that she had a good alibi so that she wouldn't be implicated in any way in what she thought of as "Jada's housewarming party." She figured the best thing to do was go to jail, because there was no place where you were photographed, observed, signed in, and signed out, the way you were there. It was kind of ironic—going to prison to be sure she didn't go to prison. But Michelle supposed that Frank wouldn't know the difference, and the DA would eventually like to know her whereabouts at the particular moment when Jada was finishing her caper.

Michelle had been busy. She'd made arrangements for Natalie to watch her kids while she called five potential housekeeping clients, received letters from four more, and had met with most of them. She'd also interviewed staff. The acting she'd done up in Boston and Marblehead helped her—she just acted like a secure businesswoman or an employer and it seemed to work. She'd only had trouble with one prospect, who was clearly a nut.

Then, nervously, she'd gone back to her house—now that Frank was jailed—with Jada and Angie. They helped her dirty it. Then she used it as a test site and training ground. Some of her prospective employees were awful; in five minutes of watching them clean, she could tell they'd never do the job right, but she did pick out two women—Gladys and Emily—who seemed capable and motivated. She figured she could find one more person, and then the four of them could cover nine or ten houses a week. Michelle was going to charge premium prices, but give first-class service, and she thought she could clear more than enough to live on.

She didn't have to go see Frank, but she felt that if she didn't, there would be something incomplete, something still childlike and frightened about her. Frank couldn't take care of her anymore, but he also couldn't hurt her unless she gave him the power to do so, which she was not going to do.

Frank had been picked up almost immediately after she had given George Douglas the evidence. Knowing that he was out of the house, she had gone there briefly to pack some essential things for herself and the children; now she was prepared to make her own move, but for some reason she wanted to touch base with him. Fourteen years meant something and although Michelle didn't want to think of them as "the best years of her life," they were certainly formative. In any case, although she was frightened, it was necessary to see Frank.

But the reality of jail was frightening—she had to go through a metal detector, be searched, and then walk down a seemingly endless green corridor, with heavily screened and locked doors at regular intervals. Imagining Frank here was worse than upsetting. The keys on the guard's ring jingled, the only noise until he unlocked one more barred and screened door and took her into a visitor's room where Frank sat behind a big table, looking surprisingly small.

He didn't look good. He was wearing gray work pants and a shirt that matched. It made him look like a janitor or a mechanic. His usually ruddy skin looked very pale against his dark hair. But the biggest change was his expression. His eyes, his whole face, looked closed—not closed as in sleep, but emotionally closed.

"Hands on the table," the guard said as Michelle took her seat opposite Frank.

Frank threw the guy a look, but complied. Then he looked straight across at Michelle and said, "Is this what you wanted?"

"No. It's not what *I* wanted, Frank."

"Michelle, in my wildest dreams I never thought *you'd* betray me like this."

Michelle had thought she was prepared for anything, but he pissed her off. It was still the old game—twisting everything so that Michelle was always the stupid one, everything he did was right, anything he didn't want was wrong. She wondered if he'd always been like this and she'd just never noticed. Well, two could play at that game.

"You gave me no choice," she said. "You threatened me, Frank," she said. "You shouldn't have threatened me. Because our deal was always that we put each other first and then the children, and each of us as individuals came last. But you, *you've* been selfish and crazy and irresponsible through this whole thing. You weren't thinking of *me*, and you certainly weren't thinking of the *children*. They can't afford to have their mother go to prison, Frank. It's just not a possibility."

"I *never* threatened you," Frank said.

"Right. And you *never* hit me," she said. She took the tape cassette out of her purse. "Want me to play this for you?" she asked. "It's what you said at the diner."

"Put that away," he said harshly. "They have cameras all over here."

"Okay. So I have children who need me now more than ever. Remember them, Frank. They're so traumatized already, I don't know how long it's going to take for them to recover. We have to leave town. All the newspaper coverage has affected them, me, and even the school. We have to leave their friends, who are no longer their friends, and we have to go somewhere else and start over—without you. Every single thing we did, everything we tried to do for them, is ruined. Do you understand that, Frank?"

"What about *me*?" he asked. "You think everything isn't ruined for *me*?"

"Your choice," she said.

"No, *yours*. You put me behind bars." His voice dropped but became ferocious. "You turned me in. I can't believe it. I just can't believe it."

Michelle recognized the rage. He would hit her again if he could. But now she was safe. She was grateful for the table between them, for the guard, for the law. "I'm sure that's true," she said. "You never believed you'd get caught. You never believed you'd be punished. You always believed you were exempt from everything." She looked around the room. Both small windows were made of frosted, bubbled glass with chicken wire embedded in it. She couldn't see the sky, or even what the weather was.

"No one's exempt, Frank."

"Doing what *you* did was the stupidest thing," Frank said. But she couldn't hear that word one more time. She interrupted him and almost jumped up in doing so. The guard looked over as if to warn them, but she didn't care.

"Oh, that's *it. That's* it, Frank. Stupid Michelle! It's always Stupid Michelle! You almost convinced me I was a simpleton. Well, Stupid Michelle has started a new business. Stupid Michelle is going to move the children to a new town, with a good new school. Then Stupid Michelle is going to support them and try to make them feel secure, even though they have a daddy who was the local drug lord and is going to prison." She paused to get her breath. "Remember, this was nothing I ever planned, but it's something that I've *had* to do. And Frank, I'm doing just fine. And I'm doing it without you."

"What are you talking about?" he bleated. "Where are you moving? Where are you taking my kids?"

"I've filed for divorce, Frank. And I'll get sole custody. Long-term, it might have bad effects on the children, but for now that's my choice. When you're out of prison—"

"I'm not going to prison, Michelle. I *know* people."

"I don't *care* who you know. I don't care what you do. I hope you have other money hidden, Frank, because otherwise you are broke as well as guilty. I don't care where you go. I'm out of here."

Frank shook his head. "I can't believe you gave over a half a million dollars to the DA. You *are* stupid, Michelle."

She wondered how many times she had heard that, whether Frank said it directly or implied it. She wondered how deeply she had always believed it, and she knew that she didn't have to believe it anymore. She also knew she didn't have to tell him anything, or defend herself. She knew that between the two of them, one of them had been really stupid. One of them had ruined a life that could have been satisfying, even beautiful. But there was nothing that she could do about that now, except never let herself be insulted in that way again. "I think visiting time is over," she said. "Oh. And I *do* have something for you." She threw an envelope on the table.

"What's this?" he asked, looking around, his dark brown eyes wide, the pupils dilating.

"The list. The list of everything you had me make. Everything torn or lost or damaged or broken. All the things the county would replace." She paused. "It's totally complete. Everything ruined or broken is on it. Except our marriage. You can add that if you want to. Good luck, Frank."

"And that's it, then? You don't expect to ever see me again?"

"Oh yes," she said. "I'll see you again. In court. I'm testifying." And she turned and left him there.

65

In which there is goodness and greatness and great balls of fire

Jada was waiting around the corner in the Volvo, ready with some empty shopping bags. She was wearing her church clothes and had already picked up the children. "Why are we waiting?" Shavonne asked.

"We're going to church with a friend." Samuel pulled up behind her. "Here he is. Now I want you to be quiet and good." She got the children into his car and tried to explain what was going on.

"Where are we going?" Shavonne asked.

"Who's he?" Kevon wanted to know. "Is he like Mrs. Patel?"

"Not exactly. He's a real friend, and now we're going to church. Mrs. Patel will be there," Jada said. "I'll be right back. I want you to sit here for ten minutes," she said. "Shavonne, you're in charge. I'll be right back—I forgot my Bible." Which was true. It was at the house.

Jada waited at the end of the street until she saw Clinton and Tonya walk out of her house and along the way that she and Michelle had walked together so many mornings. Their walks seemed so long ago. She looked around at the street, knowing she might never see it again.

Once Clinton and Tonya had disappeared into Michelle's house, Jada clutched the bags and went into her own house for the last time. She took the newspapers she'd already twisted into spills out of the shopping bags, along with two flame logs. Then she went upstairs and started by looking through every room to make sure no one, no living thing, not even a hamster, was left behind. She filled her shopping bags with some of each of the children's favorite toys and clothes, leaving newspaper behind in its place. Just as she'd suspected, in a new burst of energy Clinton had begun painting and fixing some of the unfinished spots that had been such eyesores to her for all those years. And, as she'd suspected, he'd also left paint cans, paint thinner, and all kinds of other dangerous stuff around. Perfect.

Down in the kitchen, she was amazed to see the plywood floor had already been half tiled. She wondered if he would have ever finished the other half, or whether for Tonya it would have remained half tiled instead of all plywood. She poured the bottle of kerosene on the plywood, put a flame log inside one of the wooden cabinets with piles of newspaper. Then she got the kids' birth certificates and four or five photo albums from the hall bookshelf, along with the Bible.

Nothing left on the shelves mattered to her; it was just a lot of paper. She poured some of Clinton's paint thinner on them. She put the second flame log in the messy hall closet, under the wooden stairway. There was lots of flammable junk in there, but just to be sure, she opened the paint cans and threw in more newspaper. She wondered if it would clearly be seen as arson. She shrugged. In for a penny, in for a pound. And it *might* look like spontaneous combustion or a construction accident. After all, as Michelle reminded them all the time, most accidents happen in the home.

But this wasn't her home anymore and never would be. All that struggling she'd done, all the hours of working, away from her kids, and she'd thought these walls were important. DAS—dumb and stupid.

In the living room, she passed her wedding portrait but didn't bother to take it. She was surprised that Tonya hadn't taken it down. Maybe Clinton hadn't let her? She didn't care, but she did pick up the candlesticks her grandma had given her and added them to the haul in her shopping bags. Then she poured the last of the kerosene onto the living room curtains and across the floor, where it met the bookcases in the hallway. She stood at the door, took out a box of matches, and made sure that her hands were clean and dry. She smoothed down her dress. She'd been gone eleven minutes. She had to get back to the kids.

Carefully, she stepped over the threshold and lit one match. When it was burning, she threw it into the house and watched the little line of flame run along the hall floor she had so often washed. Just to be sure, she put the whole box down and threw one more lit one on top of it. Jada turned her back and left the door just slightly open, to increase the flow of oxygen. By the time she got to the sidewalk, she thought she could already smell a tiny hint of smoke. But she wouldn't allow herself to turn around. Most accidents might happen in the home, but this was her home no longer.

Angie wasn't shocked to find that Clinton and his girlfriend were greedy. They'd both been put off when they saw her face, remembering her from the trial, but she calmly explained she was acting as Michelle's lawyer now and had them sign a release. She didn't feel calm, though. This man was a freeloader, willing to hurt his children emotionally in return for his own comforts. Rather than giving him freebies, she'd like to give him hell. But he'd get what he deserved.

Michelle had told her which pieces of furniture she could let them carry off, but Tonya had the nerve to ask for the credenza, a clock, and one of the paintings on the wall also. It had been a pleasure for Angie to say no.

She hated this plan, she hated being in Michelle's house, and she hated Clinton and Tonya. How had she allowed herself to be talked into it? Thank God she had Michael and Bill with her to help her stay calm and to be witnesses.

Now they were ready to help Clinton carry the stuff away down the block, but Tonya wasn't through window-shopping. "She need her big bed?" Tonya asked. "He go to the joint, she won't need a big bed. But we could sure use one."

Angie thought of all of Tonya's denials under oath that she and Clinton were having an affair. Maybe Jada was right—the system just didn't work. Ah, but there was justice to be had; she stopped in her restraint of Tonya's free furniture campaign and remembered the scene up in Marblehead with Reid glued in place. She couldn't help it, she had to smile. She wouldn't mind seeing both Tonya and Clinton glued to this mattress, but as far as she knew, it wasn't available.

"I'm sorry," she said coldly. "That belongs to Mrs. Russo." She had been playing the part of attorney, though why Michelle would need an attorney to give away her furniture didn't seem a question Tonya would ask. Clinton, though, was so busy taking freebies he didn't seem to care. She looked at her watch and excused herself, going into the south bedroom and looking out the window. Jada had to be on her way to church by now.

Had she actually done it? She paused. There, dark against the sky, was the answer to her question—a plume of smoke twisting in the wind. Angie shivered. *Hell hath no fury,* she thought. It would be perfect timing, she supposed. She checked to see that the wig and outfit were ready, and that she had the spare keys to the Volvo. She went back to join the other four downstairs in the living room.

Clinton was removing the cushions from the sofa so that Tonya could carry them, while the three men were getting ready to heft the sofa itself. Angie opened the door as Bill backed out and down the front steps, Michael and Clinton following with the rest of the sofa between them.

They were almost to the sidewalk, Tonya ahead of them with her awkward burden, when Angie simultaneously heard Tonya's wail and Michael's exclamation. Bill, with his back to the house, didn't know what was going on. When Clinton looked up, he let go of his end of the couch; Tonya dropped the cushions and began running. Angie herself ran to the sidewalk, and though she saw the back of the Volvo around the corner and knew time was pressing, she couldn't help it. Like the other moths, she was drawn to the flame.

Clinton's house was already burning merrily. The upstairs windows were lit with a rosy glow. The smoke she had seen was not coming from the chimney, but was rolling out the back of the house. The front door was open and inside what had once been the hall, Angie could see the floor and the walls already licked with bright orange flames.

"Oh my God!" Tonya cried.

"Is anyone in there?" Michael asked.

Clinton, his mouth open, shook his head. "The kids went to church with my wife."

"Are you sure?" Bill asked. "The children are out? No one visiting? No cats, no dogs?"

"My stereo!" Clinton said. "My rotary saw!"

"I'll call 911," Michael said, running back to Michelle's house.

But someone already had. The fire truck pulled up behind them, its scream matched only by Tonya's. "Get the pickup!" she yelled. "Get the pickup out of the driveway!"

Just as the fireman arrived, an upstairs window blew out with a whoosh. The stink of melting plastic and burning polyester and nylon carpet hit them in a nauseating wave. Firemen were everywhere.

"No one is in there," Angie told the chief. "The house is empty. No pets. Nothing." He nodded his thanks and called out to one of the men. Angie grabbed Bill's elbow. "Tell Michael I have to go," she said. "I have to tell Jada."

Bill nodded his head. Then he looked at Angie. "She didn't?" he asked, his face serious.

Angie tried to keep her face blank. "She didn't," Angie agreed. "Tell Michael. And don't you or he go near the house. No dead heroes."

"Don't worry," Bill assured her.

66

Oh, heavenly Father

Jada met Samuel outside the church. "Go in on your own," she told him as her social worker approached. Ms. Patel seemed even meeker than usual, looking around nervously at all the dark-skinned people milling forward.

"Would you like to join us in worshipping the Lord?" Jada asked her, putting it on as thick as she could. "Jesus has a big welcome for everyone." Of course, that was true, but Jada didn't think that Ms. Patel would necessarily feel that way, or want to be a part of the service. At least that was part of Plan A. And Plan A seemed—so far—to be the only one necessary.

"I will sit in the back," Ms. Patel said. "Or perhaps take some air. Do not worry about me."

Jada smiled. She wasn't going to worry at all. "God bless you, Ms. Patel," she said, and meant it. With luck, it would be the last time she ever spoke to the woman.

People were arriving and most had already entered the church, but nobody could say that Jada was late. She carried the baby in front of her, and with Kevon on one side and Shavonne on the other, she stepped down the main aisle and made sure that she said hello to as many members of the congregation as she could. They were witnesses, every one.

She took her seat as decorously as an arsonist could possibly manage. Reverend Grant was already up at the pulpit, leafing through some announcement papers. Jada folded her hands, told Shavonne to stop wiggling, and tried to compose herself.

Lord, she prayed silently, *I just did something very, very wicked. And I know that, but I can't truly say that I'm sorry. I didn't break a commandment, and I didn't physically hurt anyone. I just felt that I had to stand up for what was fair. Forgive me, Lord, for any sin I committed in Your sight, and protect my neighbors and the firefighters if they get there. But Lord, if it's possibly Your will, please let the house burn right down to its foundations. And then help me to get my babies away.*

At that moment, Sherrilee picked up the necklace from around Jada's neck and put a blue bead into her mouth. How strong was the chain, Jada wondered, versus how much noise Sherrilee would make if she plucked the necklace out of the baby's hands. She searched through her bag and took out a bottle nipple that she sometimes let Sherrilee use instead of a pacifier. Sherrilee's eyes opened with joy, as if she were greeting her long-lost and very best friend. Well, that would keep her quiet.

The service began with a hymn. Kevon sang lustily, while Shavonne, at first, tried to mumble when she could. But soon the spirit moved her, and by the last chorus she was singing as loudly as the rest of them. Jada smiled, closed her eyes, and said another silent prayer. All she wanted was for her children to be able to lead good family lives.

She opened her eyes as the hymn ended and glanced across the aisle to Samuel Dumfries. He was sitting across from her, looking attentively up at the minister. He looked stable, successful, and upright, the last person in the church that anyone would think was to help abduct three children. Just goes to show how looks can be deceiving. The man was risking so much for her. Jada closed her eyes again. *Please, Lord, help me get away with this, and be sure that no harm comes to my friends or Samuel Dumfries for helping me.*

The next hymn was announced: "The Lord Is the Only Home You Need." Jada almost smiled. Since she'd thrown the match she wasn't sure where she was going to live now, the Lord was the only home she *had.* But wasn't this a sign? She wasn't a believer in that sort of thing. The congregation sang together and some of the women behind Jada got the spirit. But it was only the warm-up. When the next hymn was announced, Jada had to cover her mouth with her hand. "We'll now sing 'Light a Torch For Jesus,'" Reverend Grant announced.

Oh, Lord, Jada thought. *Even for a woman who doesn't believe in such things, this has to be a sign. There have been some dark days, and You have certainly tried my soul, but surely this means that You are helping me.*

"Mommy, I'm hot," Kevon said. "Can I take off my jacket?"

"May I," she corrected, "and the answer is no. Not in church, Kevon."

He sighed and put his thumb in his mouth. Reverend Grant cleared his throat and began the sermon. "How many of you," he asked, "have heard God speak?" Several voices were raised in answer. "But how many of you have *seen* the Lord?" Reverend Grant inquired again. There were fewer answers but the room was heating up with the spirit.

"Not many people are granted that gift," Reverend Grant intoned. "Moses heard the Lord, but he did not look upon the Lord's face. Moses saw only a burning bush. Fire was the way the Lord showed himself to Moses." Jada's eyes opened wide. This was almost too much. "When Moses took the Israelites across the desert, the Lord appeared as a tower of smoke in the daytime and a tower of flame in the night. You had to be brave to follow the Lord. You had to be daring to leave a home of bondage and wander into the unknown, looking for the promised land."

Jada could hardly believe it. Homes, torches, burning bushes, and towers of flame. She knew she was meant to do this and her last bit of guilt disappeared. "Thank you, Lord," she whispered, and her eyes filled with tears. The sermon went on and on, but Jada heard no more. She was poised to go as soon as she could. She looked at her watch, and noticed Samuel checking his.

When they called for the choir to come up front, Jada rose and made sure that the children did, too. She moved toward the front of the church, though Shavonne gave her an inquiring look and said, "I'm not singin'."

"Shhh," Jada told her.

Discreetly, waiting his turn, Samuel Dumfries rose and joined the moving bodies. People were already making a joyful noise and Jada had the nerve to turn and see if Ms. Patel was watching, but either she was lost behind the standing crowd—she was a very small woman—or she was waiting in the vestibule for all of the noise to be over. Smoothly, moving past the rest, Jada walked past the pulpit to the side nave and out the exit door, Samuel Dumfries now right behind her.

"The car is there," he said, and she followed him. This was the moment she had feared, the moment she had prayed over. If the children didn't agree, she swore that she would make Samuel turn around. She'd face the music for whatever crimes she'd be accused of.

What if they said no? What if, at this very moment, the children decided that life with their father, that life in a known quantity, was what they desired? That they weren't willing to leave their friends, their school, their grandmother? Jada was willing to make every decision for them necessary but they had to realize what they were leaving behind and be willing to do that.

Jada got them into the backseat of Samuel's car while he got into the driver's seat, then she sat down in the passenger's seat and turned to observe her children. "All right," she said, "listen up. I wanted us to be together, all of us together, as a family, but Daddy didn't want it that way. He wanted Tonya. And he loves you—but so do I. He didn't want me to see you very much, or live with you. So we're going to leave here and go to where we can be together. Unless you say no."

"Is he going to be our new Daddy?" Kevon asked, pointing to Samuel.

"No, of course not," Jada assured him. "You only have one Daddy and you only have one Mama. But sometimes they can't live together."

"So you want us to live with you?" Shavonne asked. And Jada looked at her daughter and held her breath.

"Honey, I've *always* wanted you to live with me. Every single second. Didn't you know that? It was Daddy and I having the fight over that. I never, ever wanted anything else."

"*Really?*" Shavonne asked, her eyes growing big, the way they used to when Jada told her a fairy tale.

"Of course," Jada said. Was her daughter going to go for it? Was her daughter going to let her pull off this caper?

Shavonne leaned over and hugged Jada for the first time in what felt like months. "Really, Mom?" she asked, her cheek crushed to Jada's.

"Really. Really. Oh, baby, I love you," Jada said.

"So; where we goin'?" Kevon asked. "And who's he?"

"We're going to grandma's and grandpa's, at least at first," Jada said. "And after that, well, we'll have to see. It might be hard, at the beginning. A new school, new friends."

"Are we goin' to live down there?" Kevon asked. "By the beach?"

"Yes, sweetie. We're going to try to."

"Hooray!" Kevon shouted. "I'm going to go swimming every day! Can we live right on the beach?"

Out of the corner of her eye, Jada saw Samuel smile. "I'm not sure," Jada said. "Shavonne?" she asked. "Is this okay with you?"

"We get to be with you, Mama? Every day?" Shavonne asked.

"All the time," Jada promised.

Then, "Yes! Yes!" Shavonne said, a little less fearless than Kevon, but a lot more aware.

"Okay," Jada said, turning around and putting on her seat belt while she silently thanked God. Then she turned to Samuel. "Step on it."

67

In which the final chapter is written

Michelle pulled up to the curbside check-in, got out of the Lexus, and waved for a skycap. "Are we taking a plane to our new house?" Frankie asked.

"No, honey. We're just saying good-bye to our friends. Then we'll drive to our new house. Jenna, take your brother out of the car and stand with him over at the curb." Jenna, for once, didn't argue, and did as she was told. Michelle had had a serious talk with her daughter and Jenna knew now that they were making big changes.

"I have a lot of luggage here," Michelle called out to the porter, and began to unload Jada's new suitcases, all packed with the equally new clothes that she and Michelle had bought together. It would be a good way to start their new life. "I packed them with my sister," Michelle lied. "She's parking her car. I'm about to go park this one." She pulled out a twenty-dollar bill. "Here are our airline tickets. Could you just keep an eye on this stuff and my children until I get back?"

"Well, technically I'm not supposed to." Security at the airport was berserk. As if a real terrorist would answer questions honestly or be deterred by these guys.

"Sir," she said. "My sister has three children. They've got a lot of lug-gage. It couldn't fit in one car. And she'll miss her plane if I have to park and drag it back with my kids. She'll be pulling up any minute. Please," she said, pulling out another twenty. "I'm trusting you. I'm not asking you to check it or anything."

The man took the money and nodded. Michelle smiled at him and then drove the Lexus over to a fairly close short-term parking space, running back as fast as she could. "What are we waiting for, Mom?" Jenna asked, antsy.

"We're waiting to say good-bye to somebody," Michelle told her.

"Can I go in and watch the planes take off?" Frankie asked. "Can I get some candy? When we go to the airport with Daddy, we always get candy."

"You can get a chocolate bar in just a few minutes, when we go inside," Michelle said, bending her no-sugar-before-dinner rule. She retrieved the tickets from the skycap and she walked up and down the curb; it seemed like an endless amount of time until, at last, Jada pulled up with the children and Samuel.

Jada slid her long legs out of the car, stood up, and looked around. "We're at the wrong airline," she said, looking confused.

"Not for the Caymans," Michelle told her, and looked at Samuel, who nodded.

"Wait a minute," Jada said. "I don't have the money to go there. I've got to take my chances in Barbados."

"Let's just get checked in," Michelle told her calmly. "Everything is under control. We can discuss the latest update once we're safely inside." She looked around nervously, as if expecting Clinton or the police to pull up at any moment.

Jada looked at Samuel, who was calmly unloading the rest of the luggage. He nodded. "This had better be good, Mich," Jada said.

"It's *very* good," Michelle told her. Meanwhile, Kevon had climbed out of the back of the rental car, and he and Frankie greeted each other happily. Shavonne and Jenna acted as cool as preteens with mixed feelings could manage. "You have to check in all the luggage and answer the security questions," Michelle told Jada.

"It would be easier if I knew where I was going," Jada snapped tartly. Michelle handed an envelope to Jada and turned back to the skycap.

"Here's my sister, and the rest of her luggage," she said. He opened his eyes wide, looking the group over; five children of assorted colors; a lanky blonde; a tall, tawny-skinned woman; and a very dark black man obviously were more confusing than his sexual mathematics were up to. *Wait till he sees Angie!* Michelle thought. He shrugged and rolled the luggage cart to the terminal door, following them without another question. "Come on, kids. First class. Flight Three-two-one," Michelle announced.

"First class?" Jada asked, as the group moved together to the counter. "But Michelle, I can't afford it. And if you cooked this up, you shouldn't have, and even if you could, then I should save the money for other things—"

"Oh, relax," Michelle said. "I think it's finally appropriate to." She looked around. "So long as Clinton doesn't show up at the last minute, and Angie does, we're home free. Now just answer the security questions and let's get up to the gate."

Jada handed her passport, the kids' birth certificates, and the tickets to the very, very thin woman behind the counter and watched as the luggage was moved to the scales. Everyone in economy was waiting on a long snake of a line. The first class clerk looked up. "This is first class," she said, as if Jada had got it wrong.

"I'm aware of that," Jada said coldly.

"My sister always travels first class," Michelle added. "You got a problem with that?"

The woman recovered as best she could from her politically incorrect comment. *Well,* Jada thought, *that's the good thing about the islands. Fewer assumptions based on skin color down there. All of that may be good for my children. Maybe a white suburb was too difficult.*

"Have you packed all your own bags?" the airlines clerk asked. Jada nodded. "Have they been in your possession all the time?"

"Yes," Jada lied.

"Has anyone given you any gifts?"

"No," Jada lied again, this time looking at the tickets.

"Do you have any concealed weapons?" the woman asked, and Jada raised her eyebrows. Was that a standard question?

"Only my tongue," she said sweetly, and Samuel and Michelle both laughed.

All that was left was for Samuel to hand over his passport and ticket. They were checked in. The whole group of them moved through the metal detectors. "Are we going, too?" Jenna asked, confused, though she knew the answer.

"Kevon says they're going to the beach," Frankie said. "Can't we go? Just for a little while."

Michelle and Jada kept herding the kids as they used to do, through malls, through grocery stores, through toy stores. At least here there was the distraction of the fast food court, moving sidewalks, and a new candy store—one with every imaginable sweet displayed in big plastic dispensers that made them totally irresistible. *Oh well*, Michelle thought. It would keep them busy until Angie got there.

But where was Angie? They couldn't separate without her. Michelle moved the kids in the direction of the candy store. "You have four minutes to fill your bags," she told each of the children. "Samuel, do you think you could help Sherrilee?"

He smiled. "I think I can manage it," he said, and followed the toddler, who was already pointing to a bin of gummy worms. He was a nice man. Michelle wondered if anything would happen between him and Jada.

Left in peace for a few moments, Michelle turned to her friend. Jada looked at her. "Okay," she said. "What's going on?"

"Everything's under control," Michelle said. "You know it's much safer to go to the Caymans than to Barbados. Samuel managed to fix the legal part and I fixed the other part."

"What's the other part?" Jada asked.

"The financial part."

"The Caymans take real money. I can't go there," Jada said. "What are you talking about?"

"That's for me to know and you to find out," Michelle laughed.

Angie was driving the Volvo like a bat out of hell. She thought that Clinton had been behind her when she was on the Merritt Parkway, but she wasn't a hundred percent sure. Angie had actually enjoyed her job as the decoy. Now, driving Jada's car and wearing a black braided wig, dark makeup, Jada's sunglasses, and her overcoat, she was playing rabbit to Clinton's greyhound. And just like at the dog races, she had to get to the goal long before the dog did.

Frightened, she gunned the Volvo, though she knew that the Merritt was always filled with troopers only too happy to give out speeding tickets. She looked at her watch. She had to get to the airport and park the Volvo, filled with all of Michelle's luggage and boxes, in time to say good-bye to both of her friends and their children.

She could hardly believe that Jada was leaving the country for good. Not that she didn't want her to get away—it wasn't that. Michelle and Jada had been right—the system didn't work for them, and they had stepped outside of it. As an attorney, she might not approve, but as a woman, she did. The fire at Jada's house had been a real statement. Angie had changed into her costume and gotten to the Volvo, which Jada had parked around the corner, but as she drove away, she saw Tonya pointing at her. If she had been followed, it didn't matter—if they got as far as the airport, they'd go for the wrong airlines.

Angie pulled into the American Airlines lot, threw off the wig and sunglasses, wiped off her face, tore off the coat, and ran to the shuttle bus station. If Clinton *had* seen her, he certainly hadn't followed her to the lot. But just as she crossed the street toward the departures curb, she looked back and thought she saw Clinton's truck pull in beside the Volvo.

God! She couldn't wait for the shuttle to the other terminal! What if he followed her? What if he figured out that he wasn't pursuing Jada at all, and that they'd pulled a switch on him? Did he already know the house wasn't insured, that the kids and his meal ticket were gone? He'd be enraged.

Angie realized that she couldn't wait for a shuttle to pull up, and there were no cabs. She saw a Hertz van and waved it down, getting on as if she were on her way to her car rental. But had the van already passed Jada's terminal? Or was it on its way there? Would the driver let her off? She'd have to play very stupid. Not so easy for someone whose brain was clicking as fast as Angie's was at that moment. "Do I need to pick up my luggage before I get my car?" she asked the driver. "I'm so confused."

"Most people do," he said, looking her over as if she was an idiot.

"Oh. Then would you mind bringing the car to me at Terminal B?" she asked.

"Lady, we don't do that," he told her and laughed. "You better get off at Terminal B. Get your luggage. *Then* get on the van."

"Are we near Terminal B?"

"Next stop," he said, only too happy to get rid of her.

She looked at her watch. She only had twenty minutes before Jada's departure. She bounded down the van steps, across the terminal floor, through security, and up to the gate. Thank God she immediately saw Michelle and Jada, surrounded by the kids, all of whom seemed to be chewing on something. She ran up and hugged the two of them. "I made it!" she exclaimed.

Michelle looked around. "He didn't follow you?"

"I think he did for a while, but I lost him." She handed the Volvo car keys to Jada. Jada turned and handed them to Michelle.

"It's yours," she said, "though why you want the Volvo instead of the Lexus is beyond me."

"A new life, an old car. It makes sense to me," Michelle answered. "Anyway, you do understand. I don't want what Frank bought me." She fished into her pocket and pulled out her own car keys. "These are for you," she said, and handed them to Angie.

"Your car? Oh no. I couldn't take it. That's a forty-thousand-dollar car."

Michelle shrugged. "Eighty-eight thousand, 'cause it's fully loaded, but never mind the details. God knows where the money came from. But you're an underpaid, over-worked, do-gooding mother-to-be, you're going to need it. You can't drive to the hospital to have your baby in your hunk of junk." Michelle turned to Jada. "I also wanted to wait until Angie was here to give you this. It will explain about the Caymans." Michelle handed Jada the canvas bag she'd been toting.

Jada looked at the brown paper-wrapped, string-tied packages inside, raising her brows in question.

"What's six inches long, has a head on it, and drives women crazy?" Michelle asked.

Jada smirked. "I have no idea. I never slept with a white man."

"Money," Michelle said, ignoring her vulgar friend. "Paper money, and lots of it. You can count it on the plane."

Jada looked down at the bag and then back up at Michelle. "Samuel assures me you'll have no trouble taking it into the Caymans," Michelle said. "That's what the Caymans are for. And don't try and give it back. It's like the Lexus. I don't want any part of it. You're doing me a favor. Buy yourself and the kids a nice house—one that's finished."

Jada stood silently for a moment and then tears began to flow from her eyes. "I didn't think I'd ever have friends like you two, and now I have to leave you?"

"Flight three-two-one to the Cayman Islands is about to board. First class passengers and Premium Gold passengers may begin boarding at this time."

"That's us, Mama," Shavonne said. "Come on!"

"I don't think I can go," Jada told Angie and Michelle.

"Are you frightened?" Angie asked. "I really think it will be okay. Your parents will come for a long visit. And I think you can depend on Samuel."

"No. It's not that," Jada said. "I'm not afraid anymore. I just can't leave you two."

"Well, we're leaving you!" Michelle said. "I'm getting in that station wagon of yours and driving. I've got houses to clean and new employees to supervise." She looked at Angela then, and giggled. "Plus, Angie wants her apartment back so she can finally have somewhere to sleep with Michael."

"At least she doesn't have to worry about getting pregnant," Jada laughed.

"Hey. How do you know I haven't slept with him already?" Angie asked. "He really liked me in your wig." The women hooted.

"Well, we have a gift for you that he might not like," Jada said. She looked at Michelle, who fumbled in her big purse and pulled out a wrapped flat package.

"Oh, come on. You've already given me too many gifts," Angie said.

"You'll want this one, sisterfriend," Jada said and laughed.

Angie tore the paper away and realized it was a frame. But the picture inside was unbelievable: Michelle and Jada grinning into the camera, wearing their sex clothes.

"You saved me a Polaroid! How did you do it? The two of you in the picture at once. Who took the picture?"

"The camera. I put it on the bureau and used the timer."

Angie stared at the photo of her two friends grinning. "The best memento I've ever had," she said.

Samuel came up to them then, which made Angie blush. "I'm afraid I have to say good-bye now. And I'm going to take the kids on board," he said to Jada, "if that's all right with you."

"No," Jada said. "Just give me another minute or two. I'll be right with you."

"Are you going to sleep with him?" Michelle asked Jada after Samuel walked away.

"I don't even know him!" Jada whispered, shocked.

"That's not what I asked," Michelle said. "I slept with Frank for fourteen years and I never knew him."

"Jada, it's time to say good-bye," Angie said, reaching up and hugging the taller woman.

"Look, I don't know if I can come back here from the Caymans once I've done this thing," Jada said, "but it doesn't mean you can't visit me. We don't have to say good-bye. I mean, not a permanent good-bye."

"Are you kidding?" Angie said. "I'm bringing the baby down as soon as we can travel."

"And I want you to look around and see if they need a cleaning business in the Caymans," Michelle told Jada. "There's a lot of rich people with condos and they don't want to have to mop up that sand themselves."

"Just as long as I'm not pushing a mop," Jada said. "No domestic work for me."

They announced the last boarding call. "Agreed. You don't do windows, but you *do* have to go," Michelle said.

"Who made you the boss all of a sudden?" Jada asked.

"You did. The two of you did. I've become a boss, and I've done it on my own. I don't know what I would have done without you two. Jada, you gave me self-confidence. And Angie, you took me in. You showed me what true friends were like." Michelle kissed Jada. "I did it myself, but I owe you," she said. Then she kissed Angie. "And I owe you, too. And Michael."

Jada hugged both of them. "I do have to go now," she admitted, tears rolling down her cheeks.

"Yes, you do," Michelle said, suddenly serious. "Jada. Jada, promise me one thing. Promise us you're not really running away to the Basketball Hall of Fame." Angie giggled as Jada promised.

Then Jada turned and walked over to Samuel, took Sherrilee up, and gently pushed Kevon and Shavonne in front of her. She turned to Samuel, said something, and started toward the ticket taker. Angie, Michelle, and the two remaining children yelled and waved.

Jada turned back to look at them from the end of the jetway. The two women were standing in the doorway, arm in arm, waving.

Michelle had the Volvo back in Westchester in less than an hour. The road was open and the driving was fine. She didn't miss the Lexus or anything it represented. In fact, getting her old station wagon back felt good. She thought that Frankie and Jenna liked it, too. In fact, after about half an hour, they seemed to have fallen asleep.

Michelle thought about the jobs that were waiting for her. She had found a place to rent—just a plain little modular ranch on half an acre, but she was renting it furnished, so it was a simple and affordable decision. She couldn't put the house up for sale, because if Frank was found guilty it might all be claimed by the state. It wouldn't bother her. The Volvo had the basics, and though she knew now that life wasn't easy, she was determined to keep it simple.

She didn't know when she had begun, but as she turned off the highway she realized that she was singing. How long had it been since she'd sung? She smiled and sang a little louder. It was an old thing, something her grandmother used to belt out about a syncopated clock: "'There was a man like you and me, as simple as a man could ever be . . . '" In the backseat, Frankie, who loved the song, chimed in. A moment later Jenna's voice joined them. "'From far and wide the people flocked, to hear the syncopated clock,'" they all sang, and glancing into the rearview mirror, Michelle smiled at her smiling children.

On the plane, Jada looked down. Samuel had insisted that she take the window seat. They'd been served champagne, with orange juice for the children. Then they'd had a delicious meal, and now ice cream with hot fudge sauce and cookies, warm out of the oven, were about to be served. It was the first, and possibly the last, time Jada would fly deluxe, but she had to admit it was very enjoyable. She looked out the window again, and for the first time she could see down to the ocean. They were flying over an island, although she didn't know which one it was.

She wondered what the Caymans would be like. Samuel had told her about his discussion with Michelle, and what preparatory work he had done. Now Jada bent forward and took the black canvas bag from under her feet. Slowly she opened it, but she didn't remove the wrapped money. Instead she simply opened the paper.

They were hundred-dollar bills and it looked as if there were dozens—no, hundreds, maybe even a thousand of them! For a moment Jada thought her heart might stop. She tore all the rest of the paper off, put both of her hands into the sack, and started to riffle through one of the stacks of money. She noticed each was carefully wrapped in the middle with a colored band; they'd used the same things at her bank. Each small bunch was a hundred bills—ten thousand dollars. She began to count the bunches. After she had counted past thirty—more than three hundred thousand dollars—she was having so much trouble breathing that she simply stopped, folded up the bag, and stowed it at her feet again. Meanwhile, Samuel was smiling at her.

"Four hundred and eighty-two thousand dollars," he said. "She gave the rest to the police."

Jada blinked, tried to speak, couldn't, and cleared her throat. "And it's mine?" she asked.

"Absolutely. Michelle told me she wants nothing to do with it. She wants it to go to a good cause and we both agree you are one."

Jada shook her head. She was still having difficulty taking this in. "So the money is mine?"

"Yes," Samuel said. "And you'll need it to establish yourself on the Caymans. They're very prejudiced there, but only against poor people. With this capital, any interest you draw from it, and your new job, you'll do fine."

"What new job?" Jada asked.

"Well, there are a lot of banks on the island, as I told you. I think you have your choice, but of the three interviews I've set up, I would say that Island Bank will offer you not only the more interesting job, but also better pay."

Jada leaned back into the comfort of the plush first class seat. How had all of this come about? Should a girl simply listen to her mother and her girlfriends to be sure everything worked out perfectly? In her case, it had certainly helped. For the first time, she had the courage to look directly at Samuel Dumfries. "I want to thank you for your help, too," she said.

He smiled. "My pleasure."

Angie didn't know how she would feel going back to the empty apartment. Lonely, she guessed, so she pumped up the sound system in the Lexus and enjoyed the drive. But when she got there, the apartment wasn't empty.

"We thought you might want some company," her mother said as Angie walked in. Her father was there, too, sitting on the sofa reading a folded up *Wall Street Journal* in that mysterious way he had, turning pages in portions so the paper was no longer than his hand. That it was almost unreadable didn't seem to bother him.

"Well. What a nice surprise," Angie said.

"And nice or not, I'm here and I brought dinner," Bill added. "Lucky thing, too, because as they say in the ads on TV, some assembly required."

Angie was grateful to see them all. Walking into an empty, echoing apartment probably would have been more than she could have tolerated at that moment. But that wasn't all. Natalie moved her toward the door of her spare room, so recently filled with Jenna, Frankie, and Michelle. Now it wasn't empty—it was filled with a crib, a changing table, a rocking chair, a pile of stuffed animals, and boxes and boxes of wrapped gifts. "From Jada and Michelle," her mother told her.

"No, the rocking chair's from me," someone said, and she turned to see Michael behind her, a pair of pliers in his hand. She was very glad to see him. "And they left this," he said, handing her an envelope.

Dear Angie,

You'll only get this letter if we're not in jail. That means that our plan worked, and that we won't be wearing matching jumpsuits for the next twenty years.

We never could have done it without you (but you couldn't have done it without us, either). We both agree that we've never had a friend like each other, or a friend like you. We love you.

And don't think you'll be alone. Michelle promises free baby-sitting services, plus she'll attend all of your prenatal classes with you and be your coach (unless Michael wants to do it. Somehow we think he will). Jada guarantees you Christmas and summer vacations in the Caribbean every year until the baby is twenty-one. And, as if that wasn't enough, we enclose this special gift that we saved for you. In return, Jada would like a photo of the smoking ruins of her house.

We love you, but we already said that, didn't we?

Jada & Michelle

Angie smiled and then looked into the envelope. There, almost stuck to the backing on the envelope's fold, was another Polaroid. She pulled it out. There was Michelle smiling up at her, with Reid's face beside her, but Reid wasn't smiling at all. Instead he was looking down at his crotch, where it was clear that Mr. Happy was not living up to his name. *Well,* Angie thought, *now I'll have a picture of Daddy to show to the baby. But maybe I'll wait until the baby is twenty-one. And I'll let Jada and Michelle explain exactly how it all happened.*